Sixty-two minutes later, as the *Naniwa* completed her course correction, an alarm sounded from the Navigation station.

"*Chu-sa!*" the navigator said sharply, looking up from his console. "Unknown signature on the plot! We have an intruder in our patrol box."

"Report," Susan said, her voice calm and controlled. Her own displays were already adjusting, with threat analysis panes opening up. "Size—heading—something pertinent, *Thai-i* Holloway."

"Pretty small, *kyo*, about sixty meters long. It's piggybacking in the *Tlemitl*'s wake. Signature is intermittent—" Holloway swallowed a curse, as the icon suddenly vanished from the threatwell.

"Project location from the data we've already captured, *Thai-i*. Lock heading as soon as we've caught sight of her again." Koshō looked to Pucatli, who was sitting in at comm for the usual first-watch officer. "Signal battle stations to all hands, *Chu-i*. Immediate intercept. Unauthorized ship of unknown flag. Guns live. This is not a drill. Load missile racks one and two. Direct *So-cho* Juarez to ready two teams for board and seizure."

Then she sat back, feeling a cold shiver of adrenaline course through her limbs as the Klaxon sounded, and her bad mood vanished like the morning frost from the eaves. *Smartly now,* she thought, watching the bridge crew in action. *Mitsuharu would be pleased to see their progress.*

"*Chu-sa?*" Oc Chac looked up from his own console, his chiseled face gleaming as the overheads flashed three times. "Battlecast needs an update on our course correction. Should I—"

She shook her head, *no*. "Let's see what we've beaten from cover, first, *Sho-sa*. Then I'll report to the various admirals."

TOR BOOKS BY THOMAS HARLAN

LAND OF THE

DEAD

THOMAS HARLAN

TOR®

A Tom Doherty Associates Book • New York

LAND OF THE DEAD

A Tor Book
Published by Tom Doherty Associates, LLC
175 Fifth Avenue
New York, NY 10010

www.tor-forge.com

Tor® is a registered trademark of Tom Doherty Associates, LLC.

ISBN 978-0-7653-5053-4

First Edition: August 2009
First Mass Market Edition: April 2011

Printed in the United States of America

0 9 8 7 6 5 4 3 2 1

For Keith Laumer, K. H. Scheer, and Walter
Ernsting: That was some good reading!

Tremendous thanks are owed to my able, witty,
and good-looking advisors in matters scientific,
mythological, and military: Martin, Annita,
Cap'n Paul, Chris W., Chris C., and the "O.W."

A NOTE CONCERNING MEASUREMENTS

Though her later victories rendered the full terms of the Lisbon Accords moot, the México Empire abides by the common set of weights and measures set forth by the Accord in A.D. 1724. As a result, distances are in kilometers, weights in kilograms, and so on.

A NOTE ABOUT IMPERIAL MÉXICA NAVY SHIP NAMES

Capital ships—dreadnaughts, heavy carriers, and battleships—tend to have México names, usually of gods, monsters, or famous generals from the Conquest.

Midrange ships—strike and escort carriers and heavy cruisers—usually have Nisei, Mixtec, or Skawtish names. Very recently, some *Provincial*-class battle cruisers have come into service bearing city names.

Smaller ships—light cruisers, destroyers, transports, and fleet tenders—come in a wide variety of classes and naming schemes, usually assigned as a sop to some organization or group outside of the Four Hundred families.

THE CONCORDANCE

A wealth of detail about the universe of the Sixth Sun can be found at: http://www.throneworld.com/wiki/index.php?title=Category:Concordance.

MILITARY RANKS OF THE IMPERIAL MÉXICA FLEET, ARMY, AND MARINES

NISEI TERM	FLEET RANK	MARINE/ARMY RANK	MÉXICA TERM
Gensui	Admiral of the Fleet	Commandant	Cuauhnochteuctli (EAGLE PRICKLY-PEAR LORD)
Thai-sho	Admiral	General	Ezhuahuacatl (BLOOD-SHEDDER)
Chu-sho	Vice Admiral	Lieutenant-General	Tlacoccalcatl (COMMANDING GENERAL)
Sho-sho	Rear Admiral	Major-General	Tlacateccatl (GENERAL)
Thai-sa	Captain	Colonel	Cuauhtlahtoh (CHIEF)
Chu-sa	Commander		Cuahyahcatl (GREAT CAPTAIN)
Sho-sa	Lieutenant-Commander	Major	
Thai-i	Lieutenant	Captain	
Chu-i	Sub-Lieutenant	Lieutenant	
Sho-i	Ensign	Sub-Lieutenant	
Sho-i Ko-hosei	Midshipman		
Seito	Cadet	Cadet	Pipiltin
Heisocho Jun-i	Warrant Officer	Warrant Officer	Cuachicqueh (SHO___)
Joto-Heiso Socho	Chief Petty Officer	Sergeant Major	T___
Itto-Heiso Gunso	1st Petty Officer	Sergeant	

NISEI TERM	FLEET RANK	MARINE/ARMY RANK	MÉXICA TERM
Nitto-Heiso Gocho	2nd Petty Officer	Corporal	Tequihuah *(VETERAN WARRIOR)*
SeiHeicho Heicho	Leading Starman	Lance Corporal	Yaotequihuah *(LEADER OF YOUTHS)*
Joto-Hei	Able Starman	Superior Private	
Itto-Hei	Starman 1st Class	Private 1st Class	
Nitto-Hei	Starman 2nd Class	Private 2nd Class	Telpochyahqui *(LEADING YOUTH)*
Santo-Hei	Starman 3rd Class *(RECRUIT)*	Private 3rd Class *(RECRUIT)*	Telpolcatl *(YOUTH)*
Sencho	Captain of a civilian starship		

FROM THE ANNALS OF CUAUHTITLAN

In the beginning was the First Sun,
4-Water was its sign;
It was called the Sun of Water,
For water covered the world,
Leaving nothing but the dragonflies above
And the fishy men below.

The Second Sun was born,
4-Jaguar was its sign;
This was called the Sun of the Jaguars.
In this Sun the heavens collapsed,
So that the Sun could not move in its course.
The world darkened, and when all was dark
Then the people were devoured.

The Giants perished, giving life to the Third Sun.
4-Rain was its sign;
It was called the Sun of Rain,
For this Sun rained fire from bleeding eyes
And the people were consumed.

From the torrent of burning stones,
The Fourth Sun was born.
4-Wind was its sign, and it was called the Sun of Wind.
In this Sun, all which stood on the earth was carried
Away by terrible winds.
The people were turned into monkeys,
and scattered from their cities into the forest.

Now, by sacrifice of the divine liquid, the Fifth Sun
was born.
Its sign was 4-Motion.

As the Sun moved, following a course,
The ancients called it the Sun of Motion.
In the time of this Sun, there were
Great earthquakes and famine,
No maize grew, and the gods of the field
Turned their eyes from the people,
And all the people grew thin, and perished.

The Lord of Heaven cut the heart from his living son,
And so was born the Sixth Sun, which sustains
The universe with infinite light.
Its sign was 4-Flint.
Those who watch the sky say this Sun

Will end in annihilation, when the flint-knife
Severs the birthcord of the Sun, plunging all
Into darkness, where the people will
Be cut to pieces and scattered.

This is the time of the Sixth Sun. . . .

LAND OF THE
DEAD

THE HOUSE OF FUMEIYO-IE

A slim Nisei woman, her back straight as a sword blade, glossy black hair coiled at her neck, paused before a *shoji*-panel of laminate cedar and redwood. She took a moment to straighten the crisply starched cuffs of her dress whites, to tuck her cap under one arm, and to adjust the four tiny golden skulls on her collar tabs. Then, prepared, she placed two fingers against the door itself.

There was a quiet chime—the sound of a temple bell filtered through autumnal leaves—and the panel slid soundlessly to one side. The Imperial México Navy *Chusa* stepped out onto a covered porch, walked down a flight of broad wooden steps and out into a perfectly manicured Tokuga-period garden. A glassite pressure dome vaulted overhead, half of the armored panels polarized against the glare of the twin primaries of the Michóacan binary. Her boots clicked on a curving stone bridge crossing a swift, silent brook—the recycled water clear as crystal, reeds and tadpoles wavering in the current running over mossy stones—and she passed beneath the rustling branches of a stand of hothouse aspen.

A teahouse stood beneath the golden trees, ancient wood and paper walls meticulously assembled at the heart of the Fleet base, slate roof strewn with leaf litter. The newly minted captain knelt at the door and paused again—taking a measured breath—before drawing aside the old-fashioned panel of rice paper and varnished pine. The large interior room was quite barren. A tatami lay in the middle of the floor, a pale jute-colored island in a sea of gleaming dark fir planking. A man was kneeling on the mat, hands hidden in the folds of a plain civilian kimono. He lifted his head curiously at the sound of the opening door.

His thin face, pale and seamed from long exhaustion, was calm.

Then he recognized her and everything sure and composed about him disappeared in a jolt of surprise—delight—and then slowly dawning grief.

The woman removed her boots and padded across the spotless floor to the edge of the mat.

"Oh *Sho-sa*," the man said, shaking his head. "You should not have brought me the honorable blades. A fine gesture, truthfully, but—"

"I bear no swords," Susan Koshō said, kneeling gracefully and drawing a parchment envelope from the inner pocket of her uniform jacket. "The Admiralty tribunal has concluded its deliberations. You will not satisfy the Emperor's Honor for the loss of our ship. As of only an hour ago, you are free to leave this place at any time you please." She set down the envelope, touching the corners to align the rectangle properly between them.

"What is this?" Mitsuharu Hadeishi, recently captain of the ill-starred IMN *Astronomer*-class light cruiser *Henry R. Cornuelle*, eyed the parchment suspiciously. "This is not an orders packet."

Koshō shook her head *no*, gaze politely averted from his, attention unerringly fixed on the hem of his kimono, which was frayed and showing a small tear. She wondered, seeing how shabby his clothing was, what had happened to the old manservant who had tended Hadeishi's personal affairs aboard the *Cornuelle*. The rest of the crew—those who had lived through the disaster over

Jagan—had scattered to the five directions. *Even my feet,* she thought, *are on a strange road, every compass awry with the influence of the fates. With every step, a cross-roads appears out of the darkness. . . .*

"I have been retired?" Hadeishi's voice was thin with distress.

"No." Susan met his eyes at last. "You have been placed on reserve duty, pending the needs of the Fleet. Your record . . . your service jacket is . . . all references to the incident at Jagan have been removed. A compromise was reached—"

"But I have no ship," he said, blinking, trying to take in the abrupt end of his career as a plain envelope pinched between thumb and forefinger. "No duty, no . . . no . . ."

He stopped, lips pursed, dark eyebrows narrowed over puzzled, wounded eyes. Susan could feel his mind whirling—imagined touching his brow would reveal a terrible, fruitless heat—and her own face became glacially impassive in response to his distress.

After a moment, Hadeishi's eyes focused, found her, remembered her words, and his head tilted a little to one side. "What of the others? Or am I the only one small enough to be caught in the net of accountability?"

The corners of Koshō's eyes crinkled very slightly. "Great care was taken that no Imperial agency be found at fault. The Fleet Book shows you fought the *Cornuelle* against vicious odds—"

Hadeishi stiffened, astonished. "Fought? Fought! I was taken unawares by a *weather satellite network*—our ship crippled, our crew decimated—our only *struggle* was to stay alive while repairs were underway and the ship kept her nose up!"

Susan nodded, saying. "Representatives of the Mirror-Which-Reveals-The-Truth mentioned this on several occasions—as a mark against you. But the Admiralty has no love for spies and informers, or for the clumsy Flower War priests who sparked the Bharat revolt. They would not let you hang for a botched Mirror project. Not when it meant a smudge on their own mantle!"

"But—"

"They cannot give you a ship, *Chu-sa*. Not with so many powers quarreling over the blame." Susan frowned, then allowed herself a very small sigh. "Colonel Yac-atolli fared no better—he's been posted to a sub-arctic garrison command on Helmand—while Admiral Ville-neuve was actually *reprimanded*, with a black mark struck on his duty jacket for failing to provide *Cornuelle* with munitions resupply—and Ambassador Petrel has simply left the diplomatic service."

Hadeishi's eyes flickered briefly with anger, before he snorted in cynical amusement.

"Did the tribunal assign *any* blame in this wretched turn of events?"

Susan nodded. "HKV agitators have been blamed for inciting the local population to rebellion against the Em-pire."

"The—they are blaming the *Europeans* for this?" As-tonishment flushed Hadeishi's countenance with a pale rose-colored bloom. "There has not been a *European* resistance movement in extra-Solar space for nearly fif-teen years! Not since—"

"I know." Susan's voice was gentle. "Nonetheless, the tribunal has declared a Finn named Timonen ringleader of the whole sorry affair—and he is conveniently dead, his body disintegrated."

Mitsuharu snorted again, dismayed. "Do they even care what *actually happened*?"

Susan shook her head. "They are overjoyed with the Prince's performance."

"The P— No, you make a poor, poor jest, *Sho-sa*. Not—"

Koshō—at last—let her properly impassive countenance slip, showing a flash of dismay. She dug into her jacket and produced a carefully folded tabloid. The busyink lay quiescent while Hadeishi unfolded the paper, before flashing alive with colorful diagrams, animated graphs, tiny low-res videos . . . all the appurtenances of modern news.

A sallow-faced youth with unmistakable México features popped out, pockmarked walls visible behind his shoulder, smoke coiling away from hundreds of bullet holes, the glossy black of his Fleet shipskin spattered with blood, a heavy HK-45B assault rifle slung over one shoulder. The boy—he must have been in his late twenties, but he seemed much younger—was grinning triumphantly.

"The hero of the hour," Koshō drawled, "savior of the legation, captor of the native ringleaders . . . Tezozómoc's public image is shining and bright this week. Someone, somewhere, is very pleased with themselves for this bit of . . . editing."

Hadeishi stared at the picture, impassive, eyes hooded, and then turned the tabloid facedown on the mat beside the parchment envelope. For a moment he pressed both palms against his eyes, head down, breathing through his nose. Koshō waited, wondering if her old captain would react as she had. *I should have brought a sidearm, a ship-pistol, something . . . to stun him with. When he becomes violently angry. When he threatens to—*

"All this . . ." Mitsuharu did not look up. "Our dead—our broken ship—the wreckage on the surface—my career—it was all for *him*? To polish his reputation, to give this dissolute Prince some respectability in the eyes of the *public*?"

"The Four Hundred families cannot allow a Prince Imperial," Susan replied, voice carefully neutral, "to seem the buffoon, to be known as a wastrel, a drunkard, a party-addict . . . the Emperor is no fool. Even the least, most laughable member of the Imperial Clan *must* be seen by the general populace as a potentially terrifying warrior of unsurpassed skill. Particularly when *Temple of Truth* runs a popular weekly featurette detailing his latest lewd binge. . . ."

Hadeishi rocked back, eyes still closed, fists clenched white to the knuckle. Susan waited, feeling a tight, singing tension rise in the pit of her stomach. After ten minutes had passed, the man's eyes opened and his shoulders slumped. Hastily, Koshō looked away, giving her old commander the illusion of privacy, though they were no more than a meter apart.

"So I am the last, least fish caught in this flowery net."

Susan did not reply, her gaze fixed on the rear wall of the teahouse.

"And I am left with nothing." There was the crisp rustle of parchment. "You are to await the pleasure of the Emperor," he read, "should he have need of your service." Hadeishi sounded utterly spent. "How long, *Shosa*, do you think I will wait? A year? Two years?"

Forever, she thought, feeling the tension in her stomach turn tighter and tighter. *You will be forgotten, like so many other disgraced captains before you.*

"There is nothing to say, is there?" Hadeishi lifted a hand and scratched slowly at the stubble on his chin. "There are never enough combat commands for all those who desire them . . . who need them. Not without some great war to force the hand of the Admiralty and inspire a new building program." A tiny spark of anger began to lift the leaden tone from his words. "Not when political favor can be exchanged to see some well-connected clan-scion at the helm of a ship of war—"

He stopped abruptly. For the first time, Mitsuharu focused fully on Koshō's face. A clear sort of penetrating light came into his eyes, wiping aside the despair, but leaving something far more tragic in its place.

"You've your fourth *zugaikotsu*," he whispered, lifting his chin at the gleaming skulls on her collar. "At last."

Hadeishi bowed in place, as one honorable officer might to another. "*Sho-sa*, I regret the words just spoken. I do not impugn the nobility of your birth. Of any man or woman in the Fleet who has borne my acquaintance, you—you are worthy of a ship."

The cable of tension in Susan's stomach bent over on itself, wire grating against wire.

"The *Naniwa*, I hope," Mitsuharu ventured, recalling a dim memory. "She should be out of trials by now . . . did they hold her for you?"

Koshō nodded and felt a sharp pain in her gut, as though the imaginary cable had frayed past breaking and steel wires spun loose to stab into her flesh. "They did. She is waiting at Jupiter for me right now."

There was the ghost of a smile on Hadeishi's lips. "She is a fast ship, Susan, new and bold . . . tough for her size, but still no dreadnaught! I pulled her specs months ago. A sprinter she is, not a plow horse, not a charger . . . you'll need to keep her dancing in the hot of it—no standing toe to toe—not with the armor she lifts. In and out, missile-work and raids . . ." The momentary surge of energy failed, and his eyes grew dull again. "You'll do well . . . a Main Fleet posting, I'd wager . . . something where you'll be seen, noticed. . . ."

Where my family connections can lift me up, Koshō thought bitterly as he fell silent. *Where my advantage of birth can show its strength. Where the son of a violin-maker and a shop clerk would not even be accorded the time of day by his fellow officers.*

"*Chu-sa*—"

"Say nothing, *Sho-sa*. Say nothing."

"No. You are the finest combat commander I've ever met. All of *my* skill springs from your example. You will be *wasted* on the List, waiting for some . . . some scow to need a driver. Let me . . ." She struggled to frame the proper words, failed, and blurted out: "Enter my service, *Sensei*. You've the heart of a *samurai*; let me make you one in truth. Then you *will* command a ship again! Come with me—"

Hadeishi stiffened, almost recoiled, and a quick play of emotions on his agile face exposed—just for an instant—astonishment and then a stunning grief shown by suddenly dead eyes and a waxy tone to his flesh.

"*Sensei*," he whispered, almost too faintly for her to hear. "Your *samurai*. This is how you see me?"

"*Hai!*" she said, overcome with embarrassment, and bowed so deeply in apology her forehead brushed the mat. "Please, you mustn't lose hope. I can—"

"No, thank you," Hadeishi said faintly, staring at her as though an apparition had risen through the gleaming floor, a *yakka*-goblin out of legend to torment him and lay bare every scar carried in his heart. "An honest gesture, *Sho-sa*, but the weight of my failure will only drag your star down into shadow."

Susan almost flinched from the icy tone in his voice. She felt short of breath. Koshō blinked, forcing her face back to accustomed impassivity, falling back behind her shield of customary remoteness. "*Chu-sa* . . ."

"You should leave now," he said coolly. "Your ship is waiting."

Entirely unsure of what she'd said to put such abrupt distance between them, Koshō left quietly, gathering up her boots. Outside, the day-program of the garden had advanced into twilight, yielding mist from the streams and pools. The panels far overhead dimmed still further. The twin suns at the core of the Michóacan system were now reduced to sullen pinpoints, no brighter than the other main sequence stars in the sky.

Susan strode into the base's main departure lounge in a black mood. Riding alone in the tubecar from the Fumeiyo dome she had turned her conversation with Hadeishi through all five directions. *He does not wish your charity, Koshō-sana. He will starve and die rather than ask a friend for assistance. Idiot. Three kinds of idiot. No, four kinds!*

But it was a familiar idiocy.

How many of grandfather's retainers went the same way? Wasting away, living on less and less, refusing to admit their sons and daughters needed to learn useful skills—would it be so terrible to master a craft? To . . . to sell goods in the marketplace?

That Koshō's grandmother had steered her into a military career—the *one* paying profession which remained honorable for her caste, though the subject of intense competition—seemed now the most natural thing in the world. An admirable and direct answer to the nagging question that plagued all of the old nobility: *How does one pay the rent, when there are no koku of land remaining to till, leasehold, or sell?* Changes in Nisei tax law under a succession of canny Diet prime ministers, and the constant pressure of the mercantile classes, had eroded the vast estates of the old families. Susan was sure the Tai-Sho was quite pleased with the outcome. *No one can raise and arm men from houses filled with antiques. And the merchants pay their taxes.*

Susan's pace slowed, eyes drawn to the huge transit board filling the far wall of the lounge. Hundreds of ships were listed, heading in every direction. One of them was hers—a Fleet personnel liner bound for the home system, to Anáhuac, and the massive Akbal yards off Jupiter.

My first command. My own ship ... the dream of every junior officer in the Fleet. For a moment, she felt uneasy, aware of an incipient loneliness, and part of her devoutly wished Hadeishi had accepted her service. *I will miss him, but I do not need him to guide my hand.*

Then a half-familiar shape glimpsed from the corner of one eye drew her head around. The general ill-feeling of anger, resentment, and thwarted intent endemic to the passages of the base suddenly had a singular, unmistakably clear focus.

"Green Hummingbird!" she hissed. Koshō turned on her heel and plunged through a squad of enlisted ratings sprawled on transit couches, the floor around them littered with Mayahuel bottles and *patolli* gaming mats sprinkled with money and dice sticks, to fetch up before two men—no, one human and one alien—sitting in a quiet corner of the huge, bustling room.

"What are *you* doing here?" Susan's voice was cold.

The human was holding a package in his hands, something rectangular wrapped in twine and brown paper. He looked up, catching Koshō's gaze with a pair of green eyes deep as Tuxpan jade, and his polished old mahogany face, etched with tiny scars and sharp wrinkles, expressed nothing more than the most polite interest. "*Chu-sa* Koshō, a pleasure."

"What are you *doing here*?" A horrible suspicion had formed in her mind the instant she'd set eyes on the old México. He was well known to her—an Imperial *nauallis* or Judge, of the sort who traveled the backwaters of the Rim, poking and prying into all sorts of dangerous business, showing up at odd places and times, commandeering the *Cornuelle* or any other Imperial ship on hand as he pleased—he and Hadeishi had some kind of history, for the captain had always been generous, bending rules and regulations with aplomb to accommodate the Judge and his "business." *An Imperial agent, a spy, an assassin, a sorcerer . . . a walking career disaster.*

"I am waiting for my ship, like everyone else," Hummingbird said, showing the ghost of a smile, "and catching up with a recent friend."

His scarred hand—now empty, the package having disappeared into one of the medium-sized travel cases at his feet—indicated the alien in the opposite chair. Susan spared a glance for the creature—a slight shape with a vaguely humanoid face. Thin, ancient-seeming fingers covered with a close-napped blue-black fur held a chain of beads. Much like Hummingbird, the alien was wearing a hooded mantle over tunic and trousers, this one a faded, mottled green with a dull-colored red cross quartering its chest.

"Holy one, this is Captain Susan Koshō. *Chu-sa*, the honored Sra Osá."

Koshō bowed politely. "My pleasure, Osá-*tzin*."

Then her whole attention was on Hummingbird again, her face tight with barely repressed anger. "Did you have anything to do with this? With the Tribunal's *compromise*? With what happened to us on Jagan?"

"I had nothing," the old México said carefully, "to do with the astounding success of the *xochiyaotinime* in providing Fleet and Army with such a *vigorous* martial test. And I am very pleased Captain Hadeishi was not forced to satisfy his honor, or that of the Emperor, in some . . . final way."

"Are you?" Koshō managed to keep from curling her lip, all in deference to the old priest watching the two of them with bright, inquisitive eyes. "Then why have you done nothing to help him, when he has always rendered you aid—even in defiance of his ordered duty? Is this how the *nauallis* repay their allies?"

Hummingbird's chiseled face tightened. He was rarely challenged by anyone, much less a Fleet officer whose career he could destroy with a comm call. Susan knew this and failed to care. She had never found him intimidating—dangerous, yes, like a redwood viper loose on your command deck—but not a source of fear. Though she would be loath to admit such a thing, the Judge did not exist high enough on the slopes of the Heavenly Mountain to impress her.

"I have done what I can," he snapped. "He lives, does he not? He will have a command again, when enough time has passed to dim the memory of his enemies."

"He only has such enemies," Koshō allowed a faint exhalation of disgust, "because of his association with *you*."

The old *nauallis* became quite still, eyes narrowing, and he seemed to settle into the lounge chair like a mountain finding its footing in the earth. "What would you have of me, child, that Hadeishi would not ask himself? For he has *not* asked me for aid, though I have offered."

Have you? How many visitors has my captain entertained in his empty rooms? How many well-meaning friends has he turned away?

The admission stilled her angry rush, letting unexpected venom drain from her thoughts.

"He has to be saved," she said, controlled once more. "Before he simply fades away."

Hummingbird shrugged. "Perhaps you should let him tread his own path?"

"No." Koshō fixed him with a steady, considering eye. "He will languish and die if left without purpose. Find him a ship. Put a g-deck under his feet. Give him what he deserves."

Hummingbird rubbed the top of his head, which was brown and smooth as a betel-nut. He cast a sideways glance at Sra Osá, whose attention seemed far away, politely ignoring the argument playing out before him, rosary beads clicking one by one through pelted fingers.

"Arrangements could be made," the old México allowed with a grimace.

"Good." Koshō offered the most minimal bow, glanced up to check the transit board, cursed at the time, and then left in haste.

The *nauallis* watched her go, his expression pensive. Hummingbird rubbed the back of his head again, glancing sideways at his wizened companion. "Ah, if only she had a gram of Hadeishi's native circumspection! He will be hard to replace . . . but what is done is done. Once the arrow has flown . . ."

Sra Osá said nothing, ancient face impassive beneath the woolen hood.

Hummingbird nodded to himself, some internal judgment weighed and accepted, checked his bag for the twine-wrapped package, then lifted both cases and moved away.

IN THE *KUUB*

ANTISPINWARD OF MÉXICA SPACE, BEYOND THE RIM

The navigator of the IMN DD-217 *Calexico* frowned at her console, tapping her throatmike to life: "*Chu-sa* Rae? We're at barely thirty-percent see-through in this . . . combat reaction range is down to less than a light-minute."

At the other end of the narrow twenty-meter-long bridge, Captain Rae's grimace matched the navigator's wary expression. His destroyer had an upgraded sensor suite to match the two Deep Range scouts for which he was flying gunsight, but in this protostellar murk nothing was working quite to Engineering Board specifications.

"Are *Kiev* and *Korkunov* still in relay? Are we getting a clean telemetry feed?"

"*Hai, kyo*," the navigator responded, watching the particle collision counts on the forward transit deflectors flicker rapidly in and out of redline on her stat panel. "Feed is clean, but we're edging towards full-stop."

"I see it." Rae had the same readout running on his console. *Calexico* lacked the new battle shielding Fleet was refitting onto the capital ships, and her transit deflectors—though upgraded to match Survey requirements—were finding it hard going in the heavy interstellar dust endemic to this region of space. "Comm, patch me through to the *K* and *K*."

Rae waited patiently while his communications officer rounded up the captains of the two Survey ships. Watching the collision counts surging red did not ease his mind. The *kuub* was notorious for its hazards to navigation. Ancient stellar debris—rumor said the science team was feeling warm about a double-supernova—swirled in a hot murk glowing with radiation from the few suns still embedded in the nebula. There were solid fragments as well, the bits and pieces of planets shattered by the catastrophic detonation, mixed with cometary debris, stray asteroids . . . a nebula of incredible breadth and density.

There were hints of a massive gravity sink down at the heart of the region. A black hole, or maybe more than one. The navigator was starting to see queer distortions in the local hyperspace gradient, though they didn't look anything like the usual fluctuation patterns around a singularity. She tapped her throatmike again.

"*Chu-sa*, we're approaching transit vertex pretty

quickly. I think we'd better slow. I'm seeing . . . wait a minute. Hold one. Hold one." Her voice turned puzzled.

Rae, in the midst of offering the *Kiev* an engineering team to tear down a degraded shield nacelle, caught the change in her voice and his reaction was instantaneous. He slapped the FULL STOP glyph on his main console and barked a confirming order to his crew: "All engines, go to zero-v and prepare to rotate ship! All power to transit shielding, all stations report!"

Six seconds later, amid the crisp chatter of his department heads reporting their status, the t-relay from *Kiev* stopped cold.

In the threatwell directly in front of Rae's station, the icon representing the Survey ship winked out. A camera pod immediately swiveled towards the event and two seconds later the *Chu-sa* was watching with gritted teeth as the *Kiev* vanished in a plume of superheated plasma.

"Antimatter containment failure—" Rae's voice was anguished, but then his eyes widened in real horror. The *Korkunov* vanished from the plot three seconds after its sister ship. A second burst of sunfire stabbed through the dust. His fist slammed the crash button on his shockframe.

"Full evasion! Guns hot, give me full active scan! Battle stations!"

A Klaxon blared and every lighting fixture on the ship flashed three times and then shaded into a noticeable red tone. Rae's shockframe folded around him and a z-helmet lowered and locked tight against his z-suit's neckring. A groan vibrated from the very air as the destroyer's main engines flared and the g-decking strained to adjust. The *Calexico*—which had been about to rotate and slow with main drives—surged forward into a tight turn, its radar and wideband laser sensors emitting a sharp full-spectrum burst to paint the immediate neighborhood.

Down on the gun deck, a message drone banged away from the ship, thrown free by a magnetic accelerator and immediately darted back along the expedition's path of entry into the *kuub*. The drone's onboard comp was already calculating transit gradients, looking to punch into hyperspace as quickly as possible. A second drone was run out by a suddenly frantic deck crew, ready to launch as soon as the results of the wide-spectrum scan were complete.

A louder alarm was blaring in Engineering, drowning both the warble of the drive coil and the basso drone of the antimatter reactor and its attendant systems. In the number three airlock, Engineer Second Malcolm Helsdon turned in place, his z-suit already sealed, a gear-pack slung over one shoulder and ten meters of heat-exchange thermocouple looped around the other. Through the visor of his suit helmet, he peered back through the closing inner door of the lock, seeing the on-duty crew moving quickly—*as they should*, he thought—to action stations.

That heat exchanger is going to have to wait. Helsdon's habitually serious expression soured.

The engineer reached out to key the lock override, but the looped thermocouple bound his arm and he paused, shifting his feet, swinging the ungainly package around to his other side, to get a free hand on the control panel. Sweat sprung from his pale forehead, and the usual shag of unkempt brown hair was in his eyes.

Through the outer door's blast window, the blur of motion was so swift only the faintest afterimage registered in his retinas.

"What—" *was that?* The overhead lights in the air-lock went out.

There was an instant of darkness and Helsdon knew, even before the local emergency illumination kicked in, that main power had failed catastrophically. Without a second thought, he threw himself back against the wall opposite the interior lock door and seized hold of a stanchion. As he moved, local g-control failed and he slammed hard into the plasticine panel. The *Calexico* was at full burn and only the armored resiliency of his Fleet z-suit kept Helsdon from breaking both shoulder and arm. For an instant, all was whirling lights and vertigo.

A moment later, the engineer steadied himself and ventured to open his eyes.

Everything was terribly quiet.

Still alive, he thought, blinking in the dim glow of the emergency lights. The thermocouple had come loose and was drifting in z-g, slowly uncoiling to fill the airlock with dozens of silvery loops. *Reactor hasn't fried me yet. . . .* He kicked to the inner lock window, bracing one leg against the side of the heavy pressure door. Streaks of frost blocked most of the view, but Helsdon had no trouble seeing out.

Grasping what he saw took a heartbeat, then another . . . two breaths to realize he wasn't looking down at an engineering drawing, but rather at the heart of the *Calexico* herself laid bare. Somehow Engineering was falling away from him—along with the great proportion of the destroyer itself—every deck exposed, every hall and conduit pipe gaping wide to open space. A huge cloud of debris—sheets, *kaffe* cups, papers, shoes, the stiff bodies of men already dead from hypoxia—spilled from the dying ship.

Helsdon's helmet jerked to one side, searching for a point of reference—anything that made sense—and fixed on a section of wall jutting out into his field of view to the left. He could see three-quarters of the hallway—flooring with nonslip decking, dead light fixtures, a guide-panel—and then nothing. Only an impossibly sharp division where the ship simply ended.

We've been cut in half.

SHINEDO

ON THE CHUMASH SOUND, NORTH AMERICA, ANÁHUAC

A week's tips feeling very light in his pocket, Hadeishi trudged up a long low hill through fresh snow. In summer, the hillside would be covered with neatly cropped grass and the misty forest on either side of the parkland would be a deep cool green, filled with croaking ravens and drifting butterflies. Now everything was crisp and white, the mossy pillars covered with hanging ice. Behind him, where the sea broke against a reddish slate headland, gray waves shone with pearlescent foam. Walking carefully between the ice-slicked walkway and endless rows of grave markers, Mitsuharu picked his way along a turfed horse path. Even in this weather, the springy sod beneath the frost yielded queasily with each step. *Here,* he thought wistfully, *everything is just as I remember. So our dead sleep quietly, shielded from the restless chaos of the city.*

The other places he'd held unchanged in childhood memory were simply gone.

Fifteen years of Fleet service—and at least a decade since he'd spent leave in the bustling commercial capital stretching east and south of this quiet peninsula—had seen his old neighborhood leveled. His parents' single-story house with the green tin roof and white-painted walls was gone. The entire street—ancient cobblestones and crumbling asphalt and peeling advertisements on the garden gates—had vanished. No more little single-door shops, tucked in between the warehouses and old factories, selling tea and cakes and hot noodles. Even the narrow park along Deception Creek—which marked the southern edge of downtown—had been replaced. Ancient rows of cherry and mulberry trees sawn down, replaced by a modern promenade of expensive shops and brisk, gleaming cafés catering to the young and rich.

Civilians. Merchants, he thought, dully angered by the wall of gleaming sea-green-glass apartment towers burying his boyhood memories beneath sixty stories of luxury flats and their attendant hovercar garages. *Even a dirty industrial neighborhood should be allowed to putter along . . . without improvements, without renovations.*

But Shinedo of the Nisei had grown enormously while he'd been gone among the stars. A new high-speed mag-lev cargo railway now ran day and night to the far eastern coast, moving millions of tons of Asiatic goods from Shinedo's deepwater port to the grimy coastal cities of Oswego and New Canarsie in the Iroquois Protectorate. And from there, onward to Europe and Afriqa. The sprawling spaceport in the wetlands south of the city benefited as well. Though there were larger Fleet installations planet-side, Shinedo *uchumon* handled a constant and lucrative passenger service. The industrial districts Mitsuharu prowled in his youth had moved south to sprawl around *uchu* in a thick belt of newly built factories, smokestacks, and office parks.

But little of that ugliness was visible within the quiet solitude of the preserve. Here—and only here within greater Shinedo metro, still protected by the edict of an

Emperor long dead when the first human spacecraft lumbered into orbit from the Nanchao testing range—towering groves of old coastal redwoods remained. The entire park, save for the serpentine meadows containing the cemetery, was filled with the same nearly impenetrable rain forest which had greeted the first Nisei to set foot upon *Gumshan*—the Golden Mountain.

Beneath their broad eaves, heavy with snow, there was a deep sense of quiet.

As befits the honored dead, Hadeishi thought as he turned onto a side path—this one set with wooden steps and a railing—which climbed the westernmost hill in the park. *Let them rest, distant from the garish, uncaring noise of those who still live.*

His Fleet discharge pay had evaporated once he'd stepped off the shuttle. Shinedo was not cheap. Food, lodging, bus tickets ... everything was expensive. Even the most wretched grade of sake was a full quill the jar. Two ceramic bottles clinked in his jacket pocket, rubbing a handful of wilted flowers to pale yellow dust. There was a dole for the indigent, but Mitsuharu had prided himself on having useful skills. His comp, waiting messages ignored, and other things reminding him of the Fleet, he sold. So his old life had been eaten away by the new.

Solving a four-dimensional puzzle with seventy-six vectors in less than a second has no value in the civilian world. Knowing the little tricks of command, of gaining men's loyalty, of making them work harder, faster, more accurately as a team under fire ... who needs that here? There is no war in the city.

Very near the shuttle port, in the maze of narrow alleys and bars and tea houses making up the district called Water Lantern, he had managed to secure employment. He played the samisen in a tea house on the evenings, while the off-duty Fleet and merchanter rat-

ings wasted their money on girls and rice beer and gam-
bling at *patolli* or dice or cards. His father—who had
been very good with almost any stringed instrument—
would have been appalled to see his so-promising son
picking away at the kind of cheap lute a tea house *teishu*
could afford.

No vinegar left, he thought, passing beneath a wooden
arch wound with heavy snow-dusted vines. *All spilled
out of me at Jagan with the* Cornuelle *burning up in the
atmosphere. With all the dead. . . .*

Beyond the arch was a small clearing laid with fitted
stones—swept clean even on such a cold day—surrounding
a temple-house of red enamel and dark, polished wood.
The smell of incense hung in the frigid air, tapers twining
long loops of smoke through the rafters. Hadeishi's Fleet
boots made a tapping sound as he walked and his careful
eye could make out ideograms cut into each of the paving
stones. Ever here, in the Western Chapel, where at winter's end the Emperor came to witness the sun of the ver-
nal equinox settle into the distant sea, surrounded by the
great nobles and the deep, throaty roll of massed drums,
the dead lay close at hand.

Mitsuharu knelt in the temple, bending his head
against the floor in obeisance to the gilded idol. The altar was crowded with candle stubs, pools of melted
wax, and drifts of fallen ash. Coins, gewgaws, trinkets,
little toys, chicle-prizes, letters, twists of paper folded
with prayers covered every flat surface in the shrine.

"The city is expensive," he said aloud, shaking his
head in dismay. "I've little to leave you, mother, father."
Hadeishi dug in his pockets, found the sake, the flowers,
the hard plastic shape of his Fleet comm. "But what I
have, I will send to you, beyond the sea."

Beyond the walls of the temple-house, a late afternoon wind guttered among the stones. The first Nisei to
be laid to rest in the Western Paradise had been interred

within days of the Landing. The fleet had breached upon this shore out of exhaustion. The rough passage between the outer bulwark of Mowichat Island and the rocky, forest-shrouded coastline had taken the last burst of energy the refugees could muster. Thirty-six days had passed while the gray vastness of the sea hammered at their boats. Few of the Japanese vessels had been fitted for such a voyage, though in the mad panic to evacuate Edo and Osaka, no mind had been paid to their seaworthiness. More than half of those who fled dying Nippon had perished. But the Emperor himself had survived, carried forth from the wreck of his ancient realm in a massive Chinese *hai-po* taken in a raid off Taiwan. That enormous ship had run aground in Deception Creek, or so the children said, and the last true Emperor to be born in the Immortal Islands had splashed ashore with *katana* in hand and rusted armor upon his breast. Though the shore he faced was crowded with an impossibly thick forest, and his people were sick and weak, there was nowhere else to run.

Mitsuharu made a little space among the grave goods with his fingers and set both sake bottles among the debris left by other mourners. He considered his comm for a long time. The metal surface was chipped and worn, discolored by plasma backwash, and a sixteen-glyph was blinking on the display surface. *Messages of sympathy from fellow officers*, he thought, entirely devoid of curiosity, *I will never view.*

Hadeishi placed the flowers atop the comm and bent his head over clasped hands.

"One leaf lets go," he whispered, eyes squeezed tight, "and another follows on the wind."

I am sorry, mother, father; that I did not come home. News of your illness, your death, reached me by courier off Kodon, when vital repairs were already underway. I am late to bring you these things, to pray for you, to bid

you a speedy journey home to the Blessed Isles. I am
sorry. I am not a good son. I was not a good captain.
Now I am a wretched player in a disreputable tavern. So
the wheel turns.

The foundation of the temple-house was laid upon
the grave of that first man—a lesser courtier of the Imperial House; a *kugyo* born in Echizen—to die upon *gum-*
shan. He was not the last. Fell beasts roamed the
primordial forest and the natives were quick and sly,
slipping unseen through deep shadows with knives of
knapped stone. The weather was far fiercer than the nobles of Nara and Kyoto expected, and the refugees accounted barely a handful of men experienced in hunting,
fishing, carpentry, blacksmithing . . . by winter's end, another quarter of the survivors were crudely interred
around the temple-house. The great cemetery had begun
its millennia-long sprawl.

But the third spring had brought an unexpected
sight—long boats with many rowers toiling up the coast
from the south. The handful of Nisei ships which remained seaworthy—many had been cannibalized for
nails, lumber, cordage, and other desperately needed
fittings—met the Toltec *pochteca* on the low swell at the
mouth of Deception Creek. From the front step of this
very temple-house, a pillar could be seen on the farther
shore where the Emperor's representatives had first held
conversation with the emissaries of the great southern
kingdoms. By then the Nisei had driven the tribal peo-
ples from their villages along the shore and were beginning to clear the forest for their new city.

Mitsuharu finished his prayers and remained seated,
feeling entirely directionless.

I've done what must be done, he realized, *every com-*
mission discharged. Honor to Fleet, family, and Emperor
satisfied by the most meager effort. My purpose at an
end. His lips twisted in dismay and thin, fine-boned

hands patted at his service jacket, feeling for the hilt of a knife or blade of some kind. *Ah, old fool. You traded your service tantō for new strings for that useless scrap of wood . . . you have already forgotten yourself, haven't you? A samurai, an officer, without even the least weapon to hand? What would Lord Musashi think of you now?*

Hadeishi grunted, the harsh sound echoing in the silent temple, and answered himself. "Lord Musashi was never bothered by the lack of steel!"

An old, old memory came to mind—the fuzzing screen of an ancient black-and-white two-d set showing the calm, centered face of a samurai framed by the pillars of another temple, one in Japan itself, where a ring of ruffians—not even *samurai*, though their nervous hands held blades aplenty, but bandits and honorless men—circled the lone sword master. A strong wind was blowing, rustling the leaves of ancient trees, bending their creaking limbs. Lord Musashi had nothing in his hands save a length of willow wood.

They were doomed, Hadeishi remembered, the ghost of a child's smile in his eyes. *Though he had nothing but the clothes on his back*. The *Five Rings chambara* had played on the two-d every afternoon throughout Mitsuharu's childhood. Hundreds of episodes, rarely shown in order, depicting the long and remarkably heroic life of the sword-saint Miyamoto Musashi. An excellent reason for a youngster to run home from school and fling himself onto the floor of his parent's house in a pile of blankets, eyes fixed on the tiny screen. *Five Rings* was particularly beloved for its setting—Japan itself, during the long struggle of the Restoration, when the Nisei had returned to the home islands and driven out the vile Mongol dynasty which had terrorized their homeland during five centuries of exile.

I will have to buy a knife next week, Hadeishi thought glumly. *When I've a little money again.*

The door of the temple-house slid closed behind him with a soft click. Mitsuharu tucked his chin into the collar of his jacket, frost biting his face. A long walk faced him—back into the upper city, across the lower bridge vaulting the estuary, a hike up over the ridge separating the well-heeled Khahtsalano district from the area around the spaceport, and finally home to his pallet.

Hadeishi was descending the wooden stair into the cemetery proper when a long-drawn-out rumble reached him, carried up from the south in the cold, still air. A laser-boosted shuttle cut through the clouds, a bright red spark racing away to orbit.

They look big from down here, he thought, remembering sitting on the hillside across the river from the main launch-pits at *uchu* with his father. *Gigantic. Leaping into the heavens on wings of flame* . . . But even the largest shuttle was dwarfed by the massive shape of the commercial liners waiting in orbit, much less the vast bulk of a Fleet carrier or dreadnaught. The cold was in his heart now, and an ache was trickling along his spine.

He trudged across the bridge, bitter sea wind piercing his jacket and sweater, cap tugged low. *There was a merchanter's guild office,* Hadeishi remembered, *and I'd qualify for a senior rating's birth. Perhaps even an officer. On a miner, or a cargoman, or a bulk carrier. It would be . . . something. Better than being a samisen player for drunkards.*

The wounded sound of the *Cornuelle*'s spaceframe groaning as she twisted into the atmosphere over Jagan was suddenly sharp in his memory. The hoarse rasp of his own breath inside the helmet, the queasy nausea of shattered ribs. Corridors clogged with floating debris, bubbles of smoke, and the drifting bodies of the dead.

I killed my ship. Susan's face appearing out of the darkness, her eyes blazing with worry as her helmet visor levered up. The tightening of dismay around her almond-shaped eyes as she realized what he'd done. *I killed my own children. For pride. Because I was very good at what I did. But not good enough to deny fate.*

Neon washed his face as he walked, expression vacant, thoughts light-years away. Snow was falling again, dusting his hunched shoulders with white. He'd felt terribly cold then, too, strapped into his shockchair, hands numb with the effort he'd spent to get the ship's nose up, her orbit stable.

If I were not prideful, Mitsuharu thought, feeling his spirit sink even lower. *I could be among the stars again. But what am I beyond pride,* he wondered, *without my uniform, without duty? Am I more than a shell of starched linen and golden ribbon? Is there any reason to be anything else?*

Without a warship to command, he realized, merely shipping out was without purpose.

Lord Musashi, he remembered, *would not compromise his honor at such a pass. He would wait patiently, living on a beggars' charity, until someone deserving of his service called upon him. Even if he waited until death.*

But that was a very cold comfort, on this gray and frigid day.

TENOCHTITLÁN

The Center of the World, Anáhuac

Sahâne stepped gingerly down a flight of well-worn steps formed from compressed ash, his eyesight adjusting smoothly to the abrupt separation of a hazy, hot day and the cool dimness of a restaurant. The insect-whine of his cooling system fell below audibility and the Hjogadim priest let out a relieved hiss. His long snoutlike nose twitched, assailed by the thick, greasy smell of cooking meat, the acid bite of chilli powder, and the earthy smell of red beans simmering in an iron skillet. With a conscious effort, Sahâne closed his mouth, thick gray tongue rolling back into his jaw.

This species of indigene, young smoot, a gruff, pedantic voice spoke out of memory—one of an interminable number of teachers replaying in response to the situational prompt—*grows uncomfortable, even agitated, when confronted with the sight of our superior dentition.*

"No teeth, no teeth," the Hjogadim muttered to himself, a jaundiced eye roving around the gloomy cavern. Long wooden tables—all too small for his two-meter-plus frame—jammed against the walls, crowded by throngs of chairs. Threatening wrought-iron chandeliers hung from the domed ceiling on chains. "A torture chamber," Sahâne observed, beginning to feel nervous. *To remain demands intoxicants.*

The cool air, however, was a blessing he was loath to abandon so quickly. The superconducting threads running through his heavy fur could only dissipate so much heat when he was walking—no, more like swimming—through the thick hot air of the city. That the natives would build underground, or behind heavy whitewashed adobe walls, or install their own refrigeration systems on a massive scale, did not trouble his mind. Sahâne was keenly aware of his own discomfort, but the theoretical trials of a planet of inconsequential *toys* did not move him at all.

Circling around the wicked ornamentation of the nearest chandelier, the Hjo sat at one of the tables, back against the pleasantly cool wall, and wondered if the establishment was closed. A handful of other patrons sat at the far end of the long room, but none of them had paid his entrance the slightest attention. Sahâne's long, tapir-like head swiveled, looking for the telltale ghosting of a human comm-panel in the air. *Nothing.* He frowned, the leathery skin around two deep-set eyes wrinkling up. He could *smell* food, but . . . how did you order a meal without an interface?

"A *waiter* comes," someone said, in passable Trade. "And you tell him which ingestibles you desire."

Sahâne's frown deepened into puzzlement. The human settling into a chair opposite the young Hjo was familiar— Sahâne had been aware of him dozens of times—but they'd never spoken before. The fine coating of hollow hairs forming the top layer of his fur shivered, making the silver-gray gloss ripple. *An Eye should not speak; it is inappropriate! Its only duty is to spy.*

"Though," the human male continued, tucking a pair of sunglasses into a pocket of his mantle, "the menu here is limited. You'd be best to order an *octli* beer and perhaps a plate of *nopalli*, if you are hungry."

"I am not," Sahâne said, after a moment of consternation. "You have never spoken to me before—is there a . . . a situation? A danger?"

Every member of the Hjogadim delegation on Anáhuac, to the best of Sahâne's knowledge, had at least three Eyes fixed upon them—not all at once, of course, but in rotating shifts throughout the swift Terran day—but always from a distance. This one—tall, as the indigenes went, with sleek dark fur on its head and regular, waxy-skinned features—had always been at least a block away for as long as the Eye had observed the Hjo. That it should come closer—or even *speak* to Sahâne—implied something had gone terribly, terribly wrong.

Ah, the Hjo suddenly realized, *the wretched Eyes don't wish me to purchase trimethoxyphene from this new vendor. The previous merchant must have complained—*

"There is no situation," the toy said, quite calmly. It approximated a Hjo smile, lips tight. "You are perfectly safe. There will be only a slight delay before the priest comes."

Sahâne blinked, feeling a familiar fog of confusion congealing around him. He did not like this place—the backwater polity; the crude, barbarous planet; much less this dreadful bowl of hot smog that passed for a city—and the intrigues and plots of the local princelings did not move him at all. His master the *zhongdu* seemed to take an interest in the chattering and scrabbling of the *humans*, but Sahâne had done his best to stay far, far removed from such things. It was not, after all, his purpose.

"The . . . *hikuli* priest is coming here?" Sahâne whispered tentatively. "How would he know to come—"

"I told him," the human said, unnaturally slim fingers producing a data-crystal, "that you would be a little late, and wished to try authentic Tenochtitlán food. Where else but Tlatelolco would you find such fine grilled dogs? We will need only a moment for our business."

The Hjo's dull black eyes fixed on the message capsule, which was banded with red and seemed to shine with an inner light. "That is one of *ours*," he muttered, feeling his skin heat with distress. "How did you get it?"

The human smiled again. "This is for your master. Will you convey it to the *zhongdu*?"

"I will not," Sahâne hissed. The low ceiling pressed down claustrophobically. "It is not my purpose to exchange messages with your kind! I will be . . . ." The Hjo clamped his mouth shut before *severely punished* escaped into the open air. "I am not a Voice," came out instead, as a hiss.

"If you do not accept the gift," the human said, sharp brown eyes watching the nervous alien and wondering what a "Voice" might be, "then your 'priest' will be further delayed and there will be no godhead to accompany you to the consulate."

The Gods are not here! an ancient-sounding voice sneered among Sahâne's thoughts. *Were they, we would be exalted and these toys churned to ash for our gardens. Were the Gods here, we would not need these pasty sulfates and salts to entertain us! We would burn with—*

"I can find another—" Sahâne rose abruptly and there was a dull *clonk* as his head slammed into the iron candelabra suspended over the table. "Aaah!"

Wincing, the Hjo staggered away from the table, long fur-covered fingers clutching his tapered head. His mouth gaped wide, revealing the heavy rows of grinding molars and chisel-shaped cutting teeth lining his fore-jaw.

"I've got you," the Mirror agent said, steadying the alien arm. The smooth human countenance creased with worry. "You're bleeding, Sahâne-*tzin*."

The Hjo grimaced, wrenching his polluted limb free from the toy's grasp. Beneath his fingers, the warm oozing sensation of a cut was already fading as his scalp-skin crawled back together. "I heal," Sahâne spat. Though his legs felt loose and rubbery, the Hjo fled, staggering up the steps and brushing past a startled-looking youth in vibrant, polychromatic robes carrying a ribbed, dark green effigy pot in his hands.

Behind him, in the dim recess of the restaurant, the young México pretended not to notice the puzzled Xochipilli priest on the stair. He smoothed down his mantle before spraying a biocide on the table and chair where the Hjogadim had rested. Then he glanced around the room to make sure no one was paying any attention and disappeared out through the kitchen.

Down the street, Sahâne stumbled to a halt, leaning against a wall covered with glossy painted tile showing dozens of young boys dressed as bees, birds, and macaws sitting in the branches of a massive tree whose limbs tangled the sun and stars, while the roots twined down amongst the skulls and bones of the dead. Opposite him a stall lined with dozens of flowered cloaks caught the midday sun, casting a hot glow of brilliant hummingbird colors in his watery eyes.

This is a dreadful place, the young alien thought for the thousandth time, pawing in the pouch at his belt for a map token that would lead him to other vendors. *I will just find some alkaloids instead—*

His long fingers brushed against something small, smooth, and cylindrical. The Hjo fell still, hindbrain yielding up a list of everything he'd donned in his cubicle before setting out into the teeming anthill of the human city.

Seconds passed. Sahâne carefully pulled out and regarded the data-crystal with a jaundiced eye. He looked about, saw only the usual throng of humanity, and pitched the irritating little item into the nearest garbage can. Then he stood up, feeling relieved, and loafed off thinking: *Right Thought guides me well, to avoid the complications of lesser creatures at every turn!*

The Hjogadim had gone a good block or more, almost stepping out into the bustling flower market of Tlatelolco to buy his lunch, when another thought intruded: *What if some cunning Eye informs the zhongdu of my meeting, and Demands are made upon me to produce the contraband? If I do not hold it in my hand, it will seem I am hiding Truth or have sold something for my own profit.*

Cursing, he paced back down the alley and retrieved the crystal, which had gone seemingly untouched. Now it seemed far too heavy in his palm.

The little old Yaqui man sitting on the corner did not look up from stuffing his face with fried *chapultin*, nor show the slightest interest in the creature's self-conscious scrabbling in the garbage bin, but the event had not gone unnoticed.

DUMFRIES POST STATION

IMPERIAL CHARTERED COLONY OF NEW ABERDEEN

The leaden gray sky poured down rain as a small backwoods settlement lurched into view through streaming windows. Sitting quietly on a cracked dark green vinyl seat, Green Hummingbird watched weather-worn buildings roll past, their windows shuttered tight against a cold, damp summer. The transit bus slid to a halt before a terminal of patched glass and corroded metal. He climbed down behind a crowd of migrant lumbermen and waited patiently for his turn at the baggage claim.

"Here y'go, graunfaither," a red-faced clerk nodded politely, pushing a heavy leather satchel across the counter. "Welcome t' Dumfries."

Hummingbird paused a moment inside the drafty arrival hall, letting the crowd of travelers carrying waterproof luggage tubs swirl past and out the doors. The crowd was mostly dour-faced humans wearing heavy clothing and knee-high boots. They scuffed across a hard-surfaced floor smeared with yellowish mud and out into the rainy afternoon. A collection of heavy-wheeled vans, crawlers, and logging tenders was waiting. There were no taxis or pedicabs in sight.

When the locals had sorted themselves out, the México ica put away his hand-comp and shrugged into a nondescript Imperial Army surplus poncho. His boots rattled on the slabbed logs making up the sidewalk. Somewhere out of sight, enormous tractors rumbled past heavy with newly cut lumber. Their passage made the puddles filling the street quiver and shake. *On their way to docks at lakeside,* he guessed.

The identifying sign for Dumfries Technical College was far newer than any of the buildings, and each door was marked by irregular patches where older signs had been recently removed. Piles of crumbling, moss-eaten concrete lined the walkways between the classroom halls. Hummingbird passed from building to building, a steadily growing frown etching his face. None of the signage matched what he expected to see. At last, after passing through a grove of dour trueoak which had apparently grown up unplanned in one of the quadrangles, he found an unpainted wooden building turned dull silver with age.

Now his hand-comp chimed quietly, indicating the outline of the old laundry matched a six-week-old Identicast from a Colonial Administration surveillance satellite.

Through a scratched metal door at the end of a dirty hallway, in the basement of the building, Hummingbird found Gretchen Anderssen sitting behind stacks of archaic equipment, her desk covered with manila folders, stacks of memory crystals, and a relatively new comp—though he could see the device lacked a *pochteca* maker's mark.

"These computers were old when I was a young man," he said by way of greeting.

Gretchen did not look up. Her fingers, lined here and there by old scars, moved quickly on the old-style interface.

"There's a pitiful ghost in this corner," the *nauallis* said, forcing himself to step through the door despite an uneasy stomach. "There's no proper sign on your door, no windows . . . this whole building feels . . . ill." He patted the chest of his poncho. "My guidebook says this was formerly the Territorial Prison."

"Then leave," Gretchen said, not bothering to look up from her control slate. "I have work to do. *Paying* work to finish today."

He leaned over the table, reading her comp screen. *Disaster Communications Protocols: Classroom Lockdowns*. One of the side panes was filled with thumbnail-sized video feeds from cameras scattered around the campus. The rest of the display surface was filled with text-readers scrolling constant streams of log data. To his eye, even the fonts seemed archaic.

Hummingbird moved a stack of printed manuals aside and sat down. "ISS will make it worthwhile to listen; I've found a contract for you—a lucrative one—if you've need of more quills than this place can afford."

Gretchen's fingers paused in their movement. Now she did look at him, and her expression was cold. "Do you? Paying like the last one? Not a single quill? An oversupply of broken promises? What will it be this time? Do you know my son Duncan is . . . too old for *calmécac*, even if, at long-last, you came up with tuition and an open door!"

Hummingbird stiffened slightly. "What is this? I kept my end of *Chu-sa* Hadeishi's bargain, Dr. Anderssen."

Gretchen laughed harshly, her oval face suddenly chiseled with tight fury. "Duncan's applications were lost, so the *calmécac* deans say. So sorry. It is too late, Dr. Anderssen. All the deadlines have passed. Perhaps when your son has obtained a certification from your local collegium, he can apply for graduate school?"

Hummingbird sat quietly, his face still.

Gretchen went on. "The colonial government denied us access to the tuition funds. Your so-subtle influences meant *nothing* to these institutions. You have no power over them. I have no delusion that you are capable of paying me anything for my work. Ever. Go away!"

"How does it happen that you are not, at least, still working for The Honorable Company?"

"I am working *here* because I fit with everything *here*. We are unaligned with any of the great families, the big corporations, or the Imperial government. We cater, in fact, to the sons and daughters of the timbering crews, the land-clearing gangs, the Batrax miners, and the local rural population."

She pointed to the door. "If you leave now, you can still catch the last bus. You'll be back at your transport node by noon tomorrow. Find another fool for your dirty work."

Hummingbird did not stand up. He continued sitting quietly, watching her work. Twice, he attempted to dissipate the suffocating atmosphere of the cell-like room with a movement of his wrinkled hand.

"Stop that!" Gretchen turned and gave him a sharp look. The blue flash of her eyes showed her pent-up anger had not abated. "I like it this way. It keeps managers and other carrion birds out of my hair."

Hummingbird smiled a little at her joke, but did not reply. Instead, he continued to wait.

At last, Gretchen gathered her materials together and stood up. "Why are you still here? I told you 'no.'"

"I cannot leave until you accompany me."

She hissed in annoyance, and then shuffled through papers in one of the drawers. "See—" She handed him a closely printed page. "You must leave no later than tomorrow by eleven in the morning, or you'll be stuck here for three days longer. The bus service only runs four days a week."

"*We* should leave tomorrow, Dr. Anderssen. There are several transport changes between Dumfries and the Rim."

"The Rim." Gretchen's eyebrows twitched. Then she shook her head. "I'm late getting home already. You can't stay here. The night watch would shoot you."

The Anderssen homestead hugged a ridge well above the town. Gretchen's mother had picked the site—there was plenty of open space to discourage surprise attacks, and the house sat with its back to the wind among stands of imported spruce and fir. Night had already fallen under the eaves of the forest as they settled onto bare, rocky ground west of the house that served as a landing pad. Together, they pushed the aircar into a pole barn cut into the hillside. Heavy blocks of stone and turf formed three of the walls. Before crossing the garden—all rows of spindly beans on lattices, with some tomatoes and squash in between—Anderssen took a slow careful look around, hand light on the heavy revolver slung at her hip. "You carry a weapon, Crow?"

Hummingbird shook his head, though her tension made him wary.

"There are cats here big as jaguars. And half-humans with the same table manners. Out beyond the town-fence, you should always go armed. Never know what might come roaming by."

"I don't use them," the old man said quietly, keeping clear of her gun hand.

Inside the house and behind a pair of locked, airlock-style doors, Gretchen started to relax. Curt introductions served to identify the México to Grandmother Anderssen and the two girls. Isabelle and Tristan regarded Green

Hummingbird with interest, but when the meal arrived, they quickly fell to whispered gossip from the day. Gretchen's mother caught the wary look Hummingbird gave their sidearms and monofilament knives as she was setting the table for dinner.

"Not the Center, eh?" Grandmother cracked a betelnut and grinned at the old man. "Though we do occasionally put on a duel or blood feud for the tourists. Then it's just like Anáhuac, isn't it?"

Hummingbird ignored the aside, his attention fixed on the hulking gray reptilian shape squatting on a broad, leathery tail at the end of the table. Gretchen smiled wickedly at the old *nauallis'* pained expression when Malakar snuffled around him, her snout wrinkled up in suspicion. Anderssen was in no mood to explain anything to the Crow.

Why volunteer, she thought, *that our old friend spends her nights crouched at my bedside with pen and parchment book, listening to me mutter and sing in my sleep, writing down all the fragmentary bits and pieces of Mokuilite poetry so revealed? It is the least I can do to repay her my life, and her friendship.*

After the plates were emptied and cleared away, and the night was fully upon the house, and with all eyes upon him, Hummingbird nodded to them each in turn and then faced Gretchen. "Your particular skills are urgently needed, Dr. Anderssen."

Both girls perked up at this, but Gretchen felt a cool thread of anger boil up in her chest. *That'll get you nowhere, Crow.* She caught her mother scowling from the kitchen door and held up a finger for pause. "Excuse me." Gretchen took a handheld scrambler from the pantry and set it on the table between them. The constellation of lights on the device flickered, formed a series of random geometric patterns, and then settled into a calm blue square.

Hummingbird tilted his head to one side. He scrutinized the sturdy, if outdated, Vosk Model 12 for a moment, and then nodded approval. In a low voice he went on: "Imperial Scout Service has found something enormous, Anderssen, hidden back in the depths. Within an area of heavy interstellar dust clouds navigators name the *kuub*. Are you familiar with this place?"

Gretchen blinked involuntarily in recognition, then eyed Isabelle and Tristan, who were sitting very quietly at the table, trying their best to remain invisible. "Why don't you two show Malakar how to play that new coaling sim?"

Twin pouts met the invitation, but the code for "make yourselves scarce, this is business," was unmistakable. The disappointed girls left, gathering up their gunrigs and taking the shotguns with them. Gretchen frowned at Hummingbird.

He responded to their exit by pulling a flat packet out of his vest pocket. Unfolded, the package proved to be another, far more modern, scrambler.

"A *something*, Crow? You must have more than that? Something won't get you anything here. . . ."

Hummingbird nodded slightly. He felt more at ease now, to Gretchen, as though the two girls had been a particularly hostile audience. *And maybe they are. . . .*

"There was a Survey mission. Telemetry was received."

"And—"

"There seems to be a multiple singularity within the region."

"Black holes inside a dust cloud? Shouldn't the particles have been drawn into the . . ."

"It's artificial. The whole arrangement has to be." Hummingbird's expression—though it had not appreciably changed—seemed pinched to her. His voice dropped even lower. "Something is holding the clouds at bay . . .

and there's a weapon that snuffed out three ships in as many breaths."

Gretchen felt a flush of heat on her hands and the back of her neck. "How old?"

"You need ask, given the scale of the artifact?"

"Well, yes, Crow, I do need ask. Are you asking me to look at a First or Second Sun creation that'll fry my brain and that of all of my troublesome friends and relatives in a millisecond? Or something young enough it could actually be *studied*?"

A ghostly smile flitted across Hummingbird's face. "Old enough. Old enough to launch an Imperial task force. Under Mirror command."

Under the table, Gretchen clenched and unclenched her fist. *So. A race. And the Hummingbird is not in the thick of it yet.* "When are you leaving?"

Hummingbird grimaced. "When you come with me. What we find . . . will be beyond my capacity to evaluate properly."

She considered her palms, and the glassy scars and nicks lining her fingers.

"Huh. Well, when five hundred thousand quills are *verified* in my mother's Riksbank account, then I'd be happy to go with you. And that will be in *advance*, if you please."

She felt his inward sigh of relief as a knot uncoiling. In the same moment, she felt a sharp pinch between her shoulder blades. Just the sort of feeling you got in the alpenstand when crossing the trail of a *kilikat*.

Ay, she realized, sweating suddenly, *that was an easy catch for him. Goddamnit! We need that money, though. No, they need it.* Gretchen turned her head, relieved to see the girls and Malakar crouched in front of the 3-v, arguing about the loading capacities of the latest mine crawlers. *I don't need anything anymore.*

———

Much later, when Gretchen had sent out the last piece of reporting for her "paying work," she stood up from the scarred kitchen table and turned off the dimming solar lamp.

"*Hoooo*, now." The familiar alien voice spoke softly out of the shadows. "This old one does not trust this 'friend' of yours."

Gretchen nodded ruefully. The scrape and rustle of the Jehanan's long furred coat filled the doorway to the main hall. "You shouldn't. He is not a nice man." She moved to pass by, but Malakar placed a long, broad-fingered hand on her shoulder. Though old and hunched, the alien still outweighed Anderssen by twenty or thirty kilos.

"It stinks of disease and death." The triply lidded eyes blinked slowly, revealing deep-set irises tucked into a bony integument. "Broken shells and ash—"

SHINEDO

Winter clung tight to the city. Icy fogs daily filled the darkened streets, driving most inhabitants to hearth and bed. This day the prostitutes were asleep, the bartender dozing. Listless, Hadeishi sat on the stage in the empty tea house, plinking away at a mournful tune. He was regretting the lack of even a few quills to purchase sheet music. *How am I supposed to entertain, when*—

The traditional cloth curtain at the front of the main room parted with the slight shimmer of an environment field, allowing in a gust of chill air and a sleek-haired woman dressed in a conservative pale blue winter suit over a black sweater, pants, and high boots.

"*Konnichi-wa*," she said, drawing a 3-v card from inside her jacket. The woman held up the tiny pasteboard, which flickered to life when pressed between her thumb and forefinger. After an instant of intense scrutiny—comparing his own face to the picture—she nodded in satisfaction.

"Hadeishi-*tzin*? A pleasure to meet you."

Hadeishi laid aside his instrument and returned the bow.

She tapped a modest pendant hanging at her neck, which generated a full-featured holo in the air before him. A duplicate of the woman's face appeared, surrounded by blocks of text and a variety of commercial *mon*. In more refined circles, his comp would have exchanged greetings and security protocols with hers, verifying her identity. Here he was satisfied her amber-hued eyes matched tone and color from life to holocast.

"I am Bela Imwa, representing the Rusman Corporation. We provide crews for the major shipping concerns and liner companies. I understand you are Listed as an engineer's mate?"

Hadeishi found himself nodding. *Not for long years, woman—*

"There is a ship—"

Hadeishi was nonplussed. His mind raced, trying to frame some response, but the woman continued, blithely unaware of the abrupt struggle between pride and raw greed that seized hold of his tongue and held him helpless.

"A small ship, which has need of a junior engineer. If you are not already contracted here"—Imwa indicated the bar, the sleeping prostitutes, and the spiderwebbed curtains with a wave of her fine-boned hand—"then we may fulfill our obligation by arranging your service."

I've not served in Engineering since I was a cadet. My course seemed so promising then. Hadeishi realized he was gaping at her, while she waited patiently for his response. He resisted the urge to explain what he was doing playing *samisen* in a house of pleasure. *Now it seems I cannot even rate as an officer on some tramp steamer.*

"When—when does she lift?" He croaked out at last.

The Javan smiled prettily and drew a crisp-edged packet from the inner pocket of her jacket. "As soon as there are hands to fire the reactors."

"I will consider it," he said, and with another bow the young woman left.

Hadeishi scanned the papers to see if they were some kind of joke; then he sat down on the edge of the small, dark stage and read through them carefully. Now he regretted parting with his Fleet surplus comp and comm. Both would have made verifying the recruiting company and everything else about Miss Imwa and this . . . this *ship* . . . far easier.

I will have to go see this scow for myself, he thought, amused.

Then he realized just how tightly he was holding the papers, and how fast his heart was beating.

Despite the poor weather—morning rains had turned to sleet and then a nasty, treacly slush in the streets—Mitsuharu found himself loitering across the cargo road from liftpad ninety-two later that afternoon. The bulk of the ship was visible behind a tattered razorwire fence and a series of tar-shingled warehouses held together by broadsheet advertisements.

Small, was his first thought, looking up the sixty-meter-high shape. *Cramped inside . . . but lean. Those atmospheric drive fairings look a little big for this class of barge.*

It felt strange, to be standing groundside, sizing up the tiny starship. He felt crippled, without the constant ebb and flow of data on the threatwell, the reassuring chatter of his bridge crew in his earbug. *I'm the crew!* he realized, and perversely the thought heartened him. *Even as Musashi was always alone, yet never lacking companions. And what would the sword-saint think of this ship?*

With a more critical eye, Hadeishi waited for the latest line of lorries to rumble past, then walked quickly across, his boots crunching in the icy slush. The air was thick with fumes and constantly hammered with enormous bursts of noise. Every ten or twelve minutes a ship or shuttle lifted off from somewhere in the sprawling expanse of the *uchumon*, and each time the whole world shuddered. The gate to the pad was half ajar, but he did not enter. Instead, he walked past, craning his head to see the flanks of the little ship, the way she sat on the blast-plates, whether there was rust or grime caking her intakes—what he could see of them, anyway.

The gangway into the lower cargo deck was foul with sooty ash and oil. The painted letters identifying the registration numbers and name were almost unreadable; micrometeoroid scaling had worn them away. He could still see, however, the outline of a string of *katakana* representing the word *Wilful*.

Musashi, he thought sourly, *would be disappointed. This isn't even a smugglers' ship! It's just . . . small, nondescript, and poorly maintained.*

But in the back of his mind, a casual voice said: *She is still a ship, and she can still make transit.*

Hadeishi could not disagree, so he traced his way back to the gate. There he stood for a moment, turning the Rusman Corporation hiring packet over in his wiry hands. This one thing stood out in a peculiar way—the contract chits and packaging were all first rate, the agency far too expensive for the presumed owners of the battered old *Wilful*. There was no lack of "hiring agencies" in the office parks ringing *uchumon*, and none of them would employ an expensive-looking Javan . . . not for a contract as paltry as this.

"Hmm." *An intrigue of some kind.* But whose? Standing in the cold slush, surrounded by the scents and sounds of the port, with an actual ship in front of him, he found he did not care. He pushed aside the half-open gate and went in search of the purser.

The crew did not take to Mitsuharu. The bosun, a stringy Frank in a stained shirt and nondescript work pants, directed Hadeishi to a hammock slung behind the number two heat exchanger, in a space previously inhabited by a refrigeration unit, and mostly filled with spare boxes of ration bars. A fine layer of grime coated the floor, overlaid by discarded litter, and the walls were mottled with dings and cracks.

The cubbyhole was mostly private and Mitsuharu settled in with his few remaining belongings, including the lamentable *samisen*. Some sticktack and spare wire scavenged from the bins under the engineer's desk made a hanger for the instrument, and then he lay back in the hammock to consider the conclusion of his grand career as a musician. *And well done with,* he thought, relieved. His efforts had only embarrassed the shade of his father, which was doubtless now resting easily once more in the Western Paradise.

A day after Hadeishi had come aboard and been pointed to his hole, the engineer returned—he was a Marocâin, showing faint traces of Swedish blood, named Azulcay. The officer scowled at Mitsuharu, ordered him to "clean things up"—and then disappeared into the upper decks of the tiny ship to consult with the captain. Barely had Mitsuharu started stowing tools and making sure nothing was going to come loose the next time they turned over the engines, than the Bosun returned and detailed him off to help load cargo.

This led to a raised eyebrow on Mitsuharu's part; the cargo holds were some kind of refit—a pair of modernized transfer bays sitting on opposite sides of the ship. Though they had a passable ground-loading configuration with extending ramps and a forklift, to his eye they were custom built for open-space resupply with a matching pair of z-g gantries in each hold.

Realizing this, as he helped two other crewmen guide a heavy cargo pallet up the A-ramp, Hadeishi felt a tiny jolt of adrenaline and a tiny fragment of *chambara* rose out of his memory: *Musashi sitting under a bridge, in the rain, with twenty or thirty other rootless men, listening to them complain about the weather, the lack of food, the cold. And marking they were all missing the same* mon *from their* haori, *and the underlying colors were all of a kind.*

He started to whistle a little tune under his breath as they rolled the pallet into one of the holds.

When the loading was done, the Bosun failed to reappear, leaving Hadeishi an opportunity to investigate the farther corners of the *Wilful*. Much of the ship itself was a mess, showing signs of clumsy repair and refitting, but some things very much in order were not easy to hide. The overly large atmospheric drive fairings on the outer hull were matched by a series of interesting bulkheads ringing the hyperspace coil and the maneuvering drives.

He ran a hand along one of the bulkheads, feeling the metal tremble with the action of hidden engines. *A little overpowered, I think. There's something beyond the usual gear behind these walls.*

Mitsuharu's movements on the ship were limited—there were too many locked doors and hatchways to allow for *all* his curiosity—but he was beginning to feel her out.

She might be fast. He rubbed his hands together and grinned quietly. Not even the foul air seeping into his quarters from the fuel stowage dimmed his cheer. Sitting in the semidarkness, feeling the *Wilful* throbbing at his back, reactor idling in port, Hadeishi counted up the days and was ashamed to find his "abyss of despair" had lasted only twelve weeks. "Barely three months! Addict!"

His soft laugh drew a glare from Azulcay, who had returned from "upstairs."

"You, Nisei. Make yourself useful. The below-decks mess needs a cook. The rest of us need dinner. Move."

The mess proved to need more than a cook, but the simple act of opening the self-heating threesquares and doling out portions gave Mitsuharu a satisfaction out of proportion to the minimal nutrition obtained from the food. Out of long habit, he sat quietly watching the dozen men eating at the single long table while he nursed a cup of tea. *Possibilities,* he mused. *Under the dirt and sloth. Something could be done with them.*

The *Wilful* lumbered into space the next day and a shadow lifted from Mitsuharu's mind. The tug of gravity faded, the ship shivered alive under hand and foot, and even though his spirits sagged momentarily at the tremulous moan the engine emitted, he smiled to be home again.

"Stop smirking," barked the engineer, who was listening to the maneuver drives with a cocked head. "One of the translator circuits is going bad. Get that kit and follow me."

TENOCHTITLÁN

OLD EARTH

High on the side of a skytower rising above the neon tumult of the Tlapocan district, a thin, darkly handsome México of indeterminate years stepped from an unmarked aircar and onto a landing platform shining crimson with silken carpet. Six guardsmen had preceded him, each shrouded in combat armor, their faces invisible behind armored masks skinned as jaguars. The nobleman paused, waiting for his bodyguards to check their perimeter and signal an all-clear. While he waited on the open platform, a hot southern wind tousled his long, straight hair, carrying with it the stench of the largest city in the world—burning rubber and plastic, the smoke from countless fires, and the acrid tang of industrial solvents exuded from the endless kilometers of factories, workshops, foundries filling the old city districts climbing the surrounding mountains. Such was the heady air of the Valley of the México people, Anáhuac.

The lead guardsman snapped shut a portable sensor and inclined his head towards the man standing quietly in the center of the platform.

"Clear, my lord," growled the Jaguar-Knight. The nobleman nodded slightly, and then lifted his arms. A manservant stripped away his mantle and undertunic, leaving nothing but bare flesh. A second servant immediately ran his thumb—enhanced with a spurlike ring—along the man's shoulders, arms, sides, and down to his heels. The first servant hurried back from the aircar and now gathered up the almost-invisible skinsuit puddling at the México's feet.

Now the second servant produced a slim metallic wand and carefully ran the device around the periphery of the man's limbs, eyes fixed on a tiny readout. When he was done, the servant nodded sharply to the México, who let out an infinitely small breath of relief. He shrugged his shoulders, loosening the muscles, and then beckoned for the heavy Tatarsky coat just carried from the aircar. A sleek ermine-fur hat followed, and both servants made a careful check of cuffs, belt, and boots before whispering "all is well" in the man's ear.

The pattern word made something *click* in his mind, and the omnipresent exocortex overlay that daily informed his vision faded away.

The Jaguar-Knight stepped away from the man's side, his heavy *Yaomitl* plasma-rifle at half port. The safety interlock was sealed and peace-bonded with a texite strap, but none of the guardsmen could bear to leave their weapons behind, not even here. The circle of iron parted, allowing the México to approach the single door exiting the platform.

The portal was massive—six meters high—and formed of a single anthracite slab. The walls on either side gleamed dully, showing the refractive sheen of battlemetal. When the man's step reached a hand-span from the door, there was a soft hissing sound and the entire massive structure folded up and away into a hidden cavity. Beyond, a dark corridor receded, lit only by a line of pale blue lights on the floor. Chill air billowed out around the nobleman, biting at his high cheekbones and stinging his lips. Eddies of fog formed as the near-freezing atmosphere inside the corridor mixed with the thick, warm air of central México.

"Await me," the man said to the Jaguar-Knight before stepping away and pacing down the corridor, fog boiling at his heels. "I will return in due time."

The twenty-meter-long passage was entirely empty—and in truth, in the whole of the man's life this was possibly the only time he was truly alone—and ended in a second titanic slab of stone. As the first had risen, this one receded into the floor at his approach and again the temperature dropped. Hoar-frost now rimed the walls, though the chamber beyond was well appointed with large, heavily constructed chairs, a pair of low waiting tables, and behind them—on walls cloaked in heavy silken tapestries—a vast collection of curious artifacts.

Gorgeous masks and finely wrought amulets, tiny figurines of gold and silver, one or two delicate statues in glossy marble—a collection of treasures, all drawn from the cities, nations, and principalities of Anáhuac—and all well known to the México, who had spent many interminable hours considering them as he waited in this very room.

Thus are our museums plundered, he thought drily. Any anger had long since been schooled from him. *And our history held up to mock us.*

This time he did not pace along the walls, but rather stood quietly, attempting to conserve some vestige of the summer heat in the folds of his coat. The first time the nobleman had entered this chamber—sixty years ago, more or less—he'd come close to hypothermia and he had no desire to lose fingers or toes to hastiness.

A breathing technique, imparted by a *nauallis* of his acquaintance, settled his mind, slowing his heartbeat and moderating his metabolism. His mind, usually filled to capacity with a thousand and one details, all warring with one another for his attention, fell quiet as well. In other circumstances, the México would have welcomed a moment of quiet meditation.

Here, however, such efforts were part and parcel of his preparations.

No more than an hour later, a creature appeared out of one of the passages opening into the waiting area, and the México was curiously surprised. He guessed—and a review of historical records would later confirm—this was the shortest that either he, or one of his predecessors, had ever waited.

Odd, he allowed himself to think.

The servitor gestured sharply with a wrinkled gray-black hand and then turned away. The México followed without hesitation and moments later had climbed a flight of steep, granite steps into a second room—this one well known to him, and occupied by a being he knew far too well. Like the servitor, the creature, sitting upon a large chair of some bloodred wood, was wrinkled and gray-black with a heavy, close-napped fur. To a human, it seemed as though a two- or three-meter-high tapir had found hind legs and stood up. A pair of shiny, feverish eyes was placed far back in deep sockets on either side of a long, tapering skull which ended in a pair of slit-like nostrils. Though his scientists had not dared to dissect the rare Hjo which fell prey to misfortune in Imperial space, the México knew the alien could withstand tremendously cold temperatures, that it was very fast when startled, and stronger—kilo for kilo—than an equivalent human. In other circumstances, the suffering the Hjo must endure in the Anáhuac summer might have drawn a drop of compassion from the México, but in this case—he often prayed for even worse heat and drought to afflict his city.

"Esteemed Ekbanz." The man bowed precisely as low as required, then stood up straight with benign attention arrayed upon his face. "Guide me to Right Thought."

"Right Thought? *Right Thought?*" The *zhongdu* Ekbanz's brow furrowed sharply and his eyes gleamed with distaste. "Ever we are displeased to hear sacred words from your pitiful lips." A massive hand cut the air sharply. "Though so you must address us, as guided by Law . . ." There was a long, high-pitched hiss as the creature exhaled through a set of multivalved nostrils.

The nobleman neither spoke nor moved. He felt his own naturally smooth brown skin blotching and pitting with the cold in the audience room. He waited an unseemly period for the *zhongdu* to continue, but by continued slow breathing and a focused mind he kept from making an unwise movement, or showing any hint of the grim cold which was stealing into his limbs.

At last, the *zhongdu* stirred from his contemplations and exposed a single claw tip. The appendage gleamed with red and black lacquer as it pointed at the man's chest. "You have neglected Duty. You have broken the third agreement, human. By Law, this entire system should be forfeit to us—an example to be made, of cindered worlds and ashy skies. . . ."

What has come to his attention? And more important, who was the messenger? "Esteemed—"

"You cannot force harmony from this dissonance! My sources are accurate, timely, detailed in their facts."

Just fishing for information? I wonder. "The third agreement?"

The *zhongdu* bared his teeth. Even at this distance, its breath was hot upon the México's face. "With proper concessions, We may be satisfied with a colony world serving as an example. What do you offer to restore proper balance between us?"

"Esteemed, I still await the accusations."

The Hjo grimaced, revealing twin rows of tiny, cutting

teeth. "You are a bold servant, human. But this is not a matter for a Speaker of the Law to adjudicate. This is between *us*. Our arrangements require that you provide us with *all* evidence of the Ones-Who-Wait in a prompt and forthright matter. If you have found *anything* . . ."

Ahuizotl felt suddenly, unaccountably sad. *An Imperial security breach. At the highest levels. The Mirror, I would think. Now there must be another purge.* He straightened his shoulders. "Esteemed, I assure you that the evidence is quite poor. It consists only of three missing ships. We are mounting an effort to examine the area of space and determine if a permanent hazard to navigation exists, and if so, to determine what it might be that all might avoid the region in future."

The *zhongdu* settled back, wrinkling his long leathery snout, and took a protracted drag on a *nargile* sitting beside the chair. The sharp scent reaching the México's nostrils suggested opium, or another derivative of the poppy. *No, not just opium. Something else less subtle. Probably synthetic. Remarkable how much psychoactivity Hjo physiology absorbs without noticeable effect. It is true that in his place I, too, should not be pleased. Nor surprised.*

After a moment, the creature issued a long, coiling stream of smoke from one nostril. Its eyes had settled back in their sockets, leaving only a faint, disgusted gleam.

Ekbanz considered the human with disgust. *Look at the fragile, pink-skinned toy in the heavy jacket and fur-lined cloak! See how it mimics Us, as though taking our seeming would confer our strength! This one seems sick, too. Behold the yellowing of the eyes. But Right Thought has guided it to me, just as my patience with Sahâne wanes. Their ships are fragile—easily lost in the abyss—yes, there is Purpose to be found here.*

"We shall send an expert to review the situation," the *zhongdu* declared. "As we have great experience in such matters."

"Esteemed, such generosity is far beyond our—" the México began.

"*Hsst!* Your fleet's departure requires our emissary aboard the flagship. Do not consider otherwise."

"Of course, Esteemed." The México bowed his head. *I hope your agent is disposable.* "The expedition's departure is imminent. The last shuttle leaves this evening at the second dinner hour."

The *zhongdu* shook its head slowly. "You will wait until the emissary arrives. Go now and prepare. Your presence here is no longer required."

Despite an intense desire to begin running, the man held a measured pace as he removed himself from the chamber. Once outside, in the blue-lit tunnel, he clenched his jaw against a stabbing pain behind both temples. *A migraine and no med-band to alleviate the pressure.*

With the toy gone, Ekbanz glared down at the pitiful specimen his servitors now dragged before him. The *zhongdu* felt a painful throbbing in his forebrain, just from considering the doleful aspect of the Hjo at his feet. But, as was proper, he said nothing for a long moment, partaking of the bitter smoke provided by the water pipe.

"A punishment is in order," he declared at last, "for disturbing the right order of *my* heavens. You were sent here with great expectations, Sahâne, but you have only proven how low your noble line has fallen." The *zhongdu* made a gesture indicating large and abiding regret. His nostrils flared wide to inhale the aspect of the young priest suffering deliciously from pure fear. Ekbanz felt almost repaid for having this embarrassment cluttering up the embassy for so many months. "The Hypothesis that brought all of this about was posited by *you*, and you will prove it out."

Sahâne's nose quivered. "Esteemed, I only imagined . . ."

"Pack your bags. You will accompany the local toys to investigate this anomaly."

"Yes, of course. Guide my Thoughts."

"They shall find Guidance."

Sahâne shuffled out into the outer hallway and sank immediately into a dreadful depression. *Isn't it enough that I am exiled to this backwater?* He fished about in his pouch for a box of opium pellets. *I am too large of mind and body to be stuffed into a miniature spaceship! How shall I stand the smell and chatter of these ignorant toys? It will take too long—these foolish exercises are beyond the Rim. The universe is full of worthless stellar clusters. I am no astronomer! This is beneath the station of anyone in my family! Pah!*

"Ah, Most Honored One . . . word has it that you have received a crucial posting, a task from the *zhongdu* himself. Where are you going?"

The young Hjo straightened up, seeing two older members of the embassy approaching. Their fur was lying quite flat and still, indicating hidden amusement and delight.

"As you can well guess," he replied, trying to keep his voice level, "this is a secret mission, and not to be bandied about. I must leave you now. There is little time to prepare."

He brushed past the others quickly, but still heard the sneering whisper: "Maybe the great Sahâne can bring Right Thought to the humans and their chattels!"

"Yes, a task worthy of our esteemed holy one!"

"I do not need servants to remind me of my family duties," the young Hjo mumbled to himself. "More than a thousand generations of noble duty are more reputation than any one Hjogadim of the Sacred Line should have to bear." Once safely inside his sleeping compartment Sahâne slumped against the hatchway. "Little is more useless," he whispered bitterly to the nearest wall, "than the last priest of a race without need for Gods."

A thousand meters away, the unmarked aircar lifted from the landing stage with a swirl of dust and sped away into the thick, humid sky. A constant layer of cloud lay over the city, trapped beneath the massive dome which enclosed the Capital. The vapors and exhalations of the millions living below rose upward, forming a microclimate beneath the glassite despite the presence of thousands of air circulators in the dome superstructure. The leaden clouds replied with a constant, stinging rain.

Two kilometers from the skytower, four *Tocatl*-class airtanks dropped out of the gloom and settled into formation around the aircar. Now the entire convoy increased speed, racing northwest across the sprawl. In the comfortable passenger compartment, the nobleman coughed harshly and rubbed his temples, trying to banish the remaining chill. The servants had dressed him on the platform, resealing his armored skinsuit, applying a fresh med-band, and pressing a cup of circulatory stimulant into his hands.

The *kaffe* had gone into the disposal as soon as he was alone. He needed the warmth, but his stomach would not stand the acidity of the drink. And now his mind was full again, and ten thousand priorities vied for his attention.

The *zhongdu*'s command, however, held sway in his thoughts.

But what could be done? If the Hjogadim wanted to interfere, then he must let them. "There is too much set on this throw to provoke another crisis," he said aloud to the mauve and gunmetal blue compartment.

"Would you care for hot *cacahuatl?*" the CabinComp asked in a soothing feminine voice.

"Later." The México tapped up a panel showing the faces of five men. Four were quite alike, handsome and clear-faced, flint-eyed, each radiating a sureness of spirit which would have made another father positively glow with joy. The last was a sallow, dissolute wreck with puffy features and lank hair. Despite his intent, the man's eyes settled there and remained for a long time.

"Tezozómoc, my son," the México breathed at last, running the edge of his little finger along the side of the 3-v pane. "You were such a beautiful child. . . ." Great sadness suffused the *Tlaltecutli*'s face, here in this false privacy. The image before him melted into that of a little black-haired baby held in a woman's arms. His large, bright eyes looked out from the folds of a blanket. "Now look at you . . . my little, little boy. What has become of you?"

After a long moment, the Emperor passed his hand over the pane and it folded away. Only the four mighty brothers remained. Outside the armored windows, the convoy threaded between soaring towers aglow with neon and searchlights. Tenochtitlán the Eternal sprawled out to fill the bowl of the Valley of the México like a lake of living gold. The cold fire of his city lighted Ahuizotl's face while he considered each of his sons in turn. *Four of the finest warriors we can produce,* he mused. *Equipped with the finest training, with dearly bought exocortex overlays, genetically enhanced . . . which should I spend on this useless exercise? Who goes to the eagle's stone?*

Minutes later, he reached out from deep thought to

com Xochitl, his second-eldest, popularly know as "precious flower."

"My son," he began without greeting. "I have a task, a mission which I wish you to undertake."

"My father, I . . ."

The Emperor did not permit a response. "Someone exceptionally trustworthy must convey an agent of the *zhongdu* beyond the Rim. It is *possible* that a weapon of the First Sun has been found. Considering your capabilities, I am confident that no one else will serve. Understand that the Mirror is already on station, monitoring the device . . . and a Fleet battle-squadron will be underway within the hour."

Ahuizotl could see the combined suspicion and pleasure in Xochitl's face. *His tutors did train him to be ever wary. But he is my son, and he wishes to earn my good regard.*

"Surely one of the Admiralty would . . ."

"This is family business. You must understand that. None else can assume the responsibility." Ahuizotl smiled. "And who, then, should I send? Tezozómoc the Glorious? To command the *Tlemitl*?"

Xochitl laughed nastily. Pleasure at his father's apparent favor flushed his face. "The *Tlemitl*, you say?"

"Yes. She has just cleared the fitting yards. And it is only proper that you should command her. But carefully now," the Emperor went on, a serious tone creeping into his voice. "The Scout Service may have found something *real* out in the back of beyond, and if they have, the single most important thing you must do is make sure this Hjogadim emissary *does not find out* what it is. Too, he must be returned safely to Anáhuac. And of course, we must secure the relic or object for our own use. You understand?"

Xochitl nodded.

Ahuizotl knew his son's blood would be afire with

the prospect of reaching high enough to touch the face of *Tonatiuh* itself. As for himself, the Emperor felt exhaustion and sadness settle deeper into his bones. *We cannot afford the loss of a ship like the* Firearrow *... not now. I can spare a son, but not her ... curse the Mirror, the Judges, and all meddlers!*

He tapped the channel closed, an old song coming to mind—something he'd heard long ago, in his innocence, from one of the elders at Chapultepec:

> *Oh youths, here there are skilled men with*
> *shield-reeds,*
> *In the flowers of the pendant eagle plume,*
> *The yellow flowers they grasp; they pour forth noble*
> *songs,*
> *Noble flowers;*
> *They make payment with their blood,*
> *With their bare breasts*
> *They seek the bloody field of war.*
> *And you, O friends, put on your black paint*
> *For war, for the path of victory;*
> *Let us lay hands on our shields,*
> *Raise aloft our strength and courage.*

THE AKBAL YARDS

OFF EUROPA, THE JOVIAN SYSTEM

Koshō entered the temporary officer's mess on the *Naniwa* balancing a tray of tea, rice pudding, and sliced fruit on her right hand, while a heavy set of construction binders were tucked under her left arm. The room seemed enormous to her after the cramped quarters on the *Cornuelle*.

Due to the rush of work underway to complete fitting out the ship, there were sections of wall panel missing, and several ceiling tiles were pulled up, exposing bundles of comm and power conduit.

Two long tables ran the length of the room and both were crowded with officers of all stripes, busily digging into bowls of rice, fried egg, picken, and chillis. As soon as she'd stepped across the threshold, the nearest ensign shot up out of his place on the tatami and bawled, "*Chusa* on deck!"

Everyone paused, chopsticks in midair, and the veterans cast amused looks at the clean-shaven young man, so fresh from Academy. No one else stood up, though everyone was paying close attention to the new commander's response.

"As you were," Susan announced to the room, which brought a rustling sound as everyone relaxed. Then she nodded politely to the ensign, saying: "We are not so formal at mealtimes, *Sho-i* Deskae. A well-fed crew is a hardworking crew. Please continue with your breakfast."

The boy was back at his bowl of noodles faster than the eye could follow, bronzed skin darkening in embarrassment. Susan hid a smile as she paced along the tables towards her place at the far end. After a dozen paces she slowed, noting an empty *zabuton* between two senior petty officers from Engineering—but there was a little, mahogany-skinned man sitting cross-legged on the floor in just such a way as to block anyone else from sitting on the cushion.

Koshō stopped, looking down at his bald head and was dismayed to glimpse her own reflection. *Ay, I look haggard as a fishwife,* she thought. *Three months of sixteen-hour days wears . . . that it does.*

Her initial postings to the destroyer *Ceatl*, and then the *Cornuelle*, had begun nearly a decade after the light cruiser's commissioning, and though they'd been in dry dock or offlined for repairs many times, Hadeishi had always been in the middle of the actual repair work, leaving her to manage the local authorities and run security while he crawled around in the engines with Isoroku and the grease-monkeys. Under normal conditions, she'd have had the option to task her XO with the engineering review or take it herself—but *Sho-sa* MacMillan had not yet arrived from his previous command—and that left her very shorthanded.

Now *she* was the one in the conduits, banging her head and shuffling around after the construction foremen and *Kikan-cho* Hennig while the engineers talked nonstop about kinetic absorption rates in the between-frame armor and the spalling tendencies of the new model g-decking.

She had never felt better in her entire life, or more exhausted. Every cell in her brain had been stretched in three or four directions, and then snapped back into place. *But she's my ship, and I have—at last—my own command.*

It had not really occurred to her, until now, how long she'd spent on the *Cornuelle*, banging around in the dark, out beyond the fringes of Imperial control. She was years behind the others from her Academy class in achieving a ship command—*but there is a balance,* Koshō reminded herself, *none of the others were given a battle-cruiser.* None of them had her combat experience.

"*Chu-sa* Koshō," the man said, peering up at her with a pair of black eyes. The pupil and irises were almost exactly the same peat-dark brown, leaving only a thin white ring to outline them against his skin. He was wearing the somber black uniform of the Engineering service—not the shipboard branch, which was under the purview of the Fleet, but the station-side arm, which ran the sprawling complex of orbital habitats, forges, construction frames, and fitting stations which comprised the Akbal yards.

A Mayan, she thought with interest. *Of an old, old family. What an astounding profile.*

"Oc Chac, *kyo*," he said, bowing stiffly to her once he'd stood.

"A pleasure," she replied, then paused a split second before saying: "Is there something wrong with this *zabu-ton*?"

Chac nodded, lips thinning.

"Should it be replaced?"

He shook his head, *no.*

His silence was both amusing and irritating at the same time, and she was hungry.

Chac frowned, thought for a moment, and then shook his head. "*Chu-sa*, be mindful of this mess hall—always leave one seat empty. Always."

"What suggests this?" She shifted the binders under the tray and started picking at her sliced fruit.

"Saving yours, *kyo*, there are only twenty-five seats." He indicated the tables and Koshō saw this was indeed the case. "The last to sit will be—must be—in the thirteenth chair, regardless of how they enter."

"Ah," she said, suddenly realizing who he must be. "You are our *hafuri* priest."

"No!" He shook his bald head abruptly. "The *jichin-sai* rites to consecrate the hull will be performed by others, before you leave the yards. I am your fitting officer, *kyo*."

But our hafuri bonze *should . . .* "You're not our fitting officer," she said, voice suddenly cold. "You're our *superstitions* officer."

Chac's impassive face seemed to congeal, and Susan bit down on further angry words. *That was not polite.*

"Starmen *are* . . . superstitious, *Chu-sa*," the Mayan

hissed, trying to keep his voice down. Koshō realized she'd cut him to the quick with the heedless statement. "Do not tempt fate! You bring this ship bad luck enough, *kyo*, without provoking Camaxtli with your rudeness!"

"Bad luck?" Susan's eyes narrowed to bare slits.

"Not that you are a woman!" Chac hissed, standing his ground. Though Koshō would never be accounted tall, she had a good two inches over the tiny Mayan. But he did not flinch away from her. "Your last ship died, her crew disgraced, captain sent down to the List . . . you think no one here *knows* what happened at Jagan? And you survived? Were promoted? How dearly bought was that last golden skull, *Chu-sa*? Did your family pay?—Or did you?"

"I see." Koshō felt still and cold, the Mayan's words a well-placed dart straight to the heart. She turned, sweeping the mess with a sharp, piercing glance. Every officer sat still as a statue—staring at the two of them in varying degrees of interest, horror, and uncertainty. "Rumor is fleet of foot, they say, and your ears will be filled with all manner of calamities." Her voice echoed from the unfinished *shoji*. "I will say this—and no more—the *Cornuelle* was well and truly caught in a trap at Jagan. Her captain taken by surprise, myself trapped planet-side when the ship was stricken. The Admiralty made many excuses for us, but none of them are the truth. We had been out on patrol *too long*. We were far past tired, and our ship had worn down to nothing . . . a stupid, deadly mistake her captain rues to this day. *His* soul was in that ship, and now—with *Cornuelle* sent to the breaking yards—he is lost as well."

Koshō inclined her head towards the ensigns sitting near the main door. "Remember this lesson. *Chu-sa* Hadeishi was one of the finest ship-handlers you could ever meet—and even he was caught out—defeated—by an enemy whose first weapon was patience. The odds *always* turn against you."

"So is my belief, *kyo*," Chac said, in a voice too low for the others to hear. "And what did you learn from this excellent teacher?"

Koshō's right hand tightened on the breakfast tray. The Mayan matched her frigid stare without flinching, then raised one eyebrow minutely, bowed, and made his way out of the room. Susan did not watch him go, but stalked to her seat and sat down.

Koshō took two deep breaths, closed her eyes for a moment, and then set to eating the rice pudding. *A fine breakfast with my officers,* she thought, chewing mechanically. *Very fine.*

The next week passed in a blur of construction review, sitting in with *Thai-i* Goroemon while the Logistics officer bartered with Supply Service to fill the ship's holds with perishables and spare parts, and the lengthy business of actually meeting all of her department heads and their staff. In all the confusion of the tribunal at Toroson and the hurry to get to her new command, Susan had neglected to obtain the services of a manservant or—as she might have claimed—a maid. She'd always considered Hadeishi's maintenance of old Yejin some kind of a charitable arrangement . . . until now, when she woke one morning, twenty-one days after reporting aboard the *Naniwa*, and found she had not a single clean uniform left in her closet. The ship, of course, boasted a fine, modern laundry, but *someone* had to gather up the dirty clothes and send them off to be cleaned.

Her comm chimed politely, reminding her that *Thaisho* Kasir—the operational commander of the Yards—was expecting her on v-cast within the hour. A whole set of Fleet orders packets had arrived during shipnight and they required discussion with the *Zosen* officers responsible for the *Naniwa*'s construction, as well as other personnel issues she would have to manage herself.

Grandmother Suchiru would put her cane to the soles of my feet for this. . . . Koshō stiffened at the thought of facing a superior Fleet officer in a less-than-immaculate uniform. *All night and all day. What to do? Improvise. I will improvise.*

Frowning, Susan commed the laundry and asked the petty officer on duty to send someone around to collect everything, then she found a reasonably clean kimono and clipped her hair back.

Laughing a little at herself, Koshō sat at her desk, woke up her main comp, and unfolded three v-panes on the desk surface. *Chapultepec lower form never taught a better lesson than this!*

Her stylus skipped across the control interface in a blur as she called up a skinning module, mapped her proper dress whites onto a splice of the v-cast feed routed back from the pickup nodes to pane two, then set pane three to show her what the admiral would see.

Six minutes before the v-cast started, she was finished tweaking herself and the door cycled open to admit one of the midshipmen.

"*Kyo?*"

"Everything is over there, Jushin-*tzin*." She watched him for a moment, toying with a pair of reassignment packets from the bigger pile, as he bustled around, gathering up uniform tunics. A thought occurred to her while she was waiting. "*Ko-hosei*—do you know if our fitting officer is still aboard?"

"Chac-*tzin*?" Jushin's expression was carefully neutral. "I believe so, *Chu-sa.*"

"Excellent." Koshō considered the packets sitting on

her desk, then shook her head. *I will just have to make do with the resources at hand.*

Two hours later, Susan had an excellent view of the construction frame enclosing the six-hundred-meter length of the *Naniwa*. Beyond the spindly web of metal and the hundreds of canisters queuing to be unloaded into the cargo bays, the striated orb of Jupiter blotted out most of the visible sky. The constellation of orbital habitats holding station between Europa and the gas giant were off to her left, though invisible save for the tiny moving flares of shuttles or cargo lighters trolling between the wide-spread components of the Akbal complex.

Koshō stepped carefully, wending her way along the hexacomb pattern of the shipskin tiles. Her combat armor boots were magnetized, as were the narrow walkways installed for the final fit-out of the ship. Primary hull construction had been completed early the previous year—the last sixteen months had been spent by the *Zosen* installing crew compartments, weapon systems, fuel bladders, and so on.

With the loading bays and internal atmosphere operational, the shipskin had been laid down—a quarter-million tiles according to one of the binders now filling up the tiny office in her quarters—and punched down to the shipnet. Each tile was composed of a multi-phase composite which could deform—within limits, of course—upon command. Reflective or refractive surfaces could deploy within milliseconds, absorptive ones as well. They were tough, too. A diamond-bit saw could barely scuff their surface, much less cut the material.

But the *Chu-sa* knew there were gangs of yard specialists running hundreds of tests against the skin, looking for defective linkages, bad command interfaces, or skunky tiles which had—for unknown reasons—lost their ability to deform with acceptable speed. Her boots trampling on the quiescent surface would trigger alarms and lead to unnecessary work.

We have enough to do, she thought pensively. *Naniwa* was still at least thirteen days from being spaceworthy.

The marine walking point in front of her raised a warning hand. They had entered a region of the shipskin where long radiating fins ran out from the hull, making a queer sort of forest—all black limbs and leaf-like extrusions frilled with thousands of tiny heat-exchanging surfaces.

"Priest dead ahead, *kyo*," *Socho* Juarez muttered across the local comm. Susan could tell the sergeant major was unhappy, but who wanted their commander skylarking around outside the ship's armor—even here, deep in Anáhuac space—when they could be safely parked in Command, out of harm's way? "*Chu-sa,* do you want some privacy?"

Susan shook her head.

You're sure? he signed. *There are Mice everywhere.*

Koshō almost laughed aloud. *The Mice are always watching,* she replied with a deft movement of her gloved fingers. "Feel free to listen in. But if you are worried—I will be polite."

The officers complement on the *Naniwa*—including junior officers—stood at almost a hundred men and women. After her discussion with the Mayan *hafuri,* their attitude towards her had cooled noticeably. When she'd first come aboard, most of the five-hundred-plus crew were already hard at work, so Susan had found herself out of synch with her subordinates. There had been so much to do, however, they had started to gel into something like the team she expected.

But nothing like we had on the Cornuelle. Koshō knew that had been rare—Fleet crews usually had a high rate of turnover as specialists rotated out and the officers were promoted. A ship's complement which remained substantially intact for three years—particularly under combat conditions—was almost unheard of save in the Clan-supplied squadrons. She missed the comfort long familiarity provided.

Proper respect for the *Chu-sa* was absolutely necessary for the proper functioning of the ship, but there was an uneasy tension Susan could not ignore, particularly when the fitting officer was not in her chain of command. The Fleet was dependent on the *Zosen*—Construction and Supply Service—but did not control the logistics arm of the Imperial military. Like the Army, they were held separate from one another by the Emperor's decree. Each *Kaigun Kyo* reported directly to the Military Council. Her rudeness, therefore, had exacerbated a natural division between *Zosen* and Fleet.

Again, grandmother would have illuminated this error with a bōken *or perhaps a kettle.*

The marine signed an all-clear and Koshō stepped past him, around one of the towering fins, and onto an open area among the heat radiators much like a meadow in a forest of black battle-steel. Oc Chac was waiting, hands clasped behind his engineer's construction suit, helmet turned towards the vast eye of Jupiter burning down upon them. His mirrored faceplate glowed amber and red, as though filled with fire.

"Chac-*tzin*." Susan waved off the marine, who faded back into the "forest," his combat armor dappling to match shadow to shadow. Most Fleet officers seeking a private conversation—particularly of ship-command rank—would have ordered the sergeant-major to stay aboard ship and out of their hair, but Koshō had spent far too long beyond the Frontier to go anywhere without proper security precautions. Indeed, she hadn't even thought of *not* having Juarez accompany her. "I understand we've finished final inspections on all systems save the shipskin and the main drive coil?"

Chac nodded, but said nothing. In response, she gave him an abbreviated bow and turned to look upon the face of Jove as well.

"I would like to apologize for my behavior the other morning. It was rude."

The Mayan shifted a little, and Koshō could feel his attention focus upon her.

"I understand," she continued, "that you have been most diligent in your efforts to see construction completed and all systems readied for our trials. Engineering, in fact, sings your praises and promises to spill a thousand cups of *octli* beer in your honor. Which, from my experience with engineers, is heady tribute indeed."

There was a short, abrupt snorting sound. *He laughs. Well, now I have him.*

"These same engineers pressed me, in a most unseemly way, to let you finish your work. I must admit, as I've never served on a *new* ship before, that I do not fully understand your role."

"Truth, *kyo*," the Mayan barked, almost against his will. "Your service jacket bears such a statement out. . . ." Now he was facing her, and Susan could make out his eyes as shadows within shadows. "The *Cornuelle* was far past her time."

He paused. Koshō could hear him click his teeth together. *Thinking, is he?*

"This *Chu-sa* Hadeishi of yours was competent—this I have heard from Painal the Runner, and having read the Book, would believe. But he was reckless! Ah, by the Gods, *Chu-sa*, he was a madman!"

For a moment Susan struggled, trying to frame a proper response. *How can he say this! Mitsuharu was spinning gold from straw for six months! How . . .* Her shoulders sagged for an instant, before she straightened up again. *How could he have risked all our lives? He did. He dared Hachiman over and over again . . . even at Jagan he was still maneuvering for a way to stay out on patrol. Even at the end, when he and the ship and the crew were past exhaustion. . . .*

"He was." The words were harsh, brittle, metallic in her mouth. *But true.* "And so he paid, in the end, in blood—as we all pay."

"Huh!" Chac wrinkled up his prominent nose and clicked his teeth sharply. "Do you see why the crew fear you, *Chu-sa?* Why they are on edge? Why my work here is crucial for your success at trials?"

"So all say." Koshō spread her hands, accepting fate. "And are we ready? Could I take *Naniwa* into transit tomorrow? Could I take her into battle in a month?"

"Battle, *kyo?* In a month!" The Mayan laughed out loud. "Oh, *Chu-sa*, you know she is not ready, the crew is not ready! Six or seven months of working up, running the engines through a full maintenance cycle . . . then you can go hunting! A month." He chuckled.

Susan removed a folded orders packet from the document pouch on her suit gunrig. She held it up, letting the light of Jupiter gleam ruddy red and gold from the Fleet seal.

"We have received deployment orders," she said quietly. "To join a battle-group forming up off Europa right now. *Chu-sho* Xocoyotl is already aboard the *Tokiwa*, and the other ships are arriving in short order. *Naniwa* is expected to join them within five days, fully supplied and ready for action."

"Hsst! Impossible!"

"Tell that to the admiral. Will your work be done in time? Will everyone cease giving me such foreboding looks and turn their minds to proper work?"

The Mayan's chiseled old face twisted into a grimace.

"*Chu-sa*, you don't believe they have cause to fear? Even with all that has happened to you, even with the engineer's mighty tribute?" For an instant, it seemed as if he would spit in disgust, but then held back. "You called me the *superstitions* officer, as though such a thing had no weight in this world!"

Susan almost took a step back, hearing the fury in the old man's voice. "Instruct me, then, *Zosen*, for I have little time left to waste, not with the admiral—"

"Waste, *kyo*?" Chac cut her off with a harsh bark. "Waste is the root of my business, and the fullness of your ignorance. Listen!" He stopped abruptly, his anger having passed as quickly as it had come. "Listen, *kyo*."

Koshō said nothing, waiting patiently. Grandmother had spent a long time teaching her to grow still, to pause in the instant of action, waiting for balance to emerge from chaos.

"The mind of a warrior must be clear, *kyo*," Chac began, "undiluted by fear, unrestricted by disorderly thoughts. If he hurries the throw, his aim ever goes awry. You know this, you are *samurai*. Your family is noble with a long tradition, a great lineage. . . . Your blindness in this matter is of great concern—both to me, and to your men.

"So listen. There is no mechanism yet devised by man which exceeds the complexity of a ship of war. Our *Naniwa* is small, as the great ships go, yet she holds within her every kind of system, every kind of compnet, sensor, power plant, engine of destruction we can devise. Her armor may be lighter than a dreadnaught, she may lack so many launch-racks as a carrier—but everything is present in her. A capsulation of all we can build . . . and she is fragile. A delicate bubble."

Chac lifted his face to the vast, molten orb hanging over their heads. "Despite all her shielding and armor and bronzed hull, if *Naniwa* were plunged into the heart of Jupiter—tidal pressures would crush her shell, incinerate her inhabitants, and leave nothing but dust."

His hand moved, indicating the radiating fins surrounding them, almost invisible against the ebon backdrop of open space. "If the thermocouples fail, we roast inside, broiled by our own waste heat. If Engineering does not balance containment properly, a fusion rupture obliterates us. In battle, the slings, arrows, and stones of the enemy will seek us—and one penetrator through the point-defense leaves us an expanding cloud of superheated plasma. Everywhere, failure is waiting to consume us.

"All this, beside the unforgiving environment of open space . . . a hideous broil of hard radiation, micrometeoroid swarms, gravitational eddies—you have seen what happens to a ship which loses transit shielding in the run-up to gradient! There is no soft margin upon which to fall, not for us.

"Thus the *Zosen* crawling through every compartment, access way, and control space on this ship. All of them seeking to find and eliminate as many sources of failure in this machine as they can. Your crew, too, is deep in the work. Preparing to take her out—then the real learning begins! And I am here, *Chu-sa*, trying to keep *you* alive with my . . . superstitions."

The Mayan leaned close, the faceplate of his helmet almost touching Susan's.

"What kills more ships, Captain, than pitiless space? More than microscopic black holes, the teeming ships of the Megair or Khaid or Kroomākh? More than solar storms lancing out from the heart of some unseen sun to overwhelm shielding and armor?

"What is *my* enemy, *Chu-sa* Koshō?"

Susan tilted her head; her face a quiet, still mask. "Tell me."

"Your crew, *kyo*." His left hand stabbed at the hull

beneath their feet. "These men and women toiling inside, all effort concentrated to our safety. They are my enemy, and a cunning, devious one they are, too! More than a match for all fail-safes and interlocks, able to overcome every restraint we put upon them.

Koshō attempted to keep her expression still, but Oc Chac snarled at *something* in her countenance. "Still, *Chu-sa*, you do not understand. Listen!

"The *Agarwal* was a Fleet battleship in the *Vishnu*-class. A planetary commission financed by the colonies around Maghada Prime. Two thousand, five hundred crew. Lost with all hands off Tau Ceti during her second trials. The wreck was recovered and the *Zosen* tore the remains of the ship apart, seeking to understand her death.

"This much they found—" he held his thumb and forefinger apart by the smallest fraction. "One of the waste recirculators failed behind a bulkhead, seeping biochemical sludge into the between-hull. Line-sensors reported the initial leak, but the engineering tech investigating the alert did not enter the between-hull. Instead he checked the flow meters on either end of the line, saw they were within variance of each other, and then suppressed the alert.

"The sludge—containing a robust strain of mycelium—seeped through the between-decks, multiplying vigorously. Now it infiltrated the air circulators for a series of sleeping compartments and poisoned the men occupying those quarters. A contamination alert was triggered, but the men didn't realize they were suffering from mycotoxic infection when they went on shift. A sanitation crew arrived after they had left—and by then it was too late. Two of the *uchu* were gunnery crewmen and began suffering violent hallucinations at their duty station. *Agarwal* was destroyed by a sprint missile ignited in the launch-rack by mistake."

Susan said nothing, waiting for the Mayan to continue. After a long moment, Chac continued: "The technician refused to enter the between-hull because one of his coworkers had suffered a bad injury in the same area during construction. The man had lost his left arm when his z-suit was ruptured by a dislodged stanchion. His z-suit autosealed, of course, but the severed limb was too badly damaged by cyanosis by the time the rest of the work crew got him inside."

"And what," Susan asked, now truly curious, "would you have done to prevent this?"

"*Chu-sa*, my purpose is to address *kaach'al*—the things which are broken. To mend them. One of the most curious things to repair is men's apprehension—their fear of ill-luck. Had I been aboard the *Agarwal*, then my *huitzitzilnahaualli* and I would have attended to the compartments where the man was injured. And every crewman aboard would have known of what happened and how any ill-luck was taken away from that place."

"What?" Koshō could not help herself. "How is this *not* wild superstition?"

Oc Chac shook his head in dismay. "How is a dwelling haunted, *Chu-sa*? There is nothing that can be measured, no true apparitions to behold—but you enter and feel a deadly chill, you walk night-drowned hallways and your heart races with quiet panic. What makes this dreadful place so different from your parents' quiet peaceful garden where your heart finds ease?

"Nothing! Do not delude yourself, *kyo*, every centimeter of Anáhuac is drenched in blood. No meter of the earth has not seen murder, rape, betrayal, theft ... if you knew the provenance of every stone in that garden, you would recoil, your mind's eye filling with the blood of the innocent, your ears with the shrieks of those enslaved or betrayed. There is *no difference* between the cursed dwelling and the beautiful garden, save that *you do not know* what has occurred there.

"This is the purpose of the *huitzil*—to go into these dreadful places, to show himself to all, for his feathered cloak to shine alabaster white, to take upon himself the burden of this ill-luck, these curses, this dreadful karma—before an entire crew, a nation, a planet. And by his sacrifice, to ease so many minds and lighten so many hearts that you can, once more, lift the tool, use the chamber, send the ship of war into the face of the enemy with an unburdened heart."

He fell silent, and Koshō did not speak. Instead, she stepped away, circling among the radiating fins, her head bowed in thought. When at last her steps led back to the old Mayan, she regarded him with a new appreciation and a faint smile.

"Then you cannot leave the ship until all is done, can you?"

Chac shook his head sharply. "*Chu-sa*, you cannot have her for—at least!—another three weeks. Then you can catch up with your admiral! I will not authorize release from the yards until then."

"Very well." Susan removed the second packet from her pouch. "*Sho-sa* MacMillan will not be joining us from the *Akashi*. He has been brevetted to command in place of her late captain. And I must replace him with someone the men trust, particularly if they are wary of me and my inexperience."

"Very wise, *kyo*," the Mayan nodded sharply. "You will not interfere with my duties?"

"I will not. But I will guide them, as needed, and expect you to perform admirably." With this she presented the packet and gave an abbreviated, but proper bow. "Welcome to the *Naniwa*, *Sho-sa* Oc Chac. I've had the orderlies move your gear to the XO's cabin—a bit more spacious than your old bunk, I trust, but not palatial!"

Chac stared at the orders packet, then at her in horror. "Impossible, *kyo*. *Zosen* are not Fleet line of battle officers! I've no—"

"Due to his knowledge of the crew, the ship, and all on-board systems," Susan recited from memory, "Oc Chac-*tzin* is the most expedient and effective replacement available for MacMillan."

She squared her shoulders, regarding the older man with a stern expression. He was struggling to frame a response.

"*Sho-sa*, we have sixteen hours to finish loading supplies and get underway. The rest of the squadron is already formed up off Europa—two more battle-cruisers in *Tokiwa* and *Asama*, with the heavy cruisers *Axe*, *Gladius*, *Falchion*, and *Mace* as escorts for the Fleet tender *Hanuman* and the science platforms *Fiske* and *Eldredge*. They're our real purpose, I expect."

Chac let out a long, sober hiss of dismay.

"The Mirror, *kyo*."

Koshō lifted one eyebrow. The battle-group manifest was terse but could not disguise the throw-weight surrounding the two exploration ships. "What suggests this?"

"Sealed orders, *Chu-sa*, we've had no real-time 3-v onto the stellarcast in weeks. No regular mail coming or going. All incoming manifests under crypt, but you're doubled on every kind of ration, repair-part, and munitions they can pack in. Be gone . . ." The Mayan pursed his lips, calculating stowage. "At least nine months."

"Back of beyond . . ." Susan smiled tightly, tapping her own orders packet. "Stepping out into the big dark."

"A bad omen, *kyo*," Chac growled, "a very poor precedent. The festival of *Mictecacihuatl* is underway . . ."

"Prove them wrong, *Sho-sa*. Dispel this apprehension." She paused minutely. "Put on a brave face!"

Two days later, with her comm-panel singed by a vitriolic series of messages from her commander, *Chu-sho*—or

Vice Admiral—Xocoyotl, Koshō was on the bridge of the *Naniwa* as she matched velocity with the rest of the battle-group nearly sixty million kilometers off Europa. One pane of her command comp showed their approach to gradient as a sharply narrowing spike.

Below her and to one side, Oc Chac was standing behind the two *Thai-i* on the Navigation boards, gnarled hands clasped behind his back.

"There's the go-ahead, *kyo*," he announced. *Mace* and *Falchion* were in the lead, and both cruisers had cut maneuvering thrust in preparation for transit.

"They're not wasting time." Susan switched to the all-hands channel. "All hands prepare to make gradient. Transit in five minutes. Repeat, transit in five minutes."

Susan sat back, her heart steady, looking for a moment upon the golden orb of Jupiter arrayed behind the blue-black of nightside Europa. *Where now,* she wondered. An ancient *jisei* crossed her mind as the whine of the main coil began to shudder through the decking, lifting the fine hairs on her arms and making her inner ear sing in counterpoint.

> Rise, let us go—
> along the path lies
> the clear dew.

THE WILFUL

Hadeishi woke, feeling the ship drop from transit with a twisting sensation. Almost immediately a subsystem somewhere in the ceiling kicked into operation. With a frown he realized that a capacitor was discharging at sharp, staccato intervals. *Transit shielding is taking a hit;*

he thought and swung down easily from the hammock. His boots, a heavy jacket he'd scrounged, and his tool belt peeled off the wall easily enough. Out of habit, he tugged at the bolt cutters, hand-torch, welding arc, and other useful items on the belt. All were secure. Though the ship was under acceleration and there was gravity of a sort, he'd spent too many long-suffering hours as a cadet to trust even Fleet g-decking.

He padded to the engineering boards in the outer room and ran through a quick checklist.

We're running hot, he saw, and tapped open a series of v-panes showing exterior telemetry. There was only one hull camera patched through to Engineering—which was odd of itself—and it revealed only a confused roil of dust clouds shot with intermittent points of reddish light. But the shielding monitors were in constant motion, registering thousands of impacts a second. Hadeishi frowned and his stylus—dug out of a crevice behind the main comp panel—skittered quickly across the control surface. Two more capacitors dropped into the circuit, and the secondary fusion pump shivered awake.

"Captain didn't ask for that," growled a voice at his shoulder. Hadeishi nodded, feeling Azulcay's scrutiny hot on his neck. "What are you thinking?"

"In protostellar debris like this," Mitsuharu said, his voice level and unconcerned, "sensor reaction times degrade—sometimes masking something more massive behind lesser dust. The shielding control relays would have tried to bring more capacity on-line—but by then, we might have lost deflection . . . and even if the deflectors snapped back in time to push aside something big . . ."

"We'd already be punched full of a thousand little holes." The engineer grunted in agreement and then—with a grudging air—went through his own checklist on the panels. Hadeishi stepped away, keeping a polite distance, and took a moment to make sure his boots were strapped tight and all of the tools in his belt were in place.

When he looked up, Azulcay was peering curiously at the video feeds, one olive-skinned hand scratching at his tight, curly beard. "What *is* this place?" The Marocâin tapped the v-pane with a ragged fingernail. "Can we run for long in this much debris?"

"Depends on how fast the captain tries to go," Mitsuharu said quietly. "May I?"

The man nodded, and Hadeishi folded most of the v-panes away, replacing them with a large single pane containing the camera feed surrounded by a constellation of smaller displays showing hit rates and the status of the various shielding nodes on the outer hull. For some time he scrutinized the ocean of dimly lighted debris streaming alongside as the *Wilful* pressed onward. Thrust rates from the engines seemed to indicate the captain was pressing a hard course. The dust thickened as they watched, showing whorls and patterns in the fitful light.

Mitsuharu weighed the time since last they had passed an Imperial navigation beacon. *Out of range of Search and Rescue, I think.* One of the sensor panels dinged quietly, warning of scattered asteroidal fragments in the murk. The ship shifted course minutely and the engineer let out a soft whistle.

"Someone upstairs is paying attention . . . but we'd better get ready for damage con—"

The comp displays on the main panel wavered, blinked twice, and went dark. The engineer cursed fluently in Norman, then jerked a frayed power cable from its socket in the back of the board. "Gimme those spacers and a meter probe."

Hadeishi had the tools in hand already, and he hid a smile at how quickly the action had become second nature. For all his faults, Azulcay knew far more about the *Wilful*'s systems than anyone else. The *Wilful*'s mix of systems were not up to Fleet standard, and they made a constantly mutating puzzle to unravel.

"There!" The Marocâin scrambled up from behind the console as the screen flickered to life again, revealing even an ever-thicker murk, now glowing in long striated bands with the light of some distant, unseen star. "Damn, it's worse."

Mitsuharu nodded, though he noted the engineer did not open a comm channel to the bridge, or issue any kind of warning to the captain. *Interesting*, he wondered. *His faith in the command staff is remarkable. In this murk, I would have my damage control crews in z-suits and waiting in the airlocks to go hullside. . . .* The paucity of data irritated him immensely, but there was only a single, shielded comm run connecting the engineering spaces to the bridge. *One camera, one shipnet conduit . . . we're blind down here. Still, I should—*

"What the hell! We're right on a moon." Even as the Marocâin spoke, the rumble of the maneuvering drive hiccupped into a lower pitch. "That's orbit. To stations!"

Mitsuharu immediately took his place at the secondary console. It was the "station" he had appropriated from the beginning, giving him a reasonable view of the engineer's panel and control of some useful secondary systems. *A moon*, he saw, *but without a planet or star in reasonable distance.* Only a dim glow illuminated the indistinct sphere. One could imagine ice-shrouded peaks piercing the roughened surface, but without better sensors it looked dimly red-purple, like the passing boulders.

"Looks like a beat-up billiard ball," Azulcay muttered. He looked curiously at Hadeishi. "Where's the solar system? There's no proper star in sensor range."

"Gravitational eddies could form a moon from stellar

debris without forcing an orbit." Mitsuharu shrugged. "Or the star could have lost fuel millions of years ago . . . who could say?"

"See if you can get a read on . . ." The engineer stopped, listening.

Hadeishi heard the sound, too, and reflexively hit the ALERT glyph on his control pane.

"Explosions. Coming our . . ."

The alarm began to blare, but the wailing noise did not drown out a succession of dull, heavy thuds.

"We are attacked." *Who? I wonder. Perhaps Kryg'nth?* A dull *whoomp* came from the direction of the nearest loading bay. Something dark and jagged flickered across the camera pickup before the entire control console died again with a massive thud that made the flooring shake. *All the loading bays.*

"We're boarded," cursed the Marocâin.

It wasn't a question. Hadeishi was already sealing up his z-suit as Azulcay fumbled with his. The feeling of the suit gelling around his neck and face brought back a thousand memories. *Wind was rattling the bamboo, making the surface of the stream flowing past at Musashi's feet sparkle with tiny wavelets. A series of mossy boulders made an uneasy path to the far side. Kiyohara was poised on the largest of them, his nodachi slung insolently across his massive shoulders. "Come then," the brigand shouted, "unsheath your famous blade, King of Swordsmen!" Behind him, on the far bank, the sally drew a raucous laugh from the dozens of ronin gathered there.*

"Gun locker code?" Hadeishi was at the armored cabinet, but the battle-steel door was properly secured. The engineer nodded, his face paling. Despite obvious fear, his fingers were steady enough to punch in the authorization code and the gray metal doors swung aside to reveal a brace of shipguns and two bandoliers of ammunition.

"Pretty light," Mitsuharu muttered, pulling a Bloem-Voss TK6 from the padded cradle. The civilian weapon only carried a single kind of round, a ship-safe flechette, and lacked a grenade launcher or a thermal sight. The Nisei had the bandolier over his shoulder and secured, with the gun tucked under his arm and lanyard snugged to his tool belt before the engineer had even managed to get the ammunition and snub-nosed rifle out of the cabinet.

"Let me," ordered the Nisei, quickly righting the civilian's gear. "Follow me and shoot at anything you don't recognize. But, please, not the back of my head." The proper helmet for the z-suit slid down over Hadeishi's brow and he locked the neckring with a practiced twist of his fingers.

A moment later, Mitsuharu eased out into the main corridor connecting the cargo bays to the shipcore. The overhead lights were flickering on and off as something interfered with environmental power, so he tripped the nearest panel and killed them entirely. Azulcay's breathing was harsh and fast in his ear.

"What's—" Two crewmen bolted down the passageway towards them, followed immediately by a stabbing flare of gunfire. One of the spacers staggered and spun around, crashing into a wall. The other threw himself down, caught on the nonskid decking, and scrambled past them on hands and knees. Behind the gun-flashes, five or six bulky figures advanced at a quick pace, the muzzle of the leader's gun glowing like a hot star in the gloom.

The sideways, skittering approach of the invaders told the Nisei all he needed to know about the enemy which had overtaken them. *Khaiden*, he thought, a brief flash of memory bringing back visions of a bulky starship breaking apart under the impact of three well-placed shipkillers. The *Cornuelle* had taken severe structural damage in that affray, but shipboard losses had been light. *We were lucky,* part of his mind commented as he moved. *They thought we were too small to—*

Hadeishi squeezed off a burst just low of the enemy gun in his sights, then darted aside into the corridor, his shipgun pointed at the floor. Answering fire raked the wall, shredding the paneling and sending the Marocâin into the nearest room with a yell. One of the Khaiden was down, and the others rushed forward. Mitsuharu stepped in, emptied the rest of his clip into the nearest hostile at point-blank range and then darted past, trying to burst past the following two in the darkness.

The roar of Imperial guns filled the corridor behind him as the other crewman and the engineer opened up. Flechettes hissed past, spattering from his armor and Mitsuharu felt something clip his shoulder. He stumbled, thrown off balance and into the last of the Khaiden boarders.

The creature towered over the slightly built Nisei by at least a meter and its shipgun lashed out hard, butt-first, to slam into Hadeishi's faceplate. The tempered glassite rang with a clear, bell-like tone and Mitsuharu was thrown to the decking. Teeth clenched, he snatched a fresh clip from the bandolier and snapped open the Bloem-Voss' cartridge bay—then froze, the glowing bore of a Khaiden zmetgun jammed hard into his faceplate. Smoke curled across his vision and the glassite popped with the heat. Hadeishi groped for a suitable *koan*. *No time left*, he thought sadly. *For a proper parting.*

The Khaiden kicked the human's shipgun away, and then wrenched the bandolier from his shoulder.

Ah, Mitsuharu realized with dismay. *They do prize technicians—a life of servitude awaits. . . .*

With two of the enemy in close proximity, there was nothing to be done but clasp both hands behind his back and feel the bite of a heavy pair of steel cuffs through the z-suit gel. Hadeishi kept his eyes lowered as the Khaiden dragged him down the corridor past the bodies of Azulcay and the other starman. The Marocâin's face was invisible behind shattered glassite coated with congealing blood. The Khaiden in front of him kicked the corpses aside, ignoring their tools and comm bands.

They are in a hurry, they haven't taken my tool belt. Mitsuharu hurried along between the two invaders, chin tucked to chest, trying to see anything he could out of the corners of his eyes. The shipcore was swarming with the enemy, most in battle armor—the usual grab-bag of stolen equipment—but some were kitted out in dark blue z-suits with a gold-colored icon of some kind of hunting bird. The tight, blocky script on the sides of their helmets was hard to read, but Hadeishi thought it might be something like *Qalak*, or *Khaerak*. *Those are custom-fitted uniforms,* he realized with a little chill shock. He did not remember ever seeing a Khaiden raider sporting standardized equipment, much less uniforms or heraldry.

Mitsuharu was herded up the shipcore, following a swing-line with three other crewmen from the *Wilful*, and then into a cross-corridor marked with heavy yellow stripes warning of environment change ahead. *The port, forehull airlock,* he guessed. They had passed several more squads of Khaiden, and now he was thinking the dark-blue z-suits were officers. The boarding parties—the equivalent of the Fleet marines—showed little standardization in their arms, armor, or personal gear. *That's business as usual. . . .*

At the entrance to the airlock, he stopped abruptly as the lead guard jammed the other prisoners against the wall without warning. Four Khaiden jetted past, z-suit maneuvering jets spitting exhaust, with two more of their fellows on litters between them. Still keeping his head bowed, Hadeishi smiled tightly. *That little gun did some good.*

Ahead, the airlock cycled open, sending a gust of damp, hot air into the corridor. The medical party disappeared through without a pause. Mitsuharu weighed his chances, but then the guard behind him was pushing him forward. They passed a cross-corridor leading upship and for the first time Hadeishi caught a glimpse of the command deck. There was a drift of corpses—all of them apparently human—pinned against one wall with a net of sprayfoam. More of the dark-blue-suited Khaiden were busy at the consoles. The doors were pitted with thousands of tiny sparkling blemishes where shipgun flechettes had impacted.

Fierce smugglers in these parts, he thought, seeing a cloud of tiny ruby-colored droplets drifting in the hatchway. Then the momentary vision was gone, and the airlock was cycling around them. Hadeishi tensed, feeling the hot, humid air of a Khaiden ship wash over him.

The Qalak, *then,* he thought. *Into the belly of the carrion bird.*

The guard jammed him in the back with the muzzle of a tribarrel, pushing him forward, and as they passed into the dull, redlit space beyond, his earbug cycled frequency—losing contact with the *Wilful*'s shipnet—and for just a moment, before an encrypter kicked in, he caught a burst of Khadesh.

"—blood-drinking Maltese! A pestilence upon their—!"

THE *NANIWA*

Koshō sat easily in the captain's chair, one leg crossed over the other, comp control surfaces arrayed to the left to allow an unobstructed view of the engineering stations on her right. Midafternoon watch was nearly half over and there were crewmen at every station. The threatwell forming the center of Command was filled with light—the hard diamonds of the battle-group and a contorted maze of filaments representing the dust clouds they had been passing through for the last three days.

On her central board, the transit shielding status displays were flickering crimson and amber much like the fluttering of hummingbird wings—nearly too swift for the eye to follow. One of the graphics surged into red, and then scarlet, and a soft *ding-ding* sounded. Susan looked up from the readiness reports filling her displays and frowned, a sharp crease splitting her forehead.

Gravitational densities were fluctuating in an uncomfortable way, causing the protostellar debris to congeal in ever-moving eddies. The *Naniwa*'s newly installed deflectors were easily shrugging aside the constant stream of impacts, but she was beginning to worry about the other smaller, older, ships in the convoy. At present the combat elements made a widely dispersed globe around the *Fiske*, *Eldredge*, and *Hanuman*. The squadron was currently arrayed to prevent wake overlap and further damage to the smaller ships following the heavy warships.

Koshō brushed the readiness reports closed with a flick of her wrist, then keyed into battlecast with her stylus.

After a few minutes of considering telemetry from the

noncombatants, she tapped her earbug awake and paged Engineering.

"Hennig here, *kyo*." The *Kikan-cho* was a dough-faced Saxon of very conservative mind. Koshō found him refreshingly direct and, like many engineers, disinterested in politics of any kind. Had he shown any flickering of concern for the past glories of Imperial Denmark—of which Saxony had been long part—he would not have found a posting in the Fleet at all.

Which would be a shame, Susan thought, *because we are short enough of talented officers as it is.*

"Emil," she said aloud, "how does the shielding on the *Fiske* or *Eldredge* compare to ours, in this dust, at our current velocity?"

"Poorly, *Chu-sa*." He looked off-pane, and Koshō was heartened to see that the engineer already had the 'cast telemetry on his own monitors. "We're pegging up to five or six percent capacity—that last bolus deflected from the port shielding at nineteen percent—but *Fiske* is showing sixty or seventy percent just in the easygoing."

"You'd agree the densities are increasing, the deeper we go?"

He nodded. "*Kyo*, whatever gravitational sources are causing all of this debris to collect are—more or less—dead ahead. The closer we come, the tighter the influx spirals are going to be. Right now, if you plot back to our entry point, you can see we're cutting across deeper 'valleys' in the clouds. The interval between each ridge is growing shorter as well."

"Sensor efficiency?"

"Declining, *Chu-sa*." Hennig smoothed back short-cropped gray hair. "Have you been watching the cyclerate on the battlecast itself?"

Susan shook her head, *no*.

"Increasing as well. Tachyon relay times are starting to vary—which indicates we're getting deep into a gravitational eddy as well—and 'cast timing is starting to slow. Not noticeable to you, or I, *kyo*—but our ability to supplement the navigational suites of the smaller ships is starting to degrade."

"And if—when—we're attacked?"

Hennig showed a set of small, pearl-like teeth. "*Chu-sa*, below-decks chatter says the gunnery officer on *Mace* nearly lit off a sprint missile into the *Falchion* two watches ago . . . a distortion interposed between them and he lost ident lock. So it will be interesting."

"Delightful." Susan sat back, her face calm and composed. "Thank you, *kika-no*."

Thirty minutes later, after reviewing the incident reports from the rest of the battle-group—or at least those she was privy to—Koshō lifted her chin and caught the duty Comms officer's eye.

"Pucatli-*tzin*, I would like to talk to the battle-group commander on the *Tokiwa* directly, captain's line."

The *Chu-i* stiffened and then immediately began speaking into his throatmike. Koshō stood up, stretched, and took a roundabout of the bridge. This caused a wave of activity to move with her, as the staff checked and rechecked their status displays. When Susan came around to the threatwell, she was standing well away from everyone else. Only Oc Chac had remained on-task with the gunnery control officer, testing the launch control relays for the main missile batteries spaced along the "wing" of the battle-cruiser. Six or seven control modules had already been replaced, having failed their workup.

Now the Mayan's attention was fixed on her from across Command, and he lifted one eyebrow in question.

Susan shook her head, then tapped her earbug live as Pucatli reported the channel was open, secure, and the admiral on-line. A holocast of the *Chu-sho*'s face appeared before her, surrounded by a wedge of informational glyphs. Xocoyotl was a little overweight for a México officer, with hard cheekbones and a northern—or Anasazi—cast to his features and a deep, gravelly bass for a voice. So swift had been their departure that Koshō had yet to actually meet her commanding officer in person.

"Report."

"*Chu-sho*, battle-group 'cast is showing increasing shipskin erosion from the cloud. *Naniwa*'s deflectors are fresh from the yards and we're still failing to make a perfectly clean channel—the smaller ships are doing worse, with an increased risk of equipment failure."

"Your point, *Chu-sa*? We are still behind schedule to reach rendezvous. If we slow—"

"Understood, *kyo*. If I may—our projections show that slowing one-half—or reorienting the battle-group for overlapping coverage—will reduce the chances of losing the *Fiske*, *Eldredge*, or *Hanuman* by almost sixteen percent."

The admiral's expression did not change—it was habitually disapproving—but Susan thought there was a brief flicker in the deep-set, black eyes. She missed Hadeishi again—discussing something like this with him would have been brief, efficient, and to the point.

"We've no time to experiment," he said at last. "All ships will stay on course and make do."

"*Hai, Chu-sho!*" Koshō nodded sharply in acknowledgment. Then she paused, wondering if there was enough of an opening to—

The v-cast folded away in the air before her with a soft *ding!*

Shaking her head, Susan returned to the captain's chair, her fingers tapping in thought on the shockframe. Oc Chac was almost immediately at her side.

"What were you going to ask him, *kyo*?" The XO asked in an undertone.

Susan tilted her head, considering the engineer for a moment. Then she said, "What we discussed earlier: live-fire exercises for our command and gun crews. But given the rush, I doubt he'd approve the expenditure of munitions or time that it would require." She sat down in her chair and flicked open the v-panes on her control surface. "Not that I am easy about pulling power from the deflectors in this muck—even without the stress of gun exercises—it's eating my ship."

Oc Chac stiffened at the light tone in her words. "This does not seem amusing to me."

He stared at the convoluted patterns in the threatwell for a long moment, then continued in a low voice: "I cannot laugh, *kyo*. All this reminds me of Hunahpu's description of the road to Xibalba:

> *Here there is no light but what we wayfarers*
> *bring with us.*
> *We grapple in the dark with degraded,*
> *phantom faces.*
> *Only treachery awaits us.*"

Susan frowned. "It's long since I read the *Popol Vuh*; what canto—"

> "*It is as if we are finding our way to the*
> *underworld,*
> *To the dark stairs which bisect the sky.*"

The low, chanting tone to his voice began to raise the hackles on Susan's neck. His face—normally striking, given the strength of his features—now seemed cold and still. The long oval shape, the distinctive nose, the wide lips punctured by labrets of jade and turquoise—a living statue dredged up from the wreck of old Palenque or Copán.

"*Chu-sa*, you know the legend of Mictlan?"

"I do, *Sho-sa*. The tutors of Chapultepec are diligent in their application of México history."

He waited expectantly. *For what?* she wondered.

"*Kyo*, did they teach you that the México Kingdom of the Dead is but a weak shadow of Xibalba, place of phantoms, place of fear? That deadly trials and cruel, prankish Gods and whirlwinds of knives bar the way to that awful kingdom?"

Susan frowned. The Mayan had her full attention. "You believe we've chosen such a road ourselves?"

"Those who go that way have no choice, *kyo*. It is only for those who are dead."

Before she could reply, Susan's earbug crackled with the peculiar static endemic to the region. Pucatli was speaking, his normally calm voice tight with adrenaline.

"*Hai, Chu-i*, put him through."

"*Chu-sa* Koshō," Xocoyotl's voice rumbled in her ear. "I have decided to reform the squadron. *Tokiwa*, *Asama*, and *Naniwa* will lead with the cruisers forming a secondary wedge. Set your transit shielding at maximum extent and clear a path through the dust for those who follow. New vectors will be on your navcomm within the quarter hour."

"*Hai, Chu-sho!*"

Susan turned, feeling the chair motors kick in quietly. She tapped up the intraship channel and waited for Pucatli to confirm green across his repeater boards. Chac said nothing, his attention turned inward. Koshō's attention lingered on him for a moment, before she shook her head and opened the channel.

"All hands, all section officers. Be advised that *Chu-sho* Xocoyotl has commanded the squadron to reform our flight pattern. We will be shifting vector in fifteen—I say fifteen—minutes. Engineering sections be aware that we are going to full transit shield power. Stand by for maneuver on my mark."

When she closed the circuit, Oc Chac was standing at the edge of the threatwell, seemingly lost in thought.

"Do you truly believe what you just said, *Sho-sa*?" Susan's voice was soft, given they were surrounded by a busy Command deck. "That we've stepped onto some cursed road, leading only to destruction?"

Chac turned, his face somber. "Such thoughts come to me in this place unbidden, *kyo*—and if they assail *my* mind, they will afflict the soldiers, starmen, and scientists aboard the squadron doubly so."

He nodded sharply to her, and now everything about him seemed professional and direct once more. "There is work to be done, *Chu-sa*."

"Dismissed," she replied, and then watched him with interest as he strode off.

Can he really make the men forget—or put aside— this apprehension? That would be a boon indeed.

ABOARD THE *MOULINS*

In the *KUUB*

Gretchen sat squeezed in behind a narrow fold-out table on the mess deck, a mug of coffee clinging to a sticky-plate by her right hand and a battered field comp balanced on her left knee. The crew was grumbling in and out of the tiny space, getting their threesquares heated and coffee refreshed, and passing what gossip had managed to evolve in the last shift. The room was cold, crowded, and noisy. Every surface felt worn with age and constant, hard use. Like the rest of the ship— or the parts she'd seen—it was spotlessly clean, but the freighter was of an age that no amount of scrubbing and polishing could make the walkways, walls, or counters seem fresh.

Despite this Anderssen felt almost happy for the first time in nearly six months, her nostrils filled with the stink of cold diesel and burning rubber. Abstracts from a good year's worth of the *Extraplanetary Archeological Review* flipped past on the comp's screen. From time to time she recognized names or remembered the faces of old coworkers or rivals or long-standing dignitaries in her field. Occasionally an obituary cropped up—leaving a small, cold chill behind as she paged to the next document.

How did I get so far behind? All of the time spent toiling at the Technical College seemed to have faded from memory already, as though the whole interlude had been a fever dream, and her last "real" assignment and this one were running together with only a few idle weeks at home in between. *Easy to forget the last half year, I guess.* She hoped that was true.

The articles were the same as ever—plenty of insights promised, but the results were always a few pages of heavily censored data, some halfhearted conclusions, and hopes for further funding. The good stuff, of course, was never in the public journals. The Honorable Company, or the Mirror Which Reveals, saw to that quickly enough. *Our Secret Histories,* she thought morosely, *where the truth goes to be stuffed, buried, and forgotten.*

Her coffee cup suddenly shivered—dark liquid pulsing into a sharp spike and then collapsing. Her stomach did the same thing, at the same time.

The freighter had dropped from transit. The g-decking

in the mess area failed momentarily, eliciting curses from a crewman trying to refill his cup from the dispenser. Gretchen's mug had a clear cover, which kept it from disgorging a flight of brown-and-white globules into the air. Without thinking, she put her thumb over the drinking spout—gravity returned—and she wiped her finger on the thigh of her field pants.

Hummingbird ducked into the room, even his short frame needing to bend to get through the hatchway from the passenger cabin they'd booked for this leg of their journey into the unknown. Like the crew, the old México was kitted out in a workaday mantle over his z-suit with a broad leather belt at his waist and deep pockets. As he passed, Gretchen looked up curiously. The old man lifted his chin, indicating the hatchway to the control deck.

"Are you ready to transship?"

Anderssen nodded. *Next bus, now departing...* "How soon?"

"We'll see in a few moments."

Though he hadn't invited her, Gretchen slipped out from behind the table—tucked her comp away, drained the coffee cup—and followed along quietly. They had been in motion—hopping from ship to ship—for nearly ten days now and the old sorcerer had yet to speak more than a handful of words to her, none of them concerning their eventual destination.

When she squeezed into the door to the control space—*bridge* seemed too grand a word for the crowded warren of consoles, wire bundles, and creaking shockchairs—the sharp, abrupt impression of fear and adrenaline was a cold splash on her face. *Better than coffee!* she thought, feeling suddenly awake and on edge.

The freighter's master, a short balding little man named Locke, was standing over the pilot's shoulder, peering at the main navigational display. The camera displays were filled with a riot of iridescent color. Thick clouds of dust congealed out of the void on every side, lit with the radiance of distant, unseen stars. In comparison to the usual emptiness of interstellar space, the view seemed dangerously crowded. Hummingbird was also squeezed in, on the other side of the pilot, and his face seemed tight.

"One drive trace," muttered Locke, chewing on the edge of his thumb. "Too big for our contact."

"Maybe two," ventured the pilot. His stylus clicked on the display surface. The navigation holo shifted slightly and Gretchen, now quite alert, could see two vectors illuminated by the computer. "But this big signature is washing out the other."

"Our ship?" Green Hummingbird was watching Locke closely.

The freighter captain rubbed his forehead, and then swung into the navigator's seat. "The commercial shipping registry has some drive signatures on file," he said, uneasy. "Let's see what it kicks up."

Hummingbird waited patiently, while Gretchen—who felt an urge to start tapping her fingers—took the opportunity to examine the little room and the adjacent compartments. In comparison to the mess area, things were cleaner, and some components might have been recently replaced—but even so, there was a sense of age and hard use permeating everything she could see.

No, she suddenly thought, *that's not right—*

Locke cursed, drawing her attention back to the three men. Two ship's schematics had come up on his display— one obviously of considerable size, the other showing an outline almost exactly like their own paltry freighter. The captain sat back, covering his mouth with one hand. He pointed at the larger schematic with his chin.

"This is the flux signature of a Khaid *Neshter*-class destroyer. And the smaller one must be your ride."

The pilot hissed in dismay, looking back to the drive trails on the navigation holo.

"The smaller ship's signature is showing a couple hours newer than the entry-point for that destroyer . . . but their chrono tracks synch up on exit."

"I warrant the freighter went in chains!" Locke stood up, giving Hummingbird a hard look. "There's no ride onward for you, México. We're turning around and getting the hell out of here."

"Our agreement, Captain Locke, says you deliver me and my assistant to our destination." Hummingbird's tone was even, showing neither anger nor concern. "I will provide you with new transit coordinates and we will press on."

Locke bristled and Gretchen could feel his agitation like a sharp, prickly heat on her face. Before the captain could continue, however, Hummingbird raised a hand and looked over to Anderssen.

"Could you step outside, and see we're not disturbed?"

Meeting his gaze directly, Gretchen felt the adrenaline-heat suddenly flow away, replaced by cool calculation. *He expected this*, she realized. The old *nauallis* didn't seem fazed by the turn of events, though there was a substrate of annoyance in his voice.

"Sure, boss," she said, ducking out through the hatch. The heavy steel drew closed behind her, though she didn't let the panel lock into the socket. Three crewmen were now standing around the dispenser, their attention drawn by her sudden appearance and the clank of the hatch.

"I think," she said brightly, "that you're all going to get a hazard bonus."

The men looked at her quizzically, and then one bustled off down-ship with three cups balanced in his hands. Gretchen leaned against the hatchway and unwrapped a stick of chicle from her pocket. *I am so very nonchalant,* she thought in amusement as the hot taste of cinnamon filled her mouth. *Very much the idler.*

The remaining two crewmen ignored her and sat down to the table.

Without consciously intending to, Anderssen turned to examine some old bulletins posted on the nearest wall and let her eyes lose focus. Like magic—if sensory prioritization could be called magic—her hearing sharpened and she heard one of the men say: "Spero Lockenem maleficum eum circuagere non permissurum esse."

The other replied, equally softly: "Navarchus non stultus est. Claude os et oculos aperi!"

How odd. They're speaking—

She forced herself to step away from the door and pick up her cup of coffee. The little sound leaking through from the control space indicated a vigorous discussion was under way, and now that these two burly specimens were watching her, it wouldn't be polite to overhear. She swirled the cold liquid around in the cup, frowned, and went to the dispenser. Both of the men at the table turned away as she passed, but something about their clothing—no, their tool belts—caught her eye. *Nothing unusual about them,* she thought, wondering what had set her on edge. *You're getting paranoid . . . that's Hummingbird's business, not yours.*

Hot liquid steamed into the cup and she thumbed the glyph for extra cream, extra sugar-substitute.

Both of the crewmen stood up, pitched their cups, and climbed down the ladder to the engineering spaces.

Not their work tools, she realized, watching them go out of the corner of her eye. *They have the same sidearm.* The thought caught in her memory and other fragmentary images suddenly coalesced. *Tattoos—at least two, maybe three of these men have a crimson cross fitche on a white field. Like an insignia. Every one of them has at least one handgun. All about the same size, too, as though they were issued arms. These men must be ex-military.*

She gave the mess deck a considering glance, then cast about in memory for any other details she'd glossed over in the last two days while the ship had bounced from transit point to way station and onward into this trackless expanse. The *Moulins* was small; listed as a freighter seeking supercargo passengers, or some kind of high-value, low-mass cargo that couldn't wait for a big liner or cargo-carrier to come by. Or, she realized, for fugitives to smuggle . . . like her, like the Crow. Or information—very low mass; data-crystals or comp discs—and that could turn a tidy profit.

That familiar pressure—the constant, draining, exhausting need for quills which had been omnipresent her whole life—seemed out of place here. *That's not right. This captain, this crew, they don't taste right, feel right; they're not mercenaries.* She couldn't say quite why, but she was suddenly certain that Locke and his men were not out in the back of beyond looking for money.

A spy-ship? But not an Imperial one. Her heart skipped. None of the crew she'd seen were México or Nisei or Skawtish or any of the other nations bound by the compact of the Four Hundred families. *Could this be an HKV courier? A Resistance ship? Glorious Christ, there is still a Royal Navy at work amongst the stars?* She thought of *her* great-grandfather, a fiery old man with a neat white beard, killed in the Last War. He had served aboard a Swedish cruiser in battle near Saturn. A flood of emotion filled her and for an instant—her heart aching—she perceived something of the *shape* of the ship, the crew, even the irritable Captain Locke. She saw a *bloody spear, shining in the darkness, radiating roseate light into the void. Pointed ever outward, fixed upon the heart of an invisible, implacable enemy.*

Chilled and sweating, Gretchen slumped back against

the bulkhead. The coffee cup squeaked in her hand. When she looked down, her knuckles were white. *Oh. Well. I guess I don't need Malakar's singing to bring on this . . . this . . . whatever it is.*

The peculiar perceptual gestalt which came and went—incited by stress, or by psychotropic drugs, or the presence of another being in a state of extreme agitation—had been absent from her daily existence while she'd toiled away in the basement office on New Aberdeen. The nightly visions or dream-states which caused her to speak aloud in the tongues of ancient Mokuil had been slowly diminishing as time passed and her body recovered from being exposed to the memory-echo of the *kalpataru*. Malakar's notebooks were filled with drawings, songs, tales long lost to her people—Gretchen's troubled sleep had yielded up an unexpected bounty for the old librarian—but even that had been drawing to an end when the Hummingbird had arrived.

Now, with her mind feeling awake for the first time in months, Anderssen licked her lips in unease. *Is simply being in the presence of the* nauallis *enough to fray the veil blinding my perception? On Ephesus he had to give me a pill—a dose of oliohuiqui to part the shadows— but on Jagan all I needed was the presence of the Tree Which Gives What You Desire. And here? There doesn't seem to be even so much . . .*

The prospect of perceiving the true shape of the world around her, to glimpse the underpinning of men's purposes, was both troubling and exciting. *Now if only I could make it work when I want it to! That would be a bonus. What a tremendous tool. Just seeing the proper pattern of a broken pot would—*

Then, with her mind alert to the present, she heard through the hatchway Hummingbird's low, sharp voice speaking in an unfamiliar language, though the vowel cadence sounded terribly familiar. Locke's astonished reaction was like a bucket of ice water.

"You? *Præceptor*? Impossible!"

Peering through the partially open hatch, Gretchen caught sight of the old México's face. The *nauallis* nodded slowly, his arm lifted as though displaying some symbol to the merchanter.

Ah, a pity. Anderssen's throat felt tight with disappointment. These men were not HKV, not Resistance. *A crimson cross on a white field. A bloody spear and some secret language. No crew-women to be found. Just some marginal religious sect fallen prey to the Crow's blandishments.*

Disappointed, she gathered up her things and crawled back to their tiny cabin behind the food recyclers. Lying in the narrow bunk, with barely enough room for her shoulders, much less her feet, the hurt curdled in her breast. The thought that Grandfather's cause—noble and doomed as it had been—was still secretly alive in the wilderness out beyond the Rim, had lifted a little of the weariness upon her heart. Now the same cold weight settled again, twice as heavy, and she fell into a fitful sleep, troubled by dreams of men's voices singing beyond a golden doorway, in a lost tongue she ought to understand.

THE PINHOLE

"Transit kick in three—two—one . . ."

Susan's stomach flipped, settled, and she swallowed the faint taste of bile. At the pilot's station, *Sho-i* Holloway counted down his post-insertion checklist, announcing all systems green; deflectors intact and the ship in proper spatial position. By then, two minutes had passed.

"Status of the squadron?" Susan had already reviewed her own boards, seeing that all three battle-cruisers had kept station after dropping to normal space, but it never hurt to check. Particularly with a piglike Fleet tender along. The *Fiske* and *Eldredge* had done well in keeping up so far, but she doubted they had any legs at all if things got hot.

"All present and accounted for," Holloway replied. "We have three friendly IFF registers. Fleet says they are—" He reviewed a side-pane on his panel, making sure that the battlecast relays had come up, verified the new ships, that they matched registry entries and the *Naniwa*'s long-range cameras had confirmed their outlines in the heavy murk. "—*Temasek*, *Corduba*, and . . . no name on the third vessel, but she's registered as a 'mobile science platform'—same as ours in the registry, but the silhouette is markedly different."

That will be the Mirror hard at work. Susan nodded. Then the debris density they'd dropped into registered on her consciousness and she felt mildly ill.

In transluminal space, the physical protostellar matter collecting in the wasteland of the *kuub* was represented by both a gravity dimple and a quantum-level spore, or nugget, which interacted with the translated quantum-frame state of a ship much as a physical rock would interact—that is, smash into—the physical hull of a ship in realspace. Here, though, where physicality assumed its usual guise of solidity, the swarms of dust particles, or even micrometeoroids and outright boulders or asteroidal fragments, posed an even greater danger to the *Naniwa* and other ships trying to make realspace headway.

Everything within optical range of the battle-cruiser's cameras was a thick haze of heavy dust and debris. What dim light filtered through the murk from distant, half-hidden stars was diffuse and red-shifted. It made an appalling sight for a Fleet captain. Even a miner's scow would find heavy going in this environment.

"Impact rate?" The *Naniwa* was at very low v as she maneuvered into a parking station a safe distance from the unnamed research station.

"Forty-five percent," responded the weapons officer. "And we're nearly dead slow."

Susan nodded, leaning back in the shockchair. "Holloway, you and Konev work up some velocity metrics for me—how fast can we go, how best to configure the transit deflectors. We need to make headway in this mess. I want something by end of the watch."

"*Hai, Chu-sa!*" both voices chimed together in near unison.

"And get us a name for that station—something simple."

Holloway smiled tightly. He'd already queried the *Temasek*—the lead of the two Survey Service frigates—for the latest news. "They're calling it the *Can*, *Chu-sa*. Very imaginative."

"That will do." Koshō considered the threatwell for a moment, trying to map out the local terrain in her mind. This was just the situation—some nasty, unknown patch of space filled with hidden opponents, tangled local politics, and unsteady stellar phenomena—that Hadei-shi excelled in. *Nothing drains the strength of your opponent,* he would say, *faster than unknown ground. But if you are alert, even the most treacherous swamp can be your ally, a third arm striking at the enemy.*

A message chime on her board interrupted the memory. Susan started to grimace, seeing the *Tokiwa's mon* chopped on the header, but then smiled slightly as the message unspooled.

"*Socho* Juarez, I'll need a shuttle prepped and a guard-party suitable for the squadron staff meeting."

The marine, never far away by earbug, replied immediately: "*Hai, Chu-sa.* We'll be ready in fifteen minutes, boat-bay three."

Good, she thought, relieved to finally get a chance to meet her fellow squadron commanders and exchange proper introductions with *Chu-sho* Xocoyotl. *Now we'll find out what the devil is going on out here.*

The staff conference room on the *Tokiwa* was crowded, hot, and noisy as the last of the squadron commanders found their seats. *Chu-sho* Xocoyotl's staff were arrayed along the walls, while everyone else was present at a long oval table which folded up out of the floor. The flag battle-cruiser was an older model than the *Naniwa,* though still in the Provincial class, and this same room did not exist in the current configuration of Koshō's ship. If memory served, a suite of Logistics and Supply offices occupied the same internal coordinates.

"Admiral on deck," barked one of the *Tokiwa's* marine sergeants and everyone stood.

Xocoyotl was of medium height, carrying a bit too much flesh on his bones, and the color of polished mahogany. His high cheekbones caught a gleam from the overheads as he took his place at the head of the table. "Sit," he growled—his voice was even deeper in person than over stellarcast.

"Our business here comes under purview of the Imperial Secrets Act," he said with a scowl. "The Mirror is leading an investigation of some local phenomena and Fleet is providing security for their operations. Beyond this, I am informed we do not need to know *anything*."

He stopped, glanced around the room at all of the officers, snorted, and continued in the near-perfect silence.

"Survey informs us this area of the *kuub* is tremendously dangerous. It is also uncharted and there are no navigational beacons within range. I expect, therefore, that all watches will be fully staffed and weapons will be maintained in ready status at all times."

Xocoyotl flashed a tight, frosty smile at Koshō. "At least one of our ships—the *Naniwa*—has a fresh crew, a fresh captain and has not yet completed trials. I expect the other combatants to make allowance for this when plotting combat vectors."

To her credit, Susan remained entirely still while the *Chu-sho* went on about the combat patrol pattern he expected of the other ships, and she did not let her outrage show in any obvious way. Out of the corner of her eye, however, she could see some of the cruiser captains glancing sidelong at her in puzzlement. *How could I be more circumspect,* she wondered, *in suggesting that deployment change during transit? Losing one of the support ships would have crippled the entire mission.*

"Scientist Cuaxicali? Your turn." Xocoyotl gestured abruptly at a fat little México civilian in a Survey Service mantle who had been standing by one of the doors. One of the admiral's aides keyed up a projector panel and the lights dimmed. Cuaxicali cleared his throat, looked at the *Chu-sho* questioningly—received a snarl in response—and then began tapping on a slim silver comp with his stylus.

Behind him the projector shifted aspect and a holo of the surrounding region sprang into view. The collection of ships arrayed "south" of the *Can* appeared with Imperial standard glyphs. "North" of them, a broad area of crimson points appeared.

"Avoid this range of spatial coordinates," Cuaxicali said, indicating the beelike swarm of scarlet, "if you wish to keep your ship intact. This is the area of our—ah—*the* phenomenon. And it is exceptionally dangerous."

The assembled captains looked at one another, then a forest of arms went up to ask for details.

"No, no. No questions." Cuaxicali shook his head nervously. "This is a matter of the utmost security. There is no other information available at this time save what I've shown you—a copy of these astronomical charts has already been commed to your navigators."

"Surely you can tell us what sort of peril to expect?" a loud voice boomed across the conference room.

"I could," Cuaxicali agreed, attempting a consoling smile. "But for safety's sake I will not."

A red-haired *Chu-sa* whom Susan remembered vaguely from Chapultepec stood up and asked, "Begging your pardon, Scientist Cuaxicali, but please explain how can it be safe to not know the nature of our opponent? Or even what it looks like?"

An ill-disguised snort of laughter erupted at the back of the conference room.

Cuaxicali's face changed abruptly into a sort of maroon-olive. Susan was not sure she'd seen the exact shade before, on anyone, anywhere.

Chu-sho Xocoyotl stood up and surveyed the assembled officers with one raised eyebrow. The room settled down.

"That is all. Return to your ships. Patrol patterns will be distributed by third watch."

Five hours later, as second watch was winding down, Koshō was back on the Command deck in a fresh uniform, her hair slick from a fast shower. For the moment, the bridge was double-staffed as the crew prepared for turnover. Amid all of the commotion, she had taken a moment to comm up the two officers she remembered from the Academy. Both of them—Muldoon on the *Falchion* and Tloc on the *Axe*—had been surprised to hear from her.

"Not often you high-flying battle-cruiser commanders take the time to say hello to the plow horses," said Muldoon after they'd confirmed a private channel and triggered their own encryption. "But it's good to see you again, Koshō-*tzin*."

"Likewise," grumbled Tloc. The Ciguayan captain had acquired a bad set of burn scars on the side of his face since graduation day. "How did you get on Xocoyotl's bad side? I've never heard him rip a junior officer like that before."

"I gave him some advice," Susan said, shaking her head slightly. "I should have known better."

Muldoon laughed. "Admirals know all and see all, remember? Just like the upper form prefects on Grasshopper Hill. The Runner said you'd been the wise woman behind that formation change during transit—but I didn't think he'd take it so hard."

Tloc grimaced. "I'm on my second posting with him—he knows best and likes it that way."

Koshō frowned, feeling worse for having the extent of her misstep made so clear. "My last commander would've expected me to suggest a better course, if I saw one."

"Then you were lucky." Muldoon's normally lively

tone flattened. "I heard Hadeishi was beached. That's too bad, everyone said he was a fine ship-handler."

Susan nodded, once. "Too good, sometimes. I have been reminded—repeatedly—that being very good can lead to believing you can do the impossible *one more time* than you can."

Both men nodded, sobered. "That's the truth," Tloc said, touching the side of his face.

"So what about *this* mess?" Koshō felt the memory of Hadeishi weighing on her. "What does Painal the Runner say about this most secret of secrets?"

Muldoon perked up, laying one finger alongside his nose. "My money is on a quantum-level distortion. We could see it from here, except it's invisible to our sensor suite."

"How could—" Susan started to ask, but Tloc interjected:

"My information says a gravitational distortion's been detected around a huge volume, all of it clogged with nova debris. Almost impenetrable to scanning . . . just to twist the screw another thread."

"And I've heard if you run into this phenomena you get cut to bits." Muldoon made a throat-cutting gesture. "Word is a pair of Survey ships tried to break through and ended up literally dissected."

Susan frowned. "Do these lost ships have names? Any detail at all?"

"Not yet, but give me some time," Tloc replied. "I've got about a ton of *chocolatl* and *kaffe* in personal stowage."

Ten minutes later, after arranging a trade to keep the kitchen happy, Koshō signed off. The second watch was in the process of leaving Command, most yawning, some already busy in conversation with their fellows. The comm duty officer and the assistant navigator were a step slow and Susan beckoned them over.

"Rumor says a pair of Survey scouts caught hold of the *Chu-sho*'s phenomena by the sharp end. See if you can pick out any wrecked ships in the immediate vicinity. They ought to be the other side of the *Can*. Keep your eyes open for *anything* out of place. Something very odd killed those scouts—and I'd like to avoid the same fate."

The quiet of the off-watch officer's mess was broken by a soft voice: "*Chu-sa* Koshō?"

Susan looked up from her cup of tea. It was Navigator's Assistant Llang, trying to suppress a huge grin. Susan beckoned her over. "We've got 'em, *kyo*." Llang blurted, comp clutched to her chest. "All three. It's—"

"Not to be discussed here." Koshō silenced the girl with a sharp look. The *Chu-sa* picked up her tea and guided the young *Thai-i* back out the door at a brisk walk. "Let's use my station on the bridge instead."

In the lift, as the decklights blurred past, Susan considered the young Tagalog lieutenant. This was the girl's second duty posting—she'd come recommended from the *Mac Allan*, a frigate working shipping lane patrols around Alpha Centauri—and Koshō was sure she had very little political experience. After a moment she said quietly, "There may be those aboard *Naniwa* who will have lost friends or family in those ships. We do not want to break such sad news in a casual way."

Third watch should have found the bridge nearly deserted, but when the lift doors rotated away, every duty station was staffed and there were four or five extra bodies present, holding up the walls and checking console diagnostics that had been checked only the day before. Oc Chac nodded as she approached.

"Show me." Koshō nodded to Llang, who slipped into a seat at the comm and sensor station. The *Thai-i*'s stylus skittered across the control surfaces with admirable speed. Immediately a series of navigation diagrams appeared and a holo rotated into view, showing the science platform, the debris clouds in the immediate vicinity and then—three sharp taps zoomed the focus far, far down, showing an indistinct smear a goodly distance from the *Can*, deep into the area marked off by the Mirror as out-of-bounds.

"*Kyo*, it's really hard to see—the remains of the ships are just more radioactive junk in with all of this other radioactive junk, but we believe that this—"

Llang tapped once more, and a camera overlay sprang up, showing a sort of empty wedge in the cloud.

"That this was the *Kiev* after she lost reactor containment. The scout must have been traveling within gun range of the *Korkunov*—that's this other gap off her starboard. When they blew, the force of the explosion actually cleared an area in the nebular cloud. The densities of material around the edges of each of these gaps sort of approximate the mass of the ships themselves. At least we think that's right. And look at this—the *Calexico* has been cut clean in half!" Llang looked up, her face filled with mingled horror and awe. "Have you ever seen anything like that before, *Chu-sa*?"

Susan stared at the enhanced, high-contrast image and marveled at the clean edge of the ship's wound. "How far away is this?"

"Three light-minutes beyond the *Can, kyo*, just at the edge of sensor range in the cloud." The *Thai-i* grimaced. "Too much grit to see if there's anything else out beyond them. . . ."

Susan compared the plots and the information from the morning's briefing. Her frown deepened.

"There's an opening," she said, clenching her hands, which had suddenly gone cold. "Survey and the Mirror advance elements have been here at least a week—they'll have seen what we see, guessed what we guess. Their danger zone is well on this side of all three of those ships. The *Kiev* must have blundered into a failed component of the weapon's array, leaving just the tiniest gap . . . but not big enough to avoid destruction when they stepped out-of-bounds."

Sho-sa Chac considered the plot, eyes fixed on the Mirror research ships now snugged up against the station. "They'll be going in, *Chu-sa*, and someone will have to play watchdog . . . pray to the Lady of Tepeyac we avoid such a fate!"

For her part, Koshō felt claustrophobic. The emptiness around her ship seemed suddenly confined, filled with invisible walls. "Keep the coordinates of this . . . barrier . . . in the threatwell at all times," she decided, caution pricked by the object lesson of the three wrecked survey ships. "If we need to maneuver at speed, we don't want to interpenetrate by accident."

"*Hai, Chu-sa!*" Llang was very quick to agree. The others nodded vigorously.

"What else?" Koshō felt the tactical problem beginning to turn over in her mind, options shifting in and out of consideration, alternatives discarded as quickly as they suggested themselves.

Llang tapped through a series of detailed views of the area around the Mirror station itself. "*Kyo*, the only other thing we've found is this . . . probably a good third of the *Calexico* is the core of the *Can* itself. Looks like they dragged half of the scout back out of the danger zone and cut away the damaged sections. The other two ships lost containment on their reactors, but by some miracle the *Calexico*'s power plant survived."

"Frugal." Koshō clicked her teeth together. "Someone must have survived the attack or they'd never have found this opening . . . not without losing another dozen ships blundering around in the dark. Ask around, *Sho-sa* Oc. See if you can get names."

"*Hai, kyo!*" The Mayan nodded, his face impassive. But as he strode away, Susan caught a fragment of a prayer, muttered under the man's breath: "Hear us, O Xbalanque. Lend us your clever mind and subtle hand. Guide us in this foul Darkness which over you has no power."

Now, she thought, feeling the bone-deep ache of being up too long and running on too many cups of tea. *That makes me feel so much better. May it settle his mind, for it does nothing for mine.*

His image of a whirlwind of knives barring the dark road to Xibalba remained with her.

ABOARD THE *QALAK*

IN THE *KUUB*

Inside the Khaid ship, Hadeishi and the other prisoners were hurried out of the main airlock—a fresh squad of Khaiden marines was crowding into the space, preparing to board the *Wilful*—and immediately down a side passage. As soon as the hatchway groaned shut behind them—Mitsuharu's ear caught the distinctive sound of a pump working overtime to compensate for a fouled hydraulic line—he lifted his head in the dim, fetid darkness and glanced around.

The last time he'd been aboard a Khaiden raider his Fleet sensibilities had been affronted by how poorly maintained the alien ships were. And his reaction had been mild compared to the outrage shown by the Engineering team he'd put aboard . . . that captured heavy cruiser couldn't have been salvaged without a complete interior rebuild. Much of this, he believed, sprang from the paucity of resources afflicting the ill-defined and disorganized Khaid polity. Fleet intelligence bulletins indicated the hostile power was more a fragile alliance of feuding clans and stations than a real nation. In particular, they lacked a unified industrial base—most of their ships were captured, or stolen—and repair facilities were few and far between.

In the same situation, Mitsuharu believed he'd have taken pains to keep his ship—or ships, if he were some lucky Khaiden warlord—in the best possible condition. But then, he suspected the Khaid might do just that, for ships they had built themselves. But for a stolen ship? Some alien vessel jury-rigged to allow Khaiden operation? There was no reason to spend more than the most minimal resources on a captive vessel; particularly when it would likely be destroyed in the next raid.

Now, seeing the interior of the *Qalak*, he guessed they were being herded down to a holding facility—and from the look of the piping overhead, and the steadily growing heat, it would be close on to a thermocouple station. Then the guard behind Hadeishi interrupted his train of thought with a hard jab to the shoulder with a zmetgun.

Hadeishi fell clumsily, knocking into the sailor in front of him. The man turned, snarling. Mitsuharu took the opportunity to lose his footing and fall down. The guard kicked him, catching Hadeishi on the thigh, and then turned to warn off the sailor.

Curled up on the decking, Mitsuharu pulled his cuffed wrists under both tucked-in legs and—once his hands were in front of him—jimmied the bolt-cutters from his tool belt. Groaning with effort, he managed to twist the steel chain into the cutting blade. Seconds later, a heavy gloved hand seized his shoulder and dragged him up.

"Suk korek!" A throaty alien voice snarled in his

earbug. At such short range, the conductive comm system in his suit was picking up the 'cast from the Khaid's radio. Hadeishi turned, keeping his head down, and gritted his teeth. The cheap steel in the cuffs was resisting the cutters, and the tight pressure on his wrists was sending sharp, bright pains up his arms. "Napiyorzun?"

That's done it, Mitsuharu gasped. A sharp *ping!* echoed in his helmet and his hands were free.

The Khaid reversed his zmetgun and made to slam the metal stock into Hadeishi's chest, but the Nisei officer bounced up and slashed the alien across the neck of its z-suit with the heavy cutters. The blow sent a shock up both arms, but the creature's trachea—or equivalent—ruptured. Dark blue-black blood suddenly gushed from the Khaiden's mouth, sloshing into the bottom of his neck-ring. Its wide-spaced eyes—set into a skull resembling nothing so much as an Afriqan meerkat mated with a hyena's coloring—glazed with pain.

That was enough—Hadeishi smashed the tool down on the Khaid's gun hand, knocking the zmetgun free. The rifle skittered away on the metal decking. At the same moment, the lead guard—who had whirled at the gurgling cry from his fellow—triggered a burst from his weapon. The first of the sailors was lunging at the Khaid and caught the burst full in the chest and face. Shattered z-suit material, clothing, and blood sprayed back. The second two men rushed the guard, heads down. Hadeishi darted in behind them, desperate to silence the Khaid before he could sound an alarm. The guard knocked one sailor aside, then fired wildly—missing everything—and Mitsuharu speared the cutters into his faceplate.

Glassite splintered, turning the clear material milky white, but did not shatter.

Hadeishi hurled himself to the side as the zmetgun roared, barrel smoking red hot, and a spray of flechettes ripped across the ceiling of the passageway.

This is taking too long, flitted across Mitsuharu's mind as he backhanded the Khaid's helmet with the cutters. This time the blunt tool caught the creature in the join between neck-ring and the helmet proper. The z-suit gel—much the same technology as in a Fleet rig and designed to ablate high velocity impacts—gave way and metal jarred on bone. The Khaid staggered, clawing at its neck, and the other two sailors—hands now free—tore its zmetgun away.

One of them, his own faceplate washed red with blood, jammed the rifle barrel into the guard's chest and triggered a burst. The corpse jumped and flechettes spalled across the deck.

"Back to the ship," snarled the other sailor. He'd recovered the other zmetgun and ammunition.

"No!" barked Hadeishi, without thinking. He still had the cutters clenched in both hands and his whole body was shaking with adrenaline. Every instinct screamed to tear down the passage and lose themselves in the environmental conduits sure to be spidering out from the thermocouple into the rest of the ship. "We need to go down deck and look for a shuttle bay."

"Idiot," growled the other sailor, now armed himself. "Our only way home is the *Wilful*—and we can't let the Khaid capture her. A shuttle will only make a quick coffin. . . ."

"There are—" Hadeishi fell silent. Both men had already run back up the passage towards the main airlock. He shook his head once, and then snatched up the equipment belt from the nearest Khaid, something that looked like a document pouch on the creature's thigh and—using the bolt cutters with a sharp, violent jerk—the guard's right forearm. Then he ran in the opposite direction.

Past the next set of hatchways, Mitsuharu found himself at the top of a gangway leading "down" and paused for a moment to crack open his helmet. The smell of the alien ship was violently awful, but he forced down the urge to vomit and let the heat flowing up from the shaft wash over him.

Definitely a heat exchanger below and that sound— There was a gargling sort of wail echoing from the dripping walls.—*will be the holding cells we were destined for. Now I do need that shuttle bay.*

Which posed a dilemma: his Khadesh was limited to the barest courtesies—the human palate and tongue couldn't really duplicate the high-pitched yelping and growl undertone that characterized the diplomatic language used by the clans—and he couldn't read most of their written language. The ship itself, even if stolen from another starfaring race, wasn't a model he recognized, so he was going to have a hard time guessing where to find the nearest shuttle bay.

From in here, he realized. *I need to get outside, where I can make better time. . . .*

He cocked his head, listening again, and now—very distantly—he heard something like the roar of gunfire. Some of the overhead lights flickered and Hadeishi felt certain the sailors from the *Wilful* had found an honorable death.

No more distractions for the enemy. He picked a corridor that seemed—if he was not entirely turned around—to lead outward towards shipskin, and ran swiftly along, watching the maze of pipes and conduits overhead as he moved. A dozen meters on, a big pipe emerged from the floor and disappeared through the wall to the left. It was banded with bright mauve stripes and covered with blocky lettering.

Mitsuharu slowed, turning his wristband over to let the temperature sensor pick up the ambient radiation from the conduit. *Five-degree spike*, he saw. *Just what I need.*

Now he felt his shoulders creep with tension and a prickling at the nape of his neck, which usually meant something hostile was close by. He scuttled along the base of the wall, shining a hand-light at the joins in the passage molding. Fifteen meters down he found an unusually thick panel border and stopped.

His helmet was still open, so he squatted down and closed his eyes, listening.

Back the way he'd come, there was an echoing grinding sound. *Hatchway opening.*

The tool-belt produced a cutting torch and he thumbed the plasma emitter to quarter power and bit in along the edge of the panel. The join came apart, revealing a dark access way carpeted with mold. *Ah, brown mushrooms!* he thought, a fragment of an old song unspooling in memory. *In we go.*

The panel pulled closed behind him and, duckwalking, he scrabbled along by helmet light. After only a few moments, the shape of the huge heat exchanger conduit loomed up before him. This time the mauve striping had been replaced by bright crimson bands and, to his surprise, lines of a different—familiar—script ran between the warning markings.

This was a Hesht ship? Astounding. I thought they suicided their—well, maybe the Khaid bought it from some bankrupt pack. Or a shipyard switched clients in midstream.

He did remember a bit of low Heshok, as well as most of the more important letterforms, and what he could make out of the warnings indicated that yes, this was an air circulator attached to the heat exchangers. *On one of our ships, that means the outbound air will circulate through shipskin radiators to cool before being returned to the sterilizers.*

Feeling grimly determined—Musashi himself would have been impressed by such a stoic demeanor in the face of such calamity—Hadeishi hurried along beside the conduit until, after squeezing past a number of stanchions, he found an access port to the exchanger itself. *Finally!*

The panel popped loose with a little help from his pry bar, and then—after making sure the things he'd looted from the Khaid guard were secured to his suit by lanyards and his helmet was snugged tight—he crawled inside. Immediately, a hot wind roared around him and his z-suit began to squeak alarms about the mounting temperature. He also felt his stomach quease with the loss of gravity and guessed he'd just moved past the last of the g-decking.

Quickly then, he thought, scrambling along the pipe as quickly as he could. *I wonder how long my temperature regulator will hold out?*

Some time later the character of the conduit changed. The pipe came to an abrupt end in a wall filled with hundreds of dimples, each with a much smaller pipette opening recessed within. Hadeishi stopped, feeling the hot wind beating at his back, and then retreated. This proved difficult—going with the airflow, he hadn't realized how hard it was pushing at him—but three meters back from the diffusion wall he found an access plate. Now he pressed his temperature sensor against the opening, and saw with relief that the plate itself was quite cold.

They'd be fools to have open vacuum adjacent to the air exchanger, right? Don't want to trip a pressure alarm.

Regardless, he forced open the access plate and eeled out into a dark, congested room filled with more pipes and machines of unknown provenance. Getting the panel closed behind him was an effort, one that left him exhausted. Hadeishi hooked one leg around a nearby pipe and let himself float.

A search of his pockets found a threesquare bar, which—after checking his environment readings—he ate. That quieted his hunger, but did nothing for his thirst. He licked his lips, trying to remember how many days or hours he could survive without something to drink. *Probably the least of my worries,* he thought. Hopefully, he went through the equipment belt and pouch taken from the Khaid marine, but found nothing edible. He did find a brace of thumb-length cylinders on the belt. Turning them over, he sighed—despairing for his fellow man—for they were México Imperial Army HM-240 grenades long past their expiration date.

Why sir, I found these lying in the street. They must have fallen from an air-lorry.

Fortified, Hadeishi checked his chrono and tried to gauge how much time had passed since the *Wilful* was attacked. *No more than an hour, I hope. I've got to keep moving.* He didn't remember feeling the over-under nausea of punching into transit, which meant the Khaid were probably still cleaning up after their attack on the freighter.

Searching the machine room he found a small door and another access plate. Both seemed temperature neutral, so he eased the door open and found himself looking into a service way lit by only a thin strip of glowlights along the walls. This struck him as a proper maintenance shaft and he looked back, trying to gauge which way was skinside from the heading of the conduit.

That way? he guessed, pulling himself quickly "down" the corridor. Twenty meters on, the shaft turned to the right and a heavy lock-style door emerged from the gloom on his left. *O praise Ameratsu, bringer of daylight!*

Mitsuharu kicked away from one wall and touched down beside the lock. A control panel faced the heavy hatch, but there was no glassite window showing what lay beyond. He wanted to rub his face, but found himself nervously tapping on the faceplate of his helmet instead. The controls had a keypad with twelve buttons around a hex-shaped bezel, some kind of card-reader beside them, and a touch plate.

Time for the old guard to lend a hand, Hadeishi thought. The severed Khaid forearm had been dripping globules of blood behind him as he'd moved and now they gleamed fitfully in the air, drifting past like tiny blue-black planets. He pressed the glove against the touch plate.

Nothing happened.

Then he felt relieved—*Idiot! If they found those bodies, someone will have noticed the missing hand, and shipboard security will be on the lookout for these credentials.* That meant getting through the airlock the old-fashioned way . . . the keypad was a guessing game he didn't have time to play, the card-reader had possibilities—but a quick search through the pouch and the belt he'd stolen didn't find an access card or crystal—and the touch plate was too likely to trigger an alarm. Instead he cast around in the immediate vicinity, looking for an emergency access hatch that would let him cycle the airlock on an override. This led him farther down the corridor without success.

Back at the lock, Hadeishi felt his chances of escape eroding with every chrono tick. At a loss, he examined the control panel and its various components again. This time, something tickled in memory and he found himself staring at the hex-shaped bezel. *A ship built for the Hesht, six fingers on each hand, six packs to a pride* . . . He took out his pry bar and jammed the metal tip under the edge of the bezel, which was not made of the same heavy steel as the rest of the lock. Indeed, the plastic cap popped off, revealing a deep socket—also hex-shaped—running into the hatch.

Emergency access! he gloated, fumbling through both tool belts for something that would fit the keyhole. A moment later he was spraying some unlok into the opening—it was a fair guess no one had manually opened the hatch since construction!—and then he wedged a number six socket wrench into the opening and then ran one handle of the bolt cutters through the socket itself. Then Hadeishi braced himself against the sidewall— thankful for once that he was working in z-g—and put everything he had into cranking his scratch-built key around.

For a long, long minute the socket and cutter combination resisted, going nowhere. His arms started to burn and he felt a twinge in his chest. Then, with a creaky vibration felt through his boots, the wrench rotated a centimeter. Breathing harshly, Hadeishi stopped—sprayed more unlok into the hole—and then put his shoulder into it again.

Now the mechanism creaked again, but faster, and then began to rotate smoothly. Letting out a long hiss of relief, Mitsuharu worked the balky key around until a dull *thud* reverberated through his arms and the control panel flashed a magenta icon. At the same time, a pair of handles popped free from the metal.

Now, he thought, *I will truly be on the clock.* Before opening the door, he carefully stowed all of his tools and secured the lanyards and pouches on both belts. Even the severed hand was tacked down. Then he took hold of both handles and pulled. The hatch swung towards him a little ponderously, revealing a dull gray chamber with a perforated grating as the floor. On the opposite wall was a thick glassite panel and beyond that—the wink and gleam of distant stars.

Thirty seconds, Hadeishi counted, watching the airlock cycle. A number of warning lights had come on as soon as he'd secured the inner lock and vented atmosphere. *Thirty-five seconds.*

The exterior hatch opened and the dull, ruddy light of the *kuub* streamed in, throwing harsh shadows on the walls. Mitsuharu checked his wrist, watching the radiation indicator fluctuate and then settle into the orange zone. *Thirty-eight seconds.*

He swung out of the lock, oriented himself, and then dialed up the magnification on his helmet to thirty-x and took a quick three-sixty of the horizon line. To his right a long profusion of radiating fins emerged from the shipskin, blocking most of his view. To the left the hull arced away into nothing but the abyss of stars. Behind him, however, he felt his heart leap to see the drive cowlings of the *Wilful* rising over the horizon.

Forty-four seconds. Watching the radiation detector fluctuate wildly, Hadeishi wished he had a full EVA rig. His z-suit was airtight and temperature regulated, but it was *not* intended for lengthy stays outside of the shielding of a ship. *Beggars cannot be choosers,* he chided himself, and moved off towards the freighter as fast as his boots could adhere to the shipskin.

A hundred meters on he halted, catching sight of a pair of recessed cargo or boat-bay doors ahead. He crouched down and crept to the edge of the opening. The doors were closed, but he could see a porthole-like window not far away, on a smaller access hatch. Carefully he glanced around, checking the horizon. Nothing caught his eye, so

Hadeishi worked his way down to the smaller hatchway, trying to keep out of line-of-sight from the window. Just a meter away from the opening, he froze, feeling the hull under his hands and feet begin to tremble.

One hundred and sixty seconds.

The bay doors began to separate, spilling a frosty wisp of atmosphere out into the void, and letting a sharp white light gleam through. Beneath him, the metal doors continued to roll back into the hull, carrying Hadeishi with them. *One hundred, sixty-eight seconds.*

He scrambled to the porthole and risked a look inside before the smaller hatch disappeared. Sure enough there was a boat-bay on the other side, holding a fair-sized shuttle. With the brief glimpse, he picked out a pair of Khaiden pilots visible through the beveled windows of the spacecraft. Then he took in the rest of the bay and froze, heart thudding in his throat, back pressed against the cold metal. The loading deck beside the shuttle was swarming with Khaid marines in combat armor; some of them were climbing onto EVA carts like the ones the *Zosen* used to ferry supplies and work crews around the hulls of larger starships.

Musashi was trudging through mud, in the rain, his head bowed beneath a peasant's bowl-like straw hat, a simple bokutō *over his shoulder, when the gates of the castle swung wide. Perforce, he stopped, moving to the side of the road, and watched in interest as a great column of samurai rode out, their armor gleaming wetly and their spear points bare to the sky. Weary, he squatted as they thundered past, wrapped in silken cloaks, their faces hidden behind armored masks. At the last, the banner man rode out, and though his* uma-jirushi *hung heavy in the pelting rain, Musashi could not avoid seeing the Tokugawa* mon. *Thus knowing the evil lord remained within the castle, his heart was gladdened—for victory or death over the Mongol overlords was close at hand.*

Hadeishi glanced back at the shuttle, saw the bus-sized craft was not mounted on a launch rail like a strike-fighter, and raced to dig into his pouches. An instant later, he'd found the roll of stickytape he needed, then double-checked the grenades and the severed arm. Nerving himself, he moved to the edge of the still-moving bay door. Keeping out of sight of the Khaiden hunting party, he crouched down, tensing his legs.

One chance, he thought, feeling giddy. *Watch for it. . . .*

The bay doors stopped with a *clunk,* and then the shuttle separated from the landing cradle. Ponderously, moving only under low-powered thrusters, the craft wallowed out of the boat-bay. Crouched just beyond the edge of the opening, Hadeishi waited for the right moment—then he saw the port-side passenger door slide past—and he sprang outward, hands and feet out-stretched.

He hit the side of the shuttle with a heavy thud, let his knees and elbows flex to absorb as much impact as possible, and then flattened himself against the hull. Seconds later, the Khaid shuttle had cleared the *Qalak* and the entire spaceframe shivered as its main engines went into pre-ignition.

Two hundred seconds. A cool sensation tickled his left wrist as his med-band started to inject anti-radiation meds. Ignoring the sensation, Hadeishi scuttled forward to the passenger door and peered inside.

Perfect, he thought, suppressing a laugh. A Khaid sailor in a blue-and-black z-suit was just inside, watching an environmental control panel as the shuttle started to pick up speed. After a moment of preparation, Mitsuharu began banging hard on the porthole with the severed forearm. Then, before waiting to see what happened, he secured the limb with two quick passes of stickytape so that the bloody glove was easily visible in the window, and scrambled up and over the roof of the shuttle.

Crouching, he took his bearings and saw the shuttle was turning away at an angle from both the *Qalak* and the *Wilful*. It was hard to gauge distance with no back-drop, but he guessed the freighter was a good kilometer away. *Two hundred, fifteen seconds.*

Hadeishi pulled out the little plasma cutter, oriented himself towards the *Wilful*—looked back towards the passenger door with a wry twist to his lips—and when he saw the top edge of the door cycle outward, he ro-tated the strength ring to full and thumbed the control.

The plasma jet flickered out in a long, blue-white line and Hadeishi felt his boots tug—kicking away, he lost adhesion—and then saw the shuttle falling away below him. Long seconds passed . . . he imagined the hatch cy-cling open, the limb being retrieved, the Khaid sailor stepping back inside to examine the queer artifact. Then the portholes on the sides of the shuttle suddenly flared with a stabbing, orange-red light. The spacecraft shud-dered, spilling debris. Out of the corner of his eye, Mit-suharu saw a swarm of combat suits boiling out of the *Qalak*'s boat-bay. EVA carts winged towards the shut-tle, which was now leaking spheroids of gray-white smoke as the interior fittings burned.

Two hundred, forty seconds.

He switched off the plasma cutter and curled himself up into a ball. It was a long fall to the freighter and he hoped—devoutly prayed—that the Khaiden commander on the *Qalak* didn't decide to turn on full active scan-ning for the immediate volume around his ship. *Then I would fry like a sweet dumpling!*

At two hundred forty-five seconds a wave of metallic debris, intermixed with charred cushions, chunks of pip-ing, internal framing, and bits of z-suit accelerated past him. Buffeted by the flotsam, he looked back and saw that the entire shuttle had vanished in a blast cloud. The Khaid marines—barely visible at this range—were in equal disarray. *Score one for the army! Good thing, too,* he thought. *That combat armor will sport an IR mode for extravehicular combat.* Gritting his teeth, he dialed down his suit temperature regulator. *Can't go to zero, but I can draw down my signature. . . .*

Sixteen minutes later, his limbs numb with cold and his radiation monitor strobing red, Hadeishi collided with cargo hold B on the *Wilful*'s port quarter. Shocked out of a hypothermia-induced daze, he bounced along the pitted, scarred surface of the freighter for five or six seconds until he managed to get his hands flat against the metal hull and his z-suit adhered. The jerky stop sent stabbing pains up each arm, but he managed to hold on. *Ah, now that hurt.*

Now able to dial up his suit temperature, Mitsuharu scrabbled along on all fours, looking for the nearest airlock. If memory served, there was a cargo door between two of the drive fairings. The last six meters seemed a vast distance, but he managed to drag himself to the control panel and punch in his access code. Human-friendly lights flickered on inside the lock chamber and he fell in, feeling utterly drained. Hands shaking, Mitsuharu managed to get the outer lock closed and atmosphere cycling before he collapsed.

Gravity kicked in as he lay on the floor, inner door rotating open. For a long moment Hadeishi couldn't even lift his head, but when he could, the cargo hold access way was empty. No alarms had triggered, no sirens sounded. *Khaid haven't reprogrammed the ship yet.*

Dragging himself over the threshold, Hadeishi managed to prop himself against the nearest wall and close the hatch. His hands and feet were getting warmer, and he felt some strength returning. When he could get to his feet, Mitsuharu shuffled down to the cargo master's office—really no more than a closet with controls to manage the gangways and cranes—and rummaged through the storage bins. This yielded up a Gogozen bar—a kind of high-fat candy he usually avoided, but now stuffed into his mouth without delay—and far better, three cans of Kuka-Kolo—a carbonated *chocolatl* beverage sweetened with the sap of the Nopal cactus. When all three were drained dry, Hadeishi began to feel human again. *Ah, sugar. Very delicious. Now I need a weapon, or more than one.*

He missed the grenades, but they seemed to have done well by the Khaid shuttle.

After searching the closet one more time, Hadeishi signed into the shipboard net and paged through the security camera views available to him. Restricted to below-decks, he found nothing in ten fruitless minutes. *No Khaid down below . . . they must be up on the bridge.*

Picking up a long pry bar stowed behind the comp panels, Mitsuharu slipped out of the closet and made his way towards the shipcore with his helmet external audio turned up, listening for anything beyond the usual groaning and hissing of the old ship.

The starboard cargo lift rattled to a halt on the accommodation deck—not an area Hadeishi had ever set foot in before—and he eased out, pry bar in both hands like a bat, and stepped lightly towards the shipcore. Almost immediately he encountered a rec room strewn with burned fabric and paper, fallen *kaffe* cups, and broken plates. His boots crunched on scattered shipgun flechettes, and the walls and cupboards were badly torn up. Two bodies lay sprawled on the floor—both wearing the jumpsuits favored by the *Wilful*'s crew—and as he gingerly approached, they convulsed with a rippling wave of motion.

"Shipbugs," Mitsuharu muttered under his breath, skipping backward, face twisting in disgust.

Both corpses collapsed into a tatter of cloth and white bone. The Khaid shipbugs, an insectile omnivore about the length of his thumb, swarmed across the floor, their silvery carapaces making a queer, shimmering mass. Hundreds of antennae turned in his direction, waved about tasting the air, and then the entire swarm turned away with a rustling *tik-tik-tik*, looking for more decomposing organics to consume.

Why the Khaid—who were not one of the insectoid species known to the México—employed the shipbug, Hadeishi did not know. One intel briefing he had seen suggested the Khaiden themselves had once been a subject race of the Kryg'nth or Megair and had adopted some of their past masters' technologies and practices. Too, he understood they found the insects a delicacy. He found the bugs loathsome and stayed back, out of the room, until the swarm had departed for some other corpse-strewn pasture.

Then he forced himself to search through the remains of the two men, and gathered up their identity cards, pocket multitools, and anything else of use he could find. The refrigerator in the rec area also yielded up more to eat and two bottles of Mayahuel brand beer, which he stowed in the leg pockets of his z-suit.

Do they have a handler? he wondered, thinking of the shipbugs again. *So far they are the only sign of life. . . . Perhaps the Khaid close off the ship, let the bugs scour everything clean, and then come in to gather them up. All fat and juicy and . . .* He spat violently in the sink, then wiped his mouth. *I need to find a real command console with access to all of the security cameras.*

Hadeishi crouched at the junction between the shipcore and an access way to the main passenger airlock, morbidly amused to stand no more than a meter from where he'd been marched out in chains no more than an hour earlier. This time the roundabout was empty—all of the bodies had been dragged away and the Khaid marines were gone. Cautious, Mitsuharu held a small mirror mounted on a telescoping handle around the corner, looking for the expected guards. The airlock itself was open, but no one seemed to be in the gangway leading to the *Qalak. There must be someone just out of sight on the other side.* . . .

Wary of showing himself in the crossroads, Mitsuharu backtracked to the nearest door and slipped inside. The room was one of a set ringing the top of the shipcore and seemed to be sleeping quarters for four. On the far side was a sliding doorway leading into a shared bathroom. Hadeishi wasted no time in passing through, giving the fresher a quick once-over—no weapons or tools—and then easing open the doorway to the second bunkroom.

Here he found the bodies from the roundabout and bridge. They were thrown in a heap—and the *tik-tik-tik* of the shipbugs was loud enough to hear through his helmet. Suppressing an urge to vomit, Mitsuharu kept to the edge of the room and made a quick exit out the far door.

Breathing fast, Hadeishi forced himself to stop—now he was in a short corridor leading back to the roundabout—and he was suddenly afraid he'd walked out in full view of any Khaiden camera pointing down the gangway between the two ships. Luckily, the corridor was not in line with the airlock itself. Breathing a sigh of relief, he ducked across to the other side of the passage and was about to chance angling back to the crossroads to get to the bridge itself when he realized that the thick trail of blood and offal leading into the charnel room had a companion. Not much more than a scrape of blood here and there, but a clear sign that someone had come out of the slaughterhouse—crawled across the corridor on hands and knees—and through a door at the end of the passage.

Well now, they missed someone on their sweep. He followed the trail down a short maintenance passage filled with racked air filtration membranes and into a space holding the plumbing risers for the bathrooms.

The blood trail led into an opening beneath the gray water return. Taking a risk, Mitsuharu cracked open his z-suit helmet, set down the pry bar, and then knelt on the deck, peering under the pipes.

The dim glow of his helmet lamp glittered back from a pair of pale gray eyes.

An elderly, silver-haired woman was squeezed in among the plumbing, her jumpsuit caked with blood, her face gashed open. Now he could hear her labored breathing and see the muzzle of an automatic—a Webley Bulldog, from what he could see—pointed in his general direction.

"*Sencho,*" he said quietly, recognizing the rank tabs on her collar. "I'd better get you out of there."

An hour later, on the bridge, Captain De Molay was lying back on the pilot's shockchair, her face bandaged and a mug of instant *kaffe* clutched in hands shining with antibiotic biogel. She looked only marginally better and her breathing was still hoarse. Hadeishi was sitting at the captain's panel, carefully paging through the onboard cameras, a long machete-like knife close by his hand, and two different earbugs inserted. The *Wilful*'s systems were more of a hodgepodge than he'd believed, but on-board power was up, the transit coil was spun down to a low idle, reactors were cooking, and every kind of weapon on the ship had been gathered up by the Khaid and hauled away.

Well, he thought, *almost everything*. He patted the machete.

"You're our new engineer's mate then," De Molay wheezed, trying not to cough. "Azulcay said you were showing some promise."

"Kind of him," Mitsuharu replied, glancing over at the main hatchway. The door was locked and barred, though he knew there was a shipbug swarm busily cleaning up the blood sprayed across the floor and walls outside. The thought still turned his stomach. "Are there any explosives on board? Grenades?"

"If the bastards didn't take it," she coughed, pointing at the bridge gun locker—whose door was hanging open, the locks sprung. "There might be some blasting putty in there. I keep some on hand when we have to clear a landing zone."

Hadeishi nodded, distracted by a faint tremor suddenly running through the floor and making his fingertips buzz on the control panes. He checked the exterior camera feeds, and saw the *Qalak*'s shipskin was deforming. The forests of radiating fins were drawing inward, while the destroyer's transit drive foils were unwinding.

"She's prepping to jump and take us with her. Finish that *kaffe*, *kyo*, we're going to have to move."

"Move where?" De Molay managed to lift her mug and drain the rest of the sludge. "Two poor pilgrims are we, with only one tired horse—not even one we can fly out of here!"

"No, not yet." Hadeishi rummaged quickly through the gun locker—twice looted between the *Wilful*'s crew and the Khaid—and came up with a half-used cylinder of grayish putty, no more than a finger in length. "No triggers?"

"Not in there, child." De Molay attempted a smile, which made her cheek twinge. "Stowage bin beside the captain's chair, the one with the broken lock."

"Ah." Hadeishi fished out three putty triggers, one of which was a remote-controlled detonator. "*Dōmo arigatō.*" The triggers went into one pocket, the putty into another.

On the camera pane pointing down the gangway into the *Qalak* there was sudden motion. Mitsuharu leaned over, caught sight of four Khaid in z-suits strolling across the gangway, and motioned to De Molay. "Time to go, *Sencho-sana.*"

Moments later, with the bridge hatch propped open once more, Hadeishi was climbing down a service tube running between the decks, with Captain De Molay clinging to his shoulders. The old woman was light enough to carry, but no burden he wanted to freight for hours. A clumsy set of straps tied them together, and he could do no better with the time allowed.

He could feel, from the vibration of the ship, that the *Wilful* was underway, though her engines were still cold. Hadeishi assumed the *Qalak* was accelerating away from the ambush point and spinning up gradient. Hadeishi was hoping to find somewhere for them both to hole up before—

The dim lights in the shaft flickered—his stomach sprang up, reversed, and crawled back down his throat. De Molay groaned, her abdomen clenching in protest. She gagged, but managed to choke down the vomit.

"We're away," Mitsuharu said, when he felt steady

enough to resume climbing down. "And who can tell where we're heading?"

"I can," De Molay wheezed, "if we can get access to a control panel in engineering."

"*Hai, kyo*. At our first opportunity." They reached a junction between decks and Hadeishi struggled to step off the ladder and onto the service door landing. De Molay had to help, grasping at a stanchion with her weak hands, while he navigated the corner. Then Mitsuharu keyed through the door and saw they had descended far enough to reach the lower cargo deck.

"Wait here, *kyo*," he muttered, setting her down. "I need to set some insurance."

Back in the maintenance shaft, he tore open a series of access panels until he found an orange-colored conduit the thickness of his wrist. Gingerly—who knew how stable the substance was!—he tacked the blasting putty behind the communications main and then wedged the remote detonator into place. Working his way back to the corridor, he closed and locked the entrance to the shaft and then checked the detonator relay.

Cupped in his hand, the status light shone a pale green.

"What did you mine?" De Molay asked, peering up at him from the floor. She was still too weak to stand.

"Main shipnet relay from the bridge to down below, *kyo*."

"And how did you know it was there?" She was frowning, and had the old woman her full strength, her expression would have been formidable.

Hadeishi shrugged. "*Sencho*, I have many bad habits."

Slinging her on his back again, Mitsuharu set off for his old quarters behind the fuel tanks.

———

Winter rain was pouring down, setting the mountain-side streams to rushing, white-frothed torrents. Musashi was climbing the pass under Mount Murou, a plain wooden staff in each hand. A bitterly cold wind howled, nipping at his face, etching white streaks on the wolf-skin he wore as a cape. The old blind man clinging to his back was cursing endlessly, complaining about every jounce and jolt in the road as the swordsman climbed, step by step, his feet bleeding in the straw sandals, towards the summit of the pass. If he missed a step, the old man would strike the side of Musashi's head with a begging bowl and shout—"donkey!"—over the hiss of the wind.

De Molay slumped into Hadeishi's hammock with a relieved groan. Her face was very pale, her skin waxy. Mitsuharu pulled one of the bottles of Mayahuel from his leg pockets and popped the cap. The old woman drank noisily, but seemed a bit revived when he took the empty away.

The main engineering console had been shorted out, which Hadeishi found a crude but effective way to prevent its use, but the secondary panels were still active. He retrieved his stylus from a corner and keyed up the interface. "*Kyo*, what code should I use?" he asked, looking to De Molay.

"Hierusalem," she said, and then spelled out the Latinate word for him. The panel quickened to life, showing a wholly different interface than he'd ever had access to before. Both of Hadeishi's eyebrows rose in surprise, then he quickly navigated through the sensor options to find the transit display.

———

At the summit of the pass, where Toudai temple had once stood, there was a ring of shattered pillars and broken stones. Here the icy wind was howling like a demon, and the chill cut through Musashi's cloak like a knife. Arrayed across the road, their own furs white and almost invisible against the blowing snow, stood a line of men with drawn blades. In his ear, Musashi heard the blind man sniff once, then twice. "Ah, idiot donkey—why have you angered the shugenja? Now we shall be late. . . ."

The engineering panel was not equipped to generate a full-up threatwell display, but Hadeishi could read the swarm of glyphs and icons as well as any Fleet officer. De Molay opened one eye, peering at him from the hammock. "Well, engineer's mate, where are we going?"

"That, I cannot tell. But we have found company . . . two dozen Khaid warships, I would judge—some of them larger than I've ever seen under their colors before—and we are all on the same heading."

He stepped away from the console, thinking. "I'm going to have to find a place to hide you, *Sencho*. The Khaid prize crew will come around soon enough."

NEAR THE PINHOLE

Anderssen woke abruptly, finding herself in near-darkness, and for a moment she was certain the roof above was formed of bronze-colored metal, metal which gleamed and flickered with the light of constantly moving streams of flame. Something like wraiths, or fiery shadows, which moved throughout the tower around her, which tenanted the streets below, and darted through sullen, amber-colored skies above.

Her mouth was filled with a hard, metallic taste and she tried to muster enough spit to clear her palate. *Gods, what did I drink last night?* She could not remember drinking anything harder than tea.

Sitting in the darkness, Gretchen flexed her fingers, tied back her hair, and groped around for her comm band. She found the bracelet by touch and turned the device over. The cool blue glow of the readouts steadied her and the last of the flickering, flame-tenanted shadows faded from the edges of her vision.

"I see," she said aloud, suddenly wishing she'd brought Malakar along to watch over her while she slept. *Or Parker, or Magdalena! Where are my friends, my team? In the old days I would never have hared off like this without them.* The thought brought her up short and Anderssen realized—with a chill shock—that she had placed herself in a very precarious position. *I am out here, in the middle of nowhere, with a crazy old sorcerer and a crew of religious fanatics, looking for ... something ... which by all rights ought be left well enough alone. Holy Mary of the Roses, what was I thinking? Magdalena would give me such a cuffing!*

Then she decided that Hummingbird had jobbed her again with his measly five hundred thousand quills. *And why did he pay that out?* she wondered. *He must be desperate for ... for a washed-up, out-of-work, out-of-her mind xenoarchaeologist. He could rent a graduate student from the Company for almost nothing!*

The obvious reason was disturbing. *He knows about my talent, and how it's grown. He's expecting me to be able to find all of the pieces of some puzzle that would elude everyone else, even him. This is not going to be pleasant.*

She clipped on her medband and comm bracelet,

swung out of the tiny bunk, and found her jacket, comp, and other tools. The *Moulins* had been poking along in the dark, following an uneven, zigzag course for several days. But now, she had a sense the ship had stopped moving. *Have we arrived?* she wondered. "Time to find out."

After a detour by the mess deck to fill her mug with hot, weak *kaffe*—the dispenser seemed programmed to produce the most wretched version of anything requested—Gretchen climbed the gangway to the control spaces. Captain Locke, the pilot, and Hummingbird were sitting, watching the navigational displays with varying degrees of boredom. The screens showing the exterior view of the *Moulins* were filled with gorgeous, glowing dust clouds in every shade of red, violet, and viridian. Streamers of iridescent material arced across the field of view. Embedded in the murk—were they distant pulsars, or stars almost swallowed by this wrack?—were hot points of light.

Anderssen slipped into the creaking, cracked-leather chair beside the old *nauallis* and strapped herself in.

"What's happening?"

Hummingbird turned slightly, his weathered old face impassive. "We've found what seems to be an Imperial battle-group. Most of the ships are stationary, but some are working patrol patterns around this whole area."

"But we're waiting?" She felt itchy, knowing that the artifact—her life's work if she could but touch it—might only be light-minutes away. "What for?"

"The right ship. And the right commander." His voice was very low, only barely audible to her, even sitting in the adjacent seat.

"So, we're thinking weeks parked here in the dark, watching the pretty lights?" Her light tone did not move him.

Instead, he nodded minutely. "If need be."

A chime sounded from one of the console panels and a series of glyphs strobed on the main board. The pilot leaned over, interested. His stylus circled a moving icon on the display and the view focused in. Velocity and heading figures appeared in a sidebar.

"Reckless idiot!" Locke shook his head in dismay, and then eyed Hummingbird. "This the one you're waiting for?"

"Target's v is pushing the limit for this particle density." The pilot sounded impressed. "It's big and must be packing a serious set of deflector generators! I wonder if—"

Locke snorted, saying: "I don't think he can see any better in this than—"

"Go dark!" Hummingbird's voice was sharp as a knife and filled with an unmistakable tone of command. Without even thinking, the pilot jerked around in his seat, both hands busy on the controls. The level of ambient noise in the control space suddenly dropped and every light shaded down to a dull red, or turned off entirely. The sound of the air circulators ceased and the constant, low-level vibration in the decking stuttered and then died.

"Captain, we are at zero emissions," the pilot reported in a low voice. "Gravity generators are cold. Engines are cold."

Gretchen was interested in Locke's reaction— Hummingbird had given direct orders on his bridge— but the freighter captain seemed unperturbed. *If he'd noticed at all?* Anderssen found that peculiar, but the captain had been treating the old *nauallis* very deferentially for the last week. *I need to look up what Præceptor means.*

The icon on the navigation board continued to show swift progress and Gretchen, peering over Hummingbird's shoulder, suddenly realized that another icon—one shining green with a blue band around it—must be the *Moulins*. Which meant . . .

On the camera screens, a point of blue-violet light suddenly became visible. As she watched, it grew in size, resolving into a black speck surrounded by a brilliantly colored corona of violently excited particles. The wake of the approaching starship quickly became apparent as a corkscrew-like fan of burning motes.

The pilot cursed, looking first to Locke and then to Hummingbird. "Radiation from that drive plume is going to slam us hard. We need to—"

"Hold position." The Crow's voice was steely and his demeanor inflexible. "They are blinding their own sensors with all that electromagnetic trash. If we remain still, they will race past, unknowing. Otherwise, we'll be a fine target for a sprint missile or particle beam practice."

Locke nodded, swallowing hard. His hands clenched on the arms of his chair.

Gretchen was glad—she'd had the thought before—she'd already had her quota of children. *Though just one more . . . no, it's too late for that.*

Twelve minutes later the *Moulins* groaned, her hull hammered by successive waves of particles—all hot and glowing with borrowed radiation—as the massive ship rolled past.

"A super-dreadnaught," whispered the pilot in awe, camera interpolation yielding an enormous outline through the curtains of fire. "It must be four kilometers long, or more!"

Hummingbird was working his stylus in a quick, efficient blur on a hand comp. A lead had been jacked from the unit into the control consoles and Gretchen jumped slightly when he suddenly cursed aloud. Locke and the pilot turned in alarm.

"Xochitl!" The sound was harsh, abrupt.

Hummingbird stared at his comp, right eyelid twitching. Then, after a stiff moment with everyone staring at him, he looked up. "Captain Locke, spin up the mains as soon as we're in the thrust shadow of that monster."

"Delicate flower?" Gretchen ventured. "I've heard that name before."

"One of the Princes Imperial has arrived," the old *nauallis* answered, looking at her sidelong. She had been around him long enough to glimpse anger and unease behind his usual stoic mask. *Could our all-seeing sorcerer be worried?* Gretchen struggled to suppress a grin.

"We have to get in there immediately." Hummingbird glared at Locke.

Xochitl—I remember, that's "precious flower"—now where . . . Ah! Of course.

A flurry of 3-v magazine covers, each more lurid than the last, came to mind. Page after page of *Temple of Truth* filled with "candid" snaps of a young, heartbreakingly handsome man. The foremost of the Emperor's "Mighty Sons," Prince Xochitl was not the eldest, but he did shine the brightest in popular culture. A victorious Fleet commander—he'd driven the Kroomākh back from Al-Haram, recapturing two colony worlds and a series of critical mining stations—and a notorious duelist who had left a long trail of broken hearts and honorable deaths behind him.

So, she thought, feeling Hummingbird's tension ratcheting up with each second. The pilot had the maneuver engines on restart and Captain Locke had pitched in to bring up the hyperspace coil. But she could tell it was all going far, far too slowly for the Crow's frayed patience.

"Hm," she said, drawing a baleful gaze. "He's the pretty one, isn't he? With the hair?"

Koshō happened to be reviewing battle-group dispositions in preparation for ordering a change in heading for the next leg of their patrol pattern, when a bright spark popped into view on the threatwell. Her eyes widened, then flicked to the ident code glyphs popping up around the speeding mote.

"*Kiken-na!*" she snapped, outraged. "Evasive action, *Thai-i*, cut to starboard at maximum burn."

The lieutenants at the navigation and pilot stations were already in motion and acceleration alarm Klaxons blared the length of the ship. *Naniwa*'s frame groaned, antimatter-powered drives kicking into maximum thrust, and Koshō watched, face impassive, as they cut away from intercept.

A moment later, as the g-decking stabilized, *Sho-sa* Oc Chac was in Command as well, sliding into his own shockchair. He seemed a little wide-eyed, given the abrupt maneuver.

"*Chu-sa?*"

Susan did not answer for a moment, her face hard-set, brows furrowed. She was watching the conversation between the *Naniwa*'s 'cast system and the intruder. Camera images of the oncoming ship began to unfold on her panel, and the ident system chirped, yielding a verified identification.

"IMN SDN-6 *Tlemitl* has joined the battle-group," she said at last, her lips a tight, hard line. "Under the command of the Prince Imperial Xochitl, Admiral of the Fleet." She sat back in her shockchair and forced her hands to stillness. "What is he doing here in the *Firearrow*? There isn't a 3-v camera within light-years! I should . . ."

"*Kyo,*" Oc Chac ventured to interrupt, his black eyes curious. "Do you know the *Gensui?*"

"We were in school together," Koshō bit out. *And I will not tell you what I think of the Flowery Prince, his personal attributes, or his social history.* She tapped her earbug angrily.

"*Chu-i* Pucatli, please send appropriate greetings to Prince Xochitl aboard *Tlemitl* on behalf of myself and the crew of *Naniwa.*"

Then she turned back to her XO. "*Sho-sa* Oc, get us out of the *Firearrow's* drive plume. Send *Naniwa* wide, then curve back to the patrol pattern. That should avoid any radiation wake behind that behemoth."

"*Hai, Chu-sa!*"

Susan tried to turn her attention back to reviewing the latest supplies and munitions projections from Logistics, but the constant chatter on the battle-group stellarcast—which she had spooling on one of her earbug channels—was afire with speculation. *Tlemitl* had not 'cast the usual greeting or pleasantries, though the massive ship's course was clear—dead on to the *Can.*

The thought of Xocoyotl's reaction to being usurped by the Prince, who outranked the vice admiral in every possible way, did lighten her mood a little. But she did not relish the prospect of managing both of them.

Sixty-two minutes later, as the *Naniwa* completed her course correction, an alarm sounded from the Navigation station.

"*Chu-sa!*" the navigator said sharply, looking up from his console. "Unknown signature on the plot! We have an intruder in our patrol box."

"Where?" *Thai-i* Konev at Weapons looked keen to exercise his systems.

"Report," Susan said, her voice calm and controlled.

Her own displays were already adjusting, with threat analysis panes opening up. "Size—heading—something pertinent, *Thai-i* Holloway."

"Pretty small, *kyo*, about sixty meters long. It's piggy-backing in the *Tlemitl's* wake. Signature is intermit-tent—" Holloway swallowed a curse, as the icon suddenly vanished from the threatwell.

"Project location from the data we've already cap-tured, *Thai-i*. Lock heading as soon as we've caught sight of her again." Koshō looked to Pucatli, who was sitting in at comm for the usual first-watch officer. "Signal battle stations to all hands, *Chu-i*. Immediate intercept. Unau-thorized ship of unknown flag. Guns live. This is not a drill. Load missile racks one and two. Direct *Socho* Juarez to ready two teams for board and seizure."

Then she sat back, feeling a cold shiver of adrenaline course through her limbs as the Klaxon sounded, and her bad mood vanished like the morning frost from the eaves. *Smartly now,* she thought, watching the bridge crew in action. *Mitsuharu would be pleased to see their progress.*

"*Chu-sa?*" Oc Chac looked up from his own console, his chiseled face gleaming as the overheads flashed three times. "Battlecast needs an update on our course correc-tion. Should I—"

She shook her head, *no*. "Let's see what we've beaten from cover, first, *Sho-sa*. Then I'll report to the various admirals."

The *Naniwa* cut in quite nimbly, Susan was pleased to see, using the particle storm kicked up by the *Tlemitl's* passage as a hunting screen, and Juarez' combat teams had dropped alongside the tiny ship with two shuttles before there was any indication the intruders realized they'd been seen.

Koshō listened intently, a constellation of v-feeds from marine armor cameras unspooling on her main console, as the *Socho* and his men cracked two airlocks simultaneously and secured the ship. There was some chatter from the inhabitants, but by then the engines were locked out.

She raised an eyebrow, looking questioningly at Oc Chac.

"Registry, *Sho-sa*?"

"The *Moulins*, *kyo*. A 'merchanter for hire' out of Denby 47. No more than an asteroid with a hydrogen cracking station and fueling gantry. If memory serves, Denby lies within the jurisdiction of New Malta."

"A Templar ship?" Koshō was intrigued. "Or even Norsk?"

Oc Chac grimaced. "The Europeans would be mad to meddle in the Prince's affairs, *kyo*. But the knight-priests? They might find it amusing to trick about at his tail, all unseen."

Susan folded her slim arms and stared apprehensively at the multiplane view afforded by the threatwell. *This place is drawing far too many players. All for a hazard to navigation? No—the Mirror must think they can gain control of the weapon, or whatever it is, and turn it to our use. But why did the Prince arrive so late? He was never late to any affaire or affray before . . . curious. Very curious.* She tapped open the Marine command circuit.

"*Socho* Juarez, what do we have for passengers?"

His report, brisk and efficient as it was, was *not* what Koshō wanted to hear. Her expression turned quite remarkably sour, as though she'd bitten into a rotten persimmon. Oc Chac waited, his curiosity obvious, while the *Chu-sa* stared distantly at the threatwell. When she turned to him, he straightened, hands clasped behind his back. "*Kyo?*"

"Loading bay one between the engine ring and the main holds—do we have something stowed there?"

"*Iie, Kyo*, Fleet regulations indicate the exterior bays are only for—"

"*Sho-sa*, prep the bay to tether that ship. I want it inside our coil field as quickly as we can." She looked away. "*Socho* Juarez, we're bringing you inboard, but I want a squad on-board at all times, and bring in some *Zosen* to tear it apart—hidden compartments, look for everything. . . ."

"*Hai, kyo!*"

On the bridge of the *Moulins*, Hummingbird watched with equanimity as the gaping maw of the battle-cruiser's rear cargo hold enveloped them. He was keeping an eye on his comp, which chirped pleasantly a moment after they were fully inside the Imperial ship. Anderssen frowned—her hands were clasped on the top of her head, just like Captain Locke and the pilot—and she was staring down the barrel of an Imperial shipgun. The *nauallis'* comp was sitting on a side console, still plugged into the freighter's shipnet, and seemed to be quite busy.

"Who are you talking to with that thing?" she hissed out of the side of her mouth.

"There has been correspondence with the battle-cruiser's navigational system," the *nauallis* said. "Are your bags packed?"

"Of course," she growled, and then fell silent. One of the marines—his black-on-black nameplate seemed to say Juarez—had noticed their conversation and came over, expression grim.

Before the Imperial could say anything, however, Hummingbird nodded pleasantly and said: "*Socho*, please consider my credentials before doing anything rash. I am an Imperial *Tlamantinime*—a Judge—on official business. This woman is my assistant and we appreciate your commander's efforts in picking us up." He twisted his wrist, exposing a comm band, and then submitted quietly as the marine scanned his various forms of identification.

"Huh." Juarez pursed his lips, looked the motley set of them over, and then turned away, speaking into his throatmike.

Gretchen snorted in disgust, knowing full well there was *no way* the old México had planned this. "You know, Crow, you remind me of my first field instructor. She really didn't know what she was doing. She didn't plan. She was clumsy and forgetful. Disasters followed her everywhere, but something always happened to make her look great. She eventually wandered up a pyramid on Go-Long in the rainy season and was struck by lightning."

Socho Juarez returned, his expression thunderous. "The *Chu-sa* will speak with you." He jerked an armored thumb at two of the marines. "*Heicho* Gozen, Chayle, the captain is waiting for them in the loading bay overlook."

"We'll need our luggage," Hummingbird interjected, radiating an aura of perfect reasonability. "It will only take a moment, and save time later." Juarez just stared in bafflement. The *nauallis* slowly lowered his hands, gathered up his spare mantle, the hand comp, and gestured for Gretchen to precede him out of the control space. Both marine corporals—shipguns at the ready—followed along, a little nonplussed themselves.

Behind them, Juarez shook his head, finger to his earbug. "Are you sure, *Chu-sa*? This whole ship stinks of an infiltrator. . . . *Hai, hai.* They're on their way."

Clattering down the gangway from the *Moulins*, half-blinded by the brilliant glare of the spotlights illuminating the enormous hold, Gretchen shifted her duffle and backpack, feeling the straps dig into her shoulder. "But the native people that lived nearby said they had seen a bright angel escape from her body. So they built a shrine so they could pray to her for good luck."

Hummingbird said nothing, breath frosting in the chill air, his attention fixed on a petite figure in dress-whites looking down upon them from a glassite window half-way up the side of the bay. His two travel bags—made from some heavy synthetic and badly worn, some holes patched over with dozens of transfer stickers—hung heavy in his hands as he walked.

"I like that story," he replied, after a moment. The marines keyed open a passenger door and they stepped aboard the *Naniwa*.

The overlook was entirely lacking any amenities—no chairs, no soft couches, no dispenser filled with cold drinks. No heat to speak of, as the cargo hold was actually part of the exterior hull of the warship, which carried the shipskin, weapons, boat and cargo bays, and so on. The secondary hull—probably twenty meters inward from their current position—would be warm and toasty. Gretchen looked around, sighed, and parked her duffle and backpack against the foot of a control console. Then Anderssen leaned back against the metal, arms crossed, and nodded politely to the Imperial ship captain. *This one looks very familiar, where . . . ah now, it's Captain Hadeishi's second! I haven't seen her since that embassy reception on Jagan.*

Koshō's attention was wholly upon Green Hummingbird, and she radiated an icy distaste which matched the room temperature. The strength of her animosity was refreshing to Gretchen, for the Nisei woman evinced not the slightest fear, respect, or deference for the old Crow. *That is more like it!*

"I see," the *Chu-sa* said, lifting her chin slightly. "Now everything is perfectly clear to me."

"Excellent," Hummingbird replied, setting down his own luggage. "Then I need not explain. We require a private room with bath, shipnet access, and transport to the science station I believe the Mirror Which Reveals is operating not too far from here. And quietly, too," Hummingbird said. "This is a privy matter."

"Is it?" Koshō gave him a steely glare. "I am entirely familiar with *my* operational orders, Hummingbird-*tzin*. Your ... faction ... is not welcome here—your presence forbidden." The faintest smile threatened to disturb the cold perfection of her lips. "I could have you both shot, buying myself the favor of the Mirror with the same flechette. A bargain, I think!"

Hummingbird became very still. Gretchen watched, wide-eyed, wondering if the sense of sharp, coiled fury she felt from the Imperial officer was apparent to the *nauallis*. *Damn,* Anderssen thought, *her fingertips are on her sidearm! Is she going to chop him down right here?*

The old México's eyes narrowed and he shifted his stance subtly. Then, apparently rallying himself, he said: "Your *sensei* still lives, *Chu-sa*, as I promised. And he prospers."

"Proof?" Susan tilted her head slightly to one side, almond-shaped eyes bare slits gleaming with reflected light from the boat-bay.

"My word upon it."

"Utterly without value." Koshō's free hand made a chopping motion. Then she glanced over at Gretchen. "Dr. Anderssen, a pleasure to see you again. Do you know what is happening here? What all of this is about?"

"I do," Hummingbird interrupted at once.

The *Chu-sa* flashed a tiny, cold smile.

Gretchen wanted to smile, too, but thought it wise to

mind her own business. She could feel Hummingbird's anger starting to rise. She knew perfectly well the *nauallis* did not like to barter. *He needs something very badly, or he would not be prepared to horse-trade.* She sat down on her duffle—the console was like ice—and reached into her jacket for a Gogozen bar. *Maybe I should record this,* she mused, *for posterity.*

SOMEWHERE IN THE *KUUB*

Hadeishi sat in deep gloom, only the barest slivers of light shining on the pipes overhead. One boot was edged against the fuel valve at the top of an enormous tank of reaction mass, the other tucked under him as a makeshift seat. De Molay, tucked into the hammock again, was only a hand-span away, almost invisible in the darkness. The string net was suspended from a series of overhead pipes. Below them, intermittent sounds echoed up from the engineering spaces as two Khaid engineers banged around, trying to decipher the *Wilful*'s control systems. Hadeishi had put the rest of their supplies—everything he could gather up in the time allowed—in another bag, which also hung from a lanyard.

A burst of harsh chatter rose up to them, and the entire ship shuddered with a sharp, reverberating *clang-clang-clang*. De Molay shifted, and Mitsuharu heard her whisper: "We've separated."

He nodded, judging the sounds the same way. Their suspicions were confirmed a few moments later when the entire ship shivered awake and the pumps attached to the fuel tanks hummed into action. *We're on maneuvering drive,* Mitsuharu thought.

His fingertips reached out, confirmed the location of the machete, and then he leaned close enough to the freighter captain to feel her faint, thready breath on the side of his face. "They are preparing to take us into hyperspace."

Hadeishi twisted around, putting his back to her, and held up a comp he'd appropriated from one of the equipment lockers. The tiny screen displayed a telemetry feed relayed from the navigational system. The whole Khaid fleet was in motion.

"So many ships," whispered De Molay. "That doesn't seem like a raiding party. . . ."

Mitsuharu shook his head. "This is a fleet. The first I've ever seen—or heard—of the Khaid assembling. Something—larger—is underway."

On the display, Khaiden icons shook out into new positions.

"That is an odd formation," De Molay wheezed, trying to find a comfortable position. The hammock swayed a little.

"They're preparing for a hot combat jump," Hadeishi replied softly, feeling a trickle of adrenaline start up in his heart. Old familiar feelings—ones he'd thought lost, now welcome in their return—flooded him, watching the alien ships form up. "Heavies pentahedral at the core, lights orbiting at the edge of their combat interlink range. But . . . what is there to attack out here? No planets, no systems . . . not so much as a mining enclave in range."

De Molay snorted softly. She had recovered some color. "The hidden places are always busy, Nisei. There is an Imperial research station. Five or six light-years from here, I would venture. A secret . . . but not well kept, as we see."

He looked over his shoulder, one eyebrow raised. "You were bound there yourself?"

"The *Wilful*? Not directly." She tapped him gently on the shoulder with gnarled fingertips. "*Your* destination, Captain Hadeishi, is a little grander . . . one of our sister ships should have been waiting for us at that moon. I wonder if they suffered our fate, only earlier. Unless they were delayed and have yet to reach rendezvous."

Mitsuharu breathed deeply, calming a sudden burst of outrage. *So—I've been deceived and carted about like a sack of meal! Hmmm . . . but who would want me out in this desolation?*

"Ah, see? The Khaid fleet is underway." De Molay's voice was a bare whisper.

Indeed, the enemy was rippling out of sight into hyperspace.

"Three waves. Then us." *In this soup,* Hadeishi thought, *they'll be on top of the station without the slightest warning.*

He thumbed through a series of other views, tapping each ship's system in turn. The hyperspace coil reported coordinates for transit had been locked in and the freighter was quickly approaching gradient. Mitsuharu's eyes narrowed, but a quick flip back to the navigation feed confirmed what he'd expected—hoped!—when he'd seen the Khaid combat pattern.

We're plotted for a different vector. For some frontier depot with a prize crew aboard. Useless in a fight, but too valuable for these scavengers to leave behind. Excellent.

He thumbed a set of commands into the hand comp, one ear listening to the banter of the Khaid technicians below them at the main engineering panel. A red glyph began to flash on the little display and he covered the icon with his thumb, ready to press.

The hyperspace coil buried two decks below keened awake. His thumb mashed down—the glyph deformed—then disappeared. The ship spun up to gradient and then—with a shudder and a queasy slide—the *Wilful* was away as well, racing forward at transluminal speeds.

Vector confirmed, he thought, smiling to himself.

De Molay looked up at him questioningly. "What have you done?" she mouthed.

"A detour," he whispered. "When one door shuts, another opens.'"

ABOARD THE *CAN*

Kikan-shi Helsdon, formerly 2nd Engineer on the IMN DD-217 *Calexico,* squinted against the glare of a pair of work lights to see if he could help the shipnet specialist crammed down in the cramped bottom of a holotank housing. "Do we need to run in more power?"

The specialist coughed, his face spotted with flecks of data crystal interface cable. The sound echoed tinnily in the confined space. "Modelers always need more power, Engineer. And memory. And room. And . . . how long before somebody comes down here wanting to see a life-size model of the whole damned *kuub*?"

The other Mirror technicians in the upper chamber laughed. They were busy laying down conduit and hooking up racks of portable computation engines into the shipnet. The whine of cutting saws echoed from the outer corridor, along with the *pang-pang-pang* of a nail gun tacking up temporary wall sections.

Helsdon tried to grin. "Maybe we should have looked around when we appropriated this threatwell tank. Who knows what else Logistics threw in when they loaded up?"

"I could use less chatter in here," one of the other techs muttered, "and more computational help. The volume of this flux data is unbelievable. We're saturating the storage interface!"

"One moment," Helsdon replied, wiping his hands clean. "Got a place for me to work?" He crossed to a computer station jammed in next to the pair of double doors leading into the chamber and took a handheld v-pane unit from the Mirror technician.

The sandy-haired engineer had barely sat down on the floor—no chairs were available—and started to drill down into the configuration of the interfaces when three figures appeared, their imposing bulk blocking the entire doorway. They said nothing, but every technician in the room, including Helsdon, turned instinctively towards them.

The Imperial Jaguar Knights entered silently, their armor etched with dozens of black spots overlaid on a mosaic of pale blue and yellow lines. Their helmets, the visors currently opaque, rippled with stylized black and white feathers. Though entirely functional, the *Oceloto-tec* Mark Sixteen articulated combat suit contained a simple stealthing technology which allowed the wearer to adjust the surface patterning at will. At the moment, all three Jaguar Knights had their distinctive regimental colors and emblems dialed down—but Helsdon had seen them on military parade in Tenochtitlán itself, and knew they could, with the addition of brilliantly feathered nanomechanical cloaks, shine like the sun itself.

The officer—there were no obvious markings on his armor to indicate this, but Helsdon had a sense of the Knight from the way he carried himself—surveyed the room. The Jaguar's gaze settled on the engineer, which made Malcolm swallow nervously. *Not good; someone has realized I'm the "survivor."*

"The Prince Imperial will speak with you," the officer declared, his voice underlain by a vocoder-generated growl.

A firm grip helped him to his feet and down the hall. *I guess consent isn't required.* Wisely Helsdon made no protest, simply following along where directed. Any instinct to resist had been suppressed by his tremendous weariness. A tubecar put him and his escort at the main shuttle bay, which had previously been the *Calexico*'s cargo loading hangar. A mint-new shuttle was standing by, hull glittering with protostellar debris. He got a good look at the crest above the hatchway as he was hustled inside. *The Imperial household! They did mean "the Prince." Saint Ebba the Younger, preserve me from the attention of On High.*

The shuttle drifted into a boat-bay on the side of the *Tlemitl* which could have swallowed the *Calexico* whole. The descent of the passenger boat to the landing stage seemed almost ludicrous to Helsdon as he watched acres of freshly constructed pressure wall roll past the porthole. Even the seats on the shuttle were so new they squeaked. Professional curiosity drove him to eyeball the curve of the air intakes, and peer out at the flaps and lifting surfaces on the shuttle wing.

Two versions up, at least, from the last of these Tegus models I worked on.

Inside the super-dreadnaught, he was struck by the emptiness of the passages. An SDN usually carried an enormous complement; freighting a Fleet Command staff, whole embassies, trade delegations, and a full regiment of marines. But here—as he and his escorts zipped along on a g-sled—most of the offices, or spaces for shops, were empty.

Only a combat crew aboard, he guessed. At one point they passed a pair of technicians rooting around in a series of access panels in an adjacent hallway. *Still doing*

the fit and finish work. So this heavyweight has been
rushed into service.

The sled passed through two checkpoints—both
manned by more Jaguar Knights—and finally they found
themselves in a tenanted precinct. Officers, technicians,
and staff orderlies filled the passages, each moving with
the kind of swift direction which implied a task of tremendous importance.

They dismounted in a double-height corridor lined
with enormous mural-sized v-panes.

On the left side, as Helsdon hurried past, two towering volcanoes—the doomed lovers Popocatépetl and
Iztaccíhuatl—loomed over a vast, bowl-like city drowned
in night. But so great was the glow of lights and fires and
refineries in the valley that it seemed filled with rivers of
molten gold. Beyond the dim outline of the two peaks,
the night sky was split by the blazing white-hot descent
of an enormous meteor, which would in just moments
smash into the plain of Tlaxcallan a hundred kilometers
to the east. The streaking fire-trails of thousands of anti-
ballistic missiles—launched by the México in a vain hope
to destroy the incoming weapon—were frail in comparison.

That Blow—and even Helsdon, raised on a colony
world far from the Center knew the story, which was a
foundation stone of Imperial mythology—would shatter the neighboring province, triggering massive earthquakes which would level most of Imperial Tenochtitlán,
and inspire a new ice age due to the dust thrown into
the upper atmosphere. But all of this would not fatally
wound the Empire and, indeed, the México reaction to
the attack would carry their armies victoriously to every
corner of the globe.

Curiously, Helsdon could not—in his half-addled
state—recall the name of the adversary who had struck

the Blow. *Must have been one of the European powers—was it Denmark? I cannot remember.*

To the right, the mural panels were dark, showing only intermittent static and a wandering glyph indicating the v-server attached to them had suffered some kind of file corruption problem.

At the end of the hall, a massive, blocky stone gate stood closed. Each door post was formed in the shape of a jaguar standing on its hind legs, paws raised, talons unsheathed. The lintel was formed of a line of squared-off skulls, deep-set eye sockets filled with shadow. As the engineer approached, one of the jaguar heads swiveled towards him—and even after serving in the Fleet for nearly ten years, the sight still raised the hackles on the back of his neck—and the feline eyes burned a deep, lambent yellow for a moment. Both Knights paused, and their firm grip on Helsdon's shoulders held him in place while they were scanned. Then the gate swung open, stone valves grinding ominously. The *Ocelotl* officer stepped inside, muttered something, and then gestured for Helsdon to enter.

The engineer presumed such quarters would be filled with every kind of luxury. But instead, he found himself facing a slim, dark-haired, copper-skinned young man with perfectly regular features, in a room stacked with shipping crates and a series of oddly decorated free-standing screens. The young man was sitting on the edge of a table heaped with a fortune in papers and real books. On him, Fleet dress whites seemed more than a uniform, they seemed to glow under the strip lights in the ceiling, and the contrast with his dark skin was very striking. In full court regalia, an Imperial Prince would be almost invisible under the weight of a massive, jeweled feather-cloak and pendants and torques of gold.

But here, in this jumbled room, he exuded an effortless, almost irresistible authority. Only one dissonance caught at Malcolm's attention.

He seems . . . anachronistic, Helsdon thought. *Where are all of his electronics?* The Prince did not wear a medband or comm bracelet, or even an earbug. There was a velour-skinned sofa, but no chairs and no bed. A strange, not-entirely-unpleasant odor of musk and tobacco hung in the air. The engineer was frankly puzzled when he knelt before the Prince. As he did, he noticed the Jaguars had remained outside, leaving him—apparently—alone with the young man. He was no expert on court ritual and etiquette, but it seemed rash to let one slightly deranged Fleet *kika-no* within arm's reach of the Emperor's son. *But he must be well armed of himself. Aren't the Imperial Family supposed to be superhuman?*

"*Tlatocapilli*—great lord, son of the Light of the World—how may I—"

"Get up," Xochitl snapped irritably. "Tell us—tell me—what you saw and how you survived."

Helsdon breathed in deeply. *This isn't the real thing, it's only a story about what happened to another person. Just another debriefing. Nothing can reach me here.*

"Light of Heaven, I was going EVA to repair a thermocouple relay," he began.

He related the momentary glimpse of the "blurred thread" which cut *Calexico* in half, leading to so many deaths, and then the long desperate struggle to stay alive in the wreck of the destroyer. Eventually—and by this time his voice was hoarse—another Imperial Scout ship had arrived and recovered him.

When Helsdon finished, he found himself rubbing his hands on his trousers. *Why do they sweat so much?* Then he stood in the awkward silence, trying to focus on the Prince. The room had darkened into night cycle as he'd talked, and now Xochitl was only a vague shape, his light-colored mantle a lesser shadow in the gloom.

"Thank you, Engineer Second." Xochitl stood up slowly.

Wish I could see his face better. Didn't he believe me?

Xochitl spoke to the air: "*Kikan-shi* Helsdon is ready to return to the research station."

Helsdon's mind—which seemed oddly fogged—cleared at the thought of returning to work. *Now there it is again. A sound like a tubercular breathing; such sharp, short gasps. Where is it coming from?*

But then the Jaguars entered and escorted him, gently this time, away.

In the darkness, when the door had closed, Xochitl threw himself down on the sofa and passed his hand over a side-lamp. A dull, orange-tinted glow sprang up and the Prince raised an eyebrow questioningly at the largest of the screens at the back of the room. A pair of lambent, angular eyes gleamed back at him.

"Satisfactory, Esteemed?" Xochitl strove to put the proper deference into his voice, but knew in his heart there was only truculence and barely suppressed anger in the words. "Or shall I interview another?"

THE *NANIWA*

The lift dinged politely and a battle-steel hatch cycled open, revealing the semicircle of Command. Koshō stepped onto the bridge feeling tense and unsettled. She rolled a heavy, Fleet-style data crystal between her fingers, her expression distant. Hadeishi was close in her thoughts, but not as she often heard his voice—relating advice or giving orders in the midst of battle—rather with new appreciation for the compromises he had made while commanding the *Cornuelle*.

"Transferring ship authority, *Chu-sa*," Oc Chac said, switching the command codes from his console to hers.

"Accepted, *Sho-sa*," she replied absently, settling into her shockchair. Susan held up the crystal again and it gleamed with the reflection of dozens of v-displays circling the deck. She had never felt comfortable with the kinds of company Hadeishi had kept, or the odd side diversions he would turn the light cruiser to. Many of those excursions—too many, really—had been at the behest of shadowy figures like Green Hummingbird, who was now sitting in a cabin on deck six, using her water for a shower and eating food from her dispenser system.

I forced the terms of the trade, so why do I feel I'm the one carrying home a koku *of grass seed?*

"*Sho-sa?*" She beckoned the XO over. "Load this into the navigation system, but do not replicate the data onto the squadron 'net."

"*Hai, kyo!*" Oc Chac took the crystal gingerly, but then he stopped, trying to formulate a properly deferential question.

"It is a copy of the *Korkunov* telemetry, *Sho-sa*. Recovered from a message drone launched by the *Calexico* only moments before she was destroyed." Susan raised a warning hand as the Mayan's face twitched with surprise. "We are lucky to have the data, but do not question how the goat got into the garden."

Oc Chac nodded slowly, and then ventured to say, "*Kyo*, an access request has been received from a group of visitors on six—with your chop, *Chu-sa*. Should it be approved?"

Susan nodded, though a nagging feeling of being cheated remained.

Doggedly, Oc Chac pressed on: "*Kyo* . . . this ship we

captured, the *Moulins*, her crew is to be kept in the brig, secured? But not the, ah, guests in the cabin on six?"

"Even so, *Sho-sa.*"

"*Hai, kyo!* I'll have this data loaded immediately."

"Excellent. Run it as an overlay in the well. I want to see a comparison with the plot provided by the Mirror scientists."

Then she leaned back in her chair, fist pressed to her chin. *We'll have a better picture of this Barrier, but I'm going against the spirit of the operational orders in taking a* nauallis *aboard in the midst of a Mirror obsidian-op. The* Chu-sa *never seemed to mind,* she thought, feeling a pang at the memory of Hadeishi sitting forlorn and direc-tionless in the *fumeiyo-ie* on Toroson. Then her expres-sion hardened. *And so my sensei lost his ship and nearly his entire crew. And now we are forever apart.*

Oc Chac returned from one of the operations con-soles, hands clasped behind his back.

"New orders have come from squadron, *Chu-sa.* The *Tlemitl* has taken over battle-cast control."

Koshō lifted one eyebrow. "The whole matrix? Squadron-level targeting and countermeasures? Did this come from *Chu-so* Xocoyotl or from the Prince?"

"Everything, *kyo,* is now routing through the *Fire-arrow.* The *Tokiwa* is lead for the battle-cruiser squadron, but the Flag has switched ships. Prince Xochitl has also ordered all probes presently monitoring the Pinhole to be withdrawn."

Susan tapped her fingers lightly on the armrest. "And the scientists?"

"Ordered back aboard their transports, *kyo.* All tech-nical personnel have been transferred to the *Tlemitl.* The *Can* is being abandoned."

"The Prince is certainly decisive!" *He is cutting the Mirror out of the picture. That will be his father's direc-*

tion. So—is this a Fleet operation now? Or are Hummingbird and Xochitl actually acting in concert?

Oc Chac suppressed a scowl at her sarcasm—one which Koshō was too distracted to notice, or comment upon—and returned to his station. The *Chu-sa* remained in her seat, her expression distant, ignoring the comings and goings of Command, old memories unspooling in her mind's eye.

The *Naniwa* pressed on, following her patrol pattern, wake surging bright with particle decay.

Down on deck six, in an officer's cabin with two bunks, a shower, proper desks, and a real closet, Gretchen threw down her duffle bag and kicked off her boots. "By the Risen Christ, Hummingbird, do you think they have fresh hot water? That would be a relief after bathing in recycled spit for a week. . . ." She sorted out her field comp and notebooks from the backpack, including a little Hesht figurine that Magdalena had given her in parting. *Grrault is the god of travelers, bachelors, and the unlucky, so keep him close and remember to give him bits of meat or bone from time to time,* Magdalena had said in complete seriousness. *See this cavity? Place the sacrifice within and after a moment or two, watch the color of his eyes. Amber means the meat is poisoned, red means it is safe to eat.* Then the Hesht had paused, snout wrinkling up. *Safe for a Hesht to eat, of course. For a cub like you with only one stomach . . . perhaps not. But still, he's sure to bring good luck.*

Parker had laughed, pressing his favorite multitool into her hands and giving her an awkward hug. If you need a ride, he said, sniffling, *you just comm, right?*

Hummingbird did not reply, and when Anderssen turned around, she whistled in appreciation.

The *nauallis* had unlocked both of his traveling bags. One of them had unfolded cleverly into an entire desktop-style comp station with three large v-displays and two stylus pads. The other bag was packed tight with equipment boxes of all kinds. Hummingbird had already appropriated one of the desks and was plugging in cables as fast as he could.

After watching for a moment, Gretchen dove in beside him and started unpacking comm relays and other devices from the second bag. Hummingbird, obviously in a tearing hurry, flashed her a warning look—to which Anderssen gave a smirk in return, saying: "Don't give me that sour face, Crow, I know which end is which."

"Very well. Find a set of modules marked with double bands of green—they can be assembled into a t-relay station. It would speed things up tremendously if you could get that operational." He seemed dubious, but gestured for her to proceed before turning back to completing his system setup.

Gretchen smiled to herself and began rooting through the bag, looking for the doubled green bands. Almost immediately, she ran across a bricklike object wrapped in—of all unlikely things—a parchment envelope.

"Well now," she said to herself, running a finger across the smooth material. "What is this? A book?"

The envelope was held closed by a silver clasp ornamented with a well-worn device. Peering closer and turning the envelope to throw the sigil into relief, she made out the stylized figures of two men—were they in armor? They seemed to be sporting pointed helmets—riding on a single horse.

I've seen this sigil before, she thought, slipping a fingertip under the clasp and opening the envelope.

A heavy metal block—corroded bronze or brass at first glance—slipped out into her hands. As soon as the device touched bare skin, Gretchen felt there was a fundamental imbalance in the mechanism. Attempting to resolve this, she switched the block around and found one end was fitted with a strip of Imperial-standard interface ports. "A comp," she said aloud, though not meaning to. "It feels so old. . . ."

Puzzled, she ran her fingertips across the corroded surface, but no rust or scale came away. Instead, Anderssen realized that the surface was quite smooth, but had been mottled by tremendous heat at some time in the past. *This isn't right,* she felt, and tugged at the interface strip until it came away. *Better.* She sat down on her bunk and opened her backpack, pulling out her trusty old octopus and jacking the multilead into her own comp. Then, humming softly to herself, she began testing the tiny pits revealed by the removal of the interface strip.

After an hour, Gretchen realized she was thirsty and looked up to see that Hummingbird had quietly completed the assembly of his comp station, including the t-relay, and was running well over a hundred v-panes, all showing a wide range of data and visualizations.

"Who made this, Crow? This little comp I've got here?"

Hummingbird did not turn, but shrugged his wiry old shoulders. "It came to me in trade, Anderssen-*tzin.* I did not think it wise to show while we remained on the *Moulins.*"

Gretchen snorted. "You didn't trust Captain Locke and his devout crew?"

"Not at all." The old *nauallis* rubbed the back of his head. "Their beliefs are genuine, but while I have some standing among them, I am not one of them, if you follow my meaning. They agreed to help us come this far, but we will need a better conveyance to move forward. To reach the device."

"Hmm." Gretchen turned the bronze block over in her hands. It was quite dense for its size. The interface strip was reattached and reconfigured. She reached for her portable input panel and v-display. "You don't know where this came from?"

"I know who gave it to me," he answered, in a very dry tone. "But before that? I could not say."

"And what did you trade for it?" Anderssen regretted asking the question immediately, realizing she did not want to know the answer. *He might trade anything, for anything,* she thought, feeling a cool chill trip across her shoulders.

"Services rendered, Anderssen-*tzin*. By another, not by you—or I—if you are concerned."

"Well," Gretchen said, distracted, "then let me see. . . ."

She powered up her input devices, socketed them into the interface strip, and settled back to see what presented itself. Almost immediately a node appeared in her little local network, right alongside the tiny blue birds representing her field comp and hand comp. *Time to negotiate,* Anderssen thought, *initiating conversational algorithm.*

Three hours later, Hummingbird was sitting cross-legged on his bunk, his stylus clicking irregularly on the control surface, when a double-chime sounded from one of the v-panes open before him. A thin line of bloody spots ran along his left arm, where he'd been pricking himself with a maguey spine as he worked. Thoughtfully he nodded, closing a series of other windows and expanding the one demanding attention.

"Squadron 'cast access achieved," he said softly, scarred hand flexing. "Protocols are open with all ships save the *Tlemitl*."

Gretchen had been following along with her own systems, which seemed positively paltry in comparison to what the *nauallis* had brought into play. Still, their activities and agents were now able to move where they willed throughout the battlecast network. Only the flagship remained isolated, but Anderssen had the impression the dreadnaught's shipnet was an order of magnitude beyond that of the smaller ships, including the *Naniwa*.

Hummingbird bit at his thumb, eyes narrowed. "Who came with the Prince?" he mused. "What resources does he have to hand? . . ."

The *nauallis* fell silent then, his attention wholly focused on defeating the protections girding the *Tlemitl*. Anderssen lost interest in his struggle. The question of the mysterious weapon and the barrier it had drawn across this whole section of space was far more intriguing. She had never had an opportunity to investigate an artifact of such colossal scale before. *No way I'm passing this up,* Gretchen thought gleefully and rubbed her hands together briskly in anticipation. Her initial forays into the resources available through the 'cast network had already discovered a whole series of robotic probes deployed along the "frontier" of the hidden weapon, probes which had been under the control of the Mirror scientists working on the *Can*, but now they were drifting aimlessly, having been abandoned at the Prince's direction.

Come here my pretties, she thought, grinning. Watching Hummingbird at work had revealed his outgoing stellarcast transmissions were masquerading as authorized 'net access from the *Naniwa*. The probes were happy to recognize her request as official and socket into her network. After handshaking, they began unspooling an enormous volume of data back to her little set of comps. Almost immediately, she received warning errors from the data interfaces. Frowning, she eyed Hummingbird's constellation of devices but decided it would be unwise to steal storage from him. *What about the local shipnet, maybe I can hijack someone's . . . Hold up, what's this?*

A new icon had appeared on her main v-display; one

showing a glyph indicating it "belonged" to her set of resources. There was no description and only a generic symbol with the identifier 3^33 attached. Curious, Anderssen queried the storage available and then sat back in surprise when the node responded with a long string of nines. *That is . . . a hell lot of crystal lattice,* she thought, impressed. *Is this the public storage cloud on the* Naniwa? *No, it would have a serial number and description and all sorts of wonky detail . . .*

Now concerned, she flipped from the logical view she'd been operating through to a physical resource diagram and then stared over at the corroded bronze block. "You?" she said aloud, startled. The protocol mapping algorithm had apparently completed, determining that the device did have storage available and there was some kind of pathway to allow access.

Gretchen's first instinct was to yank out the octopus and sever the connection. But then, when her fingers touched the cable, her eyes drifted back to the long string of nines and all of the raw storage they represented. *I could build a nice dataset with all of those probes feeding in . . . I wonder how fast it can process?*

A little guiltily she glanced over at Hummingbird, who seemed entirely oblivious to her activities. His face seemed remote and unapproachable and the *click-click-click* of his stylus was swift and sure, the patter of hail on a tin roof in a high country storm.

One step at a time, she decided, and reconfigured the octopus to allow only one-way communication. *At least,* she thought, *I can store all of the data right now, then disconnect from the probes before someone notices I've hijacked them. That would be prudent.*

Five minutes later the first of the probes was unspooling its history log across the 'net and into the bronze block at a very reasonable speed. Watching the performance metrics built into her comp, Anderssen realized after about ten minutes that the limiting factor on the transfer was the octopus itself, which had not been designed for moving such enormous volumes of data.

I'm going to short the poor thing out. What else do I have available? . . .

Her stylus tapped through a series of panes, looking for alternate methods of transfer, and on the fourth one she paused, eyebrow rising, to see that node 3^33 had registered twenty-seven wireless access ports, all open and unsecured. *I wonder . . . will stellarcast let me multichannel onto this device?* Gretchen poked around some more, cursing at the arcane interface for the shipnet, until she figured out how to assign the data feeds from the sixty-plus probes across all the available access ports. Then she tapped a GO icon and sat back.

All of the probe data was loaded nine minutes later.

Anderssen blinked, smoothed back her straight blond hair, and got up to get a *kaffe*.

Well, well, well, she mused, pouring instacream into the black liquid. *Now how to model all this and find the keyhole I need, or the shape of this . . . or, or . . .* Gretchen hissed in frustration. When she held a physical object in her hands—potsherds, a broken mechanism, a bone—something would usually suggest itself to her, some clue or guide to its proper purpose. But in the comp system? There was a disconnect between the object—or truly the data trying to describe the object—and her ability to grasp its totality.

I can't go EVA and touch the damned thing. She felt daunted. *I have to figure this one out the old way.*

Across the room, Hummingbird stirred, his eyes focusing on her as though from a great distance. "How very interesting," he said. "It would seem the Prince has arrived with no Judge or Mirror oversight. No Seeking Eye commissars, no political officers."

Gretchen gave him a look over the rim of her *kaffe*

cup. "A Prince of the realm, riding the finest steed in the land, with not the slightest restraint on his activities? What a marvelous adventure for him!"

"For all of us, I fear," Hummingbird muttered, producing a small paper wrapper from his mantle. He withdrew two small white tablets and placed one of them under his tongue. "Curious—there is only a skeleton crew aboard the *Tlemitl*. Barely enough men to operate her."

"That many fewer to share the loot." Anderssen sat back down, scratching her ear, attention already sliding away into this new puzzle.

"Abominations!" Hummingbird exclaimed in outrage as he peered at one of the v-panes. "I'm bumped out."

"Oh, you'll get back in, eventually," Gretchen assured him. "You are a *nauallis*, after all."

"Anderssen . . ." Hummingbird finally looked at her directly and the shock of meeting his dark eyes drew her full attention. "Have you considered what it means to encounter, to experience a First Sun device?"

Gretchen laughed bitterly. "You mean, will fame and fortune go to my head? Isn't your whole purpose to make sure that *no one* realizes such a thing has even been encountered? There's no fortune there, for me, and certainly no fame."

The old man shook his head slowly. "Such things are only the shell, only the surface of the matter." He pointed with his chin and Anderssen looked down, surprised to find the corroded bronze block in her hands.

"Your ability to use such things imperils your very humanity. You must tread very softly."

"This? This is just a computer—one of the tools at our command. Do you think using tools threatens anyone's humanity?"

He nodded. "The men who devised the first rifle, or machine gun, or thermonuclear bomb let go of something innate in themselves. Then those who *used* them left all pretense of humanity behind. How"—he paused, searching for the right words—"how can even a warrior countenance the death of an enemy he has not faced, met eye to eye, and traded blows with in the circle? Anything else is murder. I would say that a murderer has abandoned the common thread which ties us all together."

Anderssen squinted, wondering if the Crow was mocking her, then shook her head. "None of those atrocities were initiated by the *tools*—the rifle, the machine gun, the bomb only had the misfortune to fall into the hands of men who had *already* decided upon atrocity."

Then she set the block down, picked up her stylus, and returned to her work.

Hummingbird became quite still, seeing that the European woman had turned her back on him. He watched her intently for nearly thirty minutes, but Gretchen's attention was wholly devoted to building a new analysis model. Apparently satisfied by what he'd seen, the old Crow returned to his own efforts, and the hours passed by in quiet save for the clicking of their styluses on the control surfaces.

At length, Hummingbird pushed away from his comp—breathed out a deep, long sigh—and stared for a moment at the pale blue wall behind his still oblivious companion. "The dreadnaught's shipnet is using an unknown encryption and security system. Not only is it unfamiliar to my tools, but it seems impervious to investigation."

Gretchen made no sign she had heard. Hummingbird scratched the back of his head and surveyed the rest of their cabin. Conversationally, he said: "There are the afterimages of cranes in flight, etched into this ceiling. A former tenant must have needed at least the illusion of the homeworld to ease his mind."

Still Anderssen ignored him. The *nauallis* grimaced and rose, swaying a little. After two cups of thickly sugared *kaffe* he found steadier footing. Then he sat down on the edge of his bunk and unwrapped a threesquare. Even when he'd finished, the Swedish woman was still hard at work.

Experimentally, he said: "The *Tlemitl* is one of the Emperor's personal ships—long rumored but never proven. Never have I encountered an Imperial system which could resist my overrides. Always before, the Judges have contrived to know what transpired in Imperial Space. Things are now afoot to which we are not privy. Shall even the Judges shine dim beside the *Tlaltecutli*, the Lord of the Earth? Surely the human race would be at insupportable risk if we cannot penetrate new secrets as they arise! We must get inside this mystery box that is the *Firearrow*."

"In a minute," Anderssen mumbled.

"Of course," he said, watching her with a sort of cool detachment.

At much the same time, his comp constellation completed the process of dumping a set of infiltrators into the *Naniwa*'s communications network, allowing Hummingbird to open a tachyon relay channel without anyone on the bridge being the wiser. A short, discrete burst of data was dispatched out into the wasteland of the *kuub*. A bit later, the reply filtered back to Hummingbird's console.

Excellent, he thought, setting a timer to run. *Seventeen hours and counting.*

On the command deck, another watch came on duty and *Sho-sa* Oc Chac was once more at his console, monitoring the efforts of the rest of the bridge crew and ancillary departments. Given his background, the Mayan was paying close attention to the efforts of the *Zosen* still rounding out a few tail-end projects. When *Chu-i* Pucatli suddenly tilted his head and stared at the status board in puzzlement, he was up out of his seat and beside the Comms station before the sub-lieutenant could sound an alarm.

"*Sho-sa*, we've lost sync with *Tlemitl*'s battlecast," Pucatli reported, not too surprised to find Oc Chac at his shoulder.

"Have we moved out of range?" Oc Chac asked, reaching over the younger man's shoulder to key up a diagnostic subsystem. "Is there some kind of heavy debris concentration between us and the squadron?"

"*Kyo*, we're on a return leg of the patrol pattern—distance is closing with the *Can* and squadron center-point. But the dust—it's very heavy." Pucatli slid part of the navigational display into view on his console. "I've been seeing irregular gravitational interference with comm, but we've rotated through this sector at least once before and did not lose sync."

"Mark the area. And see if there's anything on our new map of the *Korkunov* route that could explain the blackout. Perhaps we can avoid it the next time around."

Oc Chac frowned at the console for a moment longer, watching the diagnostic run.

"*Chu-i*, if anything flags red on that scan—you let me know immediately."

THE WILFUL

De Molay was lying in her hammock over the reaction mass tank, eyes closed, listening to the gurgling and chuckling of the pipes winding over and around her, when Hadeishi emerged from the darkness, his face blackened with grease. "Here," he said, parting her thin fingers and pressing the slim metallic shape of the Webley Bulldog into her hands. "I will return in a little while, but anything may happen between now and then."

She opened one eye, and then the other, seeing the Nisei had acquired a serrated-blade knife about twenty centimeters long to go with his machete. The machete was now enclosed in a crude, handmade scabbard and strapped to his chest at an angle. The knife fit into his belt. She made a face, eyebrows beetling up. "You will need to be quick," she whispered. "Do you hear that whine building in the hypercoil? We're losing gradient fast, we'll drop back to realspace soon. And when we do, even these lax fools will realize something is amiss."

"I know." Hadeishi held up his hand-comp, which was still relaying the nav system telemetry. "About thirty minutes and we'll drop out. I plan to be back before then."

He bowed in parting, and then climbed silently down to the Engineering compartment. By his count there were two Khaiden loose in the down-below decks, and both of them had left their duty stations to do . . . something. So he padded quietly from room to room, working his way around the huge bulk of the maneuver drives. Approaching the access way leading to the hyperspace coil generator he heard the sound of boots on the decking and flattened against the wall.

A Khaid engineer ambled out of the side passage, helmet back, nosily crunching on a heavy, bonelike ration bar. The alien's jagged, double-flanged teeth were making quick work of the claylike brick.

Mitsuharu's arm snapped out, the serrated blade spearing up into the underside of the Khaid's jaw. The creature goggled at him, huge eyes rolling in different directions, and the Nisei lunged, getting an arm under the shoulder joint. The alien was very heavy—massing nearly twice his own weight—and Hadeishi grunted with pain as he eased the corpse to the g-decking. Mindful of leaving a trail, he dragged the body into hypercontrol, wrapped the corpse in a plastic sheet from his other leg pocket, and then wiped off his hands and forearms, which had been spattered with cloying blue-black blood.

Then he continued on, trying to move a little faster. The down-below had never seemed so large before, but now the number of rooms seemed infinite. Finally, having almost completed a circuit of the entire ship, he approached an alcove which served as a crude reference library—there were shelves of data crystals, a comp station, and portable readers hung on the walls. Nearly twenty-five minutes had passed and his chrono was showing time winding down at a swift pace.

But light flickered on the wall of the alcove and there was a singular musk in the air. *Reading up on the new ship, is he? A Khaid seeking to better himself, how excellent.*

Hadeishi crept to a point where he could see the elbow and shoulder of the engineer, who was sitting on the bench in the alcove, thumbing through a series of technical manuals. *Laudatory,* Mitsuharu thought, feeling a pang. *I've had ensigns who refused to do so much. . . .*

At that instant, the ship began to slide gradient and the transit alarm blared. Startled by the unexpected noise, the engineer looked up in time to catch sight of Hadeishi rushing out of the dimness. The Khaid's first impulse was to drag out his comm—a handheld unit instead of the usual Imperial wristband—and sound an alarm. In the heartbeat between impulse and action, Mitsuharu hewed down with the machete, the full strength of his shoulders behind the blow, catching the Khaid's raised hand on the wrist. There was a jarring *crack* and the joint split, along with the z-suit ring.

Howling in pain, the Khaid leapt back, crashing into the shelves. Books and data crystals flew in all directions, rolling wildly on the floor. Hadeishi crabbed in, hacking with the long flat blade, and the edge bit into the engineer's other arm, drawing a deep wound. Blood slicked the floor, making his footing treacherous. The Khaid sounded a deep coughing howl and scrabbled for some weapon—a knife, a gun—nothing came immediately to hand.

Mitsuharu kicked the engineer's knee, making the creature topple over, and then stepped in, hacking down. Now the blade fell true and the Khaid's head lolled to the side, half severed. Hadeishi grimaced, feeling his limbs burn with exertion, and then felt enormous exhaustion wash over him.

The books are ruined, his father's voice echoed in memory. *What a pity.*

Hadeishi staggered into the Engineering compartment, the tool belts from both dead engineers looped over his shoulder. He was surprised—but pleased—to see that De Molay had dragged herself down to the still-working console and was trying to secure control of the ship's systems.

"You've access to environmental, *kyo?* Good. Pump one percent cee-oh to Command and the cargo bay." Mitsuharu gasped, feeling winded. "Secure air in Engineering and let's get you into a z-suit."

De Molay clung grimly to the console with both hands. "They'll be in the corridors, too."

Struggling with the stylus, the *Wilful's* captain tapped open new series of v-panes—from cameras Hadeishi had never been able to reach with his own access. The old woman leaned her head over, wheezing: "I can see another figure in the mess as well. Everything else looks clear for the moment."

"Good." Hadeishi took a deep breath and set down the extra tools. "Don't lock the areas where the gas is released. Let them believe free movement is possible." He stood at her shoulder, watching the suddenly superior v-pane displays with envy. "And where was all of this when I was cleaning the bilges?"

"That one knows there's a problem," De Molay observed softly, a blood-caked hand tapping the feed from the bridge. A Khaid under-officer stood uncertainly at the captain's station, rubbing his eyes. "He could signal for help if the comm system has been recoded since they came aboard."

Hadeishi shrugged. "I struck down one reviewing our technical manuals—but how far they've gotten beyond the nav system—"

The crewman sat down in the captain's chair, looked around in apparent puzzlement, and then suddenly pitched forward. The sound of his fall was audible in the camera pickup, and was more than enough to draw the attention of three more Khaid who had been working at consoles on the far side of the small bridge. These turned, then one of them pointed at an environmental display flashing a warning.

De Molay shook her head. "They see the air warning lights. How quickly will they be overcome?"

Mitsuharu looked thoughtful. "Not long, but it may be enough to cause us mischief. I will stand watch at the lift between decks."

After a swift review of the weapons to hand—his machete and knife were now supplemented by another Khaid shipgun—the Nisei slipped out of Engineering. As the hatch closed behind him, De Molay ventured a crooked little smile, saying: "I'll let you know if anyone resists taking a very long nap."

AT THE PINHOLE

Sitting in the junior officer's mess aboard the *Tlemitl*, Engineer Second Helsdon was acquainting himself with a fresh-baked chicken pie and a jug of Ceylon black tea. The Jaguar Knights who had dragged him before the Prince had no interest in escorting him all the way back to the *Can*—so they'd jobbed him off on Logistics to ferry over to the research station when convenient. This left the sandy-haired engineer at loose ends for six or seven hours, so cooling his heels in the well-appointed mess seemed the perfect answer.

But scuttlebutt from the ensigns slouching at the next table indicated the *Can* itself was being abandoned, with the Mirror scientists returning to their transports. Which left Helsdon with nowhere to go, but for the moment he wasn't too concerned about finding a bunk—the chicken pie was excellent and he guessed the engineers aboard the *Tlemitl* would look out for their own in a pinch. He'd hot-bunked himself, more than once, when a fellow mechanic needed a place to sleep and hadn't found an official posting yet.

A steward passed by, and Helsdon flagged her down. "Could I get another cuppa, please?"

She was pouring, the tea shedding curlicues of steam, when an alarm Klaxon sounded. The noise was harsh, shocking to the ear, and unmistakable.

"All hands to battle stations," boomed the overhead, "all hands to battle stations."

The decking itself suddenly shivered; every cup, saucer, and pot rattling on all of the mess tables. Aft of the cafeteria, in the engine ring, the super-dreadnaught's maneuver engines were flash-heating to full combat power. Everyone was already up, on their feet, sealing the regulation shipsuit under their uniforms and scrambling towards the emergency lockers for helmets.

Helsdon seized hold of the edge of the table, stuffed the rest of the pie into his mouth, and then sealed his helmet. He, unlike many of the others present, was still wearing a proper z-suit and carried his full EVA helmet slung over his back on a lanyard. Surviving in the wreck of the *Calexico* had made him intimately familiar with every piece of survival gear Fleet provided.

"Incoming hostiles at all points," bellowed the overhead. "Missile impacts expected in one minute, one minute. Brace for hull rupture, all hands secure compartments and brace for zero-g."

Oh Lord of my Sainted Fathers. Helsdon bolted for the nearest damage control station. *Work to do, I have work to do. I need to do my work,* he chanted as he ran, fearing he'd freeze up if he faltered for even an instant.

Koshō stiffened in her shockchair as the executive threatwell displayed by her console filled with a swarm of angry red icons, each circumscribed by rapidly mutating glyphs. The ship's threat assessment AI triggered, sounding alarms the length of the *Naniwa*.

"Battle stations!" Koshō barked, feeling the shock-chair fold around her automatically. A helmet was already lowering over her head and she reflexively tucked her hair in. Combat readiness subsystems were kicking in at every station, discarding the patrol-specific displays and replacing them with battle configurations. The lights shaded to red, and behind her the main hatchway sealed itself. Her eyes flicked across the storm of data flowing into the main threatwell. "We are under attack by a Khaid fleet—repeat, we are under attack by a Khaid fleet."

The Khaiden armada—or nearly so, given the usual size of their raiding squadrons—had dropped gradient directly on top of the Imperial ships loitering around the *Can*. The *Naniwa*'s sensor suite was already flooded with the fury of beam weapons igniting, and the threatwell was filled with swarm after swarm of missiles and bomb-pods spewing into the void.

Koshō spared an instant to thank Hachiman they were in motion and a fair distance from the rest of the squadron.

"Message drone away," Oc Chac barked reflexively. "Transit to hyper in one hundred thirty-six seconds."

Susan's habitual calm turned icy and everything around her narrowed down to the storm unfolding in the threatwell. She could feel Oc Chac's attention on her, hot and wavering, an unsteady flame. The other officers were still scrambling to bring deflectors up, or confirm gun crews and missile teams were standing by. Pucatli at comm was speaking rapidly into his throatmike, confirming readiness of the interior compartments and sections.

Koshō caught the Mayan's eyes. "*Sho-sa*, this is a brawl for dreadnaughts. I'll handle maneuver, combat targeting, and tactics; you keep us able to move, fight, and react. Do you understand? We're going to get hit hard, and you're going to have to put us right with all speed."

Oc Chac stared back at her for a second, almost paralyzed with panic, and then nodded sharply. "*Hai, Chusa, hai!*"

"Pilot, full ahead," Koshō grated, seeing *Naniwa*'s velocity climb. They had not, luckily, been at full stop when the attack began. The initial confusion around the *Can* had started to stabilize and she could see every Imperial ship was trying to get underway. *They've jumped in "orumchek" formation,* she realized, watching the spiderweb attack pattern of the Khaid ships unfold. *And they've caught almost all of us at zero-v, pants down, finger up the nose.*

"Weapons, all launch racks deploy, give me every sprint missile we can throw, configure for independent terminal tracking." The stylus slashed through her copy of the threatwell, describing a second "shell" of target areas around the periphery of the combat area. "Pilot, full combat power, angle for thirty-two degrees off axis. Take us hard up along the Barrier line. Transit deflectors at maximum power."

The *Naniwa* surged ahead, engines flaring sun-bright, warning lights flashing in every compartment as the crew raced to battle stations. Susan ran through a brief internal checklist, confirming all drives were showing green, no bay doors were open to space, and internal battle compartments were sealing. Already the ship shook with the vibration of the ammunition Backbone shuttling fresh shipkillers to the primary rails, while the missile racks rolled out from the hull.

"*Chu-sa*, targeting solutions are locked." Konev seemed absurdly happy. "Hardpoints are clear to launch."

"Weapons, fire." Koshō felt a sharp bolt of elation as

dozens of missile tracks sprang into view on the threat-well, spiraling out from the *Naniwa*, which was now accelerating hard. Holloway was sparing nothing to hit the mark she'd set for him.

"*Kyo*, salvo one away," Konev reported, voice tight with adrenaline and fear. "Cycling launchers."

In the center of the spiderweb, caught at a dead stop, battle-shields off-line, the surface of the *Tlemitl* rippled with white-hot explosions. Khaid particle-beam weapons savaged the enormous hull, chewing away at a shipskin four times the thickness of the armor encasing the *Naniwa*. Clouds of shipkillers rained in, flooding the point-defense network with a constant stabbing barrage of detonations. Behind them, bomb-pods stuttered, unspooling long chains of thermonuclear-pumped laser emitters. Despite being caught unawares, the *Tlemitl*'s on-duty gun crews were already in action—city-block-long emitter nacelles swiveled, flaring with the sidescatter radiation from beam weapons igniting. Missile launch rails were cycling as fast as their hardware allowed, disgorging heavy shipkillers in bursts.

In Flag Command on the super-dreadnaught, Prince Xochitl—who had been caught by the attack in transit to a meeting with the senior Mirror scientists and their political officers—staggered as a pair of shipkillers detonated against the *Tlemitl*'s hull. The internal g-field was fluctuating and even his coppery skin was noticeably pale as he dropped into a shockchair at the Admiral's console. His Jaguars had been carrying the components for a full EVA suit with them, and now the Prince was locked down and encased in full armor.

The *Tlemitl*'s captain, Ikaru Yoemon, was in Main

Command, fifty decks and half the length of the ship away, which left the Prince with whichever duty officers were within reach of FlagCom when the first alarms sounded. Despite being shorthanded, Xochitl tapped into the battlecast directly and immediately upon establishing comm lock, the Flag threatwell sprang to life, showing the whole chaotic scene in vibrant detail.

The *Fiske* and *Eldredge* were already shattered hulks, spewing wreckage and burning with radiation fires on all decks. Two of the heavy cruisers, the *Axe* and the *Mace*, were expanding spheres of ionized metal and plasma—containment lost on their reactors, weapons cooking off in a ripple of secondary explosions. By tremendous luck, the Fleet tender *Hanuman* had been at the periphery of the attack area and was now only minutes from making gradient to hyperspace.

The battle cruiser *Naniwa*, which had just rotated out on a patrol sweep, was also out of the immediate melee.

Though his first instinct was to comm *Thai-sa* Yoemon for ship's status, Xochitl knew the captain was fully occupied with damage control and fighting for his ship. Instead he confirmed the status of the other ships in the squadron and added himself to the 'cast command channel. Immediately the chatter of six or seven commanders flowed through his earbug, including the harsh bark of *Chu-sho* Xocoyotl on the *Tokiwa*.

"Battle shields coming on-line now," Yoemon reported on a channel specific to the *Tlemitl*.

The overhead lights in Flag Command flickered and the constant shattering vibration of bomb-pod impacts and particle beam detonations ceased. In the threatwell, the *Firearrow*'s glyph changed and Xochitl knew that outside—in the maelstrom of radiation, spinning debris, and streaking missiles—a wavering, rainbow-hued globe had sprung up around his ship. Within the second, one of the v-panes on his threatwell display was strobing, showing impact rates on the various shield cells managed by the massive Tototl-Aerospatiale generators embedded beneath the shipskin.

One corner of the threatwell spiked as an irregular sphere of plasma suddenly occluded the *Can*.

So much for the Mirror's sensor platform, Xochitl thought, shunting the flood of data flowing over him to his exocortex. *Battlecast is up and synchronized . . . Xocoyotl had better get—ah, good, here they come.*

The secondary beam weapons on the *Tlemitl* were now firing in staccato, sweeping the area ahead of the massive ship free of bomb-pods and penetrators. The Khaid were fond of strewing clouds of one-off mines when they engaged the enemy, then working to drive their prey into the shoals which resulted.

Four Khaiden battleships—Xochitl had never encountered the class before and his exocortex could find no references to them in the Fleet briefings and intelligence estimates—were now closing on the dreadnaught, seeking to bring particle weapons to bear behind three speeding waves of shipkillers.

An answering salvo of penetrators was already belching from the *Tlemitl*. Xochitl fought down a fierce desire to override Yoemon and take direct command of the dreadnaught, but the *Thai-sa* was doing an able job. Initial damage was already being attacked by Engineering damage control parties. Shields were up, the ship was building velocity, and the *Tokiwa* and *Asama* were closing vector with all speed.

We need to get point-defense interlock engaged. The Prince scowled, watching the intercept projections update in his 'well. The Khaid were forming up, their main body of battleships—falling somewhere in size and throw-weight between the *Tlemitl* and her battle cruisers—

screened from immediate attack by this lead group of four.

The two Imperial battle-cruisers swung in moments later, having reached interlock range on point defense. Both were spewing ECM pods and the new remote point-defense platforms as fast as their launchers could recycle.

"Combat interlock confirmed," *Thai-sa* Yoemon and *Chu-so* Xocoyotl's voices overlapped in each ear. The Prince had already seen his secondary status displays shade green. The *Tlemitl*'s spoofer pods now began to flood nearspace with a hurricane of false data. Subsystems on all three ships had been drinking in the Khaid ECM signatures for almost ten minutes now, and with interlock allowing each ship to differentiate their countermeasures, the attacking ships were suddenly moving in an electronic fog.

«*Now?*» suggested his exocortex. «*Battlecast synch time is within parameters to implement override.*»

Xochitl shook his head, though no one else could see, or hear, the exo. "No, not yet. The commanders of the other ships haven't been briefed—" Even Yoemon, who had seen the new control overrides in action during trials, wasn't ready to let the *Tlemitl* fight herself. *Well, under my direction,* thought the Prince.

«*Our direction,*» countered his exo. «*We are one.*»

"—they'll panic."

The interior airlock opening onto boat-bay nine wheezed, locking motor complaining as it attempted to seal the hatch. A fallen stanchion twisted with a squeal, crushed by the door, but refused to break free. Helsdon, face streaming with sweat, looped a magnetic block ring around the twisted battle-steel, snugged it tight, and stepped back. Behind him, a good dozen cooks, stewards, stray officers, and off-duty ratings leaned into the rope, hauling for all they were worth.

Someone shouted "Heave!" and the stanchion squealed, trying to slide free of the hatch. At the airlock controls, the Engineer Second wrenched aside the panel covering with a pry bar and shorted the mechanism. The hatch tried to cycle open and the stanchion popped loose. Almost immediately the environmental circuits triggered an alarm—the boat-bay had lost its exterior doors and was open to the void—and only the inner airlock hatch, luckily still intact, prevented the entire corridor from venting into space.

Helsdon had his hand-comp clipped in and now he thumbed a counteroverride, letting the little unit drop into a blindingly fast response cycle as the hatch requested permission to close, was told *no*, then requested it again. . . . The damage control party dragged the stanchion free with a grinding scrape.

The Engineer Second unclipped the comp—the hatch ground closed, spitting out metal shavings—and he pitched the plastic control cover away.

"Let's go," he broadcast, drawing everyone's attention. "There's a hull puncture two halls leeward and we're venting atmosphere. We've got an emergency repair closet there and one on the way, so get ready to carry what we'll need."

Their faces were blank with incomprehension, or stiff with incipient fear, but Helsdon pushed them along—using the pry bar if necessary. If they stopped, he would stop, and then he knew he'd break down. The specter of another endless time trapped in a broken, disabled ship, waiting for the cold or hunger or radiation to take him was ever-present.

———

The *Naniwa* sped towards rendezvous with the flagship, steadily building velocity. In Koshō's mind, the invisible, undetectable Barrier seemed only a hands-breadth from her flank. All sections had finally reported in, ready for battle. Damage control crews were standing by, the launchers had recycled, and transit deflectors were at full strength. In her executive 'well, she could see that the *Tlemitl* had brought the new battle-shields on line and Susan was pained by jealousy. *Curse the Prince, he has all the new toys . . . while we fight with flint and wicker!*

Koshō stiffened, agonized to see the *Falchion*— hammered by dozens of bomb-pods—shiver and begin to break apart. A cloud of evac capsules spewed away from the mortally wounded cruiser, but Susan knew her commander would not be aboard one of them.

Muldoon. May Mor-Ríoghain convey you to the West with all good speed.

The battle-cruiser held fire, munitions racks rolled out with the full weight of her shipkillers and suppression pods ready to launch. Seconds ticked past, and then—

"*Chu-sa*, transit spike!" Holloway's voice was flat and sharp. "Multiple spikes! Incoming transit across the board—estimating thirty contacts inbound."

"Launchers ready for salvo two, *kyo*," Konev barked, running through his readiness checklist one more time.

A wide arc of space shimmered, twisting aside as dozens more Khaiden ships—a swarm of destroyers, light cruisers, Fleet tenders, and assault boats—dropped out of hyperspace. Susan grinned mirthlessly. Months spent far beyond the rim of Imperial space, hunting the Khaid and Megair and being hunted in return, had gained her a hard-won familiarity with their tactics.

The *Naniwa* sprint missiles already launched into the void were now within seconds of a sudden new array of targets. The deadly little weapons sprang awake,

autonomic targeting systems fixing on the fresh signatures of Khaiden ships, and blasted forward, exhausting the last of their fuel.

Two Khaiden destroyers staggered as the Imperial
missiles streaked past their point-defense and antimatter
charges detonated against shipskin. Startlingly violet blos-
soms of plasma erupted from their engine arrays. An assault boat tore in half. Missiles raced through the Khaiden
formation, causing panic. Ships corkscrewed away wildly
amid a wave of secondary explosions. A wedge of destroyers rotated towards the *Naniwa*, beam weapons
stabbing at her through the incandescent murk.

"Weapons, fire salvo two."

The battle-cruiser shuddered as every launch rail and
missile rack triggered simultaneously.

The *Tlemitl* and her two consorts lunged toward the
Barrier at maximum acceleration, clawing for room
to maneuver. In FlagCom, Xochitl let the threatwell
feed wash over him, his attention fixed on the maneuvering of the Khaid main elements. The arrival of their
support ships had been expected, though he was surprised to see such numbers. Exo displayed comparisons of numbers of ships, types, and throw-weight
between this battle and more recent encounters with
the Khaid raiders.

A proper fleet, the Prince observed, almost impressed.
*On our model; with supply ships, a repair tender, lighter
elements, some kind of troop transports. . . .*

Swiftly approaching the danger zone marked out on
the threatwell in strobing crimson, *Thai-sa* Yoemon's
voice cut sharply across the chatter on the command 'cast.
"Prepare to change vector, rotating aspect . . . now."

Xochitl's eyes slid to the display showing g-integrity

deck by deck on the massive ship. *Time to put everything to the test.*

The constant rumble transmitted through the hull—despite a brand-new dampening system—from the maneuver drives ceased abruptly. The *Tlemitl* rotated aspect on tertiary thrusters. The status displays started to wink amber and yellow—one red spot flared up as a compartment lost its g-decking—and then the *Firearrow* was pointed on a new heading. The exchange of missile clouds and beam weapons had continued unabated throughout the evolution and the Prince was pleased to see his gun crews had kept targeting lock on the lead Khaid battleships. Battlecast was still in sync, though hostile ECM was now starting to interfere, forcing a faster encryption cycle rate.

"Main drives at full," Yoemon snapped and the rumbling vibration kicked in again. Now three compartments flared red and Xochitl cursed, knowing any man in those areas was probably dead or seriously wounded, given the acceleration they were pulling. Still, the dreadnaught had successfully swerved away from the Barrier, the *Asama* keeping pace off her port. The *Tokiwa*, however, had failed to change vector with them. Xocoyotl's battle-cruiser had rotated to reverse aspect, but now she was forced to a full-burn to avoid colliding with the invisible weapon.

The fire from all four Khaid battleships retargeted on the *Tokiwa* as she slipped out of the point-defense envelope maintained by the *Tlemitl* and *Asama*. Hundreds of shipkillers rained in, saturating the battle-cruiser's lighter point defense network. Dozens of explosions rippled the length of her hull, stressing shipskin beyond its capacity. A bright pinpoint seared through the plasma clouds as a penetrator pierced containment on the antimatter reactor. Then everything—the *Tokiwa*, the debris clouds spilling from her flanks, the corona of bomb-pod lasers igniting—was washed away by a pure white flare.

«*IMN BC-261 lost with all hands*,» Xochitl's exo commented, spooling off a log entry.

"Battlecast resynced." Yoemon's voice was harsh and flat. The *Tlemitl* was now turning, still building velocity, with the *Asama* running in tight, well inside the fire control envelope of the dreadnaught's point-defense batteries. With the four Khaid heavies drawn off by killing the battle-cruiser, the two Imperial ships accelerated into the flank of the opposing fleet. Four Khaid cruisers swung towards them, but now the full throw-weight of the *Tlemitl* and *Asama* could focus on the approaching ships.

A storm of sprint missiles and particle beams stabbed out, while the spoofer pods flooded Khaid targeting control with thousands of phantom contacts. The first three cruisers shattered, shipskin ravaged by particle beams, missile racks torn away, and then each hull punched in by a pair of shipkillers—big *Tessen*-class multiphase penetrators.

«*Resource utilization is higher than recommended per target*,» exo commented, but the Prince shook his head. "The weapons officer is showing admirable restraint, given his desire to be sure of the mark. Yoemon has noticed we've no resupply now that the *Hanuman* has fled. Very wise."

'Cast relay beeped cheerfully, showing a fresh Imperial fire-snake glyph boosting towards the protective shell of the *Tlemitl*'s point defense.

«*IMN CA-1042 Gladius has synched to battlecast*,» exo announced. «*All other cruisers have been lost.*»

Her field of view filled with an intricate schematic of potential Barrier threads, racing ship glyphs, and the still-present necklace of science probes arrayed beyond the radiation cloud which had been the *Can*, Gretchen tried to concentrate on the results from her models. The first pass she'd taken had been discarded and while searching for more computational resources Anderssen had found—to her wary delight—that node $3^3 3$ also boasted well over nineteen thousand processing nodes. Many of them were inactive, or inaccessible to her, but enough remained to offload model calculations for three alternate schemas.

The constant fluctuations in the g-decking field made her work very difficult and Gretchen had resorted to taping down the comps and her other gear.

"Crow, we'd better get tied down, this is getting rough."

The old México did not bother to look over his shoulder. His displays had reconfigured again and the Swedish woman frowned, not recognizing any of the interfaces he was now navigating. Somehow it seemed freshly minted and new, though still recognizably México in origin. "Hummingbird, are we going to get out of this?"

"I have," he said in a musing voice, "a great faith in *Chu-sa* Koshō's ability to survive."

Then everything lurched violently and Gretchen lost her seat, flying into the nearest wall with a bone-jarring *crunch*. Hummingbird's consoles tore free of the tape, one of them shattering against the wall beside her. Despite this, his attention remained fixed on flipping through the *Tlemitl*'s internal systems as fast as possible.

"Holy Blessed Mary, Bride of Jesus, that hurts!" Anderssen slid to the floor as the g-decking reasserted itself, landing painfully. "*Crow!*"

Six decks away, Koshō watched calmly as the *Naniwa*'s abrupt course change sent the battle-cruiser careening into a pack of six oncoming Khaiden destroyers. The battle-cruiser's deflectors rippled with millions of tiny impacts as irradiated dust and battle debris hammered at the electromagnetic veil. Missiles punched straight through, while particle beam traces speared past as the Khaid gunners lost lock on the elusive Imperial ship. In turn, she was designating priority in her 'well, the stylus stabbing like a dagger into the heart of the enemy.

"Weapons, target number four, give me a tight grouping!"

The *Naniwa* shuddered as the starboard missile launchers went to rapid-fire, spitting a cloud of smaller interceptors around a single big *Tessen* shipkiller. The destroyers had broken ranks, each burning maneuver mass to break away from the oncoming Imperial. The *Naniwa*'s beam nacelles strobed, capacitors discharging with a high shrieking whine that carried through the shipframe like the lament of the damned. Secondary launchers spat out a handful of spoofer pods. Target five flared with a brilliant violet-hued detonation and the ensigns on the lower tier of Command shouted, "*Seikou!*"

Susan nodded to Konev, whose beam gunners had gotten in a choice hit.

To starboard, target four had gone into a corkscrew pattern, trying to shake the outbound munitions package—but the interceptors fragmented on final approach, separating into dozens of smaller missiles, each radiating as hot as the parent chassis. Point defense lasers and ballistic munitions tore through them, causing a sparking cascade of smaller explosions. Serenely, the *Tessen* sailed through the weak ECM spewing from the destroyer's emitters and slammed into the smaller ship's hull at a hundred g. At the instant before impact, the multiphase warhead ignited, spearing a needle-sized plasma jet into the Khaiden shipskin.

A seven-meter-wide hole blew through the side of the destroyer before the *Tessen* blew up inside the hull proper. The destroyer convulsed, filling with superheated plasma, and then shattered into a cloud of molten debris.

The other Khaid lightweights scattered, dumping a cloud of missiles and bomb-pods behind them.

Koshō nodded thoughtfully, then tapped an execute glyph Pucatli had prepped for her.

Each of the fleeing destroyers had acquired a spoofer pod running passive when the *Naniwa* had interpenetrated the formation. Now they each lit off with the battle-cruiser's signature and sped off, keeping pace with the Khaid ships, each now followed by a swiftly closing pack of missiles.

"Pilot, vector to join the Flag," Koshō snapped, letting her attention return to the larger battle. "Get us into their envelope and synched up on point-defense."

She did not have time to give Tloc, his holds full of *chocolatl*, or the lamentable *Chu-sho* Xocoyotl even the brief parting Muldoon had received.

«*Enemy battlecast pattern is adapting,*» exo announced.

Prince Xochitl had sunk back in his chair, expression thunderous as he realized how heavily the odds had turned against him. The *Tlemitl* outweighed any single enemy ship by three or six to one, but now his battle-group was stripped down to only three supporting cruisers. Even the two Scout frigates had disappeared.

As he watched, the Khaid battleships coalesced—showing admirable skill, one part of his mind commented—into a tight pack. Now they veered towards the *Tlemitl*, their point-defense overlapping, with a stormfront of shipkillers, penetrators, and bomb-pods hurtling towards the Imperial ships. Behind their munitions screen, the heavy beam weapons on the Khaiden battlewagons were sparking, searching for a weakness in the battle-shields surrounding the *Firearrow*.

The shield-generator status display was a patchwork of green, amber, and red. Some of the nodes had already failed, having shorted on backfeed from the shields themselves, or failing under the massive stress. Xochitl's teeth bared, gleaming white and sharp, and he cursed the *pochtecas* who had sold his father such junk.

«*Projected failure rate of the shield nodes, from field trials, is almost thirty percent. Current failure rate is thirty-four percent.*»

"Unacceptable." Xochitl straightened in his chair, attention drawn to the emergence of a second pack of Khaiden heavies which had been screened from the *Tlemitl*'s sensors by the oncoming wave of attackers. This formation was accelerating off at an angle and redeploying on the move, smoothly shifting from their initial wedge into an unfolding "flower-box."

«*Secondary elements are targeting the Gladius,*» exo reported, and the threatwell shifted, focusing in on the heavy cruiser, which was trying to match course with the *Tlemitl* and *Asama*. «*Missile storm intercept in sixteen seconds.*»

The particle beam nacelles covering that quadrant of the envelope began igniting. Yoemon's gunnery team had reached the same conclusion. Khaid shipkillers began to wink out, obliterated by anion impacts. The *Gladius'* point-defense guns were spinning hot, filling the intervening space with ballistic rounds, and her short-range launchers were discharging as fast as the robotic loaders could clear the launch rails. Better than half of the incoming missiles were obliterated, but the remainder detonated in a staggered wave of plasma flares, washing from one end of the ship to the other.

Xochitl jerked back, his face dark, ruddy bronze as the heavy cruiser's glyph vanished from the threatwell plot.

«*Three friendly effectives remain,*» exo stated, highlighting the glyphs of the dreadnaught and two remaining battle-cruisers. «*Hostile numbers are now sixteen combatants, twelve noncombatants. Point-defense network is suboptimal, ECM cloud is suboptimal, launcher recycle time is suboptimal, munitions expenditure—all weapon systems—is excessive, and maneuver drive efficiency is—*»

"Enough!" Xochitl felt hot inside his armor and now he heard the whine of the air circulation system trying to shed waste heat like the buzz of a thousand mosquitoes. "Enough."

His head was throbbing violently and he groped for the medband override.

The *Naniwa*'s hull shook with repeated explosions as a wave of sprint missiles and penetrators crashed through her point-defense. In Command, Oc Chac was speaking rapidly into his throatmike, his status displays a sea of red and amber indicators. Koshō snarled, seeing three Khaid light cruisers and a pair of destroyers interpose themselves between her and the *Tlemitl*. The enemy ships were formed up tight, and their point-defense interlock had stopped the last salvo of shipkillers Konev and his gunners had spun into them.

"Pilot, time to 'cast interlock with the Flag?"

"Too long, *kyo*." Holloway looked up, wild-eyed, and shook his head. "We'd have to bull right through them to reach interlock range."

"Understood, *Thai-i*." Susan's attention snapped back to the threatwell, where a second pack of Khaid lightweights was barreling in on her flank, trying to get into the shadow of her drive plume. *We need to shed some of these dogs,* she thought, juggling distance, velocity, and time in a heartbeat. Her stylus slashed through the executive 'well at her console.

"Pilot, new heading. Don't spare the horses."

Naniwa responded, still agile despite the burning craters littering her hull and the cloud of vented atmosphere, splintered radiating fins, and other flotsam she was shedding. The battle cruiser shifted course, angling away from the *Tlemitl* and *Asama*, which were at the center of their own hot, constantly strobing cloud of detonations, and headed dead-on to the Barrier coordinates loaded into Susan's threatwell.

"Course correction burn complete, *kyo*," Holloway reported. "Nine hostiles now in pursuit."

"Incoming spread—one-hundred-six contacts," Konev barked. "Point-defense engaging."

Susan hissed, feeling her ship's pain deep down in her gut. "*Sho-sa*, prepare to roll mines."

Oc Chac nodded, attention wrenched away from damage control. He stared at her blankly for a heartbeat, then caught himself and nodded abruptly. "*Hai, Chu-sa!* Preparing to roll mines."

Gretchen picked herself up warily and groped from bunk to desk. Gravity wobbled again, the ship groaning around them, but this time she was ready and held on. Hummingbird had wedged himself into a corner of the room, a comp still in his hand—face tight with some tremendous effort of concentration—and she saw his fingers were a blur on the interfaces. All of his equipment, even scattered under the bunks, was still in operation. Gritting her teeth against a series of bad bruises, Anderssen found her own field comp and flipped it open. Her models were still running, and now they had resolved themselves down to only two alternatives.

"Where are we, Crow?" she gasped, fumbling at the control pad. "We've got to get all of this gear secured before we lose g-deck integrity entirely."

All of her equipment shoveled into the backpack without a problem. A roll of stickytape secured the pack to the bunk, which was in turn welded to the wall of the cabin. Her hand-comp stayed with her, though its interface was tiny in comparison to the bigger units. Hummingbird's setup was harder to deal with, particularly when her shoulders were itching at the prospect of the next abrupt maneuver. But in a few moments, all of it was stowed save the t-relay, which was a Yule tree of status lights. Grasping the main unit, she cast around for something to secure the device to.

"Leave be!" Hummingbird spared a dark, furious glance for her. "I've almost broken into the Khaid battlecast and we'll need that to survive the next hour. Pin it to the floor, if you must, but don't move it or disassemble the mechanism."

You'll sing a different tune, carrion bird, if this thing cracks you in the head. . . .

She strapped it down as best she could, feeling the metal radiating hot enough to scorch her fingertips. Then Anderssen crawled back to the other corner, wedged herself into place, and thumbed up the display on her hand-comp. *Plot position,* she ordered the little machine. On the sidebar, Gretchen was heartened to see that node 3^33 was still in synch and processing data at a blistering rate. *Excellent, but—*

Her latest modeling pass had discarded the data preprocessed by the Mirror scientists and culled from the *Korkunov*'s initial telemetry. Something nagged at her, saying it was too old to be accurate. Instead, drawing on the sheer processing power and storage offered by node 3^33, she'd asked the comps to sweep through the most basic data flowing back from the Imperial science probes and break it down, looking for gravitational anomalies at a sub-Planck scale. The descriptions of the damage inflicted on the *Calexico* hinted at a mechanism capable of dissecting battle-steel, which implied the weapon was able to break down the interlocking matrix of the armor without diffusing its impact energy across the enormous, mutually supporting weave of the material.

Her comps now revealed a new "map" of the surrounding space, one far different in detail than the Imperial data they'd received—or stolen. Anderssen cursed, her body jolted with fear. Tearing free of the restraints, she was at Hummingbird's side in the blink of an eye. She seized hold of the old man's ear, drawing a bright crimson pinpoint of blood with the corner of one nail.

"Crow! Come back to me. Captain Koshō is trying to use the Barrier as a weapon, and the Imperial data we have is *no good* for this sector. Break me into the command circuit, right now!"

"Rack eight away," Oc Chac announced, as a fresh cluster of plasma mine icons popped up on the threatwell. "We're done, *kyo*." The Mayan looked back at Susan, his chiseled face questioning.

"Not enough," the Nisei woman said, watching the last of her area denial munitions spin away behind the *Naniwa*. The battle-cruiser was pushing hard at maximum-v for the level of particulates in this area of space, and there were still nine Khaiden cruisers and destroyers racing after her. "Weapons, start dumping delayed-fuse bomb-pods into our wake. I want them on a timer and dark until they tick over on intercept."

Then she swiveled around, considering the threatwell. *Naniwa* was now closing fast on the forbidden area indicated by the Mirror scientists. Stabbing flares started to pop up behind them, catching one of the Khaiden cruisers with a direct hit. The enemy ship staggered, losing way, and then plowed through three more plasma mines.

Atmosphere began to vent from dozens of punctures, but the other Khaid ships dodged past, their captains and crews alert enough to realize the danger and begin laying down a sweeping pattern of computer-controlled ballistic rounds.

"Pilot, prepare to rotate ship," Koshō announced, glaring at Holloway. "Rotate in one minute, sixteen—"

Stop, you've got to stop!

She jerked, hearing an unfamiliar voice shouting in her earbug.

"Belay that order," Susan snarled, "who is this?"

Gretchen Anderssen, Captain Koshō. Your charts are out of date—I'm updating your display—now!

"*Jigoku-e ochiro!*" The *Chu-sa's* shouted curse startled everyone on the bridge, and Oc Chac turned to stare at her in surprise. Susan's complexion shaded almost porcelain. The threatwell display mutated wildly, the Mirror coordinates for the invisible Barrier wiped away and replaced by a series of veil-like patterns, overlapping on one another and filled with pockets and eddies.

"Forty seconds to intersection, *kyo*," Holloway yelped, his console throwing a dozen alarms.

"Pilot, hard over!" Koshō snarled, punching the collision alarm glyph on her console. Then her stylus stabbed out, marking a new course in the 'well.

"Thirty-nine seconds!"

Naniwa groaned from stem to stern, engines cutting out as the ship rotated, and then flaring as they slewed around into a new heading. Shedding velocity to make the turn, the battle-cruiser was suddenly seconds "behind" where the constant stream of Khaiden missiles expected her to be. Penetrators rained onto her newly exposed "roof," their onboard comps triggering detonation. Hammerblows boomed across the shipskin, shredding tiles and overloading the thermocouples. Radiating fins splintered all across the *Naniwa's* hull. Secondary plasma charges pierced the shipskin itself, blowing enormous gaps through to the secondary hull. Behind the plasma charge, the penetrator rounds themselves collided with the inner armor at tremendous speed. The triple layer of armor mesh convulsed, trying to shed impact energy across the whole shipframe, but dozens of tiny ruptures punched through, spewing thermonuclear plasma into two compartments just fore of Engineering. Atmosphere vented, blowing out a chaff-cloud of debris.

"Multiple punctures," Oc Chac bawled, "we've lost environment on decks nineteen and twenty. Four compartments compromised. I have a radiation fire in compartment eighty-one."

"*Sho-sa*, get your teams in," Susan barked, "Pilot—get me some headway!"

Her engines intact, the *Naniwa* accelerated away on a sharply different vector. Koshō held her breath, watching her ship veer hideously close to the shimmering veils plotted on her 'well.

In their cabin on six, Gretchen and Hummingbird were torn through their restraints and slammed hard against the wall. Gravity fluctuated violently for a microsecond and the comps ripped free as well, smashing into the walls, displays splintering into ruin. Bloody, one arm stabbing with terrible, blinding pain, Gretchen found herself pinned against the ceiling. Alarm Klaxons screamed and the bitter smell of burning insulation flooded the air. Crushed by a giant hand, Anderssen struggled to breathe. "Crow! Crow!"

Hummingbird was pinned as well, though his head lolled limply to one side.

Four hundred thousand kilometers behind the *Naniwa*, the pack of Khaiden ships reacted as well, shedding velocity to make an equally abrupt course change. Three of them managed this quite smartly, matching the battle-cruiser's relative angle. They continued to spit missiles at the Imperial ship, though their rate of fire slacked off sharply. The other five also made the turn, but too slowly. Their icons interpenetrated with the first of the veils plotted on Susan's display and abruptly winked out.

"Score on goal," Koshō breathed, only too aware of how close she'd come to blundering into the same fate. "Pilot, get me a new intercept to the *Tlemitl*!"

Aboard the *Firearrow*, Xochitl grimaced as one of his Jaguars cut away the mangled wreckage of his shock-chair. Flag Command was filled with smoke and guttering flames from a shipkiller impact which had torn through the secondary hull. Able to move once more, the Prince crawled free, shaking off bits of burning metal and fabric. Two of his bodyguards were down, along with most of the junior officers and ratings who had been at their stations.

"Raise damage control," Xochitl ordered his exo. "*Cuauhhuehueh* Koris, status of the rest of your squad?"

"Only us in comm contact, *Tlatocapilli*." The Jaguar Knight shook his head slowly. "I'm not getting a response from Command either."

«*Thai-sa* Yoemon is dead,» reported the exo. «*Autonomic systems report that Main Command has lost environmental control due to a penetrator hit. No life signs remain in the compartment.*»

"Mains are down," the Prince said aloud, replying to Koris. "Find me the secondary and let's get moving."

The intership comm channel was fuzzing with static,

making even short-range conversations impossible. "Exo, what is this?"

«*A Khaid disruptor bug has entered the ship via a penetrator. Internal communications on the regular channels will be impossible until the module is located and destroyed or damage control reroutes around the infection.*»

"Find me a clear channel, then."

The Jaguars were already moving, hustling the Prince out into the corridor. The hatchway tried to close behind them and stuck, flat streamers of black smoke oozing along the roof. A fire suppression system kicked in, flooding the hallway with foam. Xochitl wiped his faceplate clear and jogged on. The assistive mechanisms in his suit would let him run a long way without tiring.

Four decks away, Engineer Second Helsdon and two of his crew slipped pry bars behind the cover of a section of shattered comm conduit and wrenched hard. The cover tore away, revealing six meters of shredded, blackened crystal. Freezing wind, howling down the passageway from some hull rupture, pummelled their z-suits, laying down frost on every surface. Malcolm jammed a cutting tool behind the junction at his end of the conduit and popped the interface free—off to his right, the other two men were doing the same.

"Clear!" Two *Jun-i* hustled up, bearing a length of replacement crystal. They shoved the new conduit into place and Helsdon locked down his end, a hand-comp tucked into his elbow. A moment later, with diagnostic leads attached, he had a string of green lights on the status display. The circuit came back up with a few hiccups. "Done here," he shouted. They'd manually switched to a little-used comm channel when the main network went down, but there was still interference. "On to the next."

"Doubt if we have all the holes patched, Engineer," one of the warrant officers remarked with a strained laugh.

"Yeah, only ten or twenty to go," someone else's voice came through the suit-to-suit line. "What now?"

"Wait one." Helsdon grunted with exhaustion, thumbing through a succession of panes on his hand-comp, the team crowded around him, faces expectant for the next task.

The battle-steel hatchway to Secondary Command cycled open and Xochitl and his Jaguars crowded in. The *Sho-sa*, who had found himself commanding the dreadnaught when primary Command and Flag had gone off-line, jerked around, his face ashy.

"*Tlatocapilli*, I'm glad to see you! We've—"

"Out of the chair," the México lord seized the lieutenant commander by the arm and dragged him away from the command console. "You're XO now—get me damage control back on-line and report munitions inventory!"

The main threatwell was still functioning as Xochitl settled into the shockchair, taking stock of the situation. He'd been out of contact for nearly thirty minutes, but his exo jacked in to the main boards and the Prince saw the gun decks were still in operation, hammering away at the swarm of Khaiden battleships pacing the dreadnaught. The new battle-shields wavered in and out of existence, flaring bright with missile impacts.

«*Forty percent coverage remaining,*» exo reported. «*Launchers are at sixty percent, though four port-side are jammed.*»

The *Asama* had fallen away behind, crippled and shuddering from secondary explosions deep in her core, crew bailing out in a cluster of shuttles and evac-capsules.

Xochitl waved his hand and the threatwell reconfigured; the myriad points of Imperial distress beacons vanished, leaving only the combatants.

"Lord Prince," the *Sho-sa* ventured. "We have stowage to take them aboard—"

"Leave them," Xochitl growled, his command console flickering with alternate course plots at a blinding rate. At main navigation, the *Thai-i* sitting at the station had drawn back, finding his v-panes and control displays no longer responding to his touch. Suddenly the alternates dropped away and the Prince nodded to himself. "New course by my mark, full power. We need breathing room!"

Engines thundering, the decking vibrating with a deep basso roar, *Tlemitl* charged away from the wrecked *Asama*, all surviving launchers and gun nacelles concentrated on two Khaid heavy cruisers which had drawn the unlucky course to stand in the Prince's way. Both broke off, trying to change vector as multiple shipkillers slammed into their deflectors, breaking through to sear armor and shatter their engine rings. Undaunted, the *Firearrow* accelerated towards the Pinhole.

Three-quarters of a million kilometers behind the swirling firefight around the super-dreadnaught, Koshō grasped the Prince's intent immediately. The *Naniwa* was already accelerating to join him, having shrugged aside the last of the lighter ships, but now the Khaid battleships had reformed, relocking their point-defense and fire control. Swift as harriers, they came hard on the chase and stood directly between the battle-cruiser and the flagship. Thoughtful, Susan tapped up the channel to deck six.

"Anderssen-*sana*, can you get me better telemetry?"

There was no response, only intermittent static and then a "*cabin inhabitants are unavailable at this time*" message generated by shipboard comm. Face tight with dismay, Koshō switched channels.

"Damage Control, Medical. Get teams to cabin nine on deck six, immediately!"

In the 'well, her course and that of the *Tlemitl* were fast converging on the outer edge of the debris field from the *Can*. Beyond the wrecked station loomed the invisible passage of the Pinhole, though now Susan realized that even if the Scouts had found an opening—there was no surety it led anywhere save into a veil of threads which would gut her ship like a *teppan*-chef.

"Comm, any response from the Flag?"

The comm officer shook her head, eyes huge. "Nothing, *Chu-sa*. She's still moving and fighting, but I've no response from any shipside system, not even on identi-cast."

Does he even see we're here? Koshō discarded the thought. "*Chu-i*, you find me someone to talk to. If any-one can circumvent the Khaid jamming, the interference from the dust cloud, and the radiation blaze from so many wrecked ships, you can."

"*Hai, Chu-sa, hai!*"

Then she turned to Holloway and Oc Chac, who were heads down over the navigational console.

"*Sho-sa*, can we get a reading on that Barrier? Any-thing?"

The Mayan shook his head. "Sensors show a clear field, save for the omnipresent dust. Only empty space beckons beyond the shattered dead."

"Not good enough." Susan tapped her fingers rapidly on the edge of her shockchair. "Get me an update from the medical team on six. Now."

THE WILFUL

The main hatch to Engineering cycled open with a pained groan and Hadeishi slipped through the opening. The machete was sheathed, the serrated knife tucked away in his tool belt. Two bandoliers of shipguns—in a wide variety of models—were slung over his shoulder. De Molay was leaning heavily on the console, her face tight with pain.

"You're tracking blood on my deck, Engineer. But," she gestured at her leg and side, "who am I to complain?"

Mitsuharu laid down the captured weapons and knelt beside her. His lips pursed, gentle fingers tightening the press-pak on her leg wound. The bandage was saturated and the status strip across the blue material had shaded to red as well. The old woman's color had deteriorated in his absence.

"No geisha ever had a whiter brow than you, *Sencho*. I will carry you to the medbay."

Moving the freighter's captain would not improve her condition, but Hadeishi saw no other option. He was not a corpsman and there were no doctors to hand. He rigged a sling, eased her into the fabric, and then set off, his own weariness offset by a jolt of stimulant from his medband. Dead Khaid sprawled in the nonengineering corridors, their bodies chittering with shipbugs. As they moved slowly through, De Molay glanced at the tight, distorted faces, all gray with the mark of carbon monoxide poisoning. After the first dozen or so, she closed her eyes and leaned her head against his back.

"Don't sleep yet, *Sencho*, you've landing papers to sign, manifests to review . . ." He hoped the medbay, if there was such a thing on the freighter, was equipped with an autobot of some kind. *Aren't all ships as well equipped as a Fleet light cruiser?*

The reality was far more spartan, but the medical bay—more properly a closet with a fold-out bed—did have a diagnostic and treatment module for trauma cases. Hadeishi broke open a shock-pak and applied the first IV tabs. De Molay shivered from head to toe, and then her eyes fluttered open. She gave a short breathy laugh when she saw the image of her mashed thigh on the overhead display. "Just a flesh wound," she gasped.

Hadeishi peeled away the press-pak from her leg. Bright red blood oozed in tiny pinpoints from an enormous bruise easily the length of his forearm.

"Severe tissue damage. No broken bones," an androgynous voice announced from the trauma unit. "Apply anti-inflammatory agents as needed. Apply fresh press-pak. Leave on forty-eight hours. Set patient medband to dispense pain control agents as needed. Bed rest is recommended to speed recovery."

De Molay made a face at Mitsuharu. "Give me those press-paks. Where's the Bulldog?"

Hadeishi fished out the Webley and checked the magazine before handing the automatic over. "Full up, *Sencho*. But I think we've finished off the other gunslingers."

De Molay shot him a pained glare. "You're a clever engineer with the toxic air, but I'll keep my old Humbert handy. He is very reliable. Now"—she paused, clenching her teeth and waiting for the medband to kick in— "I'm already a patient. I can be my own corpsman. You—you're all the command crew we have."

Hadeishi nodded, rummaging through the trauma station. He laid out the necessary medpacks, made sure her comm bracelet was responding and the overhead v-display toggled to show shipnet. "You're the only backup I have, *Sencho-sana*."

"So I'm not permitted to die, then? I'll consider the suggestion."

Stepping around the bodies fallen at the entryway to the bridge, Mitsuharu entered gingerly—a Khaid ship-gun cradled in his hands, safety off—and checked all the corners before turning his attention to the command station.

The Khaid officer was still slumped against the console. Hadeishi grunted with effort, heaving the body onto the floor with a clatter. Then he cleared the session on the boards—the Khaid had loaded some kind of interpreter to allow them to enter transit coordinates—and authorized himself with De Molay's codes.

Much better, he thought, seeing a whole series of v-panes unfold, all seeming very modern and closely modeled on the standard Fleet executive interface. *I do believe this ship has illegal software loaded. Excellent.*

For a moment he considered drilling into the ship's manifest and construction logs, looking to see who—exactly—had updated the freighter. But then Hadeishi brushed those panes aside. His suspicions could wait, for there was far more interesting business afoot.

He shut off the transit alarm and then ran through a postgradient checklist. The hyperspace coil was still in operation, though now quiescent, and maneuver drives were primed and idling. Exterior cameras showed the *Wilful* drifting in a region of fantastically colored dust and gas plumes. As the little ship's passive sensors woke one by one, they revealed distant shoals of wreckage, multiple radiation sources, shattered ships, and the far-off wink of distress beacons. His hand lingered over a set of controls which would initiate an active scan, but then he passed on, unfolding up a comm channel to the medical closet.

"We've come to the right place," Hadeishi said,

when De Molay's face appeared. "Hachiman has passed this way with scythe and spear. I'm picking up both Khaid and Imperial transmissions, so the outcome is still in doubt."

The *Wilful* crept forward through the murk, emissions signature as low as Mitsuharu could manage with his rough understanding of the freighter's capabilities.

"Where are you taking us?" De Molay asked, watching his face intently through the monitor. Now that she was lying down and had proper meds, her color was improving rapidly. The trauma unit had also dispensed a drinking tube of complex carbohydrate-based rehydration fluid. This substance was a lambent green, but the old woman didn't seem to mind the taste.

"There are Imperial evac-pods within range," Hadeishi answered, eyes flitting from screen to screen. "And this ship needs a crew to be useful."

De Molay did not respond immediately, though Hadeishi could hear her breathing tensely as he double-checked the feed from the scanners. Their immediate area *seemed* to be clear of combat—he couldn't pick up any missile drive plumes, anion beam spikes, or the gravity dimples of mainline starships. *But then, the sensor suite on this barge is . . . limited.* His fingers tapped briskly on the console.

"You should take us out of here, back into hyperspace—" De Molay was frowning.

"Not while we can rescue some of these men." Mitsuharu felt strange—alive again, with the v-panes of a starship under his fingers. He felt the hum of the engines through the deck, the tickle of a comm implant snug in his ear canal. But he had a sensation of riding in emptiness, alone on a deserted road, astride a strange horse with no known companions. *Where is the chatter of my crew? Where is Susan's slim, fierce shape at the secondary console? There are only ghosts.*

"We're not equipped to fight, Engineer. This is not an IMN ship of war!"

"I know." Hadeishi settled himself in the command chair, feeling the cracked leather dig at his skin. Even the shape of the civilian shockchair was odd and unfamiliar. The console was too far away for his taste, and could not be adjusted. There was no threatwell, or even a holotank to give him a working view of the field of battle!

Dishes rattled in the kitchen of the little noodle shop. Musashi was hungry—starved would be a better word, he thought—and was busy shoveling udon into his mouth, feeling the first hot rush of chicken broth like the wind from Nirvana, with a pair of chopsticks. The yakuza, four of them, entered with unusual swiftness, their faces blank as Nōgaku masks, and before even he could react, their leader had snatched up his bokutō and hurled the wooden blade away, out into the night-shrouded street.

"This is the one," the gangster barked, his own katana rasping from a cheap bamboo sheath. His arms bulged with muscle, gorgeously colored tattoos peeking from beneath both kimono sleeves.

Musashi looked up, expressing dumb astonishment and curled his left hand around the bowl of soup. "The one, what?"

"Haiiiii!" The other three yakuza drew their swords with a great flourish, kicking mats and tables aside.

Musashi turned slowly to face them, rising with the bowl in one hand, the chopsticks between his middle fingers in the other. "Pardon?"

But the scanner display was dusted with the signatures of evac-capsules. Mitsuharu lifted his hand towards the screen: "We're the only chance they have to escape a slow agonizing death, or slavery. We'll save as many as we can, before we have to run."

"I gather Command has spoken," De Molay replied, her expression pinched.

"You bear a simple cross of silver at your breast, *Sencho*. Would you leave all these travelers abandoned in the dark, prey to our enemies? Where is your charity then?"

The old woman did not reply, her eyes narrowing to tight slits.

Mitsuharu shook his head. "I cannot abandon them, *kyo*. We go forward."

THE NANIWA

"The fool! He should swing back to meet us."

In her executive 'well, Susan watched the *Tlemitl* barrel towards the Pinhole, closely followed by a phalanx of Khaid battleships, the entire conglomeration ablaze with the snap of beam-weapons, streaking missiles, and the constant stuttering flare of fusion detonations. The massive radiation signature from the battle was threatening to wash out passive scans and hide the whole affray from view.

"They're not going to make it," she hissed to herself. Dragging her attention away from the doomed flagship, Koshō checked in with the repair crew cutting away the door to cabin nine on deck six. A medical team was lifting the body of the Swedish woman and the old *nauallis* out on stretchers. Susan tapped her earbug, jaw clenched. "Are either of them alive?"

In the v-pane, the *gun-i* holding a medpack to the old México's chest nodded, *Yes*.

Anderssen raised her head feebly, a bronze-colored comp clasped tight to her chest. "Captain, you've . . . got to slow the ship. . . ." She coughed as the medical team loaded the stretcher onto a grav-cart. "The outer surface of the Barrier shifts and moves, billowing like a sail . . . or a permeable membrane . . . it's not stable. All of the Mirror data is outdated, too old to use."

"Get her to medical," Koshō snapped, "stabilized and jacked into shipnet with her comp!"

What next? she wondered, turning back to the threat-well. "Pucatli! Get me *someone* on the flagship—I don't care who, the kitchen staff supervisor will do!"

Three hundred thousand kilometers ahead, the *Tlemitl* swerved into the confines of the Pinhole. Susan could see they were following the pathway divined by the Mirror probes. But the newer information the Swedish woman had loaded into the *Naniwa*'s nav system clearly showed one of the veils had begun to occlude the opening. The phalanx of Khaid battleships and lighter elements charged in directly behind the crippled dreadnaught and catastrophe ensued.

Koshō couldn't help but grin ferally as first one and then a dozen of the enemy ships interpenetrated with the invisible Barrier—a rippling string of icons winked out abruptly on her 'well plot. Moments later, the camera views on the side panels studded with the blue-white flare of ships disintegrating. A storm of chatter erupted on a channel Pucatli had picked out of the storm of electromagnetic noise. Susan couldn't understand the Khaid traffic—the message bursts were encrypted and in a tongue foreign to her—but the cadence of the staticky noise said nothing but *panic.*

For another minute the *Tlemitl* dodged and weaved, exercising her maneuver engines to the utmost, following a corkscrew path known only to—and then the dreadnaught brushed against one of the invisible threads. The battle-shields, which were mostly active at that moment, did *nothing* to prevent nearly a third of the behemoth from being cloven away in one dumbfounding instant.

At this distance, on the cameras, there was nothing to see but a jagged smear of light where the hull rupture was decompressing explosively.

On the *Naniwa*'s bridge, however, there was loud confusion. Konev and Holloway, who had access to enhanced telemetry feeds from the battle-cruiser's sensors, shouted aloud in alarm. Pucatli and the others turned, staring at Koshō in raw, open fear. The threatwell updated, showing the enemy ships in disarray.

"What happened, *Chu-sa*?" The comm officer ventured. "The Khaid battleships—"

"Are gone," Susan said steadily. "Holloway-*tzin*, tracking update please."

"Ten containment failures, *kyo*," the navigator reported, shaken. "Three more badly damaged and losing way. The Khaid battle-group is trying to reverse course. The *Tlemitl* . . . she's . . . she's a dead ship, *Chu-sa*. Battlecast status is flickering in and out, but the last report says she's lost nearly a quarter of her compartments. Reactors are intact, but her drives are dead. She's coasting . . ."

Belching atmosphere and debris, the giant ship spun inexorably into another thread. Aboard the *Naniwa*, the Command crew watched in horror as another infinitely thin razor dissected the super-dreadnaught, shearing through decks, bulkheads, hapless crewmen. . . . Now they were close enough for the cameras to interpolate, picking out the disintegrating flagship through iridescent streamers of dust.

"Gods," Konev blurted, his face shining with sweat. "They're sure to lose containment now!"

We're alone, Koshō thought, forcing herself to look away. A tight knot was forming in her stomach. *The Khaid are as badly shaken as we are—but they still out-number me by five to one, at least.*

THE *TLEMITL*

Emergency lighting sputtered, flickering on and off in a red-lit haze, along the corridor. Helsdon rotated slowly in midair, disoriented. Then his eyes caught on a door-way swinging past and his mind snapped back into fo-cus. "We've lost the g-decking," he wheezed, suddenly aware that his chest and side were throbbing with pain. "Damage control team, report."

A chorus of groans and cursing answered him. The engineer tucked in, giving himself a little momentum, and his boots adhered to the nearest surface. Stable, he found himself standing on the wall of the passageway. Debris was loose everywhere, filling the air with clouds of paper, broken bits of furniture, loose shoes—anything which hadn't been secured when the *Tlemitl* had suf-fered an enormous blow.

Swallowing against a very dry throat, Helsdon re-trieved his hand-comp—which was attached by a retract-able cord to his tool-belt—and thumbed the device awake. Status lights flickered and then a display came up. "Power is down across the whole grid," he said aloud. The others were gathering, hauling themselves along the walls and floor. "No gravity, no environmental control." He blinked rapidly.

"What the hell happened?" One of the midshipmen was staring around wildly.

"We hit the—we hit the phenomena," Helsdon

croaked, feeling a horrible constriction in his chest. "Part of the ship—most of the ship?—has been cut away from—from us."

A cook caught his shoulder, holding the engineer steady. "We've gotta get off, chief."

"There's nowhere to go," Helsdon whispered, watching his hand-comp scan uselessly for a live shipnet node. "The reactors are in shutdown, but who knows how long that will last?"

"Help the chief, he's hurt." The cook gestured for the midshipmen to lay hands on the engineer. "Anyone see an evac capsule sign? That way? Chop-chop, everyone, let's go."

A grav-sled had been thrown the length of the entryway to the flag admiral's quarters, smashing into the stone pillars framing the monumental door. Broken chunks of stone floated in a slow eddy, making Xochitl's progress difficult. Both sets of mural walls had shattered, adding a glittering drift of glassite which flared and shimmered in the suit lights as he moved. One of his Jaguars led the way, combat suit jets puffing whitely, and another followed. Here in officer's country, the internal damage seemed worse—there had been more ornamentation to rip free from the walls and smash into things—than down on the deck holding secondary command.

His men hadn't asked what had happened, but the Prince had an excellent idea.

«The Mirror plotting data was flawed,» his exo supplied, completing his thought.

"I know," he whispered, forgetting to concentrate on the thought-interface between them. "I know."

The Jaguar sergeant in the lead pushed aside the fallen statuary—his powered combat armor made the task possible—and forced open the door beyond. Xochitl swung through the opening, thankful for the moment that they were in z-g. With proper EVA gear, they had made very swift progress through the wreckage. The sitting room beyond was utterly destroyed—tables, screens, personal artifacts all jumbled together in a drifting cloud of flotsam—but in one corner, curled up into a turtle-like shell, was a larger-than-human figure in a dark metallic z-suit. In their suit-lights, the metal surface gleamed with thousands of tiny, incised glyphs and markings. Their meanings were unknown to the Prince.

«*Recording,*» the exocortex reported, tucking away thirty seconds of high definition video for later analysis. «*Seven hundred and twenty-nine distinct ideograms identified. Spawning subtasks to collate comparisons against known Hjogadim character sets.*»

Xochitl drifted close to the figure—careful not to touch the alien z-suit—and oriented himself face-to-face. The suit mask was almost opaque, but he could make out the gleam of helmet lights flickering in a pair of deep-set eyes.

"Come, Esteemed One," Xochitl commanded, barely polite. "We must get you to safety."

He was answered by a long, violent harangue in a lilting, sing-song tongue, and entirely inhuman growling. The noise was abrasively loud on point-to-point comm. The Prince grimaced, his ears ringing, and then he gestured at the two Jaguar Knights.

"No one can stay here, Esteemed One. We're taking you to a place of safety."

The Knights seized the creature's shoulders and kicked off, carrying the Hjo towards the door. There was another outburst of growling and snarling, interspersed with a long tirade in the unknown tongue. But the Hjo remained tightly curled up, trying to hide its long tapering head, and this made it possible for the two *Ocelotl* to hustle the alien along.

Back outside, once they'd left the security corridor and its intrinsic shielding, Xochitl's exo conjured up a deck plan in his field of view. "Ah, good," the Prince said aloud on the local comm circuit. "There's an escape pod rail not far from here."

The Jaguars looked at him, puzzled. Their sergeant gestured at the comp built into his suit. "Nothing on shipnet, my lord. Everything's down. . . ."

"No matter, *Cuauhhuehueh*, I've a backup copy. This way."

They turned left, jetting down a main corridor—large enough to drive two grav-sleds side-by-side—filled with drifting debris. Constellations of smoke globules parted before them, bumping into their facemasks as they sped along. Though they passed scattered corpses and even some wounded, Xochitl did not stop. Hidden by his facemask, the Prince's expression was set and hard.

THE NANIWA

Susan watched her bank of displays with a fixed, stony glare. The threatwell showed their situation only too well. On the hull of the once-great *Firearrow*, the last of the battle-shield projectors flickered and died. The Khaid ships which had survived the reckless pursuit were underway at last, pulling back from the unexpected weapon which had consumed their fellows. From what she saw on her 'well they would be successful in escaping the trap if they just reversed along their own drive trails.

They're going to figure this out pretty fast, she mused, her thoughts filled with foreboding. *They've got too much data on hand, and now they have the time to let it all sink in. . . .*

But for the moment, her way forward was clear. Behind, however, the flotilla of destroyers that had been nipping at the *Naniwa*'s heels was still there, slowly closing range, their beam weapons snapping past or flaring out as the aft point-defense knocked them down. None of these hounds had the missile throw-weight to punch past her counter-missiles and Konev had gathered up fifteen or sixteen remote weapons platforms initially deployed by the *Tokiwa* and *Asama* in the early stages of the battle.

The platforms were low on munitions, but still had some capacity left. They were keeping pace, extending both her missile intercept envelope and the battle-cruiser's sensor range, and in this kind of knife-fight Koshō would take anything she could get. Susan sat stiffly, back ramrod straight, and her eyes flickered across the arrayed data one more time. "We need to determine if there are any survivors," she said softly, drawing Oc Chac's attention. "We can take on several thousand, if we triple-bunk."

The Mayan shook his head in dismay. "*Chu-sa!* We'll overtax environmentals in a few days with that sort of passenger load! Only we remain," he ventured. "We dare not help them—"

There is no time for reckless gestures, Susan realized, brow furrowing sharply. *We have to get out.*

"Status of our hypercoil? How long to make gradient?"

The Mayan *Zosen* stared at her blankly, one dark-complected finger pressed to his earbug. "*Kyo?*"

"How long," she said steadily, staring at him with a cold, considering expression, "to make transit to hyperspace?"

Oc Chac swallowed, dark eyes darting to his status panel. "Coil is down, *Kyo*. We've taken fragmentation damage along cells nineteen to thirty-six." He looked up, expression impassive. "I need two hours to make her right, *Chu-sa*."

Susan nodded, looking back to the threatwell. "We have no more than thirty minutes before they come at us again, *Sho-sa*. Take direct command of the repair crews."

"*Hai, kyo!*" The engineer bolted from Command, speaking rapidly into his throatmike as he ran.

Plasma detonations blossomed in the threatwell, bracketing the *Naniwa* as she maneuvered.

"They're getting our range, *kyo*," Konev reported, voice hoarse. "We've lost two of the remotes."

Susan's gaze swept across her console. Though mauled, the battle-cruiser was still game for a fight, but against so many Khaid? Her eyes flicked up, fixing on the long-range sensors. The Pinhole was still abroil with radiation and shattered ships. Their emissions blocked any sign of what lay beyond in the ever thicker dust-clouds. She grimaced, tapping her earbug.

"Medical? Get our Swedish passenger up here—awake—*right now!*—with all of her possessions."

Xochitl, the suited creature, and his *Ocelomeh* arrived at the evac-capsule cluster to find only one pod remaining. The other access-doors showed only empty cradles beyond thick glassite windows. The door to the last capsule was apparently stuck, as a motley collection of officers and ratings was banging away at the hatch with pry bars and other tools cribbed from the nearest damage control closet.

"Is it working?" the Jaguar Knight *Cuauhhuehueh* demanded, his voice booming on the local circuit.

A pale, sandy-haired man with Engineer's insignia turned to face the Prince's party. His light brown eyes registered the unit insignia of the Jaguars and his face grew still. "Yes. The capsule's intact. The launch rails are clear and the release subsystems are showing green across the board. We just have to get the hatch open."

Xochitl could see the pod was last in queue on the shared maglev launch tube. *A rough ride out of Firearrow's guts. And then where?*

«*Staying mobile and capable of reacting to circumstance improves our chances of survival by several orders of magnitude,*» the exo stated, displaying a variety of helpful graphs and comparison metrics on the Prince's field of view.

Without orders, the Jaguars bulled forward and gestured the sailors away from the hatchway. Two of them—a cook and a midshipman from laundry—started to protest, but the engineer waved his companions back. He was watching Xochitl with a wary expression, his mouth a tight line.

The Prince met his gaze with a level stare. "How many of us will fit?"

The man's eyes lost focus for an instant, and then he looked down at his hand-comp. "This one holds ten, Great Lord."

Xochitl's eyelid twitched. Including his Jaguars, there were twelve people floating in the compartment, most staring at him with suddenly wide eyes. His expression hardened as he considered the larger-than-human-size of his guest with a sidelong glance.

"Three of you must remain behind," Xochitl declared, his exo whispering details of skills, time in service, and political reliability in one ear. A pistol-model shipgun was already in his hand and leveled on the two cafeteria attendants. They froze. The Prince's face remained utterly cold as the pistol snapped twice, punching a flechette through each of their suit masks.

Everyone else jerked in surprise, stunned. One of the petty officers cried out, horrified, and jetted away down the corridor. One of the Jaguars raised his shipgun, but Xochitl waved him off. "Let him go—the rest of you, get the hatch open!"

Five minutes later, the Hjo clambered into the capsule, helped by the *Cuauhhuehueh*. The Prince watched the creature, whose mere existence had caused the loss of two Imperial lives, with barely controlled fury, then followed.

Moments later there was a reverberating *bang* and the evac capsule accelerated violently down the launch rail.

IN THE *KUUB*

SIX LIGHT-MINUTES FROM THE PINHOLE

The *Wilful* moved stealthily through the debris of battle. Hadeishi had the little freighter's engines pulsing only intermittently, letting momentum carry them through the wreckage as silently as possible. With only the two of them aboard, he'd isolated all of the compartments save the bridge, medical closet, and the passages connecting them. Everything else was powered down to reduce signature. Though it made no difference to a hunter's active scan, Mitsuharu had also dialed down the lights on the bridge. He sat at the command station in darkness, his face lit only by the glow of the console and the ruddy gleam of light from the external camera displays.

Bodies, broken equipment, ruptured evac capsules, chunks of decking floated past the *Wilful*'s cameras. Where he could, Hadeishi angled the little ship to hide in the emissions shadow of larger sections of blasted hull, or to follow the agitated particle trails of now-dead ships. Where he was forced to cross unbroken "ground," he moved as swiftly as the *Wilful*'s engines would carry them.

"You make a fine mouse hunting in a stubbled field," De Molay observed, her voice low and quiet, though she could have shouted wildly and none of their putative enemies would have noticed.

"An eye out for owls and foxes all the while, *Sen-cho*," Hadeishi nodded companionably. "You've lived on a farm?"

"My grandmother's. May Our Blessed Lord guard her soul."

"Ours as well." Hadeishi put the helm over a point, nav plot revealing a cluster of wreckage ahead. A light tap on the engine control shifted their heading and a long cylindrical panel drifted past on the dorsal cameras. The structure—seventy or eighty meters long—had been ravaged by a plasma detonation. The battle-steel was puckered and wrinkled. In the coppery glare, some fragments of warnings and informational inscriptions remained on the outer surface.

"Imperial?" De Molay asked softly.

"Yes. A reaction mass tank from a battle-cruiser or strike carrier."

Hadeishi sighed deeply. Remembered faces and fragments of conversation distracted him. A tremendous feeling of sorrow was welling up in him. Thoughts of the *Cornuelle* were prominent in his memory. Now he wished he'd carried the samisen up from Engineering. Lacking the instrument, he tapped his fingers on the console, setting a slow, mournful beat.

> "A phantom greenish gray,
> Ghost of some wight,
> Poor mortal wight!
> Wandering

Lonesomely
Through
The black
Night."

Then he stopped, the shattered cylinder falling away
behind them.

"What more can you offer?" De Molay shook her
head, silver hair falling into her eyes. She brushed the
strands away. "This is the fate of all sailors on this dark
sea, to perish at last in the void, and find repose on the
surface of the deep."

Mitsuharu did not respond, his thoughts far away.
Then, as he sat quietly, watching the dust clouds slowly
change color, one of his scan alerts chirped. The Nisei's
head turned, eyes focusing once more on the present. A
familiar silhouette coalesced on the main viewer. Using
the vector from passive scan, two of the cameras had
focused, picking out the outline of a vessel. Ship's registry reported an initial identification—a Fleet *Varanus*-
class cargo shuttle.

"See, *Sencho*? A sheaf of wheat is still standing
among the broken stalks."

Though the ship's boat seemed intact and free of obvious battle damage, there was no sign of life aboard.
The portholes were dark, engines cold, and the shuttle
was tumbling end to end. Hadeishi steered alongside,
smoothly matching her rotation with a deft play on the
drive controls.

De Molay pursed her lips, eyes narrowed. "A derelict,
do you think?"

"Sensors can lie, *Sencho*. If there are survivors
aboard, would they advertise themselves?"

The old woman shook her head. "I would not!" She
paused, thinking. "Our decrepit appearance will suggest
we are some kind of scavenger."

"Just as you planned, *Sencho*," Hadeishi offered a faint smile. "Just as you planned. But as fortune has provided, they are *not* deceived by our appearance. They are correct. *Wilful* is a scavenger—of the lost. Matching airlocks now."

"Very poetic," De Molay muttered. Mitsuharu did not reply, his whole attention on matching the lock interfaces and running out the freighter's gangway. A moment later, a faint *tunk* echoed through the decking and he had a string of green lights on the airlock status board. Then he double-checked the seal on the *Wilful*-side of the lock, making sure everything was secure, set the drive controls to automatic, and hurried downstairs.

His captured shipgun slung under-arm, Hadeishi looked in on De Molay in the medical closet. He'd gathered up a portable medpack and a bag of threesquares and water bottles. The silver-haired captain was trying to sit up in the tiny bunk, which was not as easy as it seemed.

"Lie quiet, *Sencho*. I'm going to cycle the lock in a moment—so I've switched Command to this console." He reached under the medbay overhead and reconfigured the display. "You've got full control of environmentals and even the drives, if need be. But try not to run about, you'll do yourself an injury."

The look she gave him eased his worry for her safety. "And yourself, Engineer. I can manage from here." She smiled tightly, tapping the grip of the Bulldog, whose holster and gunbelt were strapped across her chest. "Watch yourself, this wouldn't be the first time the Khaid have booby-trapped an Imperial evac-capsule, or shuttle."

"Or put a half-dozen marines aboard an unsuspecting rescue ship," Hadeishi added brightly.

The shuttle hatch irised open, battle-steel partitions folding back into the hull. Mitsuharu crouched just out of sight around the corner of his own lock—standing wide open—watching the other end of the gangway via a remote. There was a long still minute, and then a wary, soot-stained Fleet ensign peered out—his own shipgun at the ready. The fellow stared uncertainly into the lighted, but vacant gangway. "Hello the ship?"

"I'm stepping out," Hadeishi called, "no trouble, *Sho-i*."

Then he stood up, shook out his shoulders—offered a quick prayer to Ameratsu to preserve him for just a few more minutes—and stepped around the corner, the muzzle of his shipgun pointed at the deck. The ensign had disappeared, though Mitsuharu was certain he—and his friends, if any—were only just out of sight. "We're the *Wilful*, shipping out of Shinedo *uchumon*. My name is Mitsuharu Hadeishi—I'm the Engineer's Mate. We are prepared to lend you aid, if you need it. Have you wounded aboard?"

The *Sho-i* reappeared, looked him over, and then held up two fingers. Behind him a tall México with lieutenant's flashing on his torn and bloody z-suit pushed past on the arm of a smaller man, a wiry little marine. Hadeishi stood aside while they limped into the freighter's airlock. Three more followed, one rating in the middle—with no boots and only one foot—was being carried by his fellows. The ensign remained on the shuttle, face pale under the black coating of volatilized plastics.

"We have no medic," Hadeishi said, watching the injured rating's face grow paler by the second. "But there is an amputee kit in the medical closet." He glanced over the five men in the *Wilful*'s airlock—to his naked eye, they all seemed properly human—before turning to the ensign in the shuttle doorway. "Are there others?"

Without waiting for an answer, the Nisei stepped far enough inside to scan the interior of the shuttle. The boat was bare, even of equipment, and stank of burning.

"No, *Kyo*. We were lucky to get out ourselves. The ship was . . ." The *Sho-i*, who seemed even younger than usual for an ensign, twitched every time Mitsuharu moved. "They came in fast. *Thai-i* Tocoztic says they—they were Khaiden."

"They still are. We cannot keep the shuttle, *Sho-i*. Move over there with the others."

He took one last look around, in case there were useful supplies to bring with them, and then cycled the shuttle hatch closed. The gangway rang hollowly under his boots and then he was back aboard the *Wilful*, fingers quick on the locking mechanism. Another *thunk* boomed around them and the gangway separated. Hadeishi keyed open the inner lock to the freighter, his refugees huddled uncertainly together. Out the viewport, the shuttle tumbled away, one more fragment of debris swallowed by the greater sea of the *kuub*.

"We should not abandon that shuttle!" the wounded *Thai-i* objected. "We'll need her if this vessel suffers the same fate as the *Falchion*."

"I do not intend to lose *this* ship," Mitsuharu replied evenly. "And a cargo shuttle will only take up valuable stowage we will soon need for the others."

The airlock chuffed, separating from its seal, and then swung aside. Hadeishi nodded at the lieutenant, whose face had acquired a formidable glower. "If you are truly concerned, we have an escape pod aboard. Welcome to the *Wilful*. Medical is that way."

The lieutenant, despite his injuries, did not follow the four ratings. He and the marine *Nitto-hei* remained in the roundabout off the airlock while Hadeishi secured the hatch. "I am *Thai-i* Tocoztic, gun deck officer from the heavy cruiser *Falchion*."

Hadeishi turned and gave a slight bow. He kept his expression meticulously polite. "Mitsuharu Hadeishi at your service, *Thai-i*, Engineer's Mate of the *Wilful* and her acting XO."

Tocoztic looked Hadeishi up and down, jaw thrust forward. The México officer was taller and wider than the norm, with a dark *chocolatl* tone to his complexion. From his slight accent, Mitsuharu guessed the young man hailed from Ciguayo or Arawak—islands in the Eastern Sea which had been part of the Empire since the fourteenth century. The Nisei was pleased to see that despite falling into poor circumstance, the boy had lost none of his fighting spirit or sense of duty. *Whether dead or alive, within two campaigns he will be worthy of his braid.*

"I am an officer of the Imperial Fleet. In the name of Emperor Ahuizotl and by the Regulations covering the use of civilian assets in a time of war, I am assuming battlefield command of this vessel! *Nitto-hei* Cajeme, secure his sidearm."

"I am also the Emperor's servant," Hadeishi said softly, his shipgun already centered on the *Thai-i*'s chest. The marine private had failed to leap into action, despite his officer's command. His demeanor remained watchful, his movements contained. Mitsuharu was impressed, for the young *Thai-i* had quite a snap to his voice. *Could the marine be a Yaqui from the south? He commands excellent stillness.*

"And my Fleet rank," the Nisei continued, "exceeds yours. You may dispute me, or demand satisfaction at a later time. But not today, for there is a great deal of work to be done."

"Your rank? You have no rank! You're . . . you're a smuggler, an outcast in a grimy z-suit! Barely human." Tocoztic's face flushed red as he struggled to express his outrage.

ABOARD THE *NANIWA*

Koshō looked up, sparing an instant's attention from the threatwell, at the sound of someone gasping in pain as a grav-stretcher floated into Command. The Swedish woman, Anderssen, arrived in the company of two *gun-i*. Her left arm was splinted, her face and visible arm badly bruised. An extra med-band had been strapped to her off-wrist, leaving her face drawn and pale. Despite this, she met Susan's gaze with equanimity.

"Put her next to *Thai-i* Holloway at Navigation," Koshō said, inclining her sleek, dark head towards the semi-circular console on the second tier. "Secure the shockchair, we can't have her jolting about."

Turning back to the 'well, the *Chu-sa* considered the movements of the Khaid ships at the Pinhole once more. Konev, now moved over to the XO spot, had dialed up a series of secondary schematics, showing the historical track of the enemy contacts over the last hour.

"They're not leaving, *kyo*," the Russian said, rubbing his eyes. He, like the rest of the command crew, was now standing their second straight watch.

"No, they are regrouping. They are curious—did the *Tlemitl* have a true goal in mind, or did it act in equal ignorance, hurling itself to certain doom?"

"They're trying to guess the outline of the passage, *kyo*?" Konev sounded dubious.

Susan smiled, watching a series of darting lights

emerge from one of the Khaid ship-icons. "But— wisely—they've stopped throwing ships into the grind- er's teeth." Her stylus circled the minute flecks, directing the 'well to zoom in. "Instead they are testing the open- ing with missiles from this leeward battleship."

On the threatwell, the cluster of missiles sailed effort- lessly into the Pinhole. Some interpenetrated with the nearest veil, winking out in seemingly empty space, while others sped on, unmolested.

"*Kyo*, what are we doing?" Konev's voice was very soft. Koshō nodded, accepting the bold question.

"Finding two more hours for *Sho-sa* Chac to com- plete repairs on the coil." The *Zosen* were behind sched- ule, for the damage to some of the hypercells was worse than initially estimated. Susan lifted her chin, indicating the partial gap amongst the thready pattern. "We have this much of a map, and I hope—" She glanced over at An- derssen, who was carefully removing a bronze-colored comp from a parchment envelope and securing the de- vice to the navigation console. The Nisei officer blinked, suddenly certain that the corroded-looking surface was actually gleaming very brightly, as though burnished and new. "I hope we have the rest near to hand."

Gretchen spread her hands on either side of the block, took a deep breath, and then tapped open a pair of v-panes on either side. *Thai-i* Holloway, who had been watching her closely from his neighboring chair, stiff- ened and shot a panicky glance at Koshō.

Susan met his eyes, nodding. *We're only alive now,* she thought, *because of what Anderssen deduced. If we try and flee into open space, the Khaid will run us to ground in no more than an hour. Chac needs time, and that means we need safe haven. Even a quarter-light-minute inside that barrier, drawing a veil behind us where the Khaid cannot follow, will be enough to complete our re- pairs.*

Holloway swallowed, eyes dragged back to a flurry of geometric diagrams opening and closing on the console. Anderssen was now breathing deeply and steadily through her nose, fingers digging in another envelope from her jacket pocket. Two pale yellow tablets emerged, held gingerly between thumb and forefinger.

Oliohuiqui? wondered Susan. A nauallis *drug—ah now, how is our other passenger?*

Mindful of the security risk he represented, Koshō attached one of her v-panes to the datastream from the security cameras in Medical. Green Hummingbird was in bay three, his small brown body curled up in a fetal position. The dull gray mantle, hooded brown cloak, and trousers he affected were stained and torn—though those limbs exposed to her sight were unmarked. The vitals feed from bed telemetry showed his heartbeat was slow, his breathing shallow, and his condition marked UNCONSCIOUS.

Susan frowned at this. *I wonder . . .*

Holloway and Konev both distracted her from the thought by abruptly stiffening in alarm. A second later her own console flashed a series of warnings. Something had entered the shipnet and begun altering the code controlling the navigational interfaces—or replacing modules wholesale—at fantastic speed.

"*Chu-sa!*" The navigator had half-risen from his shockchair. "Are you *certain* this is a good idea?"

"It is the best chance we have," Koshō replied softly. She directed her gaze at the Swedish woman. "Anderssen-*tzin*, can your mechanism perceive the Barrier as it ebbs and flows? Can it relay the telemetry we need fast enough to move through at high-v?"

Gretchen turned towards her and Konev hissed in horrified surprise. The woman's pupils had grown huge, dilated by the drugs now coursing through her bloodstream. Her face had acquired a peculiar waxy sheen. "Zaryá protect us from all witches!"

"I do not know," Anderssen said, her voice tight and distant, "if your interfaces are fast enough."

"We will do our best," Susan answered, nodding to Holloway. "Stand by for our entry run. Bring up main drives, angle deflectors tight in on the hull. Konev— *Thai-i* Konev!"

Startled, the Russian turned to face her, once more composed and alert.

"Bring the remote platforms in as well, inside our deflector array. I don't want to lose them, but we're going to be moving erratically. Gun crews stand by for a hot passage. *Chu-i* Pucatli, sound battle stations and acceleration alert." Immediately, Klaxons began to blare.

Koshō turned back to Gretchen. "Anderssen-*tzin*, you have the con."

Deep in the bowels of the ship, reaction mass channels opened fractionally and the main maneuver engines roared as Holloway advanced both of his speed controls. The *Naniwa* surged ahead, building v as fast as she could. The internal frame, already battered by multiple missile impacts, groaned with the stress. In every compartment, crewmen secured their stations and prepared for a rough ride.

At the navigation console, Gretchen settled back, letting the holocast unfold before her. Attached directly to the shipnet's fastest interfaces, node $3^3 3$ seemed to expand, releasing hundreds of the processing nodes which had previously been inactive or inaccessible. The discovery algorithm she'd loaded into her own field comp had mutated, evolved, and returned, rippling across the Imperial systems with blinding speed. Her model was now tremendously detailed, with some kind of interpolative subprocess filling in the gaps in the quantum data feeding back from the battle-cruiser's sensor suite.

The science probes had been lost in the fighting, though in comparison to the *Naniwa*'s shipskin, they were tiny black birds, pecking at a leviathan wall of basalt blocks. The warship drank data with every surface, and node 3^33 swallowed it up just as fast. There was only one jarring note in the rising symphony. Gretchen was suddenly aware that something was out of place in the block pressed between her fingers.

You're broken, she realized, feeling that same rushing sense of *rightness* which had first come to her when the last fragment of an Old High Martian Period III bowl had fit into place on Old Mars and the entire object was whole and perfect in her hands, restored after five thousand years of separation. *This piece of you is out of place.* She felt the mechanism—was it like a clock? No, more a series of orbitals constantly in motion like the arms of an astrolabe, each ring a pressure-wave interlocking with the others in their emptiness—slip and slide under her attention. But then, when she focused her internal image of what *should be*, the whirling rings suddenly conformed to the pattern she desired.

The block seemed to change, under her fingertips, though she was sure nothing visible about it had altered, and felt—for the first time—as though it was in *proper* form. Unblemished, unbroken, at last intact.

In her elevated state, Anderssen's perceptions shifted, the command deck and the tiny humans there falling away, her vision expanding to taste the dust clouds, the wreckage, the hot flare of the ship's drives like brilliant jeweled stars. Agitated waves spun away from them as they built velocity, shifting the dust, even brushing the threaded veil which lay ahead, stirring its components with a hot wind.

The gap—the Pinhole—loomed, no more than a long jagged gap of darkness within darkness.

Prince Xochitl's evac-capsule sped away from the wreck of the *Tlemitl*, the momentum imparted by the launch rail carrying them forward. Through one of the viewports Xochitl could see the great ship, now cut neatly into three sections, receding, plumes of burning atmosphere jetting from the black hull. A Khaid cruiser—now no more than a shattered hulk—was within sight as well. The Prince, his helmet faceplate levered up, bit at the corner of his thumb and considered a nav-plot on his tiny control console. There were other capsules in range, and at the edge of sensor capacity, an able-bodied Khaiden destroyer was edging back out of the danger area.

"We cannot detect the threads," rasped a voice from behind him. Xochitl turned, surprised to see the engineer crouching in the door of the miniscule bridge. Looking more haggard than ever, fear radiating from him in waves, Helsdon gestured at the viewport. "Our sensors just aren't designed to recognize such a distortion of quantum law. You will want to halt our movement, before we strike one of them."

Though he was feeling something that—in a lesser mortal—might be termed terror, the Prince essayed a feeble joke: "There are laws at the quantum level?"

"As far as these pitiful computers are concerned, there are." Helsdon squeezed in beside Xochitl, ignoring centuries of protocol and policy which would have relegated the commoner to some distant precinct of the Prince's daily routine. The engineer's fingers trembled as he jacked a hand-comp into the control console. "We were right in the middle of reprogramming everything to ignore known laws, to assume that the Planck-length components of these threads were . . . well then, you shut us down." Helsdon laughed ghoulishly, his own fear cutting through any sense of social hierarchy.

Xochitl stiffened, his jaw clenching. *Whom do you think you address, Anglishman? No one reproves me. Not even the Imperial family. It is not permitted. My father depends on my judgment. He sent me here to secure this situation. He—*

Then the Prince realized his mind was wandering, even his exocortex had fallen silent while his human consciousness whirled in a dozen directions.

«*Cognitive capability is impaired,*» the exo finally announced, «*by chemical reactions to the perception of incipient destruction. Injecting stabilizing compounds.*» Xochitl felt a cool tickling sensation in his wrists and raised his hands in confusion. A moment passed before the thudding of his heart slowed and his mind cleared.

When the Prince focused again on the engineer, Helsdon was looking up at him in puzzlement, and as if at an equal. *You shall not think me incapable of the task!* Xochitl took a deep breath. "Can this sensor array be reconfigured? Tweaked to detect the barrier?"

"It will be slow work." Helsdon squinted at the intentionally simple capsule controls. "But we—" He paused, staring at the navigational plot. "Isn't that one of ours?"

Koshō watched with interest as the Khaid flotilla in the area around the Pinhole—at last—reacted to the *Naniwa*'s approach. Intermittent bursts of message traffic came and went on the enemy channel and now they were chattering away again. The enemy battleships began to accelerate, swirling out and away from the entrance to the gap like a flock of huge, ungainly birds. Her eyes narrowed to see they were keeping reasonable cohesion and spacing, even when forced to redeploy from disorder.

But they had reacted a little too slowly, given her approaching speed.

"Salvo one away," Konev reported, and the rumbling echo of launch rails discharging followed hard on his words.

A flight of shipkillers winged away from the *Naniwa* in a black wedge—exhausting the last of her ready magazines. Konev had been refining their attack vector for the past sixteen minutes and a formation of the remote platforms winged in, leading the swarm of *Tessen* missiles. With the response time from the remotes looping back through the main t-relay, the weapons officer had shortened his reaction time to the counter-missile storm erupting from the lead battleships. They had also pushed forward the reach of *Naniwa*'s countermeasures.

"Lead remotes going to rapid-fire," the *Thai-i* announced.

The flare of antimatter detonations began to spark in the darkness, almost lost against the fantastic roil of colors from the dust clouds. The *Naniwa*'s course shifted a point, driving hard against the edge of the Khaid formation, running in hot behind the glare of the sprint missiles discharged from the remote platforms. A secondary cloud of anti-missile munitions had also hared away from the remotes and these slashed into the midst of the Khaiden point-defense, confusing their targeting and ripping up their own counter-missile launch.

The wave of *Tessens* hammered into the most exposed of the Khaid battleships. A cluster of brilliant flares erupted, each shipkiller warhead separating into dozens of laser emitters. A stabbing white glare rippled from one end of the Khaid battlewagon to the other, shredding shipskin and gun nacelles, cracking open the hardpoints at each rail launcher. The ship shuddered, veering off, and then two of the big maneuver drives blew apart, disgorging clouds of debris.

"Secondary remotes going to full burn . . . now."

The other Khaiden ships burst away from the impact point, assuming she was trying to catch them edge-on, where their own fire would be blocked by friendly ships. Missiles and beam-weapons licked out at the speeding Imperial ship. The *Naniwa* swerved, punching into the dispersing formation where the battleship had fallen from line. The battle-cruiser's beam-weapons lashed across the nearest Khaiden battleship. Anion impacts rippled over the flank of the bulky ebon vessel, but Koshō had no interest in going toe to toe with such a behemoth. Instead, the *Naniwa* slipped past, spewing a tight cloud of decoys—the last of the scavenged remotes—that raced off at a sharp angle, breaking for open space, away from the Barrier.

The Khaid ships swung round, belching more ship-killers and penetrators, their formation coalescing again. The *Naniwa*, engines dead for the moment, plunged into the Pinhole along the drive-plume of the stricken battleship. Only moments from crossing the Barrier line, Koshō jerked back from her executive threatwell as the entire constellation of icons and designators shifted abruptly. Looking up at the main holocast, she saw the familiar symbols winking out, replaced by a crude new array of glyphs flaring to life in the holo.

"What—"

Holloway pointed at Gretchen, his face ashen. Most of the navigator's v-panes now showed a stream of unintelligible symbols and distorted images. "Shift piloting control to console two," Susan barked, startling the Command watch from stunned panic.

"No," Gretchen choked out, barely able to speak. The information density flowing across her v-displays was so dense, even with the assistance of the *oliohuiqui* to focus her mind she could barely process a tenth of the flood of images, sounds, models, and diagrams rushing past. She was grappling with an overwhelming—and terrifying—sensation that node 3^33 had woken from some ancient sleep. That the interfaces she had discovered—and prodded and poked—had been operating in some quiescent, dumbed-down state. Now, with the flood of information rolling in from the *Naniwa*'s sensor array, the device had improved itself, or recalled capabilities long left idle.

Now she was giddily happy that the only communications method between her and the machine was a keypad—a stylus—what her visual perception could reveal. A more direct connection, she was sure, would have rendered her insensate. *And mad, very definitely mad.*

"I can't fly this thing," Anderssen gasped. "I'll draw a path. You'll have to follow."

"Piloting control to console one," Koshō commanded, settling her shoulders. Holloway was frozen, agog at the transformation of his control surfaces. In the threatwell, patterns of constantly shifting veils were beginning to emerge from the confusion of symbols and diagrams. Susan tried to focus, finding the hubbub amongst the Command crew distracting and the gelatinlike fluidity of the new control surfaces difficult to grasp.

Despite this, the *Naniwa* plunged through the Pinhole and into the unknown spaces beyond. Koshō's grasp of the new controls—and of the information contorting her threatwell—grew rapidly. Her hands light on the flight interface, she sidestepped past both a stricken Khaiden destroyer and the spray of filaments which had torn the warship to shreds.

To Susan's right, on the second tier of Command, Anderssen was beginning to groan in a peculiar way, as though iron nails were being driven into her eyes.

Down in medical, Hummingbird opened one eye to a bare slit. He'd heard nothing for the past fifteen minutes, which augured well. The second eye opened and he turned his head gently. No one was in sight—not a marine guard, not a medical officer, not even his lovely assistant. Alone at last, the old México sat up, moving slowly, letting his heartbeat return to normal, blood flow resuming.

The poor vitals showing on the med-panel ticked up to normal after a few minutes. The *nauallis* listened again—now hearing and feeling the vibrations of a ship operating at high velocity—ignored the warning lights blinking on the med-panel, and jacked his remaining comp into the nearest access port. Then he lay back down, clasped both hands on his chest, and closed his eyes again.

Streams of data played out on the inside of his eyelids, including a navigational feed of the various ships in motion around the periphery of the Pinhole. His t-relay—despite being bounced around a bit—was still in operation. A quick diagnostic check indicated the unit was receiving and transmitting. *Good.* Hummingbird gauged distances and times, then toggled open a subaudible channel.

Have done, winged out into the night, directly to one of the Khaid command ships.

"It *is* ours," Xochitl snarled as his exo whispered the name of the approaching Imperial ship and her commander, along with pertinent details of crew, tonnage, and weapons systems. "Set an intercept course, Engineer, and speedily, too. She's faster than Lucifer himself and will not wait!"

He turned away from the engineer, his exo supplying a visual overlay for the communications controls in the capsule. Ghostly images emerged in his sight, highlighting the necessary mechanisms. The Prince keyed up a comm channel and sought handshake with the fast-approaching battle-cruiser.

Behind the *Naniwa*, the Khaid fleet—now minus another battleship—had regrouped again. This time they did not speed in pursuit, but watched with interest, waiting for the reckless Imperial commander to obliterate his ship in the same spectacular way that had consumed so many of their fellows. The Khaid destroyers were already beginning to withdraw to a safe distance.

"Incoming comm," *Chu-i* Pucatli blurted in surprise. "Flash traffic from the Flag!"

The corner of Koshō's lip curled up. Her whole attention was devoted to gentling the battle-cruiser through the drifting shoals of threads as fast as Gretchen could pump navigational data into the threatwell. Holloway—the only officer now at loose ends on the bridge—was obliged to take the call and blanched to find himself face-to-face with a ragged-looking Imperial Prince in smoke-stained combat armor. A cluster of other faces peered over the *Tlatocapilli*'s shoulders, and none of them looked at all well.

"Slow and take us aboard," the Prince demanded. "I'm transmitting our coordinates now."

A winking dot appeared in the threatwell, drifting steadily towards an effusion of threads.

"We're maneuvering to intercept you. . . ." Xochitl continued, pausing to wipe his forehead. He was sweating profusely.

"No!" Holloway turned, staring hopelessly at his captain. "*Chu-sa* . . . it's the *Gensui*! He's on that evac—"

"Tell him to *stop* and wait." Koshō's patience had long since reached its limit. In her hands the battle-cruiser jerked and jumped from side to side, swerving around individual threads. Her nerves were stretched tight, tensed

for the instant when she missed one of the deadly filaments and the *Naniwa* squealed in agony as armor and
shipskin parted before an unbreakable razor. "*Thai-i*, if
you can devise a way to bring them aboard at speed—I'm
open to suggestions—but I am *not* slowing down. Not
for him."

THE WILFUL

Well away from the Khaid squadron concentrated at the
Pinhole, the little freighter went about her salvage work.
She loitered amongst the dust clouds, letting the dim violet glow wash over her, while the passive sensors on the
hull boom listened hopefully for the sound of Imperial
distress beacons, or the drive signatures of shuttles or
other Fleet boats.

On deck two, the pair of Fleet ratings arrived at the
medical closet, their companion unconscious between
them. Captain De Molay was standing at the entrance
to the medbay, one hand clutching the edge of the platform, the other resting on the grip of her Bulldog. Her
pallor matched theirs, though she was in better color
than the man who'd lost his foot.

"Stop right there, *Sho-i*."

All of the *Falchion* crewmen halted, their eyes fixed
on the remarkably steady muzzle of the Webley. The
ensign managed a "*Hai, kyo!*" and the start of a salute.
The other *Joto-hei* just stared, struggling to support the
wounded man.

"At ease, gentlemen," she said, lowering the pistol.
"And raise your faceplates. I'm breathing decent air. Let
your recyclers take a rest—you may need them again!
I'm not going to shoot you. At least, not yet."

The two able-bodied men opened their helmets. Together, they hoisted the wounded sailor into the medbay, though his limbs were limp and difficult to manage. De Molay examined the severed foot, which was tightly bound in someone's shirt. The fabric was caked with blood. Her lips drew into a tight, pale line. "Has this man had treatment?" Her sharp gray eyes raked over each of them in turn.

"Only the tourniquet," the *Sho-i* said wearily. "I lost my medpack and trauma kit when we blew atmosphere. There were only the most minimal supplies on the shuttle. . . ."

"You're a medic, then?" De Molay took the opportunity to slide to the floor, breathing fast, and get her back to the wall. "Your name, please."

"*Hai, kyo.* I'm Ensign Galliand, *gun-i* from the *Falchion* and this is Gunner's Mate Tadohao."

"Well met, gentlemen," she said, then gestured weakly at the med closet controls. "Do what you can for him. . . ."

Galliand wiped his face, which was caked with soot and sweat, then began unsealing the injured man's z-suit. Tadohao joined in, holding the man steady. After a few moments, medpacks were secured to the damaged leg and their status lights were winking amber. The corpsman paused again, using some antiseptic towelettes from the bay to clean his hands and the rest of his face. Tadohao didn't seem to mind the grime, hunkering down beside De Molay with his head in his hands.

"I am Captain De Molay," the old woman said. "Your z-suits are severely damaged. The *Falchion* was destroyed?"

Galliand nodded. "She's gone, *kyo.* We were in the throughway between the forward magazines and the gundeck—Tado and I were clearing out some men wounded when one of the launch rails jammed with a sprint missile in the tube. No one noticed it had hung fire, and then the weapon blew—taking out the whole rail and an adjacent compartment. Then we got hit by something big and the throughway was engulfed in flame. The *Thai-i* dragged us out—I must have been unconscious for a bit—but we made it to a cargo shuttle." He shook his head, only just beginning to grasp what had happened. "Risen Christ, that was close!"

De Molay nodded, and then patted Tadohao on the shoulder. "*Joto-hei*, can you help an old woman stand up?"

Both men moved to assist her, and the freighter captain took a moment to look them over carefully.

"You need new z-suits. If you look through the cabins on this deck, you'll find something that fits—but hurry. *Sho-i*, I need you to prep this whole area for multiple injuries and the swiftest triage you can manage. I believe there are more paks for the cabinet in those bins down there. We will be recovering more evac capsules and who knows how many more wounded."

Galliand nodded and began stripping off his z-suit, which started to disintegrate as soon as he released the seal. De Molay dug in the pockets of her jacket, finding a threesquare. She broke the peanut-flavored ration bar in half, giving each of them a section.

"Now, *Sho-i*, I need Tadohao's help to get up to Command, but I will send him back to you as quick as I can. I am certain you'll have great use for him soon."

"*Hai, kyo!*" Both men nodded in agreement, chewing noisily. De Molay leaned heavily on the Iroquois *Joto-hei* and took a moment to get the worst of her hair tucked back and the Bulldog stowed inside her jacket. "Your *Thai-i* and my new XO need us, Tadohao, before they both need the medbay!"

Meanwhile, Hadeishi had managed to chivvy Tocoztic and the marine up to the tiny bridge, where they stared around uneasily. The Nisei could tell they were put off by the ancient-seeming equipment, the cramped quarters, and the grime apparent on often-used surfaces. *It takes time to see her noble heart,* Mitsuharu thought to himself. *For she is a willing steed, and does not complain of the load.*

"This is a small ship," he said aloud, drawing their attention back to him, "compared to your *Falchion*, but you will find her able. Do not underestimate the quality of the ship's fittings. Though not much to look upon, she is neither antique nor decayed. All critical components are in first-rate condition. I will wager they are the equal of anything found in the Fleet. *Thai-i.*" Hadeishi pointed to the pilot's chair with the muzzle of his shipgun. "Your duty station."

Expressionless, the México officer sat. Immediately he began wiggling around, trying to find a comfortable spot on the old, cracked leather.

"Marines?" Hadeishi tilted his head towards the little *Nitto-hei*, who—despite the Nisei's paltry height—was still shorter, though nearly as wide as the doorframe. "Cajeme, I believe?"

"*Hai, kyo.*" The marine clasped his hands behind his back for a moment, then—glancing sidelong at the lieutenant, who was grimacing at the Pilot's controls—offered Hadeishi a proper salute.

Mitsuharu returned the gesture, trying to keep from bursting into a wide smile. The little man's accent had confirmed his guess—*Out of the Atoyaatl Mayo, if my ear is still good.*

"What was your duty station, *Nitto-hei* Cajeme? Your badging reminds me of the engineers."

"This and that—*Chu-Sa.*" The Yaqui shrugged.

"You can be specific. I've been below-decks of late, plugging boilers and shoveling coal."

The marine drew himself up. "Repair hand first class, *kyo*."

Hadeishi nodded smartly. "There is much to do, *Nitto-hei*. If one of your fellows is able-bodied, round him up on the way to Engineering. I've shut off environmentals in nearly all the compartments, but we'll start flushing in atmosphere as you work. Khaiden dead go out the airlock—but strip their gear first, even z-suits if they are operable condition. We don't want to give up *anything* which might be useful later—guns, ammunition, identity packets, even shoes. Secure what you find along the main shipcore until someone can do inventory. If we are fortunate, there will soon be other hands to help you."

Mitsuharu tapped a printed map of the ship tacked up on the bridge hatch. "Medbay is one deck down from the roundabout outside, and to port-side."

Cajeme nodded, checked the equipment belt on his z-suit, accepted a spare hand-lamp, and double-timed out the hatch.

His immediate concerns addressed, Hadeishi turned his attention back to *Thai-i* Tocoztic, who had swung his pilot's chair around and was giving him a sullen, obstinate glare. The Nisei affected to ignore this, pointing with his chin at the navigational display. "Check the plot, *Thai-i*. There were twenty or thirty evac capsules within range of our sensors when last I looked. Route us to the nearest—but take care with our engine signature. We should be underway at the first opportunity, but we want no attention."

"I won't take your orders, civilian," Tocoztic declared, eyeing the shipgun angrily. "Certainly not under duress. Never at gunpoint!"

"I am not a civilian," Hadeishi said calmly, keying up

the internal surveillance cameras on the captain's console with his free hand. A mosaic of v-panes arranged themselves and he could see the wounded man was under care in the medbay. De Molay—and a helper—were on the move.

He then settled his grip on the shipgun and met the young México officer's eyes directly. "I am a Fleet reserve officer of superior rank," Mitsuharu said patiently. "Commanding this ship in a theater of war. Now that you are aboard, *Thai-i*, you will take my orders or I will consider you mutinous." He frowned at Tocoztic. "And I would be well within Regs to shoot you for a treacherous and disloyal dog if you continue to be obstinate."

The youth's face assumed a mulish expression. "You can't be a reserve officer—"

Mitsuharu reached into the document pocket of his z-suit and then paused; realizing he'd discarded every trace of his old life while languishing in Shinedo. He laughed softly. "I am—"

"Hadeishi, Mitsuharu; captain of the Imperial México Navy," croaked De Molay from the hatchway. Both men turned. The old woman was leaning heavily on *Joto-hei* Tadohao, but still had both feet under her. "Late of the IMN CL-341 *Henry R. Cornuelle*, discharged from active duty four months ago. Service ID 9874662. Decorated three times for valor under fire, credited with eleven capital-ship kills against Khaid, Megair, pirate, and Kroomākh opponents."

Wincing, De Molay slumped into the navigator's chair next to the lieutenant. "Here"—she said, rather breathless from the effort, tossing Tocoztic an identicard packet—"are his papers."

The *Thai-i* caught them, flinching as though from a water moccasin, and stared at the Fleet packet as though the snake itself were winding its coils around his hand. "A forgery—" he started to say.

"Read them!" De Molay growled, before leaning back in the chair with a relieved sigh. "I have—they are quite interesting. Particularly his duty jacket."

Tocoztic made a sour face, but began paging through the packet, brows furrowed over dark eyes. While the youth convinced himself, Hadeishi studied the mosaic of v-panes from the cameras. Cajeme had made his way halfway down the shipcore, taking apparent delight in stripping the Khaid bodies, but he was alone. Mitsuharu looked up, catching the old woman's eye.

"Another hand is needed with the cleanup. Can you spare your assistant, Captain?"

"Indeed. Thank you for your help, *Nitto-hei*." She crooked a finger at Hadeishi. "There's no point in wasting time making this gunner play pilot. I was a navigator in the old days; I can lay a plot for you better than he—with my own ship, no less!"

"He needs something to do, Captain, and he needs to be up here." *Where I can keep an eye on him*, went unsaid.

"Second seat then," sniffed De Molay. She made a puckered, terrible face, as though sucking on a salted tamarind. "You'll be useless yourself unless you've my spot—I knew it from the first."

"Well then," Mitsuharu said, settling himself into the captain's chair. "We are certainly overqualified on this watch, aren't we?"

De Molay nodded, head held high. Her fingers were not as quick on the controls as they once had been, but in a few moments the navigational displays were reconfigured into a pattern closely approximating those used by the Fleet. Hadeishi clapped his hands, unexpectedly pleased to have all of the v-panes, slide controls, and other mechanisms in their familiar places.

"Thank you," the old woman said, sketching a bow from her seat. "Now there's one thing more you're missing, I believe." She tapped through a series of obscure panes, hunting for *something*, and then, after changing this and that, the air forward of the captain's chair and behind the pilot and navigation stations shimmered with the distinctive heat-haze of a holocast projector. After several false starts, De Molay—frustrated by her inability to remember where the proper settings were—conjured up a threatwell. Not a large one, or as detailed as the data collection allowed by a warship, but a threatwell nonetheless.

"Excellent." Hadeishi smiled in thanks. Then he leaned forward a bit, studying the display, while rolling a stylus between the fingers of his left hand.

"How about this one? Not too far away," he said. "This heat signature implies a cooling plasma cloud, if the color coding is accurate."

"This analysis program is at least as good as anything you've ever worked with, *Chu-sa*." The old woman's voice was aggrieved. "But one lifeboat is as good as the next. Engaging drives on your mark."

"Underway then, Pilot."

The *Wilful*'s maneuver drive flared briefly, and then the secondary thrusters kicked in, reorienting the freighter. On their new heading, the little ship glided forward into the darkness, hurrying towards its next rescue.

THE *NANIWA*

Once the battle-cruiser had entered the Pinhole proper, Koshō was tempted to put on more speed. Unfortunately, only a thousand kilometers into the aperture the topology of the threads grew more complex, and she was forced to cut speed to three-quarters. This ended the brief respite from Khaiden bombardment. Fusion detonations began to flare around them, scattering the clouds of chaff which Konev and his crews had been liberally ejecting to mask their position. The scavenged remotes had been expended on their approach, so the *Naniwa* was back to her own resources.

The space-frame shook, rattling the consoles in Command, as a series of bomb-pods blew apart off their ventral quarter. The Khaid battleships were refining their firing solutions. Compartment alarms sounded, but Susan had no attention to spare for them.

"*Chu-sa*, we've about three hundred sixty sprint-class contacts incoming," Konev warned.

"Understood," Koshō gritted out through clenched teeth. She cast about in the topology rushing towards her, looking for a pocket she could lay the battle-cruiser into. Nothing sprang into view. . . .

"*Chu-sa!* We have to try and rescue the Prince!" Holloway had muted the comm channel, but his voice was near panic at the thought of abandoning the most superior officer he'd ever come into contact with.

"Sixty-five seconds to missile storm impact," Konev announced, his voice flat. The weapons officer's fingers were flying across his control surface. "All point-defense engaged."

"Weapons, rolling aspect in thirty-five seconds." *That'll bring the dorsal batteries into play.*

"*Hai, kyo!*"

Susan spared a glance for Holloway. "I won't lift a finger for the Prince, not if it places my crew and ship in danger—he won't be the first great lord of the México to die gloriously in battle." Koshō managed a tight, wintry grin as her fingers danced lightly on the control console. The threatwell was now fairly choked with gleaming strands of Barrier threads, yet the "passageway" had not completely closed. A fresh plume of the invisible razors now emerged from the chaotic storm on the sensors. The constant detonations of Khaid missiles were fouling the ship's perceptions, and the *Naniwa* had lost enough shipskin to seriously degrade her capabilities in the best of circumstances.

"Incoming!" The ship rolled aspect, jets of propellant erupting along her flanks. A second later the decking vibrated violently as the dorsal point-defense erupted—clouds of counter-missiles erupting from the launch racks; beam nacelles discharging, the smaller gun-pits hammering away with ballistic munitions. The Khaid missile cloud staggered, nearly two-thirds of the incoming birds shattered or knocked aside. Konev's spoofing pods and emitters whined into high-output, sending another sixth of the sprint missiles into electronic catatonia, or off into the void, chasing phantoms.

The dorsal armor took the rest head-on. Koshō felt the ship lurch, hammered by nearly a hundred impacts. Huge swathes of shipskin went dark, ruptured, and the damage control board—just visible off to her left—flared red along a jagged S-curve. The ship crabbed behind the plume of threads she'd picked out.

"*Chu-sa*, we're down to minimal load on the external batteries," Konev reported. "I've no shipkillers left on the rails and resupply is backed up. Magazines three, four, and seven are off-line."

The bridge was filled with a sea of beeping alarms and the tense chatter of damage control teams reporting in. Only Holloway was still turned towards her, finger pressed to his earbug, his face growing longer by the moment. The *Thai-i* shook his head. "*Chu-sa*, he orders you to retrieve the capsule."

"What does the Prince offer in return? What does he have to say to me?" Susan's voice was Kelvin-zero cold. Holloway flinched back, saying nothing.

"Konev," Koshō said levelly to her weapons officer,

"let the next wave of missiles break on this plume"—
her stylus indicated the formation—"don't engage them
with point-defense so far out. Be frugal—we're a long
way from a Fleet depot."

"*Hai, kyo!*" The Russian nodded, then tried to focus
on the threatwell. Susan turned back to the Pilot. "Well?"

"*Chu-sa*, I didn't tell him what you said!" Holloway
was obviously terrified at the prospect of bartering for
the life of a member of the Imperial household. Susan's
expression hardened. Holloway shook his head. "I cannot, *Chu-sa*."

At least he has enough gumption to say no to me.

"Very well." Furious, Koshō overrode the comm
channel from her console. A sharp close-up of the Prince
appeared on her holo. He had aged a little since the last
time she'd seen him. "Hello, Sayu, can I help you?"

"Yakka?" Xochitl grinned in a strained way. "Get me
out of here!"

"I'm sorry, did you say something?" Desperate to keep
her heading and velocity, Koshō finessed the *Naniwa*
around a spiral of filaments, and now the wreck of the
Tlemitl was dead ahead. She aimed the battle-cruiser a
quarter-point off, intending to slide directly over the shattered dreadnaught. "Did *you* ask *me* for help?"

"Yes," the Prince hissed. "*Please*, Yakka, slow down
and pick us up. I've got a capsule full of men."

"Do you?" Koshō kept her face impassive, throwing
in a little shrug for good measure. "Sycophants, bodyguards, a concubine or two . . . just like in school, eh?
I'm so sorry, Sayu, but *Regulations* are very clear—evac
capsules are recovered *after the battle is over.*"

"Yakka!" A glint of real fear was in his eyes. The
Prince licked his lips as he slumped back in his seat.
"What do you want? If you're going to tithe me, tell me
how much! Give me a chance."

"I'm not asking you for *anything*, Sayu. I'm just doing my duty." She finally let the tiniest fraction of old, old anger leak through into her expression. "Sit tight, and we'll be back for you after the—" Koshō stopped in mid-sentence. Behind the Prince, she suddenly caught sight of a familiar profile—sandy hair, a habitual hunch; the man's attention was far away, working some problem on a console—in the second chair.

Helsdon.

The Prince's eyes followed her gaze. "My engineer is reprogramming the sensor-suite here. To detect the weapon's knives, but our equipment is not—"

"One moment."

Susan closed the channel with a fierce, sharp motion. "Pilot, assume maneuvering on my mark—three—two—one. Hold current course for the next eighteen seconds." She ignored Konev's curious stare and whipped through the personnel manifests of the ships reported on station. Helsdon's record popped up a moment later. She skipped through a lengthy entry detailing his assignment to the *Calexico* and his ordeal in the wreck. *One of my old Cornuelles is in trouble. That, I will not have.*

"Recovery crews, stand by," Koshō announced abruptly. "All stations—we're slowing to one-quarter speed. Damage control crews, stand by. Prepare for missile impacts! *Socho* Juarez—get down to the forward boat-bay with a medical crew and an honor guard. Now!"

A flurry of acknowledgments came back to her, settling on her shoulders and in her heart like evil crows. Relieved of having to fly the ship for a moment, Susan sank into her combat chair, her heart filled with great foreboding. *If Naniwa is lost because of him—if even one of my men dies on his account—there will be no death evil enough for this cursed Prince.*

Just forward of the command chair, Gretchen suddenly roused herself, straightening up as though from a deep sleep, and looked around, blearily aware of an immediate world of physical things she could touch and feel once more. Her whole body was buzzing, as though millions of tiny golden bees were dancing just beneath her skin. "We're stopping?"

"We're slowing, but don't let the navigational updates stop," Koshō replied. There was a surly edge to her voice. "We're taking aboard survivors from the flagship. As soon as they're secured, we'll have to press on." She considered the threatwell, seeing that the latest Khaid barrage had outlined the thread-veil in spectacular manner. But beyond the illusion of safety, the enemy was in motion.

Gretchen frowned, memories of the immediate past finally forcing themselves past the brilliant geometries which had filled her sight, informed her hearing, and ordered her thoughts. "You called him *hot water*?"

The corner of Susan's mouth twitched. Her eyes slid sideways, checking to see if anyone was standing close, then she said: "On the Hill of Grasshoppers, Old Chapultepec, you could not keep your child's name, and you could not yet take an adult name. So the Sisters chose one for you. Randomly, they said, but they always picked ones which fit—or we grew to fit them, I suppose. He was *sayu*—water almost boiling, hot enough to scald—and they called me *yakka*, which is—"

"—annoying little girl." Gretchen finished with a grimace. Her head was throbbing. She groped for her medband, mashing the override glyph, hoping for a flood of cool relief.

"Or in a gruesome tale my grandmother was fond of telling on stormy nights, a goblin."

THE WILFUL

From a discreet vantage inside a cloud of radioactive debris leaking from one of the broken Khaid destroyers, the little freighter waited to see if the raiders would dare to cross the Barrier in force. Hadeishi watched the situation unfolding on their jimmied-up holocast with interest, forefinger smoothing his ragged mustache. The Khaid squadron had resorted to pitching missiles one at a time into the Pinhole.

"They're stuck," Tocoztic offered, looking up from the Fleet identity packet. "They'll never get anywhere that way."

Mitsuharu raised an eyebrow. "In comparison to the Khaid commanders I've encountered before, *Thai-i*, this one is the very model of a modern naval officer. He is circumspect, wary, and mindful of the resources he has to hand—which are greatly reduced from considerable strength."

"We would do no better, Lieutenant," De Molay remarked, only her eyes visible above a pile of blankets Tadohao had brought up from the living quarters. "They—my sources—say the guardians of this place are like whipping knives, and they move from place to place, unaccountably."

"Interesting." Hadeishi looked across the darkened bridge at the old woman. "Perhaps their pattern mimics the changing currents of some ancient sea. And the dreadful weapons drift like shoals of kelp on an unseen, ethereal wind."

"Or schools of stinging jellyfish, O poet," De Molay retorted. She was tired and cold, despite the blankets. "Dare we continue with your good work while they are fishing?"

"Not yet. They are in motion again." As they watched on the holocast, the Khaid squadron began a maneuvering burn. Soon the majority of ships withdrew from the area around the Pinhole entrance. The lighter vessels that remained began quartering the area of battle, apparently recovering survivors. "They will not go far. They *know* something valuable is here—even if they do not comprehend what that might be."

Mitsuharu looked expectantly at the old woman. "Do *we* know, Captain?"

De Molay avoided his eyes, taking a long drink of hot tea. "These raiders seem to have come out of nowhere. What do you suppose brought them here in such numbers? And at just the right moment to encounter and destroy so many Imperial ships?"

Hadeishi's lips twitched, closely observing De Molay. "Why—it could only be treachery, Captain. But now— they know there is a prize to be won, as well, and I do not think they will wish to give it up." He lifted his hand, palm up. "The Khaiden *Kabil Rezei* commanding this hunting pack has paid a dear price—he will want payment in kind. And this—weapon—if it is such, would make him more than a chieftain—it would make him king, or emperor."

"I doubt they have the means to mount a long campaign." The old woman made a circular gesture, encompassing the whole of the *kuub*. "It's very expensive to field three squadrons in this wasteland, no matter how rich you are." Then she peered curiously at Tocoztic, who had made a strangled noise in reaction to something he was reading.

"The prize is too great," Mitsuharu replied. "When you are a pirate, the taking of even one treasure ship can secure your clan for a lifetime. If left alone indefinitely, these Khaiden *will* find a way, even if they have to bargain with Mictlantecuhtli himself and take his skull and meatless bones for their own."

"A cheerful assessment." De Molay gulped the rest of her tea and indicated the holocast. "Now only two remain."

Hadeishi leaned forward, tapping through the various sensor logs and displays. Neither ship matched anything in the commercial registry, but then he suspected these were a brand-new class, quite possibly the first the clans built and fielded themselves. *They're surely not stolen from us, not with those drive signatures and hull outlines. And they don't look like anything the Kroomākh would build—they would be the most likely power to sell the Khaid some heavy metal.*

"Battleships—probably the least damaged," he said at last.

De Molay shrugged. "If they remain near the station wreckage, then we will know they are playing watchdog. After all, any ship that exits might reveal the gap in the Barrier."

"And would be attacked." Hadeishi thought of the lone battle-cruiser they'd seen escape on long-range scan. That ship had vanished into seemingly clear space, by which he assumed the weapon was actually blocking passive scan on some level. *There is a hidden pocket here, tucked away inside this wall of knives.* "Against these Khaid we need at least a heavy cruiser. Anything less will only buy us tea in Yomi. *Thai-i* Tocoztic, switch your panel to run sensor analysis. We must be about our business."

The *Thai-i* pushed Mitsuharu's identity papers away with a scowl. "You lost your ship!" he said in an accusing voice. "You were discharged from service by the court of review! And you still—"

De Molay glared at the pilot, but Hadeishi's rueful laugh cut him short.

"You were aboard the *Falchion*, *Thai-i*?" Mitsuharu gave the young man his full attention.

Tocoztic nodded stubbornly. "What does that—"

Hadeishi drifted his hand across the holocast controls. A section of nearby space expanded, revealing the scattered wreckage of a heavy cruiser. "There she lies," he said sadly, grief plain in his voice. "A fine ship, now gone to destiny, to die in the service of our lord. . . . I fear, *Thai-i*, you are the last of her officers to survive." Mitsuharu fixed him with a steady, unnerving stare. "Have I done you disservice, by saving you and your men from death? Did you wish to join your ship, your *Chu-sa*, your fellows in final repose, in this funereal pyre of cooling plasma? That is a noble end."

"No!" Tocoztic drew back, horrified. "A useless death—"

"And there you have my own desperate strait," Hadeishi said quietly. "My ship died—as yours has done— yet I lived. Do you know the *Hagakure* of Tsunemoto?"

"Of course," the *Thai-i* replied huffily. "It is required reading in the Academy. . . ."

"Have you hit your target?"

Tocoztic frowned, not grasping the reference. "I do not—It is an old text. Written by one long dead. How do those legends apply here?"

Mitsuharu nodded. "An excellent question. Tsunemoto relates the words of a vain young samurai: 'If you die before striking your enemy, then you die the death of a dog.' Many believed this to be a truth, and thereby found cause to avoid battle, to avoid sacrifice, to avoid risk. What did Tsunemoto say to those men?"

Tocoztic's face turned a rather mealy color. "I am México. I am not afraid of death. I am an officer and sworn to sacrifice my life for the Emperor."

"He said: If you put death foremost in your thoughts, if you resolve yourself to death each time you wake, then you will always strike your enemy with the utmost force."

"To embrace death so readily! I don't—This has nothing to do with—"

Hadeishi's face suddenly became calm and still, as though the grief and weariness and fear etched in his features had been washed away by a sudden, unseen rain. His eyes were upon the holocast, looking far beyond the puzzled face of the *Thai-i*. De Molay's attention snapped around, following his gaze.

"Stand to battle stations!"

Before the command was fully uttered, De Molay had activated the ship's internal alarm. Tocoztic jumped, startled by the blaring sound, and then switched all his attention onto the pilot's console. Thousands of hours of Imperial drill seized him up and put his hands, his thoughts, his entire purpose on the right path.

At the limit of their sensor range, a Khaid destroyer nosed through the dark towards them.

THE LAND OF THE DEAD

The *Naniwa's* acceleration faded off a point, and under Koshō's gentle direction, the battle-cruiser slid around a particularly dense accretion of the veils. Beyond this—to her surprise—there was nothing on the navigational display. No queer, interlocking geometry of billions of infinitesimal razors, only emptiness. The *Chu-sa* blinked, easing off on the engines, dropping her acceleration to almost zero. The ship continued to speed ahead, but she left her velocity undiminished.

"I think we're clear," Anderssen announced to a hushed bridge crew. She took her hands away from the corroded bronze rectangle. As she did the threatwell's sketchy, alien display faded away—showing only a few trailing quantum distortions at the edges—and then, nothing. The normal navigational plot flickered in and out of view, and then stabilized. A moment later, keyed up by *Chu-i* Pucatli, the long-distance camera feeds appeared on the main v-displays behind the threatwell.

There was a hiss of surprise from nearly every member of the bridge crew. Susan smoothed back her hair and then turned to the communications officer. "*Chu-i*, pipe this to all of the news displays shipside. I'll make an announcement momentarily."

Then the *Chu-sa* turned to consider the long-range scan display now building on her console.

The plot confirmed what the eye beheld. Beyond the Barrier, deep at the heart of the *kuub*, the protostellar debris folded back to reveal three diminutive stars in a tight cluster. Between their sallow pinpoints, the hard white slash of an ejection jet speared "up" and "down," bisecting the visible universe. Illuminated by its radiance, towering plumes and great walls of dust glowed with a brilliant, jeweled fire. If the gravity scan was to be believed, the rosette of stars concealed an infinitesimal black hole in their center. On the ship's plot, the gaudy roil of an accretion disc spiraling into a maelstrom of distorted gravity reached out to lap around the suns. The dim stars were shedding long sinuous trails of mass, drawn down into the hidden maw of the singularity.

The sound of the main bridge hatch cycling open was jarringly loud in the silence.

Koshō looked over her shoulder, seeing an exhausted and work-stained Oc Chac limp onto the bridge. His combat armor—a necessity for engineers working in the midst of battle—was scored with dozens of impact dimples on the battle-steel. The Mayan's face was uncharacteristically open, his lips parted, the muted glare of glowing night reflecting in his eyes.

"Mictlan," the *Sho-sa* sighed. "Beneath the cold lands of the north from whence Quetzalcoatl retrieved the bones of the first people, a tomb filled with decay and rivers of ash, where reigns the dreadful god Mictlan-tecuhtli, his face covered with a bony mask, sitting amongst owls and spiders, ruling the land of the dead: The destination an unfortunate corpse must strive towards for four long years: first through a whirlwind of knives, then against icy winds, daring all the dangers of the underworlds, at last to cross nine waters and dissolve into the void. A dreadful place where the living dare not tread. . . ."

"Approximately three light-years from us—three superjovian brown dwarfs in perfect balance," Susan said quietly, fingernails brushing across the navigational plot. The images tightened, zooming in. Her med-band was pulsing, flooding her with stimulants to keep onrushing fatigue from overwhelming her mind. The tension of battle and headlong flight was beginning to fade, leaving her entire body throbbing with pain. "And a singularity at their center, drinking their mass like blood."

At the navigational console, Gretchen stirred—tearing herself away from the wonder resplendent before them—and looked back to Koshō. The civilian's face was fairly glowing with desire.

"No." Koshō's eyes were half-lidded, but her voice was firm. "We'll be going no closer. Pilot, find us somewhere to lie up and rest the crew. We'll repair what we can, and then we'll move a goodly distance away from the Pinhole and see if we can reach gradient. . . . Yes, *Sho-sa*?"

Oc Chac had moved to Holloway's station at Nav and was shaking his head. "Even when repairs are complete, *Chu-sa*, and the coil is back in operation . . .

Gravitometric readings around us are off the scale—we've passed over some kind of equilibrium point, where the curve of physical space has inverted—we can't make transit out of this . . . this *pocket*. That inversion is forcing gradient well beyond ships' capacity to punch through into hyper."

Susan suppressed a curse. "What about inside the pocket? Can we reach superluminal *here*?"

"Perhaps." The Mayan adjusted the scan controls on the navigational console. "We'll need to move deeper in—see if gradient slopes off abruptly." He turned back to Koshō, jaw clenched. "It may be, *kyo*, that the pinhole we've slipped through has taken us into a captive universe."

"What do you mean?" Susan felt the tide of cold reach her sinuses, which abruptly made her head feel both light, empty, and clear. The engineer's statement hung before her, seemingly profound, but also beyond practical reach. "What does that mean to us, *Sho-sa*?"

"It means, *kyo*," Oc Chac said, considering his words carefully, "that *here* we may be able to punch through to hyperspace—but we won't have anywhere to *go*. The Barrier itself may be wrapping gravity—and the core fabric of realspace—back around to the other side of the pocket. Indeed, if we traveled the six light-year-width of this place from end to end, we may well wind up at our starting point."

Holloway—who seemed as confused as Susan—scratched the back of his head, then said: "But there's a break in the fabric, right, because we just came through from the 'outside.' So the only way out, would be right back the way we came—and into the waiting claws of that Khaid battle-group."

The Mayan shrugged. "*Thai-i*, such may be our fate." He lifted his chin, giving Koshō a questioning look. "Hennig's crews are ready to tear into the coil and replace those damaged cells—if we're done maneuvering at high-g for a couple hours."

Koshō nodded. "Get to it, *Sho-sa*. Keep the duty officer informed of your progress and estimated time to complete. As soon as we can find somewhere to lie up, we'll go off battle-stations."

Gretchen stirred expectantly, her parchment-wrapped block tucked under one arm. The Swedish woman looked ghastly—her face was a sallow frame for enormous, fatigue-blackened eyes—but she was still game to plunge ahead into the unknown, seeking the thrill of first-light shining upon something lost eons ago.

"I said *no*." Susan eased herself out of the shockchair, feeling every muscle and bone throb violently. "*Thai-i* Holloway, we need to get third watch on duty stations and send everyone else to the showers. Myself included. Chac is busy, and you and Konev are due for a break, so see if *Thai-i* Goroemon survived the last sixteen hours and get her up here to stand in as officer of the watch."

"*Hai, kyo!*"

Stiff beyond measure, Koshō limped through a slow circuit of Command, checking in with each duty station. As she approached Comm, Pucatli popped up with his hand extended. The young México was holding a glass vial filled with a pale rose-colored fluid. "For you, *Chu-sa*."

Susan frowned. "An antibiotic?"

"No, no, *Chu-sa*." Pucatli grimaced. "Those are poison! What's bad for microbes can only be bad for people. This is a tincture for the weary, made from the root and flowers of *chunuli* plants in my mother's garden. Mix it with very hot water and partake gently."

Drink it with sayu? Susan converted the near-hysterical laugh that rose in her throat to a polite nod. "Thank you for the kind thought, *Chu-i*."

THE WILFUL

The Khaid destroyer—another classified as *Neshter*-class by the commercial registry, though Mitsuharu's practiced eye had already picked out a number of differences between this ship and the *Qalak*—loomed in the threatwell, its icon surrounded by a constellation of informative graphics.

"Launch signature," Tocoztic announced suddenly, his voice tight. "Looks like a one-rail sprint missile." In the 'well, a glowing streak appeared, following the track of the weapon. "Vectors do not overlap."

Hadeishi had already seen the target and his face stiffened in fury.

"An evac capsule," De Molay said, a moment later. "We picked up their signal about an hour ago."

"As did the Khaid," Mitsuharu bit out with difficulty. "They haven't a chance."

The missile icon intersected the capsule's graphic and both winked out. A quarter-second later, a tiny bright flare appeared on one of the camera displays, and then faded away. Against the slow roil of the dust clouds—all ruddy red, purple, and orange luminescence—the explosion went almost unnoticed.

Hadeishi was motionless, his face in shadow on the darkened bridge, staring at the 'well. *And I was unable to do even the slightest thing to save the men aboard.*

"She's turning," the *Thai-i* announced into the silence. "We have—we have vector overlap if they hold course."

The Nisei stirred, forcing his attention back to the 'well and the movement of ships, wreckage, anything else which might affect his tiny command. He rewound the 'well through the last three hours of data, the myriad icons a blur of motion. "They're into the return leg of their patrol pattern."

He clicked his teeth, seeing that the intercept solution was very poor for the *Wilful*. "We're going to have to go to zero-power and lose steering way, hope they pass over us as wreckage. We're too close to—"

Tocoztic gave him a sick look. "They're sure to catch us on active scan—we're not Imperial, we're not Khaid—they will *know* we're a scavenger that didn't get caught up in the battle. That fate"—he stabbed a finger at the location of the obliterated capsule—"will be ours!"

"Going dark," De Molay announced, when Hadeishi failed to respond immediately. Her face drew tight with concentration and Mitsuharu could see that another set of v-panes had appeared on her console. The markings—and he could not see them clearly from his vantage point—did not seem to be formed of human letters.

"Hostile is less than a light-second away," Tocoztic breathed, sounding anguished. "She's accelerating. We're getting side scatter from an active scanning array—"

"There!" The old woman sighed in relief. "Memory still holds true!"

At the same moment, the *Wilful*'s engines died and the lights dimmed markedly. The constant vibration of the reactor drew down, and then entirely faded away. Hadeishi watched with intense interest as each on-board system shut down in swift succession. On his console, the myriad v-panes and controls faded away—the threat-well went dark—and the environmental monitors indicated that every compartment had dialed down air circulation and scrubber activity to the absolute minimum. The only activity registered on the shipskin, which was assuming a new aspect—one that Mitsuharu had never seen before. Part of the forward hull was visible in the camera display, which was still active, and there he saw that the hull had deformed into a strange, "fuzzy" configuration, the surface extruding millions of what appeared in close-up to be tiny matte-black cilia.

Truly we have turned into a creature of the abyss!

He gave De Molay a curious glance. "We're in an absorptive mode?" he asked quietly.

"We are," she replied with the hint of a smile. Hadei-shi hid his reaction, suddenly mindful of Tocoztic and the other Fleet ratings who might be listening down deck. *There's no heat sump on this ship capable of absorbing the impact radiation on the skin. Nothing big enough to swallow our own emissions, not for more than a few seconds. So—what lies behind those closed-off compartments on the Engineering deck? Something to hide us completely?*

The thought gave him a chill down the back of his neck.

"Here it comes," the *Thai-i* breathed, "we'll have visual in—"

The Khaid destroyer emerged from a screen of stellar dust, black bulk dwarfing the *Wilful*, flanks etched with the landing lights outlining her boat-bay doors. On the camera display, Mitsuharu could make out rows of launcher hard-points, the shallow pits of particle beam emitters and point-defense guns. The hypercoil ring to aft and the maneuver drives were arranged in an unfamiliar pattern, but close up the Nisei could guess at her manufacturer. *A refitted Megair Vampyre-class light cruiser. Interesting—the Khaid Zosen must have bought her as a hulk and replaced all of the internal systems— the Khaiden body form doesn't fit very well to the arthropod. Those drives look new, too.*

Regardless of her provenance, the destroyer sailed on past, showing every sign of being unaware of their presence. Tocoztic stared at his console, stylus busily tapping away. He checked and double-checked the paltry stream of data available. "Their active scan is pinging right over us!" he whispered loudly.

Suddenly Hadeishi had to suppress a full-on grin; not a proper hint of a smile or a careful mask of command, but a fierce, predatory snarl.

The Khaid rolled on past, and the *Wilful* shuddered a little as the wash of radiation from her engines pelted the shipskin. Mitsuharu, properly somber again, paid close attention to the status displays from the hull configuration. *What excellent engineering,* he thought. *The emission wave from the enemy radar failed to spike our surface temperature. The drive wake has been absorbed as well. But . . . how could shipskin cool to relative zero so fast?*

The Nisei sat back, nearly overcome with wonder. Then he noticed that the subsonic vibration of the reactor interface had soared up, almost to an audible level. He looked to De Molay in concern, but the old woman just shook her head minutely. Her gray eyes rested steadily on him. For the first time in a long time, Mitsuharu felt nervous, jumpy. *A tramp freighter, eh? I am six kinds of a fool.*

Tocoztic squirmed in his chair, looking around curiously at the walls. "What's that weird vibration?"

"Engine phase-transition, *Thai-i.* Every ship has its own quirks and noises," Hadeishi replied with deliberate calm as he reviewed his console again. *Power output is up 300 percent. But—we're not leaking heat, the internal temperature is actually cooling. . . .* The reason was obvious, but Mitsuharu was having a hard time believing the data before him. *Every engineer in the Empire would fall on his sword to bring this secret home. Someone has developed an effective thermodynamic shunt. And it's working and it's on this ship, on my ship.*

"*Thai-i* Tocoztic, eyes on your console, mind on the mission." Hadeishi's voice was sharp, ringing with hidden elation. The tone gained the younger officer's complete attention. "Pilot De Molay, plot a course for the next surviving evac capsule. We still have work to do, even if the Khaid are careless and blind. The next patrol ship may be more attentive."

"*Hai, Chu-sa!*"

Hadeishi felt something tight in his chest release at the long-familiar words: *Ah, now my heart is beating again!*

THE *NANIWA*

The last of the officers and ratings who'd ridden through the Pinhole had crawled off to their bunks by the time *Thai-i* Goroemon managed to reach Command. Koshō was still in her shockchair, reviewing the telemetry captured by shipnet during their passage, looking for somewhere to hide her battered ship.

"*Chu-sa?* Holloway-*tzin* said you needed me to stand officer of the watch?"

"I do, *Thai-i*. I am very glad you survived. Can you handle another eight hours awake?"

Goro shrugged, broad shoulders stretching the gel of her z-suit. "Hard to sleep with all the racket, *kyo*—but we didn't get hit too hard down in the Backbone. Two magazine conveyors went down due to jams, but nothing punched past into the inner hull where we were."

The lieutenant rarely stood a Command watch, though she was technically fifth on the roster. Her usual duty station was in the munitions roundhouse controlling the network of high-speed magnetic railways threading between the primary and secondary hulls of the battle-cruiser. The *Naniwa*'s main magazines were spaced along the shipcore itself, as far from hostile fire as possible, while a network of secondary—or "ready"—depots served each hard-point, launch-rail, or gun-pit. Managing the Backbone ammunition network was third in complexity among the ship's systems, behind the engines and shipskin.

"How soon will we be reloaded?" Susan asked, frustrated with herself that she hadn't already checked in with logistics.

"Another hour, *kyo*, and we'll have all the conveyors back in operation," Goro replied. "*Kikan-cho* Hennig's men have both of the jammed ones torn apart right now. He said there's some fabrication problem with the pass-along sensors, so they're getting pulled, hand-tested, and replaced as needed."

"Better than I expected." Koshō was pleased. For a ship so fresh from the yards, the *Naniwa* had experienced very few outright component failures. "What I need you to do, *Thai-i*, is—"

She turned to the navigational plot shipnet had pieced together from data recorded during their passage. Oddly, the changes made to the navigational interfaces—and to the threatwell and other Command systems—when Anderssen had taken them over, had all reverted to their Fleet-standard configurations. Even the massive rush of topology information which had allowed Susan to navigate through the Pinhole had purged itself. Only second-by-second Command camera images of the threatwell remained, but from them shipnet had reverse-engineered a model of their exit point and the surrounding area.

"—find us a place to lie up while all immediate repairs are completed. We've moved into a peculiar area of space—one without charts, and which may obey different physical laws than we're used to—so I don't want to rush about until we've laid down a tight nav plot. But here"—Koshō indicated a convoluted set of folds in the nearest dust clouds—"is a region free of the Barrier threads, and excited and dense enough we may be masked from passive sensors if someone comes along, banging on the temple-wall with a stick. Drop a remote to watch the Pinhole for us, and then move the *Naniwa* in there and go to zero-v. The engines need maintenance as well—we've taken enough dings, dents, and outright punctures to warrant a thorough inspection."

"*Hai, kyo.*" Goro covered a yawn with her salute and settled herself gingerly in the command chair.

Susan looked around the bridge one last time, saw that Anderssen had already been taken away, nodded to herself, and strode off to find her own cabin.

A monofilament saw shrieked, cutting away at the airlock on a badly battered evac capsule. Two burly engineers, their combat armor awash in a flood of sparks, were sawing away the last of the hinges holding the hatch closed. The portal itself was badly scarred and had been slightly twisted in the framing socket by some massive impact. The evac capsule had fared no better—carbon-scoring had turned nearly the entire surface black and the view ports were milky with tiny fissures. Another crew of engineers were dragging away a couple hundred meters of high-v cargo netting—the net *Thai-i* Holloway had arranged to snatch up the capsule at speed, while the *Naniwa* barreled past in the Pinhole—though its landing in boat-bay one had been . . . rougher . . . than the navigator intended.

"Clear!" barked the *Joto-Heiso* bossing the team of engineers. He stepped back, swinging the saw up onto his shoulder. Hot hexacarbon fragments littered the deck, filling the air of the cargo bay with thick spirals of smoke. "Get 'er open."

The hatch squealed as pry bars dug in around the

periphery, then popped free with a *ting!* Four of the *Joto-hei* on hand seized hold with magnetic grapples and wrestled the enormously heavy block of battle-steel, hexacarbon, and glassite onto a waiting grav-sled. As soon as the portal was removed, there was movement inside the capsule and two battered-looking Jaguar Knights emerged, shipguns at the ready. The *Joto-Heiso* stood his ground, unsuccessfully hiding a sneer behind a thick walruslike mustache. "Muddies," he muttered under his breath to the engineers standing behind him.

"Xochitl-*tecuhtzintli*, welcome." *Heisocho* Von Bayern was waiting for the next man to emerge. Prince Xochitl stamped out, his armor streaked with vomit and stippled with fresh dents. The México lord's face—his helmet was now canted back—was glacial with fury, his dark eyes flashing dangerously. One of his high, chiseled cheekbones had acquired a dark, purpling bruise. The Diplomatic Service warrant officer bowed appropriately, and then saluted sharply. "*Gensui* on deck," he barked.

A dozen meters back, *Socho* Juarez and the full remaining complement of marines aboard the battle-cruiser stamped their right feet in unison, presented arms— they'd scrambled to unpack their Macana assault rifles— and then held rigid while the cruiser's piper wailed through the Imperial March.

Xochitl stared at the welcoming committee, his expression congealing into something very much like icy mud. Nothing about the reception was in the least irregular, though rousting out a piper for the March was generally falling from fashion. Von Bayern offered the Prince a gracious smile, hands clasped behind his back, until the drone of the bagpipes had ceased.

"My lord, I hope you will accept our apologies for detaining you and your crew within your evac capsule during transit. Your physical safety is of tremendous concern to *Chu-sa* Koshō. And . . . here are the medics."

A pair of corpsmen had arrived with orderlies and stretchers. They immediately climbed in through the mangled airlock to help out the men still inside the capsule. The first to emerge was the hulking, seven-foot-high shape of the alien, in its unfamiliar armor. The marines and engineers stiffened, hands going to personal weapons. The creature looked around; head tilted back a little, and then saw the Prince. Xochitl looked back to the warrant officer.

"Take me to the *Chu-sa* immediately. Quarters for my men can wait. I will not. This one"—he pointed to Sahâne—"send to whatever cabin is reserved for *me*. I will take something else, anything else."

Von Bayern nodded amiably, apparently unaffected by the fury radiating from the Prince like a furnace draft. "Of course, my lord Prince, our transport is standing by." He gestured to a nearby grav-sled—a regular cargo carrier which had a pair of bench-seats bolted on and draped with fabric in colors approximating the Imperial eagle crest. Xochitl shook his head, now beyond words, and climbed aboard.

As the grav-sled whined away, one of the corpsmen helped Helsdon out of the capsule, supporting his shoulder. The engineer looked ghastly, but was able to keep his head up as they loaded him onto a stretcher. The *Joto-Heiso* from the work crew was waiting with a flask, along with Juarez and four of the marines.

"Welcome aboard, *kyo*. The *Chu-sa* says you're straight to a spare cabin and twenty, thirty hours of sleep." The engineer flashed a broken-toothed smile behind his white mustache, pressing the flask into Malcolm's hands. "Here, this'll set you right. She sent it down. A twenty-year malt *uisge-beatha*—like velvet!"

Helsdon laid his head back on a pillow, puzzlement pushing aside his exhaustion for a moment. "Who—who sent this?"

"*Chu-sa* Susan Koshō, Engineer." Juarez patted him gently on the shoulder, and then motioned for the marines to escort him away. "Welcome aboard the *Naniwa*. The captain apologizes for keeping you in the can so long, but there wasn't time to peel you out properly until now."

All Gretchen could see was corridor roof, gleaming with overheads, and occasionally the superstructure of a hatchway as the grav-stretcher zipped along. A corpsman was jogging along beside her, though she could hear his voice only intermittently. Her left arm was throbbing with tremendous pain hidden behind a wall of meds, and now the rest of her had seemingly converted into an enormous ache. *At least the bees are gone,* she thought blearily. Her skin had settled down, which was a mercy. Whatever had happened when her hands had been on the corroded bronze block seemed to have faded, leaving only a faint golden tinge at the edges of her vision.

The stretcher whisked through a double-wide hatchway, and she was suddenly enveloped by the smell of antiseptics, blood, and urine. A face appeared above her—a junior medical officer, his lean visage spotted with crimson, his eyes hollow with sixteen hours on watch. Despite his appearance, however, he flashed a cheerful smile and palpated her arm. His touch made everything whirl around her like a sudden *tchindi* and someone, somewhere, groaned aloud in terrible pain.

"This temporary block is shot," a voice said. "Load her up and knock her out. Back to room eight for her, with the old—"

There wasn't even a needle-prick, just sudden sleepiness and then . . . nothing at all.

The orderly guided the stretcher into the second base station in the assigned room, confirmed the med-interlocks were set and showing green on their little status panel, then covered Anderssen with a blanket and adjusted the pillow under her head. Given the possibility that the g-decking might fail if combat resumed, he strapped her down and lowered a protective glassite shroud from the ceiling. Then, given he was in the room, the medic raised a similar covering over the old Náhuatl man in the next bed and tested his retinal responsiveness with a hand-light.

"Nothing," muttered the orderly, shaking his head in dismay. "Facial pallor, weak and thready breath, heart arrhythmia . . . grandfather is in poor condition." He charted the necessary notes with his stylus, then turned out the lights and closed the door behind him.

Once the room was dark and empty, however, Green Hummingbird let out a long, slow breath, and then wiggled his fingers and toes. After a moment to let his body stabilize, the old man turned his head sideways, looking at Gretchen's supine form in the next bed. His forehead creased with worry, wrinkles drawing up at the corners of his mouth and eyes. Deftly, he worked an arm free of the restraints, and then raised the shroud himself. The monitoring panel on the stretcher beeped questioningly, to which the *nauallis* responded by keying an override into the machine.

With his bed showing nothing but green status lights, Hummingbird padded to Anderssen's shroud, raised the cover, and then drifted his right hand over her face, forehead, shoulders, and then down the length of her body. He was careful not to touch her skin or the fabric of her shirt or trousers. Instead, eyes half-lidded, he seemed to be feeling for something perceptible only a centimeter or less from her body.

"Hsss . . . that was near too much for you, child." He

frowned, green eyes dark with worry. His gnarled old hands had paused over her wrists, where there was a sensation of terrific heat. So, too, at her clavicles and the right side of her face. This was apparently unexpected, for Hummingbird drifted his hands away from each location and then back again several times.

Still frowning, his lips tight with concern, the *nauallis* opened the stowage bin under the stretcher and drew out the parchment envelope holding the bronze-colored block from Gretchen's jacket. Curious, he examined the device carefully—but could see no signs of change or transformation in the corroded metal. Shaking his head, he put everything back where he'd found it, closed Anderssen's shroud, and then crawled back into his own bed. This time, before strapping himself down and closing the glassite cover, he made sure both earbugs were inserted and responding, then yawned mightily—activating his dropwire—and pressed a fingertip into the cavities beneath either side of his jaw, turning on his throatmike.

Immediately, his earbugs filled with interesting chatter. As he lay motionless, his heart slowing, diagrams and images began to play out on the inside of his eyelids. One of his search *dorei* active in the v-network stitched through the fabric of the battle-cruiser was waiting with a video feed—complete with sound. Prince Xochitl had been shown into *Chu-sa* Koshō's private quarters.

The México lord stared around obstinately at the subdued colors and simple, even spartan furniture that Susan maintained in her suite of rooms. Koshō was sitting at her desk, the collar of her uniform undone and her jacket hung on the back of a chair which swiveled out from the wall. She seemed entirely unimpressed by his battered appearance and lank hair. He, in turn, could not help but see the *Chu-sa* was worn almost to the point of exhaustion. And that, somehow, she had aged during the past ten years, becoming a formidable-looking woman with more than a passing resemblance to her maternal grandmother.

"I'm the ranking officer here," Xochitl growled, trying to summon an authoritative snap in his voice.

"Then you'll be on the secondary bridge," Koshō replied evenly, not even bothering to look up from her personal comp. "As befits the *Gensui* commanding the battle group. My apologies—we are not fitted with a flag bridge. Be aware, *Tlatocapilli*, that *I* will remain in command of *my* ship and all operational matters at all times."

"You will follow *my* orders!" Xochitl responded, outraged.

"Only if they exhibit a shred of sense." Susan turned, looking him up and down with a measuring eye. The Prince stiffened, not used to such judgmental scrutiny, or the sensation that he had been found wanting.

"Right now," Koshō continued, her voice harsh with exhaustion, "there is only *one* thing to do—get out of here as quickly as possible. We're in no shape to deal with the Khaid, much less the powers which might dwell in this benighted sinkhole. My ship has been hammered up one side and down the other, our magazines are low, we've battle damage in every department and almost every section. Do you honestly think we can do *anything* here, other than blunder into another defensive system and make a quick exit to Mictlan?"

Xochitl started to speak, and then paused, his attention drawn away, listening to some voice only he was privy to. Then, with a sharp, deep breath he stepped back and rubbed his brow fiercely. Beads of sweat glistened at his temples.

"No," the Prince said, having collected himself.

"You're right. Without our science teams and the support ships, we have no way . . ." He paused, seeming to look inward again. "Thrice-cursed Huss and his league of devils! I am a fool and fool's fool." Xochitl glared at Susan, eyebrows drawn together as his whole face transformed into a furious mask. He ground a fist his palm. "*Someone* brought the Khaid down on us, didn't they? The raiders haven't been reported operating in this area before."

"No." Koshō's lips twitched and she clasped her hands. "Not in the last ten years of working the Rim. Someone was expecting *you*—Lord Prince, or someone like you—to come along."

"You make that title sound positively dirty," Xochitl jested weakly, trying to summon even a spark of his usual ebullience. The anger had already faded from him, leaving only a pensive weariness. He groped for a chair, found a low-cut Nakashima fiddleback, and collapsed into the elegant seat. "How many men did you lose, Yakka?"

"Nearly a hundred. I welcome the replacements you brought."

"Huh!" The Prince's laugh—to his own ear—was a tired bark from an exhausted dog.

"You still owe me ninety-three more."

In the darkness of the medbay, Green Hummingbird frowned, watching the Prince and the captain stare at each other in weary silence. He blinked, switching the feed to another of his *dorei* infesting the shipnet.

This v-cam showed the armored alien who'd come aboard with the Prince. The creature was cowering in the corner of a well-appointed cabin with its long tapering head hidden in his hands. A constant muttering wail issued forth from the helmet, which was loud enough for the room security camera to pick up and relay to the

nauallis. The sounds were unintelligible, though the Méxica had a more than passing knowledge of the Hjo
trade language used in Imperial space.

What a pitiful creature, the old man thought, and
subvocalized a series of commands into his throatmike.
*A pity the zhongdu didn't send someone more . . . aware.
Still, one uses what tools are to hand.*

"How are we going to get out of here?" Xochitl paced
back and forth across the bamboo-parquet flooring of
the *Chu-sa*'s private office. His boots ground into the
sealant layer protecting the light-grained panels, leaving
tiny gritty black marks. "How did you navigate through
the Barrier? Can you get us back out?"

"Don't you wonder," Koshō said, in a musing tone,
"if the Khaid knew our full strength when that pack
made transit . . . or do they habitually hunt Imperial
scouts with such numbers? It seems very odd their *Kabil Rezei* would go loping around in this wasteland
with a *fleet.*"

The Prince glared at her. "You are *still* just as annoying as in school."

Koshō shrugged, meeting his eyes with a calm, direct
gaze. "They were hunting for you, Sayu. They jumped
in hot, right on top of us in this cursed murk, and they
came loaded for capital ships . . . so tell me this, is it
safe to take my ship back into Imperial space with you
aboard?" Her expression flattened. "Are you running
from someone, Lord Prince? We've been out of comm
contact for weeks—is your father dead? Is there some
new Emperor on the Quetzal throne? One that finds
you displeasing?"

"What do—" Xochitl stopped, his expression suddenly frozen. "Yakka, that is a cold, cold thought."

"The Princes of the México are notoriously cruel, my Lord. Particularly when they war upon one another."

"My father sent me *himself*," Xochitl allowed confidently, but felt his jaw twitch as he gave the words life. Susan shook her head minutely in disbelief, her eyes filling with pity. Suddenly, he felt naive. "He . . . no one else knew my destination or intent. No one. We left Anáhuac under complete blackout and emissions control; my own ship, my own picked men. He . . . couldn't send anyone else . . ." The Prince's voice trailed off and his vision grew dark with growing fury.

Now I know how sensei *felt at Jagan,* Susan thought, abruptly gripped by despair. *The fate-cursed retainers of a doomed Prince, conveniently sent into a wilderness from which they will not return . . .*

"No," Xochitl said slowly as he tried to rally his wits. "No, I will not believe that, not yet. Many hands touched the planning of the Mirror expedition—or the Khaid may have been snooping here already—anyone might have . . ." A thought occurred to him and his face lightened with relief. "The embassy! Someone had informed the—" He stopped abruptly, blinking as an overlay appeared in his field of vision.

«*Security Warning! Koshō, Susan,* Chu-sa *in command of IMN BC-268, does not hold ring-zero clearance!*»

Susan looked at him expectantly. Xochitl felt suddenly, terribly alone.

I can't tell her. She's not cleared to know such things. How—

"There is another explanation," he said coldly, rising and going to the door. "Which is a privy matter. Expedite your repairs, *Chu-sa*. We will need to be underway as soon as possible. As soon as it is safe to move, begin looking for a way out of this . . . place. And send all current telemetry to the secondary bridge for my review."

Susan watched him leave with a frown. *Now what did he almost say? What "embassy" was involved with this?*

Down in Medical, Hummingbird's impassive face showed the faint ghost of a smile. In his other Eye, the z-suited alien had removed his helmet and was stuffing a long-snouted face with fried dumplings, a veritable buffet table of freshly delivered food laid out before him. Beside the table, a trolley cart had been provided, filled with gleaming glass bottles of liquor.

Now our feet are on the proper road.

THE WILFUL

Hadeishi stepped onto the bridge—such as it was—of the little freighter, with a light heart. The search pattern laid down by De Molay had let them recover no less than five evacuation capsules from a variety of Imperial ships. In each case the capsule had been maneuvered into one of the cargo bays with the *Wilful*'s z-g loading cranes and clamped down. Gunner's mate Tadohao and *Nitto-hei* Cajeme had grown quite proficient in the art of undogging the capsule hatches and sorting out the dazed, wounded, and confused men inside. Nearly every *Sho-i* and *Thai-i* they'd rescued had protested the command structure, complained vehemently, threatened mutiny, and finally settled down after a thorough reading of Mitsuharu's papers.

Hadeishi found it quite interesting—more so with each conversation—that none of the Fleet officers seemed to find it strange or unusual to be rescued by a tramp freighter commanded by a reserve *Chu-sa* in the uttermost wilderness. *But then*, he remembered, *this was a Smoking Mirror operation, which means every man and woman of them came expecting the strange, the untoward and the downright peculiar to happen.*

Mitsuharu stepped to the captain's chair, seeing that De Molay was dozing at her station, still wrapped in a variety of blankets and now wearing a hand-knit shepherd's cap. He was about to sit when he noticed the shockchair had been reduced to nothing but the bare frame, without even the cracked leather seat he'd grown used to.

"What have you done to my chair?" He gave the old woman a questioning look.

"Hm? Oh, the cushions?" De Molay yawned elaborately, stretching both skinny old arms. "All of your lost children needed something for their heads; these floors are quite cold if you've not even a blanket."

"Yes . . . that is true." He fingered the hexacarbon framing and eyed the recessed bolts in the seat.

The old woman scratched at the half-healed wound on her cheek. "So—how is our new crew adjusting to their reduced circumstances?"

"Some of the wounded won't last, but their spirits are good." Hadeishi sat, his good mood evaporating. "We'll lose nearly ten, I think, if we can't find better medical facilities for them."

De Molay nodded, watching him closely. "My apologies, but I cannot offer anything better. . . ."

"That you—that we—are here has already given them a priceless gift." Hadeishi's eyes narrowed, thinking of the hidden compartments he knew existed downdeck. "Now, *Sencho*, is that really true? This is a ship of many surprises! I've not gone through every centimeter of the holds—have you a whole medbay down there? Along with this"—he indicated the hull with a wave of his hand—"very interesting shipskin and heat exchanger?"

In response, she frowned, jutting her chin forward.

"So far the rescue campaign is going well, you would say?"

Hadeishi started to nod, his expression brightening. "Very well! We need to kit up some more bunks, as you've said, and take a close inventory of our supplies, but—"

"*Chu-sa*," De Molay said sharply. "How many men and women have we taken aboard?"

"Sixty," he said after a moment of mentally reviewing the rosters from each capsule.

"We are at one hundred twenty-five percent of environmental capacity, *Chu-sa*. The scrubbers are showing amber across the board, the sewage recycler is backed up, and we're out of hot water. In fact, we're going to be out of water *period* very soon because there is waste and leakage in these *Knorr*-class freighters and we're pushing the system too hard! But that," she concluded, her voice rising angrily, "won't be an issue much longer because we are almost out of *food*."

Hadeishi sat back, scratching at his beard, which had begun to twist into an ungainly white-streaked tangle. Reluctantly, he walked mentally through the ship, comparing the numbers of compartments to the number of men aboard. *These capsules are coming in with some emergency rations aboard, but this freighter didn't come prepared for a search and rescue mission. We're just over carrying capacity.*

"You're right," he said at last, brow furrowed in thought. "We still have capsules on the plot, but nowhere to bunk the survivors for more than a few hours. Where to put them . . ."

"Success will defeat you if we do not find a way." De Molay settled back into her blankets. "Or you will have to be satisfied with the souls you've already saved, and let the rest go."

"No." He shook his head vehemently. "I won't abandon them."

"Then what will you do?" The old woman's exasperation was clear. "There is *no room* at the inn."

Hadeishi nodded slowly, his face clearing. "Your point is taken. Plainly, we need another ship."

"Another ship?" Tocoztic—who had come in while they were talking and sat down quietly at his station—exclaimed. "But—"

"Then get one." De Molay replied tartly, glaring at Mitsuharu. "I am content to watch from here while you do the heavy lifting, but I would appreciate just one tiny favor, *Chu-sa.* I would like *my ship back* in operable condition!"

"Of course."

Musashi swung the axe in a light, looping arc—striking the end of the log square center—gravity and the full power of his shoulders splitting the wood from end to end with a sharp crack! *He reached down, tossed the two sections aside into a large and growing pile, and then reached for another log.*

"Pardon me, sir," came a polite but authoritative voice. Musashi looked over his shoulder, tattered kimono stretching over his muscular arm. An elderly, balding man was standing at the edge of the inn's wood lot—no, not just a man, someone who had once been a samurai officer. That much was instantly apparent to Musashi from his horseman's stance, his calm and level gaze. Such men were rare in Japan under Mongol rule—well, rare that they walked the streets and were not in chains, or laboring in some work gang in shackles.

"I understand that you are ronin—and needful of employment?" The stranger tilted his head slightly, indicating the woodpile.

"I need to eat, like all men," Musashi replied, straightening up. "What's the job?"

"Tax collectors are going to level their village." The samurai gestured politely to two farmers cringing behind

him, their faces drawn with hunger, their bodies thin with starvation. "As the harvest has been short this year."

"You're going to stand in the Noyan's way? You are a man of great bravery."

"Not the Noyan." The elderly samurai essayed a grin. "A local gang—no more than bandits, forty or fifty of them—the governor has parted out the collections, being too indolent to do this himself."

Musashi felt a spark of interest flare in his breast, so he settled his shoulders, picked up the bokutō and bowed politely. "Now this I need to see," he said. "How many of us are there?"

"Five others," Kambei said. "Did I mention all the farmers can pay is our meals?"

ABOARD THE *NANIWA*

INSIDE THE POCKET, FOUR LIGHT-MINUTES
FROM THE PINHOLE

Koshō woke to the sound of a reminder chime from her comp. Lying in the dimness of her cabin, she felt perfectly fine for approximately three seconds—then she moved her head, looking over at the screen to see what needed doing—and every muscle, joint, and tissue in her body complained. *Oh Queen of the Heavenly Mountain,* she thought blearily, *did I take that many meds in the last two days?*

The bone-deep achiness in her back, legs, and shoulders argued that she had, in fact, taken way too many stayawakes for her body to process in only four hours of sleep. Regardless, she swung out of her bunk and padded on bare feet to the comp.

Ventral end of magazine conveyor thirty-two, in fif-teen minutes? Susan scratched her head, feeling an irri-tating graininess in her scalp, and realized she'd collapsed into bed without even washing her face. The sensation of grime clogging every pore on her body made the Nisei woman shudder, so she tapped a quick "acknowledged" into the comp and fled to the shower.

Fourteen minutes later, in a fresh uniform and with a bulb of tea in her hand, Koshō stepped out of the tube—and nodded in greeting to a junior engineer waiting for her in the little offloading station. *Socho* Juarez had at-tached himself to her as soon as Susan had left her cabin.

"*Kikan-shi* Ige, good morning. *Sho-sa* Chac is wait-ing for me?"

"They all are, *kyo*. This way please." The Mixtec en-gineer gestured for her to precede him.

They all *are?* Curious, Koshō drained the rest of the bulb and followed along. *What is Chac up to now?*

Almost immediately they descended a gangway pass-ing through two layers of battle-steel and stepped out onto a hexacarbon walkway running the length of a rail-way tube. Susan recognized part of the Backbone from all the work they'd done during trials to get the maglev sys-tem up and running, but the number of crewmen stand-ing along the sides of the tube ahead of her was surprising. There were at least thirty *kashikan-hei* with logistics flashes on their z-suits lined up along the walkways on either side of the rail. At the far end of the group, she could see Oc Chac's polished visage watching for her, though the slim figure at his side was unfamiliar.

The Mayan's companion was young, no more than a cadet, and what she could see of his face indicated he was straight from the Center, possibly from Tenochtit-lán itself, with shining black hair like smoke tied back behind a smooth copper-colored neck. What piqued her interest, however, was the elaborate and beautiful costume he was wearing. A classical Náhuatl mantle formed of tiny gleaming white feathers was draped across his shoulders and back, leaving the front open to reveal a fitted shirt ablaze with green and gold and iridescent yellow. The shirt was also made of feathers, even smaller and more downlike than the mantle. Most of his face was hidden by a hummingbird mask figured in black and red and green—and the mask itself seemed to be formed of beaten gold inlaid with semiprecious stones and jade. His feet were bare on the platform, though tiny conch shells were braided around his ankles. As she approached, the *kashikan-hei* lining the side walls bowed respectfully, their caps pressed over their hearts, and Oc Chac saluted smartly.

The Mayan officer had set aside his z-suit and uniform and was wearing a hooded cotton cloak and tunic. Like the young man, his feet were bare, though unadorned.

"*Chu-sa* on deck," Juarez announced, his voice echoing in the tubeway. With a rustle, everyone knelt save the *Huitzitzilnahualli* and Susan. She glanced questioningly to Oc Chac, who motioned for her to step to the edge of the tube beside him and remain standing. When she had done so, the Mayan squatted down with a drum between his legs. A flat, calloused palm struck the stretched leather and a deep, basso *boom-boom* sounded. In the rail tunnel, the sound reverberated in each direction, generating a skin-tingling vibration.

In the first silence, the hummingbird dancer raised his arms, lifting one foot. As he did, the white mantle stiffened, conforming to his muscular arms, and the ends extended, becoming proper wings.

Stamp! His bare foot fell, striking the platform. In the same instant, Oc Chac struck the drum again. *BOOM!*

Thus the youth danced, first in an irregular pattern

which wended this way and that, each light footstep ring-ing in the tubeway with the slap of his bare feet swal-lowed by the deep voice of the drum. Watching him, seeing the rapt faces of her crewmen and feeling a tension singing in the air, Susan felt chilled. Back and forth along the section of rail, the *Huitzitzilnahualli* danced as though flying, an irregular, swooping motion. From one end of the watching crowd he passed to the other, some-times spinning, sometimes leaping in short, tightly con-trolled hops. The walls of the tubeway began to vibrate in time with the drum—faster now, as the dancer pushed himself, speeding through the intricacy of the pattern—and both of the Mayan's hands were a blur on the *hue-huetl*.

Suddenly, as the hummingbird dancer completed a high leap, the drum stopped cold.

The boy landed, instantly still, wings draped over his face, covering his head and shoulders.

Not even a breath disturbed the silence. Susan could feel her heart thudding in her chest.

A new sound entered—the soft wail of a conch-bellied mandolin—and the dancer contorted, flinging back his wings, exposing his iridescent chest to the roof of the tubeway. Koshō stiffened and more than one crewman gasped aloud. A thick crimson streak had ap-peared over the boy's heart. It seemed as if blood were leaking from beneath the feathers, pooling under the green and gold. The *Huitzitzilnahualli* leapt straight up, flinging himself backward in a stunning reverse, and as he did so, the white mantle and the gleaming wings be-came speckled with irregular black spots.

He landed square on both feet, but now his stance had changed. No longer did he move with such delicate grace—instead he spun, wings inward, showing his broad back and mantle to the watching men—and with every revolution, swinging into ever tighter circles, the whiteness was pierced again and again by black, corrosive streaks. In a flurry of motion, the dancer was suddenly prostrate before Chac and Koshō at the end of the lines of watching men—and his mantle, his chest, his legs were all but consumed by stippled gray-on-black darkness, as though his limbs had washed away in a tide of corruption.

BOOM. The drum sounded fully one more time, the boy head down on the platform before them, his breath coming in audible gasps. Then Oc Chac struck the sides of the drum sharply with stiffened fingers, drawing everyone's attention away from the *Huitzitzilnahualli* and onto himself.

"A poet once said:

> *Be joyful, there are intoxicating flowers*
> *in our hands.*
> *Put on these necklaces*
> *of flowers, flowers from the season of rain,*
> *fragrant flowers opening their corollas.*
> *Here flies a bird, he chatters and sings,*
> *he comes from the house of the Risen Lord.*
> *With flowers in our hands, we are happy.*
> *With songs upon our lips, sadness disappears.*
> *O great-hearted ones, in this way,*
> *your sorrow is put to flight.*
> *The Giver of Life, the Sacrificed One, he has sent*
>   *them.*
> *He invents them, the joyous flowers,*
> *These put your sorrow to flight.*"

When the Mayan's basso voice fell silent, Susan realized the hummingbird dancer had vanished like smoke among the fir trees and the faces of all the engineers and Backbone *kashikan-hei* were open and glad, empty of fear or fatigue. Even she felt refreshed, in a strange way, as though some of the weight upon her shoulders had been lifted.

Several hours later, after taking her station in Command, Koshō saw Oc Chac enter, once more in his usual Fleet uniform. She beckoned him over, her expression curious. "*Sho-sa*, my thanks for this morning's invitation."

The Mayan nodded grudgingly. "You were most welcome, *kyo*."

"Did you need me to be present?" She tilted her head to one side, watching him closely. "Should the commanding officer attend these ceremonies?"

"*Chu-sa* . . . No, it is not necessary. Most captains do not appear."

"Was my presence helpful?" Koshō leaned back a little in the shockchair. "You let me stand—you made me part of the ritual. Were I absent, would you have taken my place?"

Chac shook his head. "No, *kyo*. The officer in charge of the damaged area would usually represent the Risen Lord—but Goroemon was off-watch, having stood in for mine, and I thought . . . I thought you might find it interesting."

"It was." She looked him up and down, nodding to herself. "I am glad to see you back on duty, however. Look at this." Koshō turned to the executive 'well displayed by her console, stylus light in her hand, and marked a semicircular area deeper into the Pocket, partway between the *Naniwa* and the singularity and its attendants.

A dark mass emerged from the scan as the 'well zoomed in.

"There is an enormous amount of debris," Susan said, "between us and the event horizon. Shoal after vast shoal of matter, all of it dark and cold. The dispersion pattern is very stable—only in a few places have we been able to pick out infall from the cloud towards the black hole. And it seems to be old."

"Ancient!" Oc settled at his own console, keying up a copy of what she was looking at. He grimaced at the figures displayed on the sidebar v-panes. Other displays unfolded, showing him the results of the latest navigational scans. "We're not receiving much data from deeper in the system, either, but look at the initial analysis on this formation: very heavy—metals, radioactives, high-order elements. And the size of the field—I wonder if the planetary systems from those brown dwarves made this up—after something pulverized them into rubble."

Koshō nodded, rubbing her chin. "Or something cut them up into tiny pieces."

Thai-i Holloway, who had been poring over the same data, hoping to find some clue in the pattern of dust clouds to indicate another Pinhole-like exit, looked up and caught Susan's eye. "*Chu-sa*, I think there's something solid down at the horizon." He stepped to the main threatwell and jabbed his stylus deep into the projection. "I can see just a faint ghost—here—on my long-range plot."

The *Chu-sa* nodded. *It must be enormous to show up at this range, but what else could we expect? All of this didn't come into being by accident.*

Koshō straightened her uniform, keyed up her own image in a v-pane looping from the comm system, and then tapped open a channel to Prince Xochitl in Secondary Command.

"Lord Prince?" she said briskly, when his grim visage appeared. "Status update. Still no way out, but we've confirmed the pocket is just more than six light-years across. We have also found indications of an artificial structure very near the event horizon of the singularity."

Xochitl frowned, his expression impassive, as though carved from stone. "All of this was built, you say? The whole of the *kuub* and this hidden realm as well?"

"Almost certainly, *Gensui*." Susan remembered the raw greed on Gretchen's face very clearly. "I will keep you—"

"Let us consider our situation carefully, *Chu-sa* Koshō."

The cold formality in the Prince's voice stood the small hairs of Susan's neck on end.

"The Khaid will have summoned reinforcements," he continued. "They will not abandon the watch at our badger-hole. Indeed, they will be aggressively seeking a way in after us. A six-light-year-diameter surface will take years to search properly, and I do not believe we have years of supplies aboard this ship. If all of this is a 'made-thing,' then the structure at its core will be a control apparatus of some kind—"

"Or cheese!" Koshō interrupted in irritation. "Or the hostile fortress all of this was built to protect! Certain destruction in any case, as it will be defended—"

"Make course for the structure, *Chu-sa*," the Prince growled. "Every recording device aboard on continuously. Dispatch message drones with the contents every half-hour."

"Of course, Lord Prince." Koshō closed the comm connection, then stifled a sigh and picked up a stylus to lay in a new plot. "So, down into the black heart of the *kuub*," she muttered. "And then out again as quickly as possible." *Grubbing for something to show his beneficent father, some prize to buy back favor. There's a cold thread of fear in his heart now . . . and we'll all likely pay for it. I should not have suggested he'd been sent out here to die.*

Holloway and Oc Chac were waiting, faces pensive, when she looked up again.

"Yes, *Sho-sa?*"

The Mayan made a disgusted face. "And where, *kyo,* does he expect these message drones to *go?*"

OUTSIDE THE BARRIER

Once more, Hadeishi was sitting in the darkened bridge, the *Wilful*'s day having wound down into the third watch, watching sensor traffic spool past in the holocast. De Molay was seemingly asleep in her chair—she rarely moved now, having given up her cabin to the worst of the wounded—and Tocoztic and a Mirror comm officer who just needed a place to lay her head were snoring on mats on the floor behind the Navigator's station. The Khaid fleet at the Pinhole was still busy, various scattered ships returning to the main group, and the battleships standing watch were now gathering up and accelerating battle debris into the opening. At this range, Mitsuharu couldn't follow the details of their mapping process, but he was certain they were making headway.

His hand moved on the controls, rewinding the last thirty-six hours of data, then letting it run forward at sixty-speed over and over again. *Where are you,* he wondered, keying up the commercial registry one more time. *I can feel you're there, given a fresh coat of paint, or at least a new nameplate . . .*

His earbug fluttered with snatches of Khaiden message traffic as well. Their encryption was spotty, and some-times they broadcast in the clear—though, to their credit, only on line-of-sight laser when in close proximity—but Mitsuharu had time, and the passive scanners stitched into the hull of the *Wilful* were very good, just as the old woman had promised. What he heard was mostly unintelligible, but occasionally he made out the names of ships, or *Kabil*-commanders, or perhaps curses used over and over again.

They are not pleased. That much was very clear. Mitsuharu also gained the impression that an argument was underway between the ship captains—some seemed bent on leaving, the others on wrinkling out the one Imperial ship to escape their trap. A battle-cruiser which, from what he could gather from fragmentary appearances on their long-range scan, had disappeared into the "passage" the Khaid were attempting to reconnoiter. *So one of us got away with a working ship—excellent piloting—but now De Molay's "whipping knives" are shown to have a chink in their armor. And what might lie beyond? That is a powerful draw for the* Kabilizar. . . .

Movement in the active holocast caught his eye. Three of the smaller Khaid ships had gotten underway, each building velocity with a steady burn. The corona flare of their engines stood out on his plot—and each seemed to be departing the main group on a different vector. Hadeishi scratched the back of his head, reached for a plastic jug of water someone had left in Command, and then grew very still.

Three drive flares, three ships—but not the same engine signature. His stylus was immediately busy on the console, capturing all three emissions profiles and then routing them into a spectral analysis module the freighter's comp maintained for finding hydrogen strata in gas giants. *There! There she is.*

One of the three ships—perhaps a light cruiser from the mass index—was what he was waiting for.

"The Goddess watches over the patient," Mitsuharu said to himself. His stylus tapped rapidly on the console, setting a new course. He frowned as the nav comp calculated the intercept, as the resulting numbers were not good. *This gives us a very poor angle of approach. We need to trim that up.*

De Molay opened one eye as the timbre of the *Wilful*'s vibration changed, the maneuver drives going into their pre-ignition sequence. "And now?"

"We need to pick up some velocity, *Sencho*. How high can I push these engines?"

Both of the old woman's eyes opened. "Are you mad? If you go to maximum burn, the Khaid will pick us up on long-range scan."

"I know." Hadeishi offered her a lopsided smile. "I want one of their light cruisers to come looking for us—or at least change their course enough to scan our area." He paused, thinking. "The absorptive mode will work again, correct? It wasn't a one-time getaway device?"

"Yes," De Molay said, sounding wary, "it will work again. . . ."

"And unless a Khaid camera is pointed directly at us as we occlude the star field—which is luckily very sparse here—or move across one of the more excited dust clouds, their sensors won't pick us up?"

"That is the idea." An acerbic tone crept into her voice.

Mitsuharu stood up, straightened his battered leather jacket, and gave her a very proper bow. "Then we've a great deal of work to do. Thank you, *Sencho*."

Several hours later, Hadeishi climbed awkwardly up one of the gangways to the command deck, having trouble adjusting to the restricted field of vision and clumsy weight of his new armor. The bandolier of grenades strapped across his chest and the bulky *Yilan*-class ship-gun over his shoulder banged against him with every movement. *Maybe,* he thought—a little late—*this wasn't a good idea.*

Clomping in his heavy boots, the Nisei made his way onto the bridge and fetched up beside Tocoztic's station at Navigation. The *Thai-i* looked up at the sound, about to snarl something rude, and yelped in alarm. Trying to leap backward while snatching out his service sidearm earned the lieutenant a hard collision with the second chair, a bruise, and a seat on the deck.

"Resume your station, *Thai-i.* I am no Khaid." Mitsuharu opened the visor of the salvaged combat armor to expose his features. His face seemed a little small inside a helmet designed for the larger Khaidite cranium and jaw, but the foundation of the suit itself was composed of a gel similar to that used by the Fleet, and had sized itself to his frame as best it could. The chitin plates riding on the gelcore were now awkwardly distributed, but he hoped they'd still serve.

Tocoztic recovered himself smartly, climbing up from the floor with a doughty, "*Hai, Chu-sa!*"

"Status of that light cruiser, *Thai-i?*"

"Still holding course, dead on for the end of our burn, *kyo.*"

"Hm." Hadeishi frowned, turning to the holocast to check their vector.

De Molay, working on a thermos of tea, raised an eyebrow at the Nisei officer. "I thought you wanted them to come hunting for you?"

"I *want* them to come—look—find nothing—and return to their initial patrol pattern." He tugged a stylus from the holder at the edge of the Navigator's console and sketched out a trajectory in the air. "Like so. Then, when we overlap course here—roughly—we'll match velocity for nearly thirteen minutes."

Mitsuharu looked over at the old woman, his face

filled with speculation. "Unless . . . can your absorptive mode swallow our engine flare as well?"

"No, it cannot!" De Molay sat up, wincing at the pain in her side. "It is a passive system, as you can well guess. It is not a weapon, but a defense."

Hadeishi laughed, brightening for a moment. "We will make do, *Sencho*."

Feeling well enough to stand, the old woman limped over to him and examined the Khaid armor from top to bottom, testing the dark black-and-green fittings and running a fingertip along the tight, blocky lettering on the upper arms. Nodding in approval, she said, "You make a fine raider, *Chu-sa* Hadeishi. I think you've been in the wrong business all along!" Then her face grew more serious. "How many are you taking in with you?"

"I leave you our esteemed *Thai-i* here as pilot," he said, "plus two in Engineering and Galliand in medbay. But not Cajeme, he's in the first team with me."

De Molay's expression darkened and she rapped him sharply on the arm, making the chitinous armor ring hollowly. "That would be fifty-five men sent to their deaths, *Chu-sa*, if your calculations are wrong."

"*Wilful* carries no missiles, no guns, *Sencho*. We cannot overcome this Khaid from a safe distance. We must do this the hard way, as *your* ancestors did in the old days." He flashed a brief smile. "And so we need at least eight minutes at zero-delta, but thirteen would be better."

"We could abandon this place, take these men to the nearest Fleet depot." The old woman's voice was beginning to sound tired. Her fingers tightened on his arm. "Saving some would be better than losing all, would it not?"

Hadeishi shook his head. "These men and women are Fleet, *Sencho*. It is not in them to flee the battlefield when their comrades can still be saved, or when they can still strike out at our enemies."

Then he carried her back to the shockchair, and the *Thai-i* helped him tuck her into the blankets.

"Ten minutes to intercept." Tocoztic's voice echoed in Mitsuharu's earbug. Within the *Wilful's* port cargo-bay, ship-comm was still working. The *Chu-sa* had the Khaid radio in his armor working as well, which let him hear the rasping breath and muttering of every man and woman crowded into the bay with him. The alien armor was lacking any number of features—no personal vitals, no med-band-style dispensers—but it would hold pressure, the chitin-scale armor was tough, and the maneuvering jets had propellant. *No complaints.*

"All teams, equipment check," Hadeishi announced, rotating to the crewmen who'd drawn Team One duty with him. There were five—Cajeme and his two assistants, who were heavily laden with demolitions packs and a pair of magnetic rams—then a marine for security, and the junior comm officer from the *Eldredge*, who had survived the destruction of her ship by an utter miracle, and was kitted out with the most powerful field comp they could salvage from the *Wilful* and a satchel filled with tools, spare parts, and data crystals. Mitsuharu ran through a careful check of Cajeme's z-suit and his demolition packs. "Can't have you lose air while we're working, *Nitto-hei.* You might drop something that makes a loud bang."

The Yaqui's leathery face remained impassive as he waited, but his nut brown eyes were sparkling. "The *Chu-sa* relates an excellent joke, *kyo.* Knowing how difficult it is to drop things in z-g."

"Eight minutes." The *Thai-i's* voice was growing tenser by the second.

"All teams, sound off by section," Mitsuharu ordered as Cajeme finished checking the *Chu-sa's* armor. Team

Two was also six men—two engineer's mates and the rest of the blasting plastic, along with a portable monofilament saw from the *Wilful*'s shop and a plasma cutter carried by two more able-bodied men—then another two marines with salvaged Khaid grenade launchers. Team Three was next—eighteen men in the heaviest armor and shipguns, either Fleet or Khaid, they could scrape together—and then Team Four, the cleanup crew, which comprised the remaining twenty-five. These men were armed, in some cases with no more than their personal sidearms.

"Six minutes, *kyo*. Target is holding steady course."

Hadeishi nodded to Cajeme and the junior comm officer. "Load up."

Cajeme and his cutters swung up into the first tray on the cargo gantry. Hadeishi and the comm officer followed, spacing themselves equidistant across the second tray, with the marine to her left.

I'll miss our little talks, De Molay's voice came in his earbug, *when you've had your guts pulverized on the side of that ship.*

Mitsuharu clicked his teeth, switching channels. "The cruiser's still off-vector?"

By a point and a half. The freighter captain's voice was very dry. *You'll only have three minutes and you won't be coming in at a right angle.*

"As long as our velocities match, we'll be fine." Hadeishi felt his blood quicken, his vision sharpen, everything begin to grow preternaturally clear. "Just keep a steady hand on the tiller, *Sencho*."

"Five minutes." Tocoztic's voice had settled, becoming hard and flat. "We're in their wake. Powering up the gantries."

A set of rails embedded in the roof and floor of the cargo bay rattled to life, warning lights blinking and their motors whining. Team One was on the ventral rail, crouching in their successive loading trays—each a large, X-shaped rectangle a few centimeters larger than an Imperial-standard cargo pod. Team Two had already secured themselves to the second tray—and directly "below" them the rest of the teams were swarming into the second rail.

We're in the drive-plume full-on, De Molay reported, though Mitsuharu could already hear a roar of background static on the Khaid radio as the exhaust of the Khaiden ship's antimatter drive washed over the *Wilful's* hull. *Three minutes and we're popping out like an appleseed. Primary hull temperature is soaring and we're getting radiation damage to the secondary.*

"All teams, secure yourselves!" Hadeishi craned his neck, eyeballing everyone. He secured his tether to Cajeme, who was already linked to the others. "Three minutes, thirty seconds to the bay doors, four minutes to contact!"

Time dragged as Mitsuharu breathed slowly and steadily through each nostril in succession, steadying his heartbeat. The radio circuit was filled with tiny noises—men praying under their breath, the rasp of someone with smoke-damaged lungs, the *tic-tic-tic* of someone nervously clicking their teeth together.

Musashi's sandals slid on black sand, the whole slope under his feet breaking free and cascading down towards the beach. Behind him, the jagged crown of Suribachiyama loomed up against a darkening sky, filled with the outriders of the taifun blowing up out of the Western Ocean. This time the trusty bokutō had shattered on whale-bone armor, leaving him with nothing. He tossed the splintered rattan away, keeping his balance with a shift of his hips. The beach itself was hard and flat, the sand gleaming wet as the tide ran out. Heke

*and his retinue were waiting, weapons drawn, some of
the younger men leveling muskets at the ronin.*

"*Nowhere to run, Pākehā,*" *the chieftain shouted, his
tattooed face twisting with anger.* "*Put down your sticks
and take up a man's blade!*"

*One of the other Maori overhanded a bolo at Musashi,
which he caught from the air with a twisting motion.
The long, flat steel blade felt tremendously heavy in his
hands—far heavier than any katana. Then Heke and his
men came on at a run, their war-cries booming against
the counterpoint of the surf.*

"One minute, thirty seconds, *Chu-sa.*" Tocoztic announced, his voice barely a whisper. "Maneuvering
burn—now!"

The ship quivered, the motion magnified by the cargo-
rails, and Hadeishi felt the engines tick up to barely a g of
acceleration. The momentary burst, he hoped, would be
obscured by the Khaid ship's own engine flare. The immediate roar of static faded slightly as the little freighter
slipped out of the drive plume.

"Cycling bay doors," the *Thai-i* announced. Warning
lights along the sides of the fifteen-meter-wide cargo
doors flared to life as the motors kicked in. An audible
alarm blared in their ears. "Vector match in—wait one,
wait one."

Hadeishi stiffened, suddenly wild to see the navigation plot and the holocast. The bay doors rolled aside,
revealing the glare of the Khaid ship's drive plume falling away above them.

She's lit off her own maneuvering burn, De Molay
snapped, her voice tight. *She's preparing to roll aspect
and change direction. But we don't know which way—*

"He's turning a dog-leg, doubling back on his trail."
Mitsuharu's blood was singing. "This one alternates in

thirds—he's going to swing to port, *Sencho*, to port. Match course and give me thirty percent power for seventeen seconds, then snap the gantries and we'll take it from there."

You are *mad.*

"Do it!" Hadeishi reached down and unsnapped his tether from the cargo tray. "All teams! Release your tethers. The Khaid ship is rolling aspect and we need to match v on her. No step-through, repeat no step-through. We're going to make contact in free flight."

There was a flurry of activity, but the Nisei officer had already turned to watch the bay doors thud back into the hull. A vast expanse of boiling dust and hidden, gleaming stars opened before him, swallowing all sight and vision. The beauty of the *kuub*—the intricate traceries of debris plumes and the shining coronas of distant stars—poured in, filling the cargo bay with a hot jeweled light.

The appearance of the black shape of the Khaid ship was an abrupt jolt as the *Wilful* went into a hard burn herself. It loomed up suddenly, still in the middle of its own maneuver, the drive-plume blazing like a rising sun off to starboard as the massive ship turned inside their own course.

"Velocities match!" Tocoztic and De Molay's voices overlapped. "Gantries away!"

Rail one slammed forward, safety interlocks disengaged, and Mitsuharu and his two crewmen were suddenly blown out of the side of the freighter as the tray slammed into the end of the rail and flipped down and out of the way. The successive trays on the gantry banged away, one every three seconds. Clouds of men hurtled across the void between the two ships, suddenly enveloped in a coruscating radiance.

The Khaid light cruiser continued her burn, the hull swelling before them like a basalt cliff, a jagged landscape of thermocouple fins, airlocks, gun emplacements . . . Hadeishi's eye grasped her outline in a flash and exulted. His intuition had been right, the drive signature confirmed.

"She's an old *Spear*-class cruiser," he barked on both channels, hands light on his suit propellant controls. "Cargo locks are dorsal mount, to our right and high. All hands, maneuver on my mark. Mark!"

Mitsuharu angled to the right, jets hissing, and the black wall came rushing on. Even without a suit-comp to feed him intercept times and distances, his eye was keen enough to gauge the right moment.

"Team one, braking!" He blew the last of his propellant, but even this was not enough to avoid slamming hard into the shipskin of the old *Spear*. The junior comm officer hit next, then the marine. Off to their left, Cajeme and his team had done a better job, touching down at almost zero delta. "Team One is down, repeat Team One is down."

Hadeishi staggered up, letting his boots adhere to the shipskin. The marine was cursing, his right arm injured, and the comm officer was just clinging in panic to the hull with both hands and feet.

"Up you get, *Sho-i*," Mitsuharu growled, seizing her by the shoulder. The ensign yelped but got her feet beneath her. "*Joto-hei*, are you mobile? We've thirty seconds to get inside."

The marine nodded, his face parchment-pale behind his helmet visor. "Good to go, *kyo!*"

The hull shivered under Hadeishi's feet and he moved left, a lanyard snapped to the *Sho-i*'s belt, another cast to the marine. Cajeme had already scuttled towards them, sparing only seconds for himself before the demo plastic he'd slapped down around the periphery of a maintenance hatch offset from the set of massive cargo doors blew—a hard white flash stabbing at their eyes, sending everyone's visor polarized—and the shipskin peeled away from the edges of the portal. A pair of remote-controlled antipersonnel guns had also taken the brunt of the explosion, and their short, stubby barrels were now pointed off at the distant stars.

"Team One, go!" Mitsuharu was at the side of the two crewmen with the magnetic rams as they slammed them into place at the edge of the hatchway, where the locking bolts were now exposed. Each ram consisted of a half-circle of molybdenum-steel wrapped around the magnet array and a fusion-pumped capacitor. The crewmen snapped the adhesion arm into place, stamped down on the locking mechanism to fix the rams to the shipskin and then—bracing themselves—triggered the two devices on a count of "And one!"

Hadeishi's radio squealed, flooded with radiation, and the bolts tore free. Chunks of metal spalled away, spiraling off into the void. The crewmen cranked back the rams, peeling away the hatch.

"Team Two, go!" The engineers' mates with the blasting plastic swarmed into the hole, their tethers taut in the hands of the men behind them. Mitsuharu spared a glance for the comm officer, seeing she still had hold of her comp and the data-crystals. The marine was right at her side, shipgun at the ready, his face a blur of sweat. The two engineers popped back out of the hatch, shouting "Clear!"

A jet of plasma erupted from the hatchway, boiling the shattered edges and licking out thirty or forty meters into the jewel-hot sky.

You've got company coming, De Molay suddenly announced in his earbug. *We're getting a storm of chatter on that circuit you pirated.*

"Team Three, go!" Mitsuharu rotated in a quick circle, picking out the rest of his men, spread out across the hull.

"Cargo doors first, then punch through to the shipcore." He clapped a hand on the *Sho-i*'s shoulder. "We need to get Ensign Lovelace as far into the hull as we can!"

Then he toggled the throatmike channel. "Get out of here, *Sencho*; they can't miss seeing you now."

We'll hold on just a little longer. I have an idea, but you've got to get clear of the outer hull.

Hadeishi's heart skipped, catching a wild tone in the freighter captain's voice. "You have to leave *my* ship in one piece, too, *Sencho*."

De Molay laughed and at this short distance, he could see the black outline of the *Wilful* rotate on her maneuvering jets, swinging the main drives 'round to face him. Marines were dropping through the hatch as fast as they could, but Mitsuharu was suddenly certain they wouldn't all get through before De Molay lit off her drives.

"One hundred eighty-six seconds to get them all inside," squeaked a tiny voice at close range. Hadeishi looked down, seeing Lovelace crouched on the hull, her satchel clutched to her chest and one hand gripping a twisted piece of metal. Her eyes were huge and he suddenly realized she was susceptible to vertigo. "Three seconds for a marine, five seconds for a crewman."

"You're next," he barked, seizing her by the lanyard loop on her belt and handing her off to the last of the Team Three marines ducking into the hole. "Get her coreward, *Gunso*! There's an engineering console at the junction of the fourth spaceframe and compartment ninety-six on this class—she needs to be there, and working, in eleven minutes!"

Get inside, Chu-sa; I've got gun emplacements in motion up here.

"My men are still outside, *Sencho*, keep your rotation and head back down the drive-wake. They'll punch you full of holes other—"

The *Wilful* suddenly rippled from one end to the other

as a wave of burning pinpoints and wild color swept across her. Mitsuharu gaped, watching in stunned surprise as the freighter pulled the raiment of heaven over her head and disappeared from visual sight. "Goddess of the dawn," he breathed, "I've been sold a lame horse!"

Team Four was inside the hatch in less than one hundred and sixty seconds, though the time lag dragged into an eternity for the *Chu-sa* as he crouched at the edge of the hatchway, urging them on. As far as he could tell, the *Wilful* had entirely vanished. He couldn't see maneuvering jet flare, star-occlusion, anything to tell where she was. Despite this, he guessed De Molay was waiting it out, hiding in plain sight, so when the last of his men had dropped inside the hull, Mitsuharu climbed down himself, squirting "twenty-four seconds" on his earbug before the shipskin cut off the transmission.

The maintenance hatch airlock was a wreck, all plasma-burns and torn metal. The inner airlock was no better, and as soon as Hadeishi was inside the hull proper, his radio burst alive with the combat-chatter of men running, fighting, being killed, the roar of gunfire and the distant unmistakable whine of a monofilament saw cutting into hexacarbon. The interior of the ship seemed mostly unchanged, at least on this deck, though the old Imperial signage had been torn down and replaced, or pasted over, with Khadesh equivalents.

The marine *Gunso* commanding Team Three was waiting as Hadeishi kicked through a secondary interior door, just past the corridors servicing the cargo bay. "Shut this hatch," the *Chu-sa* snapped. "We've artillery incoming."

A pair of Team Four *kashikan-hei* slammed the portal closed, rotating the manual locking mechanism. "Report, sergeant."

The marine grinned, his faceplate scored with black streaks. "*Kyo*, this compartment's secure and we've punched through to the shipcore along the immediate axis. Cargo elevators are knocked out, as is the tube car system. There's atmosphere in most compartments, but not all. We blew out a set of blast doors at frame three and I've got the combat team pushing downdeck towards frame four—"

At that moment, the ship groaned and everything shuddered. The overheads flickered, shading from a Khaid-friendly bright white to a more normal yellow tone, then popped back. The alarms, which had been blaring since Mitsuharu had entered the primary hull, shifted tone—now they squealed like a pierced bladderfish.

"We're hit!" The *Gunso* stared at the ceiling. "Sounded like a bomb-pod going off at short range."

Hadeishi shook his head, starting to grin ferally. "The freighter's lit off her maneuver drives. I doubt she'll punch through the shipskin, but we need to abandon this corridor. Move everyone downdeck towards the engineering ring. That's where we'll settle this."

Then he—and the others—were thrown violently to one side as the light cruiser went into some violent evolution and the g-decking on their whole ring fluctuated. Hadeishi hit the wall hard, feeling chitin splinter, and then bounced back as the decking failed entirely. He tucked in tight, getting his feet under before hitting the far wall. The marine had done the same. One of the *kashikan-hei* was floating limp, his faceplate filled with crimson bubbles.

"Move!" Mitsuharu pulled himself along the guiderail set into the wall, heading downdeck as fast as he could. The *Gunso* followed with the other *kashikan-hei*, the two men dragging a spool of comm-wire and a repeater with them. The hammering roar of shipguns swelled in on the radio feed, and from the sound of his team commanders shouting, the *Chu-sa* guessed the Khaid on board were counterattacking along the shipcore.

Fifteen minutes later, Hadeishi swung himself through a jagged hole hacked from a sidewall and into the engineering station at frame four. The room, controlling the cruiser's dorsal power mains and shipskin sensor nodes, was tucked in behind a thermocouple relay and the motors for a pair of the big cargo elevators. Dead Khaid were webbed to one of the walls, and everything was scorched by plasma-cutter backwash.

Lovelace had found the main console, but she was engaged in a furious shouting match with one of the engineers when Mitsuharu reached her.

"*Kyo*," the *Kikan-shi* pleaded, turning towards him, "she's going to get us all killed—she wants to—"

Hadeishi stopped the engineer with a cold glance. His face was rigid when he turned to the comm officer. "We're four minutes behind schedule and you've already been here at least that long. What's wrong?"

"This idiot," Lovelace spat, wrenching her field comp from the *Kikan-shi*'s hands. "Is trying to convince me we can crack the authorization codes for the shipnet interface by *guessing them* with something he's hacked together on his hand-comp."

"We don't have time. Give me that cutter." Hadeishi hooked one boot under the console, took the proffered plasma cutter—a small one, not the big industrial version they'd used on the wall—and sliced open the paneling directly under the display panel. "There are thirty-six billion combinations allowed in the authorization interface of a *Spear*-class cruiser, Engineer. There's a lockout after fifteen tries in the base software—and we don't have time to work around that." He shoved aside a handful of hard-wired data threads, and found—by feel—a comm node nestled behind them in the kind of socket that Defense Consortium salesmen liked to say was "easy to service, but hard to dislodge accidentally."

"*Sho-i*, you ready up there?" Mitsuharu plucked a multitool from his belt and wiggled half his shoulder into the panel.

"Ready, *Chu-sa*." Lovelace's voice was tight and trembling on the edge of open panic. "Are you really sure—"

"It worked before," Mitsuharu said, trying to sound as cheerful as possible. *At the academy, on a different class of training cruiser—but from the same manufacturing yard and design shop—if memory serves.* "Shorting the shipnet relay for this compartment—now." He jammed the tool's screwdriver into the node's service socket and twisted to the right, grinding his wrist against the bundle of data threads. There was a sharp, bright flash and he felt his glove spark. "Done!"

The lights went out. There were a series of explosions very close by, followed by the high-pitched whine of shipguns on full automatic opening up. *I didn't mean to do that.*

"They're in the corridor," barked the *Gunso* on the team radio. "Power's down in the whole compartment!"

"Hachiman's spear, they've cut the mains!" Hadeishi popped up from under the console, finding the room had cleared save for *Sho-i* Lovelace, who was staring at him with wide eyes. The engineering panel was dead, along with the overheads and everything else in the room save one emergency light which had flickered on to shed a feeble reddish glow.

"No power," she bleated, pointing at the lightless displays.

Mitsuharu glared around the room, and then caught sight of her field comp, which was still humming away.

"Powercell—pull the powercells from everything you've got. Move!"

Lovelace's face cleared and she tore open the satchel, dragging out two Fleet-standard cells, just like the ones that ran her comp. "Here—and I've an adapter!"

Hadeishi was back under the panel, one ear listening to the scrum in the hallway, with both cells in his hands and the adapter wrapped around one wrist. The *choonk* of a grenade launcher punched through all the other noise and he hooked an arm out, grabbing the *Sho-i* by the foot. "Down!" She yelped, pitching over backward, just as the doorway billowed with smoke, shrapnel, and the whine of flechettes. Two sharp *booms* followed, and then the marine *Gunso* ducked back in.

"They're coming again, *Chu-sa*—I can hear 'em howling up past the bathrooms at that junction."

"One minute," Hadeishi replied. "Jacking power to the console—now."

Lovelace rose up enough to see the display, watching as the interface flickered to life. An unfamiliar set of v-panes unfolded, filled with the tight columns of technical Khadesh, but the arrangement was familiar enough, and some of the icons were still Fleet standard issue. "Panel's coming up; switching to maintenance—"

Under the console, Hadeishi rotated the comm node to face him and saw the main power feed was still in place. Gingerly—there was no telling if the Khaid up on Command would decide to flip the mains back on—he levered the connector out. "Node is dead, no power!"

"I'm in maintenance mode on the console, *Chu-sa*. Overwriting the diagnostics suite now."

Lovelace's field comp, plugged socket-to-socket into the sub-comp running the console itself, chuckled and whirred for approximately four seconds, reloading the tools, interface image, and 'net matrix which ran the display itself. All of the v-panes went blank for an instant, and then reappeared, now showing the Fleet-standard interface.

"We're live," Lovelace said, keying a blur of commands with a stylus in either hand.

The *Gunso* at the door caught Hadeishi's eye, signing *They're coming.*

Mitsuharu nodded, flipping himself out from under the console. He had the second powercell in his hand, thumb on the safety switch. "Twenty seconds, *Sho-i*, and you'll be back on the shipnet."

"Ready," she snapped, back in her element, thin-boned face gleaming with the reflected light of the v-panes unfolding like a thousand blooming flowers on the display. Hadeishi flipped the switch, feeling the cell come to life, and his earbug suddenly woke up as an Imperial-standard comm frequency flooded the room. "Hit it."

Lovelace keyed a complicated, thirty-six ideogram sequence. A screaming howl rose on their radios—the sound of a hunting pack in full cry—and the *Gunso* at the door ducked out, his shipgun hammering away at some unseen target. A pane popped up on the display, filled with warning notices in white lettering on a red background. Mitsuharu leaned over the panel, waiting for the authorization glyph to appear.

When it did, he keyed the reset code distributed by the Fleet to all commanding officers in the event of their encountering—or capturing—a starship of Imperial manufacture in inhuman hands. There was a tidy business in reselling retired Fleet spacecraft—some of which found their way into service with hostile powers. Too, the Fleet did—occasionally—lose ships in battle, ships that might be refurbished or rebuilt by those with the technical infrastructure to do so.

Another blast, larger than the last, smashed at the doorway, flinging the *Gunso* back into the room. Smoke billowed from something burning, filling the air with thousands of tiny black globules. A hulking figure, easily a meter taller than any of Hadeishi's team, bounced through the opening.

The *Yilan* bucked twice in quick succession against Mitsuharu's shoulder, his thigh braced against the console, and the Khaid was thrown back, chest armor splintering as the blast hit him square-on. Lovelace squealed, ducking under the console.

"*Sho-i*, back to your station!" Hadeishi shouted, dodging across the room with a kick. He got an angle on the corridor, saw there was hand-to-hand fighting amongst a swirl of figures—nearly all of them in Khaid armor—and double-tapped the tallest attacker he could see. "Seal every hatch, door, ventilator, and compartment partition from frame four updeck, and flood the Command ring with fire-suppression foam!"

THE *NANIWA*

The battle-cruiser had accelerated inbound at superluminal, having found the hyper gradient dropping off precipitously as they moved away from the Barrier. Now, having leapt three light-years from the Pinhole to the immediate vicinity of the rosette, her forward big eye filled with the ever-growing glare of the ejection jet. With initial repairs complete and Command fully staffed again, Koshō watched the plot unfold with a weather eye. The near edge of the vast shoal of debris was quickly approaching and she was on edge. There were more spectators on hand than she was used to. Prince Xochitl was still camped out in Secondary Command, and a v-pane showing his handsome but worn face had acquired a permanent—and unwelcome—place on her console.

The camera displays revealed static undulations of deep purple hue, crested with orange from the glare of the plasma stream, which gradually resolved into strings of gigantic beads, and then into enormous individual entities drifting in a black soup of smaller, irregular material. Ship's comp began scanning, trying to pattern-match the jagged shapes.

Susan stood up slowly, both eyes on the screen, one hand on the edge of her console. She had already recognized what lay before them and the sheer scale of it held her speechless for a moment.

At the XO's console, Oc Chac stiffened as the first models began to flow onto his display from the comp analysis. "Ships!" he exclaimed. "They're starships."

"All wrecked." Holloway started to bite at a fingernail, before forcing his hands to the console.

"A fleet of hundreds—no, thousands!" Prince Xochitl's expression was a study in mingled awe and excitement. He looked off-screen, and then said: "Initial analysis detects four thousand, thirty-four objects in this debris field which are likely starships of some provenance."

"The Prince is impressed," Susan said without emotion. *What will he want to do with an armada of leviathans that perished deep in the abyss of time, leaving us only traces of their titanic struggle? And Queen of Heaven, four thousand ships? There might not be four thousand starships of this size in the entire Empire!*

Oc Chac sat down again, spreading his hands to indicate the spectra telemetry duly generated by ship-comp. "This is all old. Ancient. Who were they, *Gensui*?"

Xochitl did not respond, seemingly lost in his own thoughts. Koshō stirred herself, saying: "We have more pressing concerns, *Sho-sa*. Radiation levels from that accretion disc are climbing by the hour. Reconfigure the shipskin for maximum protection and pull in any sensor booms or nodes which may be adversely affected."

In his v-pane, the Prince stirred, anger shading his expression.

"However," Susan continued, shooting Xochitl a quelling look. "We want as detailed a scan as we can manage, while maintaining hull integrity and our protection, as we pass through the wreckage. Pay close attention for energy sources! *Thai-i* Holloway, please find us a path through with as little debris as possible."

The *Naniwa* edged through the ancient armada, her engines at one-quarter, booms extended, and the shipskin deployed for maximum data absorption in those parts of the battle-cruiser which were not inhabited. Koshō was back on the bridge, a great feeling of unease riding her shoulders, as the massive shapes drifted past on the camera displays. The alien vessels were enormous— far larger than even the *Tlemitl*—and formed of three "wings" joined at a central core. Most were shattered, showing gaping wounds in the unknown metal, but despite this—to her eye—Susan was gaining the uncomfortable impression that all of the ships were of a very similar kind.

"Even the smallest is the size of one of our colony stations," the Prince mused. He had not left Secondary Command in almost thirty-six hours, obsessively reviewing every data-point as it flowed across the sensor network.

"*Chu-sa.*" Konev's voice barely concealed his eagerness. "Should we dispatch an exploration team? We could board one of the smaller wrecks! Maybe there is something useful to be gleaned, like a memory core or a switch capable of controlling the thread-barrier? Even a training manual?"

Prince Xochitl interrupted before Susan could reply. "A waste of time! I need something in operation, *Chusa*. This is all"—he made an angry motion towards the wraparound v-display configured in Secondary Command—"a diversion."

That would be "no," thought Koshō, hiding her reaction behind an impassive, cool mask.

"*Hai*, Lord Prince," she replied, then shook her head at the Russian. "Not one energy source has cropped up in the scan data, *Thai-i*. We'd need a proper science team to evaluate all of this."

Xochitl nodded, satisfied, and then turned away to stare at the vista playing out on his screens.

Susan was not pleased. *So we leave Chekov's famous pistol lying beside the road at our backs. What can the man want with an "operating mechanism?" Does he believe that we can divine or control something of this magnitude without any technical resources to draw on?*

More troubling was the intuition that the Prince believed exactly that. Koshō tried to put the issue from her mind, tapping up the latest data from the remote she'd dropped at the Pinhole. Nothing had yet appeared from out of the Barrier, but she didn't believe her luck would hold in that respect either. *Wish we'd had more mines left. . . .*

Six hours later, they had completed their passage of the wrecked fleet and come within viewing range of the structure, which stood at a resonance point formed by the gravity wells of the three brown dwarves—now huge, distorted discs on the display, shedding a ruddy glare which the v-panes automatically blocked out—and the swirling vortex of the accretion disc hiding the singularity. Each sun was distended, extruding a long tail of mass corkscrewing down into the black hole.

"*Kyo?* We've lost hyper gradient—the local g field is tremendously distorted." *Thai-i* Olin licked his lips nervously. "Something emanating from that—object—is maintaining field equilibrium. While we're inside its influence . . . there's no way we can punch through to superluminal."

At this close range, the *Naniwa*'s hull was completely locked down, all booms drawn inboard. Hull temperature was rising as well, for the ambient radiation storm in this area of space was intense. Their external sensors were now limited to a set of battle-hardened scanners built to operate during a bomb-pod storm. Despite stepping down the fidelity of their data capture by orders of magnitude, the "structure" was of such colossal size they could not help but make out some detail.

General silence prevailed in Command as they watched the visuals unspool. *Nothing in the natural world contrived this,* Koshō thought, trying to wrap her mind around the sheer scale of what they beheld. *Nothing in the world of men could have built it. It cannot even hail from this eon in time. Why aren't we dead right now?*

She tore her gaze away, looking to the Prince for fresh orders. He was silent, eyes hooded, fingertips steepled beneath his noble nose. *Now which way will Sayu jump?*

Presently, Prince Xochitl frowned hugely at Susan and grumbled, "I agree that caution is required in dealing with . . . with this relic. Dispatch an exploratory team in a combat shuttle as soon as possible. They can perform a short-range scan and begin detailed mapping of the surface."

"*Hai,* Lord Prince."

Koshō gestured for Konev to join her at the command station. When the weapons officer was within range of a quiet conversation, his hands clasped behind his back and veritably vibrating with desire, she looked him up and down, troubled by the eager expression on the Russian's face.

"If you wish to try your luck—out there—find two other volunteers and refit one of the cargo shuttles to fly by wire. We'll run the boat out, and you can fly in on camera." She raised her hand sharply, cutting off the boy before he could protest. "If you're successful with a close-in approach, and can drop some sensor packs onto the surface with the shuttle's cargo arm—then we'll work up a manned landing. But until then—you've your orders."

"*Dōmo arigatō, Chu-sa!* I know just who to ask."

Bowing, he left. Koshō stared after him for a moment, and then flicked the Prince's v-pane away from her display. *Now the Prince owes me a shuttle,* she thought, suppressing a wave of irritation. Unable to sit any longer, she rose and paced over to Oc Chac's station, where the *Sho-sa,* Pucatli, and Holloway were poring over the detailed model of the structure being assembled by the ship's comp as measurements flowed in from the ship-skin.

The Mayan's face was filled with delight as he shifted views, drilling down to successive levels of detail. "Looks like a *Chimalacatl*—the shield-reed, doesn't it, *Chu-sa?*" he remarked, looking up as she approached.

Susan nodded. *If the Gods made sunflowers as big as a large moon, and gave them long, spiked metallic petals, and a center formed from triangles within triangles . . .*

Xochitl's face was visible on Chac's console as well, his visage equally bright—though not with the joy of exploration or curiosity, but naked greed. "Each petal is comprised of hundreds of thousands of folds—do you see them? Set one within another . . . such scale! We're still waiting for an estimate of age, but surely this is something from the First Sun!"

Koshō felt her gut clench. She looked to Pucatli. "No erosion rates from the surface?"

"Nothing, *kyo*. The skin should be pitted by micro-meteoroids or cosmic ray impacts—but we're seeing nothing at all—just like it came from the fab yesterday."

"*Chu-sa*." Oc Chac's voice shaded into awe. He was indicating a fresh set of scan data, from shipborne receptors pointed towards the singularity itself. "Look at this. . . . A tether or beanstalk of some kind?"

Something with barely any cross section at all traced a hard, straight line down from the "flower" towards the boiling fury of the accretion disk and—one supposed—the event horizon of the black hole.

The Mayan rubbed a hand across the back of his head. "Could they be *powering* this structure from the electromagnetic field generated by the infall? Gods, that would give them almost unlimited capacity!"

"It is possible," Susan replied, resisting the urge to fold her arms. Instead, she kept both hands clasped behind her back, forcing her mind to consider the implications of such a place to her ship. Her gut churned, triggering her med-band to dispense antianxiety meds in a sharp, cold burst.

Gretchen was standing in a portal, her tripartite shadow thrown sharp on a glassy floor by a harsh, brassy glare at her back. Before her, a massive chamber stretched off into a hazy distance, the room spined with endless ranks of sharp vaults. Everywhere there was motion—long streams of the white-garbed Chosen flowed up from the vaults below, and then passed out through the triangular exits, shepherded by guardsmen who loomed above

them, armor glinting black and crimson. The air rever-
berated with the sound of their feet on the floor, their
bright, carefree chatter, and heavy tread of the protec-
tors watching over them. With stately grace, she de-
scended a phalanx of steps. As she moved, the nearest of
the Chosen looked up, their faces emerging from the
haze like flowers opening before the rays of the first sun.
Three of them cried out, seeing her, raising their hands
in greeting. Now she was close enough to touch Isa-
belle's hair, see Tristan's bright blue eyes shining. Dun-
can was looking away, his attention caught by something
speaking in enormous, earth-shaking tones. She put her
hand on his shoulder, and he turned. Anderssen saw—

—the roof of the medbay as she blinked away tears.
Anderssen gasped, drawing a ragged breath into lungs
starved for air. A queer humming died away, replaced by
the sound of someone drinking soup and the distant rattle and clink of men and women working in an enclosed
space. The smell of the soup—picken, she guessed—
struck her hard, turning her stomach into a twisted ball
of hunger.

"Oh sweet Jesus." Gretchen rolled sideways, feeling
utterly drained. A parchment envelope slipped from her
hands, landing amongst the blankets. "There had better
be a liter of that for *me*, Crow, or I'll murder you where
you stand."

Hummingbird looked back at her, dark green eyes
curious over the edge of his bowl. "There has been a full
breakfast the last two days, Anderssen, but you have
been sleeping—so I've done you the favor of cleaning
the plate."

Lacking even the moisture to spit, Gretchen managed
to sit up and found that—indeed—there was a full tray
set beside her bed. More soup, a bowl of red gelatin,
kaffe, two bottles of hydrofast. Fingers shaking a little,

she popped the top from the first of the orange bottles and began sipping carefully.

After a few minutes, Hummingbird set down the bowl and Anderssen drained the last of her bottle.

"So, Hummingbird—I confess confusion about the purpose of the Judges. Once you said to me your duty was to protect humanity from those powers or even ideas which could destroy us, particularly alien influences we might encounter in the depths of space."

He nodded minutely, watching her with an impassive face. Gretchen drifted her fingertips over the parchment envelope and the block hidden within. "What is this, then? An experiment with my mind, my physiology? Do you even know what this is?"

"A tool." The old Náhuatl stood up, leaning heavily on the bed. "One you can operate, where others cannot—where I cannot."

"Really?" The Swedish woman looked up at him sidelong, tasting deception in the air. "A tool that you needed working when you came—here, to this hidden place."

He nodded, face somber. "My powers are not infinite, Dr. Anderssen. Even beyond your professional skills—which are well regarded, you should know—your other talents have not escaped notice."

"By who?!" Gretchen felt chilled at the thought. *How long have I been under surveillance?* Another part of her mind answered, mockingly, *Always, idiot!*

"Not all of the *nauallis* are . . . are Judges," he said, framing his words carefully. "There are those who collate data, who watch for trends—not the trivial ones of concern to the Emperor or the Mirror—but who sift for changes in *who we are*."

"Humanity, you mean?" Anderssen frowned, gaining an unmistakable impression he was skirting around a deep and slippery pit. "What kind of changes?"

Hummingbird did not answer immediately, pursing his lips and watching her with a steady, unwavering gaze. At last he said: "It is not well known, Doctor, but there are—in broad strokes—three perceptual capacities expressed within the human species. There are those who accept the conceptual framework of cultural memes, who perceive only the *nahualli*, the disguise or mask of the world; they live and work and bear their children happily within this house of paintings. What they perceive is *ahnelli*, unrooted, inauthentic, a montage of lies and expectations, merely the replication and self-deception of contagious beliefs. There are those—to take a specific example—who express a belief in the Heavenly Creator, in the Risen Lord, in God—if they are asked. These are the people who attend religious services because everyone else does—who find a sense of community there, a sense of sharing which comforts them, or an avenue to power over their fellow men." He raised one finger.

"Then there are those who do not partake of these collective memetic frameworks, who must question, seek out for themselves the *nelli*—the rooted, true, authentic cosmos. They must look beyond the world of dreams and illusion towards the *teotl*—the heart of things. They seek, but few succeed. A *tlamatini* instructs and teaches his pupil, but he cannot lead them beyond the disguise unless their heart opens of itself to become *neltiliztli*—well-rooted, authentic. When the second group express their belief it is not because they are infected by communal memes. When they worship, they do not do so because all around them do, but because of their own undiluted vision, whether it be false or true. If they do not believe in a thing, you cannot make them. For them the Mother of Tepeyac is seen to come down Her hill, roses rising with each footstep, to lift their chin and pour mercy into their eyes, *or* She does not. You *cannot* make them become believers, though they may *tell* you that they are believers—but if they are not, they cannot become so, even under the lash or when put in irons." A second finger raised.

Gretchen snorted. "I know both of those sets of people!"

"Then there is the third group who are born with the potential for full wisdom and revelation," and now the old Náhuatl's voice shaded into an unconscious gravity. "Who need neither a church, nor a sermon, nor a book. They *know* the truth, the flower-and-song of reality, the constant becoming and motion of the world, and only the confusion of men and machines and the roar and tumult of society drives this sight from their minds." The third finger joined the first two. "And these men and women are whence the saints and prophets come, the greatest artists and poets, the worst madmen and monsters without conscience or humanity—for they see that which most cannot, finding either everlasting splendor or unending horror behind the placid mask of the universe."

Anderssen made a face, drawing back from Hummingbird, whose face had contorted into a tight forbidding expression. "You," he continued, "are among a minute fraction of the third population—a genetic pool which is quite small to begin with—but then hidden among them, are those with the propensity to *see*."

"You have got to be—"

"I am *not* joking, Doctor Anderssen." The Crow's voice was hard and flat, cutting her off. "I may be able to focus my mind, attain clarity of vision which eludes other men, perform feats which seem miraculous—but I am only a Second, not a Third. I was *taught* the arts of intuition to perceive the authentic world. And thus . . ." He gestured at the parchment envelope. "Such mechanisms are beyond my capacity to understand."

"That," Gretchen said, drawing a breath to steady herself, "is the kind of insanity which gives rise to racial genocide, and forced breeding, and tyranny! Human beings are *all the same* at the genetic level, Crow! That's been shown thousands of times, on multiple worlds! Our differences are minute, one or two pairs of chromosomes fallen out in some random coupling of mitochondrial mitosis!"

The old Náhuatl shook his head in disagreement. Anderssen found herself reduced to glaring at him in outrage.

"This," he said at last, "is not so. There are distinct and identifiable differences between the Firsts, Seconds, and Thirds. There is—" Hummingbird paused, jaw clenched against what he had almost said. "I cannot provide you proof *out here*, Doctor. But it does exist. You are a Third and the only one with your specific gift we have yet found amongst the current human population."

"Current?" Anderssen gave him a mocking look. "What about the past, then? Who falls into your special society that I might, say, know from a history book? Or have seen on the 3-d, or perused in some wet-dream *manga* peddled by evil old meddlers like yourself!"

Her shout echoed from the walls of the medbay and Gretchen was suddenly aware that all of the noise outside, in the main sickbay, had stopped. She felt furious—used and deceived—and it was an effort to keep from picking up her breakfast tray and smashing it across Hummingbird's masklike face.

In the moment before the door opened, the old Náhuatl said: "One of your distant relatives had a similar power—she could see what other men intended, sometimes even before they decided a course of action themselves. You would know her—the brightest star in the firmament of your people's history—for she saved mankind from a truly dark path. But over seven hundred years have passed since—"

One of the medical orderlies opened the door and poked his head in, a professionally cheerful smile on his olive-skinned face. "Up and around, are we? Feeling better? Excellent—*Chu-sa* Koshō has been comming me for your status, Doctor Anderssen, at regular intervals."

"Great." Gretchen looked around for her jacket, fingering the medical tunic they'd put on her. "Where did my clothes go?"

The orderly was about to answer when a sudden noise erupted in the corridor outside. Someone shouted: "Ho there! Corpsman, secure quarters for the ambassador immediately!"

Gretchen peered out to see a pair of marines escorting a wretched-looking creature—obviously nonhuman, nose deep in a white plastic bucket—into the adjoining medbay. Medical staff converged on the alien from all directions, though most of them were taken aback by its peculiar appearance. To Anderssen it seemed most closely to resemble a grayish black anteater or perhaps a kind of erect sloth or tapir. A cloud of alcohol fumes drifted in their door and she grimaced at the smell of regurgitated rum. Then Hummingbird quietly closed the door, his head tilted in an attitude of listening.

"A heavy guard for such a pitiful-looking specimen," the Crow said after a moment.

"It doesn't look particularly dangerous. What species is it?"

Hummingbird gave her a considering look. "You heard the soldiers—an ambassador."

"From where? Out here?" Gretchen's eyes narrowed in suspicion. "Wait a moment . . . is this whole business an embassy to—whatever is hiding in this place?"

The old Náhuatl tilted his hand this way and that.

"The Flowery Prince brought this one along at another's command. But despite his poor appearance, the ambassador is quite dangerous—to us, to humanity. He is Hjogadim and they are quite rare in Imperial space."

To Anderssen's eye the Crow seemed to hop from one foot to the other, wings rustling nervously, before he took hold of the door latch again. "I need to speak to the ambassador—find your clothes, get dressed, and packed up. The *Chu-sa* needs you, remember?"

Then he slipped out quietly, the door barely making a noise as he passed over the threshold.

"Huh!" Gretchen began digging through the storage bins. *Now I do truly need Magdalena and Parker and even Dai Bandao, if he were available. I need backup. I should not have lost my temper with the Crow.* She sighed, suddenly weary. *I am an idiot. I could have done this just as easily back home on New Aberdeen. But no—I have to come haring out here to the back of beyond, just on the off-chance I'll touch the face of the unknown one more time.*

Finding a shirt, spare field pants, and the leather jacket, Anderssen had managed to get herself together by the time Hummingbird reappeared, radiating pleased satisfaction. "Quickly now, Doctor Anderssen—we are accompanying the Esteemed Sahâne to the bridge."

Gretchen was holding the parchment envelope by her fingertips, careful not to actually press against the bronze-colored block inside. She shook her head angrily. "Why do you think I'll come anywhere with you? You've used me as an experimental test subject to see if this . . . tool . . . would do me harm. Do you really think I would continue helping you, once I found out?"

Hummingbird paused in the doorway, watching her with an inscrutable expression. "If you do not come, Anderssen-*tzin*, then you will not see what they have found." Then he nodded to the envelope. "Bring the device—one text I have seen names it the *Adh'atr*, which is the easiest for us to say—I think you will need its capabilities soon."

Goddamnit. Gretchen tossed the block from hand to hand, then stowed it in her backpack. Dragging everything with her, she hustled out into the corridor, where she found the Esteemed One clinging to Hummingbird's shoulder, its face a ghastly hue. The plastic bucket had disappeared, but the z-suit—or armor or carapace—was liberally streaked with regurgitated fluids. Together, they were shuffling towards the nearest lift.

"I will compel action," the Hjo declared loudly, long gray nose raised in defiance. "Someone will be Instructed for this. There is a Certainty!"

"If I may suggest—" Hummingbird said, his voice low, "there is a small but well-equipped ship aboard that could easily receive your person and take you to a safer location. . . ."

"No!" The creature's reaction was abrupt and violent, though for the moment it lacked the strength to do more than flail one arm. "Order and harmony must be restored without resort to flight! Flight in a tiny, ill-equipped cylinder, crowded with apes and their acrid stench . . ." Sahâne muttered. "*They* will try again to destroy me, the last of a noble and laudatory descent. No . . . Take me to the place of authority!"

"But Esteemed One, the Prince is at the focus of action, in Secondary Command . . ." Gretchen started to speak—seeing Hummingbird gesture towards the glyph for deck thirty-nine on the lift controls—but kept her peace, wondering what the old Náhuatl intended.

"Yes. There shall be a confrontation." The creature was mumbling again. "And explanation!"

Hummingbird bowed obediently and pressed the call button for the lift. When the doors cycled open, the Hjo lurched inside—making a snuffling whine upon seeing the confined space—and then Hummingbird and Gretchen slipped inside as well, keeping to the corners and out of the way of the long, furred arms. The creature swung its head from side to side as the lift raced between decks.

By the time the blast-doors to Secondary Command irised open, the ambassador had managed to straighten up to his full height and—somehow—his z-suit and exposed fur had shed the vomit. Anderssen found the creature tremendously interesting; when first she'd set eyes upon it, the Hjo seemed shrunken and withered. *He—yes, this is a male, I'm sure of it—felt incomplete. But now it is filling out, becoming more sure of itself.* She eyed the armored suit curiously. Was a med-band at play here, injecting some kind of confidence-building med into the creature?

"Account for this wretched treat—" Sahâne stopped, long mouth yawning open, his dark eyes reflecting a hot white glow. All of his newly won assurance staggered, quailed, and then fled. A pained whimper emerged from his throat. Gretchen looked away from the creature in surprise and then her own eyes went wide with delight.

Secondary Command had been reconfigured to create one massive v-display which stretched from floor to ceiling and wrapped around three-quarters of the chamber. The Command consoles had been relocated to the sides and back of the room, their smaller v-displays filled with ever-changing data. On the vast canvas, a live camera feed of the Sunflower filled the room with the hot white glare of the ejection jet boiling up out of the singularity. The three bloated orbs of the brown dwarves studded the sky and the dark mass of the accretion disc formed a backdrop for the tri-lobed structure. Those surfaces at an angle to the jet glared with reflected light, throwing the *Chimalacatl* into high relief.

"How big . . ." whispered Anderssen, fumbling in her jacket pockets for a hand-comp. "My god, it's five thousand kilometers on a side!"

A Jaguar Knight in combat armor suddenly blocked her view, a gauntleted hand crushing her fingers and plucking the comp from her grasp. Another *Ocelotl* had moved in on the other side, immobilizing Hummingbird, who was standing quite still, all of his attention focused on the Hjo and a slim, handsome man of middle age rising from a shockchair placed at the center of the room. Seeing him in the flesh, Gretchen felt a pang of disappointment—*he's not nearly so pretty in real life*—but then caught sight of the Prince's face and felt a bolt of adrenaline flush through her limbs. *He is furious, though!*

The Jaguars picked up the wave of displeasure radiating from Xochitl as well, and the one holding Anderssen seized her neck with an armored hand. Servos whined in her ear and the metallic grip dug into her flesh. *Oh god, he'll just twist and—*

"Esteemed One." With a visible effort, the Prince halted his angry pace and bowed, face contorted with the effort of mouthing peaceful words. "I am relieved to see you are feeling better, but I urge you to return to Medical. You will be safe there and your diverse stomachs set in order."

The Hjo trembled from head to toe, but managed to squeak out: "Turn us about, mad creature! The radiation levels in this sector must be immense. Have you no care for your offspring to come? We must depart immediately!"

Anderssen experienced a strange sensation, watching the ambassador swaying before the Prince. The jolt of fear which had struck the alien dumb now seemed to supplement the earlier sense of assurance. She could taste a stark, unadulterated desire to live, and wondered if the creature had ever felt that particular spike of self-awareness before. Then Gretchen blinked rapidly, half-blinded by the glare from the v-display, and wondered if she was hallucinating. The air around the creature seemed to be flickering or twisting with tiny fleeting gleams of light. *A reflection? But of what?*

As she turned her head—feeling the armored fingers still digging into her neck—the spectacle on the v-display drew her eye like a magnet. The panorama seemed terribly familiar—something she'd seen, or read in a book, or—*What is it? Those triliths are . . . damn, but it's just beyond reach!*

Behind her, Hummingbird had somehow moved closer to the Hjo, a supportive hand under one arm, and she could hear him whispering: "Departure, yes. An excellent idea, Esteemed One."

Anderssen and the Prince spoke simultaneously: "It is not!"

Xochitl turned towards her with a scowl, jaw tight. "Get her out—"

"This object can only be a First Sun artifact," she blurted, catching his eye. "The Ik-Hu-Huillane tablets speak of an 'abode of the waking mind' which is formed in threes and multiples of three—this structure is the very image the Yithians speak of!"

"Yes . . . At last." The Prince's face cleared, the words striking a chord in him. "I've a remote going aboard that structure within moments, and we'll—"

Out of the corner of her eye, Gretchen caught sight of an entire console filled with v-panes wink out. The comm officer sitting at the station cried out in alarm.

"*Chu-sa!* My Lord Prince!" A man's voice echoed in the air. "We've lost contact with the shuttle."

A section of the Prince's console unfolded into a large v-pane, showing *Chu-sa* Koshō's face, which was now cold and alert, her eyes flickering from side to side. Xochitl stepped back to his shockchair, intent on the Nisei officer.

"Well?" he demanded.

"The cargo shuttle has exploded, *Gensui*." Susan's lips were a tight line, her brow furrowed. "No warning, no energy emissions . . . we're rewinding the telemetry, but I don't believe there is anything left to recover."

The Prince cursed, unable to keep rein on his temper a moment longer, and slammed a fist into the side of the shockchair. The Hjo recoiled, though Hummingbird's grip was tight enough to keep the creature from falling down. "We must flee," Sahâne wailed, "reverse your course, human. Reverse now!"

Without considering the ramifications, Gretchen slipped free of the Jaguar's grip—the Knight was staring at the console display, his attention distracted for a moment—and slid into a shockchair beside the horrified comm-tech.

"Roll that feed back, my dear," she said, voice calm and commanding. "Frame by frame."

The parchment envelope was opened and one of the octopus arms snaked from her pocket into a socket on the console without anyone noticing. Gretchen snugged her earbug tight against the background noise. The Prince and Koshō were disputing the merits of sending another shuttle towards the Sunflower. "Give me broad-spectrum passive scan at 20X for surface of the structure directly adjacent to the explosion . . ." *Should be some impact scarring now, from the debris. Crude—but I'll take the infopoints.*

"My lord . . ." Xochitl turned away from Susan's impassive visage, feeling thwarted at every turn, and advanced on the Hjogadim with a fierce expression. "We must determine the provenance of this—object—and if it poses a threat to México space! Then we can—"

"*Stand away*, toy!" Sahâne yelped, frightened by the Prince's fierce movement, reflexively making a form of obedience with his hand, as though the human were a servant in the house of his fathers. Xochitl staggered, eyes wide, his face draining of color.

«*Heart failure induced*,» his exo said brightly. «*Cortex shutdown expected within ten seconds.*»

The Prince collapsed to his knees, and then tipped to one side when his arms failed to support his weight. A great rushing sound roared in his ears. He saw the two Jaguar Knights lunging forward, weapons out, striking at the Hjo with all the speed they could muster. Sahâne's exposed fur shifted color and tone, and the first body-guard to reach him—butt of his shipgun reversed as a club—saw his knockout blow glance away from a sudden effusion of spiked scales which covered the Hjo's z-suited arm in a blur.

The creature, furious and sick at the same time, back-handed the marine with a long, gray arm. There was a *crack* of electricity and the Jaguar Knight was flung back, armor coiling smoke, to strike the floor, limp and lifeless.

«*Cortex shutdown in seven seconds.*»

Everyone in Secondary Command froze. The other Jaguar fetched up, weapon raised, suddenly unsure of how to attack the fully armored apparition. Sahâne stared down at his arm, the dark, rune-scribed z-suit now glittering with a spiked metallic shell, in astonished horror. "I did not do that," he declared in a weak voice. "I could not. This is *impossible*."

"Esteemed One, stay your merciful hand!" Hummingbird's voice was clear and direct, ringing in the air as the *nauallis* prostrated himself on the deck. "These *shiau har-e* will not serve without their lord being *shun tzing*. If he bends to your will, then all will be harmonious and we may flee this accursed place in speed and safety!"

Xochitl, barely able to see, gasped for life on the deck. The exo's implacable voice continued to count down the seconds left before his brain starved from oxygen deprivation. The Hjo loomed over him, blocking out the light of the overheads. A pair of black eyes stared down and the long mouth twisted in a snarl.

"Let this toy live, when it has raised a paw against me? Why should I?"

"Think, Esteemed One," Hummingbird said, his voice controlled—persuasive—without a hint of disobedience, "Think of your offspring in their thousands to come—we must be away from this accursed place swiftly and *this one*"—the *nauallis'* boot toed the Prince's side—"is their Authority. Through him, you control the others and may achieve a swift departure."

«*Four seconds to cortical failure.*»

Xochitl fought to form a coherent thought, and found he *could* still command his conscious mind, despite the annoying overlay of the exo. Desperate, feeling his mentation slipping away, he brought to focus a string of numbers—*three, five, five, seven, eleven, thirteen, seventeen, nineteen, twenty-nine* and . . . the voice of the exo abruptly stopped. There was no audible sound, no flashing overlay informing his vision of the event—but the fail-safe tripped, shutting down his implant.

Wheezing, his chest thudding with pain, the Prince closed his eyes, hoping to avoid further agony. His mind, suddenly, seemed quiet and empty—desolate. His limbs weak, helpless. The Prince began to panic, realizing that his interface to the shipnet would now have to be managed manually—and he didn't even have a hand-comp stowed in his luggage.

"Get us underway, *nongmin*." The Hjogadim stepped away from Xochitl's body, careful to keep his eyes averted from the vast panorama filling the v-display. Then he loped from Command, making a beeline for the lift a corridor away.

Gretchen looked up questioningly from her pirated console, trying to catch Hummingbird's attention. The *nauallis* had tilted his head, watching with great interest as the Prince struggled to his feet. Xochitl's skin had turned waxy and he blinked incessantly. Without the exo to refine his vision, he did not see well at all.

"My Lord?" The old Náhuatl offered the Prince his hand.

"We're not leaving," Xochitl rasped, his throat raw. He slumped weakly into the command shockchair. He pointed at Gretchen. "You—the one with the ugly hair—what happened to our probe?"

Turning slightly in her chair, Anderssen shrugged. "The relic is guarded by the same kind of protective lattice as the whole star system." She caught the Prince's eye and grinned. "But if we stay, I can get you inside."

"We should leave," Hummingbird snapped, glaring across at the Swedish woman.

Xochitl looked the *nauallis* up and down, realizing he did not know who the old man was or where he'd come from. "Who the devil are—wait, you're one of the *tlamatinime*!" His face contorted in a snarl. "*Cuauhhue-hueh* Koris—get this old witch off my bridge! Put him in the brig—someplace locked tight! With nothing on him but his skin."

The remaining Jaguar Knight rose from inspecting the body of his comrade. The master sergeant's visor was opaque, having shifted into combat mode, but his voice boomed hollowly. "As you bid, Lord Prince."

Hummingbird clasped his hands behind his head without a fuss and was escorted away. Gretchen watched him go with interest, wondering what the old Crow was up to now. *He'll be closeted with that alien in sixty seconds,* she wagered with herself. *He doesn't really want us to leave—just nudge the Flowery One in some direction of his choosing. But,* she thought, *two can play that game.*

Seeing the initial results from her analysis of the *Chimalacatl*'s surface—even just on the battle-cruiser's shipnet, much less after node $3^3$3 had taken the datastream apart and put it back together—had solidified a chaos of options vying for her attention. *I need to set foot on this thing, if that can be managed safely; even a half-hour would make all of this worthwhile.* Another certainty had formed in her heart, crystallizing out of a thousand points of long-held despair, anger, hatred, and delighted curiosity. *Hummingbird needs to be there, too. Oh yes, he does.*

"Now you, woman, what is your name?" Xochitl blinked owlishly at her, trying to glare in a properly Imperial manner.

"Doctor Gretchen Anderssen, xenoarchaeologist, University of New Aberdeen, Lord Prince."

"Are you now?" The Prince sat up straight in his chair, surprised and pleased at the same time. "How did you get out here?"

Gretchen said the first thing that came to mind. "I was supposed to be with the others, but I missed the survey ship, so I came on this one." She spread her hands, encompassing the whole of the *Naniwa*.

"How fortunate for you. . . ." Xochitl's attention, now that he still lived and breathed, was drawn inexorably back to the enormous shape of the Sunflower. He bit nervously at his thumb. "Do you . . . do you know what this thing is?"

Anderssen felt something like an electrical shock, a tingling jolt from crown to toe. In that instant, something blossomed in her mind and, for an instant, she was back under that overhang on Ephesus III, staring up at a rock-face which had grown so impossibly detailed and distinct in her vision that she could barely process the flood of sensation streaming into her from the totality of the world. But now there was a sensation of discrimination and all of the extraneous data could be discarded, leaving the Flowery Prince isolated in her perception and laid bare before her.

She absorbed all of the Prince's frailty, fear, doubt, ignorance. She glimpsed a fading half-image of a peculiar, inhuman second self which had shrouded him like a ceremonial mask. A façade which had worn *him*, completing his persona, investing him with a thousand subtle cues to authority and rule. Without that, he was only a shadow, less than half himself.

"No, *Tlatocapilli*." she said, supremely confident. "But if you give me leave, I will peel back all of its secrets for you—every last one. But . . . didn't you tell the ambassador we were leaving? What will you do about him?"

Xochitl swallowed, blinking again, his hand trembling in physical memory of incandescent pain twisting in every nerve. "I'll have to kill it—kill him—and atomize the body. Or, or cast it into the sun—or . . ." The Prince seemed paralyzed by the decisions before him. Without his exo providing summaries and risk-vectors, everything seemed suddenly gray and murky.

In Main Command, *Chu-sa* Koshō watched the Prince and Doctor Anderssen discussing the attributes of the

Chimalacatl on her surveillance cameras. Though her mien was impassive and controlled, she was deeply troubled by what she'd seen. A command sequence was waiting on her console, constructed in great haste during the scuffle and now refined, to vent the entire compartment to the void, and flood the evacuated rooms with hard radiation. *Would that be enough to kill this "ambassador" with the self-generating combat armor?* She was furious with herself for not attaching more security to the alien.

Susan had never encountered a "Hjogadim" before, and shipnet had nothing for her—no detail, no rumors, and no warnings—despite the fact that the creature spoke passable Náhuatl and was obviously well known to both the Prince and the *nauallis*. The thought of Hummingbird loose upon her ship made Koshō's stomach twist. Brow growing thunderous, she tapped up the security cameras for the ship's brig.

The remaining Jaguar had brought the old Náhuatl to a primary security cell and stripped him naked before locking him inside. Oc Chac, at Susan's direction, had already scrambled the codes and reviewed the list of those crewmen with access to the compartment.

His kind will not remain contained for long, Sayu.

Alone in the bare room, the old man looked up into the cameras and the faintest hint of a smile crossed his lips as he lowered himself gingerly into a cross-legged position on the floor.

Koshō sneered back, wishing once more that her *sensei* Hadeishi were on hand to deal with his "old friend" and all these intrigues. *I am not cut out for this,* she thought darkly. *We should flee this place, not stay, poking at a dark hole in the cliff with sticks . . . no matter what the Emperor demands.*

ABOARD THE KHAID CRUISER

Hadeishi wiped a coating of yellowing foam from the captain's console of the light cruiser. His armor was blackened and scored by flechette impacts and all of his grenades were gone. Cajeme and the other Team One survivors were dragging the last of the Khaid corpses away, for the enemy had tried to make a stand on the Command deck. The console was flickering in and out of focus—part of the glassite surface had shattered—and the Nisei officer shook his head in dismay. Disgusted, he shut down the entire console, then went to the Navigator's station where he was pleasantly surprised to see the Fleet standard interface was up and awaiting input.

He clicked channel. "Found one working, *Sho-i.*"

Lovelace was still far down the ship, barricaded into the Engineering compartment, with the remains of Team Four as her guardians. Between them, the shipcore was momentarily in Fleet hands, but there were still gangs of Khaiden roaming the side passages, exchanging intermittent gunfire with the Team Three commandos. Locked out of all of the control interfaces, the enemy had little chance of mounting an effective defense, but the Khaid were nothing but persistent. In some places they had cut their own way through the internal doors—but none of them had any heavy equipment, which meant the frame bulkheads and the main hatches were a serious barrier. "Keying in."

Got your login, kyo, she responded a moment later. *Handing off shipnet on deck one to your console.*

"Received." Weary, he sat down in the chair, ignoring the foam which spilled onto the floor. His first thought was to check in with De Molay, so he activated the intership channels and pinged around until one of them locked onto the *Wilful*.

The freighter captain's face appeared on the display a moment later and she brightened to see him. "Well, if it isn't our Engineer's Mate, gone missing the last day."

"Fortune has smiled," Hadeishi replied, glad himself that she still lived. "Did you take any damage?"

De Molay shook her head. "Your wounded have been coming over in a steady stream—didn't someone tell you?" She looked off-screen. "There are at least a dozen more laid out in what space we can spare. But we're entirely out of meds and ancillary supplies."

Mitsuharu levered up his faceplate, scratching a terrible itch beside his nose. "The sickbay here is all Khaid supplies, but I'll have *Gunso* Ad-Din peel someone off to search the holds—there may be useful meds somewhere . . ." A shipbug scuttled across the console, wearing a crown of foam. "Are you low on vermin? We have more than I can stomach over here."

She shook her head. "I can live without them. How stands your new ship? Does she have a name?"

"The Khaid called her the *Kader*. I haven't found a hull-plate or record to indicate the Fleet designation." Mitsuharu rubbed one eye. Adrenaline was draining from his system, leaving only the ache of lactic acid buildup. "The Khaid failed to destroy the communications equipment and their sensor records. *Sho-i* Lovelace reports we have all of the telemetry of the attack on the *Tlemitl*, the Research Station, and the IMN escort fleet—if I understand her correctly. But she is speaking far too quickly today for me to follow. Can you come across and take over cleanup here in Command? I need to go back downdeck and make sure the Khaid holdouts are run to ground."

De Molay nodded, pursing her lips. "You want me to break down the Khaid battlecast?"

"With Lovelace's help, yes." Hadeishi suddenly looked thoughtful. "Also, you will want to bring a cushion."

"A cushion?"

He shrugged. "Khaid chairs do not fit us so well. There's no sign any of the Fleet interior fittings survived, which is a great pity."

De Molay laughed in delight. "You *are* having trouble sitting down these days. I will see you in an hour or two."

Three hours later, after one of the burlier Team Four *kashikan-hei* had carried her up from the cargo bay where the *Wilful* was now docked, De Molay stared around at the wreckage of *Kader*'s Command deck and wrinkled up her nose. The thick musk of Khaid blood was mixed with the astringence of fire suppression foam to make a particularly foul smell. Beyond that, the chair at the weapons officer's console she'd been offered by a slightly built, worried-looking *Sho-i* gave her serious pause. "A beetle shell?"

"Yes, ma'am." Lovelace offered an apologetic smile. "Haven't found anything better."

De Molay shrugged and fitted an instafoam pillow into the peculiar dished chair back, then sat down gingerly. "We're underway again? I felt the drives light up while that big fellow hauled me up ten decks on his back. . . ."

"*Hai, Sencho*." The *Sho-i* called up a navigational plot, showing the past track of the *Kader*, as well as the projected patrol pattern. "I recovered this from one of the engine control nodes—when we flashed the whole ship, temporary storage went too—but some of the secondary systems had working copies, and this was one of them." The route spidered out from the main Khaid elements near the Pinhole, covered an irregular section of the stellar vicinity, and then angled back to join the pack again. "The *Chu-sa* wants us to be as inconspicuous as possible—so we follow the ordered route, submit status reports at the requested times, and so on. I've already sent one, cobbled together from the last transmit from the t-relay system, but we're due for five more before getting back to tau zero."

"This course was intended to cover the area of battle?"

"*Hai, Sencho.* The Khaid commander peeled off these three ships to mop up."

De Molay smiled, tapping through the navigational interface. "Well, let's press on then, shall we? I believe these three signals are Fleet evac capsules." Her stylus sketched in a slight change in vector to overrun all three icons on the plot.

Mitsuharu frowned, reviewing a comm-system composition pane. *The Monkey of Fate,* he thought with considerable irritation, *is laughing. Now I have to submit status reports to some Khaid overlord!* He looked over at Inudo, lately of the Scout *Corduba*, who was now sitting pilot for the *Kader*. "How many men have we recovered in total, *Thai-i*?"

"Over a hundred now, *Chu-sa*."

Hadeishi sighed, and then picked up his stylus again: *Our mission continues to be successful. We have found and destroyed nine Imperial escape pods. Additionally thirty useable z-suits, numerous small arms and edged weapons were recovered. Return to the hunting pack is expected within twenty-three hours.*

A firm tap on the running-man glyph spooled the message off into the t-relay system. *Done,* he thought, *with that exercise—for another six hours.*

"Isn't that strange," De Molay said from her seat at Navigation. Somehow the old woman had acquired a puffy black expedition jacket and mittens. Hadeishi didn't think it was so cold in Command, but he allowed that the Khaid had not set environmental to warm either. "The ship's previous course indicates they took no prisoners, captured no equipment . . . just a missile or beam into each pod and on their way."

Mitsuharu tried to swivel the beetle-chair at the captain's console, found that the chitin was sticking again, and stood up. He had been sitting too long in any case. "That is an odd course for a military so very in need of technical expertise, as well as slave labor. Haste overthrew their normal procedure, I think. They always took the time to dig every last beet from the fields before."

The old woman shook her head. "Wasteful."

Then she frowned, indicating the navigational plot on his console. "Do these raiders believe they can pick up the mystery weapon and use it like a shipgun? Every vessel we've seen is a warship—have they no scientists along, to analyze these phenomena?"

"That is an excellent point." Hadeishi nodded thoughtfully. "Do we have a breakdown of the battle around the science station yet?"

"Five minutes, *Chu-sa*." De Molay yawned and turned back to where Lovelace had continued unraveling the encoded Khaid 'cast logs. "Five minutes."

An hour later, Mitsuharu was sitting on the edge of the uncomfortable chair, wholly engrossed in stepping through the debacle around the science station one more time. The *Spear*-class light cruiser had gone out of service fifteen years before his old *Cornuelle* had even been laid down, so it lacked a wide variety of modern innovations. No threatwell, no reconfigurable consoles. But the dedicated v-display built into the side of the captain's station was enough to show him what he needed to see. To his eye, structure was slowly emerging from the seeming chaos of racing ships and sun-bright detonations. One ship, in particular, stood out amongst the confusion. An Imperial battle cruiser. A brand new one, he guessed, from the drive-flare and the outline the Khaid cameras had captured during the fighting.

Ah, she is beautiful. And her commander will win himself more than one medal if he sees home again. See how deftly he handles her . . . so sure in every maneuver, parsimonious in his launch patterns . . . and if my eye does not deceive, still alive, having fled down this opening in the Barrier wall.

"*Chu-sa?*" Leaning over from her console, De Molay broke his concentration. "I think our toil is showing fruit. Listen, isn't this the Khaiden battlecast?"

"Wait." Hadeishi signaled Command for quiet. "Please confirm that we are not broadcasting, *Sho-i* Lovelace. The Khaid have acute hearing." The old women handed over her earbug—though internal comm was operating again, the Khaid-specific systems were still cut from the main loop. He wiggled the uncomfortable object into his ear, listening closely to the resulting ebb and flow of alien chatter.

After a few minutes he nodded to himself and signaled for Lovelace to kill the circuit.

"I think you're right. Now we need a working real-time translator." He smiled wanly at the two women. "In about twelve hours?"

De Molay made a face, looking sideways at Lovelace. The *Sho-i* shook her head in dismay. "I don't think that's *possible, Chu-sa*. I know they exist—but *we* don't have one!"

Mitsuharu frowned, sitting back in the beetle-chair. Now he was thankful for the rigid armor which kept him from being stabbed in the side every time he moved. "Do we have a lexicon at least? My Khadesh is very poor—is anyone on-board fluent?"

"You mean besides the four Khaid we've captured?" The old woman shook her head. "Can we get a couple hours of shuteye, then try and work a new miracle for you?"

"Of course, *Sencho*. There are mats in those rooms down the main corridor. Lovelace-*sana* can show you where they are."

A full watch later, Hadeishi had coaxed the display into allowing him to zoom in on sections of the battle, even though the *Kader*'s shipnet core complained when he used so many computing cycles. De Molay and Lovelace had settled back into their seats, some kind of hot, nasty-smelling beverage in their hands. He rotated the shattered hulk of the *Tlemitl*, examining the debris field the super-dreadnaught had generated.

Sure enough, a cloud of evac capsules is huddling behind the wreck. He scratched behind one ear with his stylus.

The warship had lost two major sections to the Barrier weapon, but had remained largely intact. Whoever remained aboard had managed to cut the engines, contain the reactors, and get the surviving crew away into the evacuation pods. They had not kept the two severed sections from continuing forward, to be diced into ever smaller debris by whatever lay beyond . . . but the main mass of the hull had halted its rush to destruction. *Affording a paltry shelter to the survivors.*

"Here, *Sencho*, here are the ones who need us most. Their oxygen, water, and food is ebbing away like the outgoing tide. Even the *Firearrow*'s corpse will not shield them from the Khaid much longer."

He turned to find De Molay regarding him pensively. "You don't intend to leave a single man behind, do you?" she asked. "Even if this means risking nearly two hundred lives you've already saved and this fine ship you've taken?"

"It is not my ship," Hadeishi replied absently. "I cannot be held to account for its loss. But there are skilled officers and men out there waiting to die in the dark, either by fire or from cold, and their spirits will weigh heavy upon me if I do not try."

"Even if they would leave *you* behind without a second thought?"

Hadeishi gave her a sidelong look. The rest of the men and women on the bridge had paused in their work and were listening intently—though, out of deference to the two senior officers, not openly. Save Lovelace, of course, who was just staring at the two of them in dismay.

Mitsuharu tapped the helmet ring of his captured Khaiden armor, which he had not had time to take off since boarding the *Kader*. "I am already dead," he said quietly. "While they still live and breathe. I would keep grave-dust from their mouths as long as I can. In this way, even a spirit can serve."

De Molay made a disbelieving face. "I do not understand this fatalism, *Chu-sa*. It is not my way."

Hadeishi spared a moment to regard Tocoztic, who had taken the weapons officer's station. The young man looked pale, trying to escape notice by shrinking down into his seat. "With time and experience, that which was once obscure becomes clear," Hadeishi said softly. Then he picked up his stylus, eyes again fixed upon the little display, his whole attention focused on the tactical puzzle before him.

THE *NANIWA*

Though proper quarters had been provided for him, Prince Xochitl remained in Secondary Command, staring fixedly at the incomprehensibly large shape of the artifact four thousand kilometers from their bow, and doodling on his console. Doctor Anderssen and a rotating set of sensor techs and weapons officers had been working through all of the data captured by Konev's shuttle before its destruction, along with everything else flowing into their limited set of radiation-hardened sensors.

Chu-sa Koshō, who seemed to have taken up permanent residence in Main Command, had directed the technical team to modify one of the remotely controlled bots used for hull repairs and use the resulting "probe" to plumb the convoluted architecture of the structure without loss of life.

Xochitl found it interesting, in a nasty way, that the Nisei officer was concerned for the life of even the least of her crewmen. *Yakka won't last long in the Fleet,* he decided, *without someone to sponsor her. I wonder . . .* He paused a moment, half expecting his exo to kick in and present a list of advantages and disadvantages accrued by his patronage. When nothing happened, Xochitl felt the absence as a kind of unquenchable hunger, twisting his stomach into emptiness. He had not realized, having the exo present his entire adult life, how heavily he relied on the device.

My eyes are flawless, the Prince reminded himself, *but how do I see when the world around me is not annotated, described, outlined?* It was difficult for him to even navigate the hallways of the ship—no map presented itself, directing his steps, and the *kanji*-lettered signs and warnings were unreadable. Xochitl was a little stunned to realize that he did not actually know the meanings of all of the rank badges, flashes, and glyphs which informed the knowing observer of all of the hierarchies and authorities within the Fleet. Exo had always been whispering in his mind, guiding his interactions with the military, with the provincial governors, with—with everyone in his life.

I'm a cripple. The thought was bitter ash in his mouth. *While the Hjo remains in my proximity.*

This, Xochitl realized, was both the core of the problem and the obvious solution. He stood up abruptly and paced over to the xenoarchaeologist at the comm station.

"Follow me," he said before turning away, scanning the doors leading off of Secondary Command for a room which would suffice. *There! Thank Yacatecuhtli, Guide of the Lost, that someone's put up a sign in Náhuatl!*

Xochitl gestured for Anderssen to enter the conference room, and then closed the door lightly behind them. She sat on the edge of a fine-looking red mahogany table which made a hollow circle. The base apparatus for a holocast projector filled the center of the room. Gretchen looked the Prince up and down with open interest, wondering what was on his mind. *Something is, for certain.* Then she narrowed her eyes, trying to gain a sense of him, wondering if her gift—if it was a gift, and not the product of drugs or the unknown influence of the *Adh'atr*—would work on a person as well as a potsherd.

Xochitl said nothing, leaning against a cedar-paneled

wall ornamented with recessed watercolor paintings of flowers—they looked like pansies to Anderssen's eye, but she was no expert on the flora of old Earth—and scowling at her with a disturbingly unblinking gaze.

This is very strange, Gretchen thought—but she played along, saying nothing, idly kicking her feet and trying not to fidget. She felt the desire to be back at her console, digging through the reams of 3-v data, or the spatial model, or measurements of the enormous structure, as a physical pain. But still, she waited.

After quite a long time, the door recessed into the wall with a soft *chuff* and *Chu-sa* Koshō stepped in, her white dress uniform as immaculate as ever, her fine-boned face perfectly composed.

Seeing her, the Prince snorted rather rudely in amusement and then lifted his chin at Anderssen.

"This is the one who led you through the Barrier?"

Koshō paused at the edge of the conference table, regarding him levelly, and then nodded slightly.

"Then we have a problem," he declared. "The *Naniwa* must leave this area immediately. My noble guest, the *sian-fengh*, has made his desire to flee very clear. I cannot refuse him. Yakka, I need you to keep a close eye on him for me. He's truculent, difficult and, as you saw— unexpectedly dangerous, but I don't think he'll give you much trouble if you put a nargile and some opium back in his hands."

"Where are *you* going?" Koshō clasped both hands behind her back, falling into an easy parade rest.

Xochitl smiled, showing a large number of perfectly formed white teeth. "I've been thinking about what you said before, about my father—I'm going to do *exactly* as he asked. I'm taking that little merchant ship in the rear cargo hold and staying behind, while you return to the Barrier wall. I understand she's well shielded, and won't cost you something off your manifest if we suffer the same fate as that cargo shuttle."

He tapped the side of his head sharply. "Find us a way out, Yakka. We have to get out of here before we starve or are baked inside the shipskin, and there's no sense in you wasting time *here* while we poke and pry."

"Thus your *problem*," Koshō said coolly. "I'll need Anderssen-*tzin* and her comp models to find a way out, but *you* can't get inside the artifact without her. She can't be in both places at once, can she?"

The Prince nodded, clapping his hands lightly together. "That would seem a puzzle, save I have an answer." He smiled tightly at the *Chu-sa*, an expression which made the little hairs on Gretchen's neck rise.

"That pale, nervous Anglishman you've got stowed away in Engineering—yes, I know where he is—give him the telemetry from your passage through the Pinhole and he can reconfigure your sensors to reveal the spiderweb trapping us."

Beyond a slight nostril flare, Koshō showed no reaction. But Gretchen could feel the woman's entire body stiffen from across the room, and the answering surge of pleasure in the Prince. *What a foul dog he is*, she thought, watching the two of them as from a great distance.

"Helsdon is not wholly himself—"

"All the better," Xochitl snapped, "near-mad as he is may prove to your advantage! I am taking Anderssen here into the artifact, *Chu-sa*, while you find us a way out of this hole. Is that perfectly clear?"

"*Hai, Gensui.*"

Anderssen felt an enormous surge of delight, like golden honey welling up within her, suffusing her arms, legs—even her thoughts—with anticipation.

Two hours later, Koshō looked up at a soft tapping at the door to her private office. "Enter."

The door slid open and Green Hummingbird stepped in, his feet bare, attired in a simple Fleet undershirt and off-duty trousers. Without his usual cloak and hood, he seemed surprisingly small—until one met his dusky green eyes and then his true stature asserted itself.

"*Chu-sa* Koshō," he said politely. "A word with you, if I may."

"I believe," she said, rising and stepping to the door, "that you were confined to the brig, by order of the Prince Imperial himself."

No one was in the corridor, though Susan was unpleasantly aware that nearly every centimeter of the *Naniwa* was under surveillance by some kind of recording device.

The old Náhuatl nodded. "I am. Thank you for your concern for my comfort. Your hospitality has been most adequate, but I am on my way to pay respects to the Esteemed One and shall not keep you further."

With that, he made a polite bow and then slipped out the door again. Koshō stared after him, wondering if she should summon the marine ready squad, have the *nauallis* clapped in chains and then, perhaps, locked in a room for which there was no key. *But then*, she thought, starting to feel rising amusement at the thought of seeing the Prince's face when the escape was discovered, *he would wrinkle his way out of that, too. I wonder . . .* Another thought brought her up short. *Does Hummingbird believe he will cheat death, too, in the end?*

Juggling the possibilities in her mind, Koshō came to the unpleasant conclusion that letting the *nauallis* go about his business without interference was less dangerous than following the Prince's orders. Particularly since she was quite certain that Hummingbird knew what he was doing, even if she couldn't stand him personally.

However, she thought, *I do need to keep an eye on the future.*

Susan then went to her console and tapped open a channel to the brig. The marine officer on duty responded immediately, his young face intent and dutiful.

"*Heicho* Adamsky, has someone thought to provide the prisoner in cell one with something to eat?"

Then while she waited for the alarms to sound, most of her attention was on the supply manifests *Thai-i* Goroemon had forwarded up from Logistics for her review. They were desperately low on every kind of munitions, and only marginally better off for parts, meds, and food. *Six months of supplies left, eh? Only if you don't get a quarter of your stowage vented by a penetrator.*

Some time later, the tramp freighter *Moulins* maneuvered out of the rear cargo hold under its own power. The ship had been hurriedly resupplied with water, food, and other perishables. Reaction mass for the engines had been topped off and Prince Xochitl, his remaining Jaguar Knight, Doctor Anderssen, and a handful of marines borrowed from the *Naniwa* were on board. In the cramped Command space, Captain Locke and his pilot were watching the external cameras and docking control status with a weather eye. The Prince and his bodyguard had appropriated the Navigator and Comm officer's seats and were glowering at the backs of the Europeans during the delicate maneuver.

Gretchen watched them all from the hatchway while the ship was decoupling, then left them all to stew and banged downdeck to the cargo area where all of their luggage had been piled by the middies from the *Naniwa*. Her duffle had disappeared, to her disgust, under an enormous quantity of marine gear.

And, she thought, rather morosely, *here I am again on this damned tiny ship with these fanatics.*

Locke had accepted this new commission without protest, having apparently spent his time in the brig playing cards and smoking a succession of foul Novo French cigarettes. Now free of the battle-cruiser and at the helm of his own ship again, his hostility towards the Prince and the Fleet marines cluttering up his decks was banked, but simmering. Löjtnant Piet was doing less well at hiding his antipathy, but Xochitl apparently did not care, showing not the slightest awareness of their anger.

They'll find a way to get along, Anderssen thought cheerfully, dragging olive-gray duffels aside. "There's my—oh, what the hell are you doing in there?"

Beneath the pile of luggage, with his head resting on Gretchen's field pack, Green Hummingbird had made himself a bit of a nest using a pair of folding kitchen tables. As she moved aside the last of the ammunition crates with a grunt, his lips fluttered with a soft snore.

"Does the Prince know you've come along, Crow?" Anderssen pinched his brown old ear as hard as she could. The old Náhuatl opened one eye, squinting at her, then sat up carefully and eased out of the tiny space under the tables.

Briskly chafing his wrists and ankles, he observed: "*Tlatocapilli* Xochitl is noted for his admirable qualities in battle, not for his legendary acumen. *Chu-sa* Koshō, on the other hand, is beginning to understand how to operate in the wide world, as befits a gifted student with an excellent master."

Gretchen shook her head, retrieving her pack. She began digging through the compartments, confirming that everything she'd stowed was still in place and undamaged. "Why did they send him then? They knew what was out here, right?"

Hummingbird shrugged. "I believe he was judged the most expendable of the Emperor's sons."

"More so than the one that's always on the 3-v? Tezozómoc the Glorious?" Anderssen was appalled.

"Not all stone flakes the right way," the old man replied, pulling on a pair of boots he'd lifted from one of the other duffels. "What use is a pretty piece of flint if it cannot take an edge?"

"And Tezozómoc *can*?"

Hummingbird did not reply, instead he dug around in the bottom of his gear and came up with a plastic container filled with cheesecloth. Holding the jar up, the old Náhuatl turned it this way and that, checking the contents. Then he turned back the lid, smelling the small egg-sized rounds inside.

"Lady of Light!" Gretchen coughed, eyes smarting. "Those are strong! Is that *opium*? What the devil are you doing with a basket of knuckles?"

He smiled serenely at her, tucking the container inside a field jacket he'd stolen from someone, somewhere. "My traveling companion needs a little coaxing to leave his shipping container."

Anderssen shook her head in dismay. "You know, Crow, I had a friend who had a fascination for doing archaeology in the ancient home of the Chichimecas. It was always dangerous, uncomfortable work. The land is harsh, the people were poor, running contraband was the only way to make money. All social hierarchies began and ended with some *pilli* in his fortified house surrounded by an army of goons. Not the kind of lord who likes strangers—particularly inquisitive ones—to come knocking around.

"But Harriet especially liked taking a gaggle of impressionable students out to do big ground surveys and to excavate just enough of an old city to intrigue the historical agencies, who would then give her more money and permits to do whatever she wanted so they could learn the next bit of the story she was telling. I think the reason *she* did it was because the challenge of facing sudden death and coming home with the bacon got her out of bed in the morning.

"As long as I knew her, she specialized in visiting the resident gang lord with a gift bottle of *uisge-beatha*. By the time she'd spent an hour chatting with him in an entirely charming manner, the fearsome and despicable toad had been transformed into her special, professional chum. I never knew her to break any laws, and somehow she always brought her crew home with all their fingers and toes."

Green Hummingbird raised an eyebrow. "An enviable record, Doctor Anderssen." He stood up, patting his pockets. "I believe you are going to need all of your equipment in a very short time."

Six hours later, the *Moulins* had reached the edge of the *Chimalacatl*.

Gretchen had appropriated the Comm station from the Jaguar Knight and now watched her v-displays eagerly. Endless ranks of jagged architectural forms glided past as the freighter plowed along at right-angles to the surface of the artifact. The structure was apparently composed entirely of triangular sections, each holding a second inverted triangle recessed within. The bronze block was tucked into a pocket of her equipment rig, now strapped on over her z-suit. Her field comp and secondary equipment were tacked to the console, all components recording at maximum fidelity. Just for good measure, her interface to the *Moulin*'s shipskin, cameras, and the single sensor boom was running bidirectional—which allowed her to offload some processing to the shipnet itself when needed.

For the moment, she had not connected the bronze block to anything. Despite this measure, it seemed heavy against her chest, and warm to the touch, as though some internal process was underway.

Even without node $3^3 3$ in operation, however, enough data was flowing into her conceptual models and analysis matrices to leave her feeling slightly drunk. Fingers trembling, she unwrapped an *oliohuiqui* packet and pressed the acidic tablet beneath her tongue. Her skin was singing with the tension congealing in the Command compartment, but the promise of so many wonders to come pushed all of her concerns away.

"Radiation levels are rising," Piet reported, tapping a winking glyph on his display to expand the warning message. "Captain?"

"Reconfigure the shipskin for maximum protection," Locke replied without bothering to consult with the Prince. "Let's try not to fry!"

Anderssen paid them little attention, though part of her mind wondered what had happened to the shipskin, for the flow of data into her analysis array did not diminish at all. The exterior configuration of the ship *had* changed however, shifting into an unfamiliar alignment.

But for the moment, Gretchen didn't care about the crew's machinations. *As long as we're capturing clean data . . . wait a moment.* A subtle change had occurred in the visual flow of the artifact. Nothing obvious—the intersecting triangles had a vertiginous effect on the eye—but the consistency of the shadows pooling in their depths had begun to thicken. "There!" Anderssen suddenly spoke, half-rising from her seat. "Quadrant six by sixteen—that's a lock entrance."

"How can you tell?" Xochitl glared over her shoulder in disgust at the flurry of bizarre glyphs and patterns dancing across her v-displays. "What *is* all of this static?"

"Our eyes in the darkness, Lord Prince," she replied

distantly. "Löjtnant—slow a bit . . ." Her stylus danced across a v-pane cross-connected to the comm system. A burst of indecipherable noise flooded from the ship's tachyon array. "Now, wait . . . wait . . . there!"

One of the triliths moved—its motion obvious even to the naked eye—receding into sudden darkness. The constellation of other triliths around the missing triangle followed, sliding backward into shadow without evident mechanism. An opening emerged with fluid suddenness—a channel or corridor leading into the interior of the structure. Measurements popped up on Gretchen's console and she whistled softly, breaking into a huge grin. "Six kilometers on a side, Lord Prince. I think the *Moulins* will make easy passage."

"This was built for truly giant ships," Xochitl said, his voice tinged with awe. "Like the thousands of wrecks in the debris cloud."

No one replied. Locke and Piet were motionless, their faces settled into expressionless masks. Gretchen felt a current of raw fear circulate among the men in Command, but the taste was distant and of little consequence. "Go on, enter," she directed. "We'll be shielded from the radiation storm inside."

The freighter passed in, maneuvering drives flaring, and was swiftly enveloped by abyssal darkness. Behind them, the constellation of triliths reformed with admirable speed, abruptly cutting off sight of the hot, glowing sky outside.

"It seems the artifact is not entirely dead," Gretchen said cheerfully. "No matter. I believe we can open the passage again, when the need arises."

In the suddenly dim bridge, Xochitl scratched his nose and—taking a deep breath—began to compose a series of numbers in his thoughts. *Zero, one, one, two, three, five, eight, thirteen, twenty-one . . .*

ABOARD THE *KADER*

"We have comm intercept available, *Chu-sa*," De Molay announced in an offhand way.

Hadeishi's command chair rotated to face her with an audible whine. Apparently the Khaid refit had failed to properly seal the gimbals, and fire suppression foam was eating away at the mechanism. The Nisei officer shifted restlessly. "We're synched into their battlecast? Is the translator running?"

"Such as it is." De Molay shrugged, her thin shoulders swallowed by the expedition jacket. "Channel eleven."

Mitsuharu pressed a finger to his earbug, jumping channels until the hissing growl of the enemy flooded in, making him wince. Dialing down the volume, he found the jury-rigged translator circuit could use a great deal of improvement—about every fourth word of Khadesh echoed back in Nihongo on channel two. He grimaced, feeling a truly staggering migraine coming on, before settling back with his eyes closed, trying to parse some kind of meaning from the staticky roaring.

After thirty minutes, he wrenched the earbug free and stared cross-eyed at Lovelace and De Molay. Hadeishi said nothing for a moment, keying his med-band to dispense as much painkiller as it would allow.

"This won't work. Your efforts are tremendous, but the shipnet comps just can't keep up with all of the cross-conversations. Have you been recording all of this traffic?"

The *Sho-i* nodded vigorously. "We have sixteen hours in the can, *Chu-sa*."

"Can we translate that, if the comp has time to grind away?"

"*Hai, Chu-sa.*"

Mitsuharu shook his head slowly, beginning to despair. "Without following the 'cast in real time, there's no way we can insert ourselves into the formation ... we'd trip ourselves up the first time someone commed to discuss the weather!"

De Molay spread her hands. "Then we give up and go home. No loss."

Her nonchalant expression sparked a flare of anger in the Nisei officer. He glowered at the freighter captain, which drew an amused snort from the old woman, and then he sat back in the uncomfortable chair again, thinking furiously.

The youngest of the Seven Sisters pressed her forehead to the straw matting covering the floor of Musashi's hut. "Please, sensei," she begged earnestly, "none of us can defeat Möngke; he is a monster, gifted with inhuman powers, surrounded by an army of tens of thousands of men. Osaka castle itself is a maze of fortifications, towers, moats ... We've tried sneaking in, but he's suborned the ninja clans as well, and they watch by night while his archers watch by day."

"He only has one weakness," Eldest said, kneeling beside her irrepressible sibling. "He believes himself the finest swordsman in all of Asia—not just Nippon—and if you challenge him, then he will come forth to meet you in single combat, for his pride will admit no other rival."

"I no longer travel the sword-saint's road," Musashi croaked, his voice raspy from disuse. He indicated a small stone statue of the Buddha with a seated bow. "I no longer seek conflict in the world of men. Ieyasu and I strove to overthrow the Yuan seven years ago, and failed utterly. Now he is dead and I have found sanctuary here on Mount Iwato. Only the Dokkōdō remains." He gestured to a series of scrolls sitting on a small side table.

Eldest glanced sidelong at Squeaker's twin, who was standing in the doorway, keeping watch.

"What if the Emperor summoned you, called you forth to do battle with the invaders? Would you deny him, foreswear your duty to all Nippon?"

Musashi shook his head sadly. "The last Emperor fell at Nara generations ago."

"Not so." The third Sister turned in the doorway. "The Imperial line is sustained even today. Would the plea of the Son of Heaven move you to action?"

The hermit fell silent, eyes downcast, for a long time. When he looked up, at last, the sunset was gilding the rough-hewn timbers of his hut. "It would."

The third Sister extended his hand. "Then stir yourself, Musashi Miyamoto, Nippon calls you."

"Attention the bridge," Hadeishi announced, standing up. The low murmur in the circular room died away. The regular watch had swollen to include the leaders of the various ships' crews rescued from the abyss. Mitsuharu looked about slowly, considering each man and woman as though seeing them for the first time. He stepped to the center of the bridge, where Lovelace had rigged up a holocast projection in place of the old-fashioned plotting display which had formerly served the *Kader*. *It's no threatwell*, Hadeishi thought, *but will do for now*. He marked off the area of interest with his stylus. A series of vector tracks appeared in the 'cast.

"The *surtu*, as the Khaiden name their hunting pack, has dispersed over the last forty-eight hours." Mitsuharu's tone was crisp. "Four of their *Hayalet*-class battleships remain at the entrance to the Pinhole. They are supported by six destroyers, several tenders, and what seems from message traffic to be a troop ship. It is difficult to keep track of their movements under the current conditions, but I would hazard they are making a serious attempt to chart the outlines of the aperture. The other surviving ships have scattered to police the battleground, and to search along the periphery of the Barrier for another way through." The corners of his eyes tightened minutely. "One of their prey—an Imperial battle-cruiser of the *Provincial*-class—has escaped the battle by navigating through the Barrier itself."

"How?" An officer from the *Mace* blurted without thinking. "Our sensors can't even . . ."

"We do not know how," Hadeishi said quietly. "But the telemetry we've deciphered from *this* ship indicates they did so. It is also possible that the battle-cruiser took aboard at least one evac capsule from the super-dreadnaught which was destroyed in the Pinhole itself—"

"Surely your Prince Xochitl left the field of battle in haste, then!" De Molay said loudly, drawing a round of glares from the Imperials seated or standing around her.

Hadeishi continued, unperturbed. "Speculating about who may have lived or died is useless.

"And we are not concerned with the Prince." The stylus in his hand circumscribed a constellation of glowing dots on the plotting board. "There are sixteen evac capsules from the *Tlemitl* hiding in the sensor-shadow of the dreadnaught's hulk. We are going to go in and get them out." A smile lit his face for a moment. "And if some Khaiden ships fall afoul of our passage, well then—all the better."

"Impossible," breathed an ensign, now the sole officer remaining from the *Gladius*. "We haven't a third the weight of a single *Hayalet*! We'll be shot to bits within moments of our initial missile salvo!"

"Therefore," Hadeishi said, turning and surveying them all, "we will not attack until it is too late for them to respond. And preferably, we will not attack *at all* while achieving our goal."

The Imperial officers stared at him in confusion. Then there was a babble of questions.

"Show us," De Molay said loudly. That quieted the group. Her seamed old face showed skepticism, but Hadeishi saw that her eyes were merry with anticipation. "Show us what you plan to do, *Chu-sa.*"

WITHIN THE SUNFLOWER

The *Moulins* crept forward through the dark, exterior floods stabbing into a colossal empty space. Hints of enormous structures wreathed in shadow ghosted by on either side. On the bridge, Gretchen had her eyes half closed, fingers drifting lightly across her console. The *oliohuiqui* she'd taken was burning at the back of her throat, and the flood of data populating her v-displays had coalesced in her perception, becoming a fluid thing, shifting and deforming with each passing moment, as more and more information flowed into the array of comps. Dozens of passageways branched off in all directions as they moved, but only one thread through the maze seemed proper to her. If pressed, she would have said the volume of the channel they were following felt the *most used*, though nothing obvious about the ranks of triliths they passed would have indicated this.

"Six hundred k from the entrance now," the pilot said quietly. "How deep are we g—"

"As deep as necessary," Xochitl snapped. His mood, if possible, had worsened while sitting in the darkness at the back of the bridge. *He doesn't like it that Europeans are handling the ship.* Gretchen clearly felt the nervous tension throbbing in the Prince, as though a wire were being twisted tighter and tighter around some fulcrum. His discomfort was now beginning to cause *her* physical pain.

Xochitl stirred, glaring accusingly at Anderssen. "We have passed several hundred thousand openings into the structure, Swede. Why haven't we stopped?"

Though her attention was focused far from the Prince, after a lengthy pause Gretchen remembered to reply: "None of them are suitable."

"How so?" The Prince brought up the internal map of the structure being constructed by the sensors on the Navigator's console. "We've passed numerous secondary openings—are these doors?—large enough for a dreadnaught to enter—how are they not suitable for *our* entry?"

"They are closed to us," Gretchen said, attempting to smile reassuringly at him over her shoulder. The resulting expression was almost feral, for a wild, heedless light had come into her face. "We need just the right kind of way in . . . nothing fancy, *Tlatocapilli*. That would be dangerous."

"And you can tell that which is dangerous and that which is not?" His attempt at sarcasm sounded shrill, for his voice was tight with fear.

"We are still alive, aren't we?" Gretchen turned back to her console. *Oh, what is this?*

Illuminated by the *Moulin*'s running lights, a constellation of new structures emerged from the darkness. Tall pylons ascended from pooled shadow below to disappear into equal indigo above. Between them, another of the structures which seemed to be a portal door had appeared: a triangular shape several hundred meters high, comprised of four smaller triangles. Each of the inner triangles contained a further inverted, and recessed, triangle. This arrangement, unlike many others they had passed, held a darker hue—almost night-black itself, but irregularly mottled.

Anderssen's console flickered, all of the v-panes abruptly closing and then reopening again. She stiffened, feeling a flood of heat warm her chest, even through the z-suit and the equipment rig. The edges of the analysis displays on the console began to distort, the lettering transforming into the unintelligible glyphs which had overcome the *Naniwa*'s navigational system during their transit of the Pinhole.

Uh-oh. Node 3^33 is connecting—but it's not plugged in! Gretchen felt the pattern of her analysis matrices shifting. The pulsing back-and-forth of her comps and storage nodes shaded as well, starting to move faster—much faster than she could follow. Dreading what she might feel, Anderssen slipped her right hand under her jacket, fingertips brushing against the surface of the bronze block. It was very warm and vibrating faintly. She looked down and was stunned to see that a hot, golden glow was shining between her fingers. *What the*—

"Anderssen, what *is* that?" Xochitl had finally noticed the grouping of pylons.

"We are very close," she managed to say. Löjtnant Piet, without even a look to Captain Locke, had turned the freighter towards the four-sided diamond. Their speed slowed, now the *Moulins* was inching along. The exterior floods angled forward, trying to illuminate the blackened surface. The beams played across the portal, but did not even generate a reflection, as though the material were drinking in the light.

Then a point of hard jewel-like radiance appeared at the center of the innermost diamond. A distinct collimating beam stabbed out and washed over the *Moulins*, causing the forward cameras to polarize, reducing their view to nothing but a scintillating white point. In Anderssen's equipment rig, the bronze block stopped vibrating and went cold. Gretchen gasped in pain as her perceptual gestalt abruptly collapsed, leaving her blinking owlishly at her console, which had terminated all of the v-panes simultaneously.

Behind her, the Prince stiffened in alarm.

The vision overlay generated by Xochitl's exo was awash with unknown and indecipherable datagrams and hieroglyphs. Voices were speaking in his mind in a lilting, singsong tongue like calling birds; but though the cadence of the sounds seemed terribly familiar he knew none of the words. Alarmed, he surged upward out of his shockchair. "What the—"

"A Gate opens before you," said an unexpected voice. A seamed old hand, hard as bog oak, settled on the Prince's shoulder and forced him back down. The México looked up, astounded to see that Green Hummingbird— now clad in a Fleet z-suit—had slipped quietly into the back of the bridge. The dyspeptic face of the Hjogadim Sahâne peered down over his shoulder, red-rimmed eyes staring accusingly at the Prince. The *nauallis* met Xochitl's gaze with a serious expression. "I advise you not to enter this structure."

"You would exhaust God's patience, sorcerer." The Prince threw aside the old Náhuatl's arm and pushed up from his seat. "You *do not* command me! You serve the Empire and in this place I am—"

"It is my purpose, *Tlatocapilli*," Hummingbird interrupted, "to keep humanity from harm—and this *place* is beyond our skill to use, our power to hold, and our intellect to understand. We must leave before we come to grief. Or worse, bring disaster home with us."

"You threaten me?" Xochitl bit out the words, struggling to keep his temper.

The Prince's exo had already summoned *Cuauhhue-*

hueh Koris and the marines, who now appeared in the hatchway. The Jaguar Knight ducked inside, shipgun leveled on Hummingbird's back.

Sahâne found himself surrounded by the marines, who were watching the alien warily, but they kept their distance. The Hjo licked his lips, long head darting from side to side.

Hummingbird affected no notice of the activity: "My duty to your father compels me to try and save your life."

Xochitl drew his sidearm, thumbing off the safety. "Unwise choice, old man. You are utterly—"

"Lining up a new approach vector," Gretchen's voice cut in. She had ignored the Prince and the Judge and their spat, even the appearance of Sahâne, instead watching the progress of the diamond-hard light which had traversed the hull. Now the radiance flickered out as swiftly as it had appeared, and the Navigator's panel in front of her woke to life again. Now, however, all of the v-panes and controls were displaying the tight curlicues of the alien hieroglyphics which had come and gone from her vision over the past days.

Landing beacon locked, one of them suggested to her and, nodding in acknowledgment, Anderssen tapped the glyph. The nav system on the freighter kicked in, adjusting their approach. Piet started in alarm—then looked to the captain for guidance—his face tight with distress. Locke shook his head *no,* the movement barely visible even to Gretchen, who was seated only two meters away. Both men watched her intently and Gretchen suddenly tasted a little of their desire, which matched tone and color with hers.

Let us see what lies beyond, a memory echoed, bringing with it the smell of oiled wood and a perfume she'd last worn as an undergraduate. *Beyond the door of the unopened tomb, beyond the rise of the next hill, within unplumbed space, beyond our conception. This is the fever which drives us to create, to innovate, to overcome.*

Outside, the mottled black wall had divided into three parts, and each triangle receded from sight. Beyond, in a chamber whose comprehensible size—only a few hundred meters in each dimension—seemed puny and cramped, was the age-etched shape of a landing cradle.

"Entering an active g-field," Piet reported, taking over the controls. "Docking jets adjusting . . ."

THE KADER

INBOUND TO THE PINHOLE

Hadeishi listened intently to the z-suit radio, his throat-mike replaced by a vocoder Cajeme had assembled from the components of an entertainment 3-v scavenged from the main mess deck. As he listened, the eager voice of a Khaiden *Kabil Rezei* aboard the battleship *Sokamak* buzzed away into silence.

"Yes, my lord." Mitsuharu keyed into a v-pane on his display. A second later, the 'coder produced a yipping bark ending in a sibilant growl. To Hadeishi's poorly trained ear, it sounded like proper Khadesh. . . . "One of the Imperial capsules had a scientist aboard—he sought to barter service—and questioning has revealed a way to detect the Wall-of-Knives. I am bringing him to you now with his instrumentation."

Out of the corner of his eye, Hadeishi observed the other officers standing watch in Command were keeping their mouths shut, as ordered. They were, however, grinning and signing "victory" to one another. *Morale is good,* he thought, waiting for a response. *As befits those snatched from Mictlantecuhtli's dreadful embrace.*

The *Kader* plowed through the dust at a swift pace, transit deflectors up full, shrouding the ship in a cascade of brilliant interference. The Pinhole was now only moments away. The *Hayalet*-class battleships deployed around the broken hulk of the Imperial research station showed clearly on her sensors.

Five minutes to deceleration burn, Thai-i Inudo keyed to each of the other stations.

Hadeishi bid proper farewell to the hunt-lord, then closed the circuit. *I miss Captain De Molay. But she has her ship back, only a little worse for wear.* The old woman had not been happy about the mess they'd left behind on the *Wilful,* but accepted it as the cost of survival. A handful of the walking wounded had been left with her as well, to crew the little freighter.

In their last conversation, on comm between the two ships, she fixed him with a bellicose stare, saying, "If you were my fosterling, I would rap your knuckles sharply, *Chu-sa.* You play recklessly, risking yourself at every turn—but I cannot fault your consideration for the other children. They are always in your thoughts, and you are always the first to offer them a hand up from the ground. I hope—and I doubt we will meet again—that you will consider that *your* life may be just as precious, to others."

The *Wilful* had slipped away hours before, vanishing into the vastness of the *kuub,* leaving no trace of its passing which the *Kader's* sensors could detect.

"All stations secure?" Mitsuharu asked on the command channel. A frenzy of confused activity followed amongst the Imperials on the unfamiliar bridge. "Weapons—confirm that guns are cold? Missile racks and penetrator pods are locked down? All hands, brace for combat acceleration."

A ragged chorus of *Hai, Chu-sa* arose, both in Command and on the channel from downdeck.

Hadeishi nodded to Inudo. "Pilot, point-and-a-quarter to ventral. Begin deceleration burn."

The *Thai-i* rotated a glyph on his display just a fraction and then slid a gauge lower. "*Hai, kyo*. Point-and-a-quarter, ventral. Beginning deceleration burn."

On the plot, the *Kader*'s icon closed swiftly with that of the *Sokamak*, the largest of the Khaid battleships. Lovelace's translation of the 'cast chatter had gleaned only fragmentary information for Hadeishi, but he knew some of the ship designators now, and a little bit about his enemy. He knew that one of the more vocal Khaid commanders was named Zah'ar, and he had at least two rivals. The late, unlamented captain of the *Kader* had been Begh-Adag—and that fellow seemed to have been the least respected of the clan-lords involved in this escapade.

"*Chu-sa*, point-and-a-half turned. Deceleration burn complete." Inudo shook out his shoulders and hurriedly called up a new slate of course and speed settings on a side pane.

"*Joto-Heiso* Cupan, ready shuttle in bay three for launch," Hadeishi said into the throatmike. "Damage control parties, starboard wing, stand by for decompression."

The chief petty officer from the *Asama* tapped in amongst the chorus of *Hai, kyo* from the damage control teams. "Shuttle in bay three, ready for launch, *Chu-sa*."

The light cruiser matched velocity with the *Sokamak*, and the shuttle jetted away on an intercept course for the battleship. A v-pane on his console showed Mitsuharu the boat-bay-three doors cycling closed.

"Shuttle away, *kyo*," Cupan confirmed.

Hadeishi shifted uncomfortably in the shockchair, one eye on a replay of the missing battle-cruiser's escape, the other on a series of panels showing thermal readings from the profusion of broken ships, fusion detonations, and other hot-spots in the immediate area. The dust clouds, which seemed to have thickened around the invisible Barrier, were slowly shifting color as the component particles soaked up the hard radiation.

"Pilot, turn two points to starboard, one point dorsal."

Inudo nodded, his neck shining with sweat. "*Hai, kyo.* Two points starboard, one dorsal."

The *Kader*'s maneuvering thrusters flared briefly as she turned away from running parallel with the *Sokamak*, her nose angling towards the entrance to the Pinhole itself. There, the walls of dust were burning with a deep orange and azure, making a sea of fire to blind the unwary eye.

Against this background, Hadeishi thought, *the thrust-signature of our so-able friend would be nearly undetectable if one did not know exactly what to look for.*

But Lovelace and Tocoztic had painstakingly reassembled the course taken by the battle-cruiser, and now Mitsuharu was watching for traces of her drive plume wending its way amongst the hidden shoals and reefs of the depthless ocean.

Musashi stands poised on the bridge at Windlodge, goose-feathers brushing the enamel of his cheek-guard, the Iroquois swarming up the levee in a numberless, copper-skinned mass. One of their ohnkanetoten *surges through the ranks of charging pike men astride a roan stallion . . . sun-dogs gleaming from his garishly ornamented plate-mail, his long sword shining silver in the summer light.*

THE NANIWA

The battle-cruiser had clawed its way back up out of the interlocking g-fields wrapped around the singularity in realspace, finally reaching a point where the hypercoil could punch them through to transluminal. In Command, Koshō sat in her shockchair, one slim leg crossed over the other, watching the threatwell rotate slowly. The cloud of broken ships was fast approaching as they climbed gradient, and the sight of such colossal devastation weighed heavily on her thoughts. Helsdon, having completed his mandatory sleep cycle, was sitting at the Nav station with *Thai-i* Olin. Together they had reconfigured nearly half of the shipskin to watch for the kind of quantum disturbances the engineer suspected heralded the movement or presence of the Barrier threads.

Better than nothing, Susan thought tiredly, *but I am already missing Doctor Anderssen's presence.*

She paced over to their console. "Any luck, *Kikanshi*?"

"There must be a defensive Thread array associated with the Sunflower," Helsdon muttered, one pale hand trembling over a plot of the broken armada. "Most of these ships were cut apart, just as ours were. . . ."

"An attack?" Koshō leaned over his shoulder, puzzled. "They're bunched together so tightly . . ."

"No . . ." Helsdon replied, scratching nervously at a week's beard. "They've fallen into a balance point in the gravitation of this system. This is an eddy of flotsam . . . the ships might have all been destroyed out by the Barrier itself . . . or even closer to the artifact."

"Why not a battle?"

Helsdon seemed to shrink, shoulders hunching in, and an expression of pain flitting across his face. "These weren't warships, *Chu-sa*." His stylus tapped unevenly across the control panes and a series of comp-projected reconstructions sprang to life. The alien craft were revealed as sixty-kilometer-long trihedrons with bulky drive fairings at the rear.

"Tens of thousands of cargo containers—suspension pods, I would guess—are held in each of those three lobes. But that's only what we see nearby in this image. In the whole of the debris swirl, there are over four thousand ships, the comp says. . . ."

Koshō's eyes widened, taking in the lift capacity of the dead fleet. "Troop transports for a million-man army?"

"Colony ships?" Helsdon shook his head. "I don't know what to make of it. Maybe refugees? A million isn't much to lift from some dying world—but it's sure better than what *we* could pull together."

"Was all this a fortress?" Susan wondered softly, her eyes turning to the system plot and the delicate balance of the brown dwarves, the singularity, and the *Chimala-catl*. "It must have been, hidden behind the wall of knives. But not a refuge, not in the end . . ." Her voice strengthened. "Engineer, can you find out if these ships were empty or full when they were destroyed?"

Helsdon nodded. Koshō turned to Oc Chac. "Meanwhile, we need another way out of this pocket, one that is not barred by the enemy. You've the search-pattern set?"

"*Hai, Chu-sa* . . . starting from the Pinhole and spiraling out."

"Excellent." Susan nodded approval.

"But *Chu-sa*, if what Engineer Helsdon mentioned is true—if the whipping knives destroyed this great fleet of souls—why haven't we been attacked?"

"I do not know, *Sho-sa*, but I hope our luck holds." Koshō returned to her station, intending to comm up

Engineering and see how Hennig was getting along, then stopped, looking quizzically around Command. *Something's not right ...* Frowning, she tapped open a v-pane showing the guest quarters, then scanned through a series of empty cabins with rising alarm. *Damn his scrawny bones!* She commed Ship Security, *"Thai-i,* can you determine if either of our diplomatic guests are available to meet me in the command bridge conference room? This is urgent."

Beside her, Oc Chac glanced up nervously, saw her stormy expression, and ducked back to the search pattern. Five minutes went by with no word from the brig. "Very well," Susan said. "Full speed ahead, *Sho-sa.* We've no time to waste." *Hummingbird would not have taken that "ambassador" with him—contravening the Prince's express order—if the creature were not part of the old witch's plan.* Another ugly thought came to her. *He has his own ship—if he knows a way out of here, then we've been left behind to decoy and delay the Khaid. But even so—I would not trade places with Sayu now.*

WITHIN THE SUNFLOWER

Forty minutes after the *Moulins* was secured in the landing cradle and Captain Locke's crew had completed their set-down checklist, the marine fire team disembarked from the freighter in full combat armor, assault rifles at the ready. They confirmed what the exterior cameras had already shown Gretchen and the others on the bridge.

The rest of the chamber was filled with an enormous drift of bones, plasma-scored metal, and the desiccated corpses of thousands of inhuman creatures. Fifteen minutes after the marines had signaled the all-clear for the immediate vicinity, the Prince, Gretchen, and a very nervous Sahâne stepped out of the cargo elevator and crunched their way across a slope of crumbling bones to a platform facing an exit door.

There Xochitl stopped, panning his helmet light across the ossuary in grudging wonder. "Battle," he commented, eyes drawn to the shattered limbs and broken armor thigh-deep in the bay. "But not here . . . these bodies were dumped." His gaze traveled upward, the light picking out the angled shape of a monstrous crane hanging over the chamber, and beside it another, and another. They were folded up against the ceiling like a resting spider's knobby legs. The Prince turned to Gretchen. "What kind of entryway did you choose for us?"

"Garbage disposal," Sahâne said, his alien voice thick with bitterness. He knelt and lifted one of the cadaverous skulls. It was long-snouted, with a tapering jaw, and a mouth filled with rows of crushing molars aft and shredding incisors forward. Some remnant of a pelt remained, preserved by vacuum, apparently a mottled black or dark gray. "For discarded husks which could not be properly cremated."

Looking over his shoulder, Anderssen nodded, unsurprised. *I will send Professor Griffiths in the Comparative Languages Department a thousand roses, should I ever see Imperial space again!*

She wanted to handle the bones, but wondered if the ambassador would take offense. *A skull much like that of a Hjogadim, though larger in cross-section. Perhaps only a difference in nutrition, but if I could look at the whole thing, it might turn out to be a genetic difference. Maybe the old Hjogadim were a different sub-species. Wouldn't that be interesting!*

Curious, Gretchen moved off across the midden, her fingers brushing lightly across the most exposed of the corpses. Most of them seemed morphologically similar, though there were other, more alien-seeming races among the dead. *Has the history of these others been wholly lost? Is this where they became extinct? How long ago did all this occur?*

She stopped, going to one knee, and pulled out her field comp.

"This is your *suitable entrance*?" Xochitl crunched over to her, his voice a harsh rasp. "How far are we from a control structure? From whatever mechanism manages the entrance to the Barrier?"

Anderssen flashed a wintry smile up at the Prince. Her field comp had flickered awake and she was scanning one of the better-preserved skulls with her sensor wand turned to short-focus x-ray. "I am not sure *we* can enter the control spaces of this device. But I believe that *he* can." She indicated Sahâne with a tilt of her helmet. "If he chooses to lead us there."

Looking back at the alien, the now-familiar sense of disassociation stole over her, filling her chest with pleasant warmth, drawing her mind far from her body, which seemed to recede below her. Standing in this ancient place, her eyes filled with glorious Sight. The snap and glare of plasma guns, the screams of the wounded and dying dinned against her ears. A swirl of faint ghosts washed over her, as the ancient Hjogadim struggled and died, slaughtering each other in the corridors and control spaces. Then machines came, bearing the dead, laying them in ordered rows in the disposal bay, even as the tide of battle washed on to other shores. In her vision, a solitary Hjo—in comparison to the others, seeming almost solid—moved among the dead, giving some kind of last blessing. His skin and armor were anointed with the same glyphs and markings as Sahâne bore.

Watching the—priest?—passing among the dead,

Gretchen became peripherally aware of a golden tinge tainting her sight. Tentatively, her fingers moved, drifting to touch the bronze block. They stopped short, encountering an aura of heat, almost hot enough to scald.

"We had best move on—if we are to stay," she said, forcing herself to focus on the Prince. "If you intend to carry through with your purpose. . . ."

"I do," Xochitl said, his face pinched and pale.

He's removed his mask again. Only a frightened man remains in Huitzilopochtli's place.

"Sahâne-*tzin*, what do you say to this?" Xochitl asked.

The living Hjo's face greatly resembled that of the long-dead priest walking in Gretchen's golden vision, a ghastly mask of suppressed horror. His limpid gray-black eyes fixed on Gretchen for the first time. "*You* know what this place is . . . how can this be? How can a *toy* know what I—one of the Guided Race—do not!"

"There are legends," she replied carefully, "and fragments out of the past that still endure. Not all fantastical tales are false . . . but all that *I* know is that this whole enormous structure"—she extended her arms, taking in the entirety of the *Chimalacatl* and the singularity—"is the work of *your* people. Are you not pleased to look upon their greatness?"

"I despair," Sahâne croaked, voice thick with emotion, "to find myself amid this ruin and find the greatness of my people is ash!"

Xochitl seemed confounded. His face went blank. Gretchen caught a fragment of his helplessness, but made no move to enlighten him.

Sahâne favored them both with a contemptuous stare. "Apes! Such skills as tore suns from their orbits and compressed matter into ultimate annihilation, such skills as made this . . . this mausoleum . . . are *lost to us*. This place, it might as well have been made by the gods themselves! By the Living Flame which Guides! We are so petty now . . ." His voice trailed away into a disgusted, lamenting mumble.

A flicker of emotion lighted Xochitl's face. He scrutinized Gretchen warily. "Team one, to me." The Prince ordered half of his men forward. "Team two, secure the ship. Doctor Anderssen, you help the Esteemed Sahâne here *find a command structure!*"

With the heavy black assault rifles of the marines at her back, Gretchen reached up to place a gentle hand on the young Hjogadim's armored wrist. "Lord Sahâne, let us go further on. Is this not a cathedral of your caste? Has not the place of it been lost to your line? Have a care here. So many lie untended."

She led the Hjo onward, picking their way out of the disposal chamber through a triangular doorway. As they passed through, Gretchen caught sight of a faint radiance shining in the metal. *After all this time there are still glimmers within the material. What marvelous alloy could this be? Or are there bioluminescent organisms trapped within?*

"Ah!" The pale gleaming strengthened rapidly, becoming a floodlight of gold. Glyphs inscribed beside the entrance swam and cavorted in her sight, a vision now drenched in brassy light. On the floor, on the walls, as high as their hand lights could reach, meanings leaped out, indicating direction and time and purpose in an ever-dancing overlay to the solid world. Murals began to emerge from the plain-seeming walls, showing the edifice of a great civilization—towers piercing cloud-streaked skies; endless multitudes moving below, in enormous cities. Thousands of races were represented and not one of them seemed to be placed above the others, though the massive Hjogadim were well represented.

Oh boy, Anderssen thought. *Is this how the structure*

functions? Or did the ancient Hjo see the world this way all the time?

"Keep moving," Xochitl gritted. They stepped out into a leviathan hallway, stretching off far beyond the reach of their lights in either direction. Only a few meters from the doorway, a row of diamond-shaped compartments was visible at floor level. The Prince, curious, advanced to the closest one—his marines pacing him ahead and behind. As their lights moved, Gretchen bit her lip, seeing another row of compartments above the first, and then another, and then another. . . .

Xochitl rapped on the closest door, then shone his light inside. "It's like glassite. Sealed, but empty." He stepped away from the dark, silent chamber and swung with the beam of his lamp off into the distance, following the wall.

"They go way up, too," the marine behind Gretchen added. "Way up."

Sahâne stared morbidly into the sealed spaces as he passed by. The gleam of the helmet lights was swallowed up by the enormous spaces surrounding them. After walking fifteen minutes without seeing any end in sight, Xochitl ordered a halt.

"Koris—take two men back and get us a grav-sled from the freighter."

Once aboard the sled, they made excellent time, zipping along the massive passageway. After nearly an hour of travel, they reached an intersection.

"I think, this way," Gretchen urged, seeing the glyphs flowing and dancing in the air congregate around the right-hand avenue. "Yes, definitely."

Sahâne peered into the darkness, staring at the patterned sigils cut into the walls of the intersection, and then shuffled over to stand beside Anderssen at the cargo rail. She scrutinized what she could see of his face within the helmet. *He's interested. Not as tired. Not as fearful.*

The Jaguar Knight turned the sled, sending them down another long vaulted hallway. More rows of compartments appeared, yet like the others they were spotless and empty.

THE *KADER*

<small>Approaching the Pinhole</small>

"Pilot, acceleration up a point," Hadeishi announced, preternaturally calm. The light cruiser moved forward, picking up speed as the realspace drives burned mass. In his earbug he could hear a sudden rise in chatter from the Khaiden battleship. *Someone is paying attention— but the shuttle is far more interesting than we are.* Before him on his plot, a faint, faint trail gleamed.

"Pilot, course one-quarter point to starboard. And not one meter more."

Warning! the navigation officer on the *Sokamak* barked in alarm. *You're too close to the . . .*

"All hands, brace for impact!" Hadeishi snapped into his shipside comm.

The *Kader's* starboard wing, a long pylon holding missile racks, bomb-pods, and an array of other weapons, sheared directly into a Thread and neatly separated with a squeal of metal Mitsuharu could hear in Command, and then spun away from the light cruiser. Secondary explosions cauterized the shattered pylon almost immediately. Damage control parties rushed down suddenly vented corridors to patch the ruptures. Mitsuharu felt the whole ship tremble. He punched new course settings into the plot. "Full speed, *Thai-i*."

A stabbing azure flare burst from the engines and the *Kader* leaped forward like a scalded cat, racing away from both Thread and the *Sokamak* at maximum acceleration. An instant later, the México officer at the *Kader*'s comm station punched up a prerecorded distress call— translated to Khadesh—on all frequencies, interspersed with pleas for "a clear path, give us a clear path!"

Hadeishi's attention stayed on the plot as the battleship receded in the viewing screen. The shuttle carrying the "Imperial scientist" was only seconds from entering the assigned docking bay. Mitsuharu nodded to Lovelace, who was poised with a preprogrammed transmission burst ready to send. "Comm, go."

The shuttle floated delicately into the open boat-bay of the *Sokamak* and set down in a rush of maneuvering jets. As soon as the landing pads had touched the deck, the entire boat blew neatly apart into six sections. Four Khaiden penetrator pods deployed out of the debris cloud. Their on-board comps recognized the environment, sorted out targeting in a nanosecond, and burst away from the broken shuttle.

The Khaiden sub-officer in the boat-bay shrieked "Penetrators aboard! Incoming! Incoming!" into his comm an instant before being obliterated by an energy flare. The penetrators raced away down loading corridors and access ways, their plasma cutters shearing through locks and bulkheads.

Mitsuharu considered the likely effects within the *Sokamak* with satisfaction. *It is a poor Khaiden commander who has not prepared for the day when he must put the knife to his superior.*

As the severed wing spun away behind the *Kader*, the on-board weapons systems woke up and spewed a cloud of free-seeking missiles, bomb-pods, and chaff. The other two *Hayalet*-class battleships reacted to the sudden appearance of live munitions on their plot by lighting off their own engines and swerving away from both the invisible Barrier and the "weapons accident." The attendant destroyers and support ships followed, while their commanders were tremendously amused to see a brace of sprint missiles from the "accident" flare across the prow of the proud *Sokamak*.

Their 'cast chatter was quick and violent, but now Hadeishi was beginning to pick out sentences and phrases:

"See, Begh-Adag covers himself with glory again!"

"Fireworks to celebrate his demotion."

"What other captain could guide his ship to such renown, eh Hunt-lord Zah'ar?"

"Are you volunteering for something, Geh'zir?"

"No!"

"God of a Thousand Eyes forefend! The Sokamak!*"*

The battleship was still quite clear on Mitsuharu's v-display. The massive hull convulsed, ripped by four fusion blasts deep within its core. Then it shattered as jets of plasma erupted from gaps in the outer hull, tearing apart in a rapidly expanding cloud of superheated radioactive debris.

Hadeishi smiled, nodding to himself. *At Kurētāko Shrine, Musashi slew sixteen adversaries with only a wooden* bokutō *when they ambushed him at prayer. Not one of them believed he was truly in danger.*

The *Kader* cut her main drives, lighting off a hard deceleration burn as soon as the ship had rotated aspect. Inudo laid the light cruiser into the shadow of the *Tlemitl* as they slowed. Hadeishi watched him handle the old *Spear*-class cruiser with great appreciation. The helmsman was exceeding himself today, despite wrestling with an archaic control system. The Nisei officer was gladdened by his men's undaunted spirit.

"All boat-bay doors open, recovery teams stand by,"

Mitsuharu ordered. Then he tapped open a broadcast channel to the cloud of Imperial evac capsules hiding in the shelter of the stricken flagship. "All Imperial survivors, stand by for identity confirmation."

ABOARD THE *MOULINS*

In the Garbage Chute

Green Hummingbird found himself in the tiny mess area of the freighter, two seats down from the *kaffe* dispenser, his hands secured with a pair of zipcuffs. The Fleet marines remaining aboard had sorted themselves out—three were on the bridge, one was keeping an eye on the *nauallis* and the shipcore, while the remaining man was downdeck in engineering. All of them had armored up while the first team deployed into the landing chamber, but the men inside the ship had slung their helmets over their shoulders on a lanyard.

No one, the old Náhuatl observed, *likes breathing their own recycled waste.*

For his part, Hummingbird was sitting quietly, being as unobtrusive as possible, while the marines and the crew went about their business. Captain Locke and his men, particularly Piet the navigator, had acquired a still, waiting quality over the last hour. The marines were all listening to the chatter of the Prince and his party banging around amongst the dead corridors of the artifact. The expedition had been dropping repeaters at every junction as they moved. The Europeans—Hummingbird had made careful note that all of the freighter crew were of a distinct genotype—were listening as well, but for something else.

The old Náhuatl could do nothing at the moment—guarded and bound as he was—but Hummingbird could let himself become aware of the tenor of men's voices, the speed and direction of their movements, even their smell if they passed by close enough. What he absorbed from all of this was troubling. The very character of the *Moulin*'s crew had gradually transformed from the ne'er-do-well collection of roustabouts he and Anderssen had first encountered, to a far more focused team with a well-defined air of something he could only describe as *fierce intent*.

They, too, have a mission here. One unknown to the Prince, or he would have warned his men.

The great unknown in the *nauallis'* mind was—were they Maltese, or some other as-yet-unknown faction who had decided to step into the great game? The Knights he believed he understood and could manage, if they kept their tempers, but if it were some other organization? *There is no path to take, yet, while they—ah, now, how interesting!*

From his vantage in the mess, Hummingbird could pick out the respiration of the navigator and Captain Locke on the bridge, as well as two crewmen climbing up from downdeck. And in this very moment, each of the four men was breathing quietly and deeply in unison.

Now, a path is opening. Hummingbird tensed without open movement, preparing for violence.

"Captain, want a *kaffe*?"

Through the hatch opening onto the bridge, the *nauallis* saw the gray-eyed Pilot stand up, his motions easy and assured. Captain Locke looked over from his console, shaking his head. "No, not right now. But—"

Without the slightest hesitation, Piet slapped a gel-tab against the neck of the marine watching the main boards. The man stiffened, paralyzed before he could shout a warning. The Imperial toppled backward into

Captain Locke's waiting arms. Hummingbird, watching with interest, noted that both civilians moved with an admirable and soundless efficiency.

The other two marines on the bridge were out of sight, but Piet and Locke both produced slender, matte-black pistols from their jackets—sighted—and there was an almost unnoticed *pfft*. A series of clunking sounds followed, which drew the attention of the marine *Heicho* sitting across the mess from Hummingbird. The corporal rose, shipgun in his hand, eyes swinging to check the *nauallis*, then darting back to the two crewmen coming up the gangway—they were chattering about a zenball scandal on Langkasuka colony—and in that moment of inattention, Piet was behind him. Another gel-tab downed the Imperial, and the two crewmen were across the mess deck at a run to secure the fallen marine.

Locke emerged from the bridge, exchanged a series of complex hand motions with the other three—patterns which, to Hummingbird's great interest, were neither Fleet nor Army battlesign—and then remained behind while Piet and one of the other men disappeared down the gangway.

Ignoring the old Náhuatl, Locke and the remaining crewman dragged the three marines from the bridge and lined up all four men in the middle of the mess area. When the captain removed a breakerbox from his jacket, Hummingbird decided that he was impressed by Locke's resources and expertise. *These men can only be Knights out of New Malta, and see—he is being so very careful not to violate the compact between the Grand Master and the Emperor.*

To that end, Locke shorted out the combat armor on all three marines before tucking the tool away.

"Deft," Hummingbird said quietly, watching the Maltese with intense interest. "Am I still a captive?"

Locke nodded as he removed the comm crystals from

the marines' headsets and pocketed them. When he did look up, his greenish eyes were cold. "The Old One said you would be carrying the tablet, but you're not. Regardless, the Saints smile upon us. Better by far for *her* to be his messenger than one of your kind."

Hummingbird's eyebrows rose and he shifted slightly, testing the zipcuffs. *Patience!* he reminded himself. The Templar raised the slim little weapon. One *pfft* and Hummingbird felt a chill wash over him. Then . . . darkness.

DEEP WITHIN THE SUNFLOWER

The very long hallway ended in a sloping wall of dark metal pierced by a triangular door. This particular portal seemed to have become jammed, for at the top of the triangle they could see a portion of the valve itself. The edges of the massive frame were also mottled and streaked with carbon scoring and sections of the metal had melted before cooling into odd shapes. Beyond the door, illuminated by the hard white radiance of their helmet and hand lights, stood a nonagonal chamber of moderate size—only thirty or forty meters across.

"Nine walls." The Prince's voice was filled with irritation. "Three was sacred to them, then? And a dead end, Doctor."

"I think, Lord Prince, that they are doors," Gretchen amended. "All alike save this one, which has been damaged."

"Massive." Xochitl did not spit on the floor, but his impatience was very clear.

"They fought hard here." *Cuauhhuehueh* Koris traced his light across the signs of ancient battle—huge discolorations from plasma discharges covered the walls, there were melted panels here and there, and the inlaid floor was scored with deep gouges. The Jaguar Knight dug at the wall with his monofilament combat knife, but left no mark. "Huh!"

Sahâne offered no comment, standing amid them with his shoulders tucked in, radiating unease.

The glyphs and signs ghosting across Anderssen's vision pointed her to the right, collecting like ephemeral birds over a collection of interlocking triangles scribed into the floor.

"Which way?" the Prince snarled, nervously swinging his assault rifle from side to side. "Is this a transit nexus? Swede, all we need is—what are you doing?"

Gretchen had nudged Sahâne down onto the floor, just where he could step onto the triangles illuminated by her hand light. At the touch of the Hjogadim's boot, there was an almost imperceptible tremor. Eight of the walls shuddered, spilling faint clouds of dust into the air. Behind them, the triangular door slid down with unexpected violence, grinding along hidden tracks with a squeal. The party turned in alarm, their lights sending a cluster of gleaming circles dancing across the battered walls. The door failed partway down, momentarily revealing the hallway beyond dropping away with dizzying speed. This brief visual cue was the only indication they were in motion. Then the door closed as firmly as its eight counterparts, vanishing into the larger expanse of the wall without leaving a visible join.

Xochitl cursed—a long, bitter oath—and his face suddenly cleared, dark eyes glinting through his faceplate. Anderssen felt his "mask" stir. In her Sight, hidden signs and symbols flared to life around the México lord as though he were wreathed in ghostly flame. Fascinated, she watched them solidify first into a wholly alien symbology and then flicker into the more recognizable glyphic alphabet of the México.

Customized, she had time to think, before a dissociative jolt jarred her mind. There had been no noticeable physical sensation of movement, but Anderssen was suddenly sure they had passed over a threshold. *What a peculiar sensation—as though we'd stepped through a doorway within a doorway, leading into a room within the room where we were already present.*

Slowly, she withdrew her gloved hand from Sahâne's arm and turned to stare at the alien. "Revered Sahâne," she breathed, as though addressing him for the first time.

"Get away from him," the Prince ordered. The marines and Koris turned as well, catching a peculiar tone in her voice.

Ignoring the threat in Xochitl's command, Gretchen marveled as the Hjogadim's periphery gleamed brightly with a dizzying array of symbols. Far more in number, and far more varied, than the ghostly effusion accompanying his outburst in Secondary Command on the *Naniwa.* Now his z-suit and fur were literally crawling with signs and symbols of all varieties. Yet as she watched, they began to settle down, consolidating into a rotating, half-seen mesh of glyphs which almost entirely obscured the alien.

Apparently unaware that *he* had changed, Sahâne returned her gaze with one of great curiosity.

Her awareness of the symbology congealed as the glyphic aura around the creature settled down. Vectors of meaning began to emerge, revealing the shadow of a greater pattern. Anderssen found she could not—did not want to—look away, but at the same time she felt her own memories begin to fray. . . . *Hummingbird,* she howled mentally. *You evil old man! Nothing ever happens around you by accident.*

"Your eyes are . . . quite golden," Sahâne said in puzzlement. The Hjo didn't remember if this toy had expressed such a peculiar appearance before. Then he flinched back as the Prince's *Macana* assault rifle jammed past his snout and against Gretchen's head, muzzle wedging in between her neckring and helmet.

"Where are we going, Swede?" Xochitl's voice was flat, menacing, much like the flash-suppressor digging into her ear. "Is this a transit car?"

"You know it is, *Tlatocapilli*," she squeaked, forcing her unwilling tongue to form human words. The peculiar jolt in her perception made her aware of two distinct identities occupying the same physicality—her old self and now something new. This evolving Gretchen rode at the edges of her nerves, altering her perceptions of the universe . . . supplying meaning, context, and direction. Constellations of glyphs began to appear in silhouette around the Prince, the marines, the Jaguar Knight—even Sahâne had his own annotations. A Hjogadim epithet suddenly sprang to mind: *A sure and certain Guide to my thought!*

"I assure you, Lord Prince, we are going where you wished to go."

"I do not think so," he said, eyes narrowed. His exo—and by the Risen Christ, it was a vast relief to have his exocortex operating again—was reporting a flurry of unexpected changes in Doctor Anderssen's breathing, in her kirlian field, in the tension visible in her skin and bone. "I think you have become *infected* with something."

Gretchen raised her arms, turning fully towards him. The flash-suppressor clinked across her helmet, coming to rest square on her faceplate. "I am very sure, now, that Hummingbird did not expect you to be here, Lord Prince, nor indeed, the Holy One." She opened her hand towards Sahâne. "He expected to need just *one key*—myself."

"Key?" Sahâne said, curiosity winning out over naked fear. "Key to what?"

The transit core suddenly came to a halt and everyone froze as they felt the ancient device grow still. In motion, none of them had been aware of anything, but now that the room had completed its travels, each of them felt their equilibrium settle. The door that showed the worst battle damage ground up, shedding dust from long-unused mechanisms, allowing a pale roseate light to shine through the opening. Armored corpses spilled into the nonagonal room, tumbling away from the hulks of shattered war-meka. Even Xochitl jumped back in surprise as a cascade of broken battle-steel bounced away across the floor.

There was a buzz of static on their comm channel, but then the earbugs cycled frequency and the irritating sound died away. The Prince was the first to regain his composure. He whistled in astonishment at the size of the chamber revealed behind the long-dead combatants.

"Now, Swede, now you've found us something." Xochitl felt a great lightness rise in his chest. "We are the first beings to look upon this vista in ten thousand years," he said. "Marines—patrol pattern! There may be automatic defenses left active, even after so long . . ."

Sahâne's long snout peeled back from his fore fangs in horror to see the faded signs and symbols emblazoned upon the shattered fragments of armor. Hundreds of corpses slithered down out of the doorway, many of them bearing recognizably similar diagrams.

"The place of the Celestials," the Hjo whispered, unable to believe his eyes. "And The Fallen Thousand . . . the Banner Crimson and Black. My revered ancestors. This is . . . *impossible. This is a children's fable!*"

"All too real, Esteemed One," Gretchen said in a thick, hollow voice. Her facial muscles jumped randomly as her old self struggled to regain neural control from the gold-tinged invader. "My Lord Prince, your *control structure*." She pushed his assault rifle aside and stepped down from the sled, hands spread wide to frame the vast chamber lit through a clear wall by the glare of the accretion disc's light-year-long plasma jet shining far, far away to her left. Beyond the wreckage at the doorway, where some ferocious battle had denied an equally forgotten, unknown enemy entrance, long rows of triangular crystalline cradles rested upon the floor in such numbers as to vanish, uncountable, into the distance. Far, far away, a tall pylon rose from the flame-lit darkness. It shone with subdued green and gold lights, crowned in shadow.

Xochitl pushed past a seemingly frozen Sahâne, following Anderssen cautiously, gun at the ready. The xenoarchaeologist moved slowly, trying to keep control of her limbs, the visible world a riot of conflicting data. The México prince signed for one of his marines to shadow her, while the other four set themselves to the points of the compass. Koris followed slowly in the sled.

Left alone in the transit core, the Hjogadim heaved violently into his waste-tube and wept purple tears into his matted, unkempt facial pelt. He trembled uncontrollably, leaning against the door frame, overcome by stunned fear. *Oh Guide of Thought,* he blubbered to himself, *why have you sent your worthless servant into such a terrible place? I am no priest, no demagogue—I know nothing of the rituals of greeting or awaking! What cruel, cruel fate has placed me here, among barbarians and slaves and discarded toys, at such a time? To place me before the Gods themselves?* He could not bring himself to step across the threshold.

But the toys are already inside the Holy of Holies. The voice in his mind was faint and hard to understand;

by far the most ancient of all his teachers. The others, who had begun babbling in counterpoint, fell silent.

You must go in, young smoot. Your only way home lies forward.

THE *KUUB*

Loitering in the dark, shipskin aligned to full absorptive mode, the *Wilful* lay at the edge of the debris cloud generated by the destruction of the Khaiden battleship *Khorku*. The region of radioactive metal ash left behind by fusion containment failure served the little freighter as an extra screen, hiding her from the intermittent lidar scans emitting from the enemy ships still in the vicinity of the Pinhole. On her bridge, De Molay had moved back to the captain's station, her puffy black jacket, blankets, and the shepherd's cap supplemented by thick woolen gloves. The environmental systems were still trying to recover from their ill-use during the rescue efforts.

The old woman had her eyes closed, and a faint snore escaped her lips.

Thai-i Patzanil—who seemed very young to De Molay, far too young to be aboard a ship-of-war, much less acting as her navigator—was watching the plotting projection and the status boards. Weary himself, he stood and paced around the periphery of the tiny Command, peering at the old-fashioned dials on the equipment and idly fingering the cracked leather seat-backs. When he'd returned from the head, something had changed on the plot and he sat down hurriedly, red-rimmed eyes scanning the boards.

"*Sencho? Sencho* De Molay?"

The old woman opened one eye halfway, squinting at the boy.

"The Khaid main fleet is in motion, *kyo*. They're making for the Pinhole."

De Molay sat up, rolled her neck, and gestured for him to update the plotting projection. When the holo had refreshed, she pursed her lips, brows drawing tight. "Tired of testing the waters, hey? Has there been any sign of the *Kader*?"

Patzanil shook his head. "They've been down behind the radar shadow of the *Tlemitl* for at least two hours. Recovery operations must be complete by now, so I don't know—"

"*Chu-sa* Hadeishi has something in mind, I'm sure." The old woman scratched at the edges of the gel sealing her face wound. On the plot, the Khaid battlewagons had formed into an evenly spaced line and were picking up velocity. The other, smaller ships were also in motion— save one.

"What are they leaving behind, *Thai-i*?"

Patzanil was already correlating the emissions data. "Something in a destroyer's mass-range, *kyo*. Might be a *Mishrak*-class—we'd identified a couple of them in the attacking force before the *Gladius* went down."

"We'll stay well away," De Molay said, settling back into her cocoon. "Any others left behind?"

"*Hai, kyo*. Three others—same general class—at the corners of the box."

"Sentries, then." On the plot, the last of the Khaid heavies had disappeared behind the seemingly invisible veil of the Barrier. She nodded to herself, making some mental calculation. "Very good."

The boy looked at her expectantly for a moment, but De Molay closed her eyes again.

"Ah, *Sencho-sana*?" His voice was tight, hinting at an internal conflict between well-ingrained Fleet duty and the plain fact that the old woman was *not* a Fleet officer.

"Yes, *Thai-i*," De Molay responded. "You can get something to eat."

"Thank you, *kyo!*" He was up and out of his seat and through the hatchway before she could open both eyes. When she had sat up fully, he was long gone. De Molay laughed softly to herself, then keyed into her console and—after negotiating several authorization screens—brought up the t-relay interface. Then she sat for a moment, considering the plot and tapping her fingers slowly on the edge of the console.

Not that much time to dither, the old woman thought. *The boy will be back soon, and I've no surety the Khaid will not return swiftly, or that reinforcements have not been summoned. The iron is hot, so we must strike.* She wondered if Hadeishi and his reclaimed cruiser were still busy recovering the crew of the super-dreadnaught, but her window of opportunity was terribly short. *The Order masters would say to act in the moment of balance,* De Molay remembered from an old book she'd been forced to read in the *collegium.*

She shook her head and keyed open a comm channel. The message had been composed in her mind for at least a day, but she had needed the bridge to herself before risking a transmission.

Peregrine, Pervicax transmito. Cohortes imperatoris deletae sunt. Khai sepulchrum intraverunt. Quinque custodes Khaianes consisti sunt, whispered out into the aether.

De Molay felt a mingled sense of relief and wary anticipation. There had been a dozen times in the last week that she'd expected to be incinerated, or captured, or simply vanish in the blossoming flare of an antimatter detonation. But—somehow—she had won through, and now her entire purpose had been discharged with a single message. *One which will likely go—*

The console chimed softly, indicating an incoming message spooling through the relay. She stiffened, startled to receive such a quick reply.

The message read: *Venimus. Signa transitu pone pro insertio directio teleportano. Evigila.*

Ready we shall be, then. By the Lord, they must be close by.

Her attention shifted to the plot. All four Khaid destroyers on sentry duty remained in their watchful pattern. No missile launches were detected by the forest of sensors extruded from the hull of the *Wilful*, no movement towards her on their part. De Molay settled back, wincing a little at the enduring pain in her face, her side, and her leg. *I am far too old for this,* she grumbled mentally.

Which, said a voice much like her own—damnable conscience!—*is why you'd retired. Why exactly did you volunteer for this excursion?*

Patzanil clattered onto the bridge, a large bowl tucked under one arm. The smell washed over her like the tidal return from Port Valletta on a long, hot summer day.

"Is it meatlog?" she asked politely.

The *Thai-i* gave her a devil-may-care smile. "I don't know, but if the Khaid can eat it, I can, too."

De Molay suppressed a laugh. "Back to sleep for me, then. Nothing new on the plot."

THE *NANIWA*

Koshō felt her stomach quail and the lighting in Command pulsed twice as the battle-cruiser dropped gradient into realspace. Brisk, well-practiced chatter flowed across the bridge stations as the officers of the watch confirmed they had made transit properly, that ship's systems were on-line and they had a solid navigational fix. The threatwell began to refresh as the remote watching the Pinhole unspooled the last eight hours of captured data. Oc Chac was working his checklist in a low fast voice, ensuring they still had maneuvering drives, nothing had lost pressure or vented during the transition, and all compartments were secure for combat.

Only Pucatli was frowning, and the tense line of his head drew Susan's eye like a magnet from her consideration of the survey plot. "Comms?"

Puzzlement clouded the *Chu-i*'s face. "*Chu-sa*, there's a recorded transmission on one-hundred-ten you need to hear."

Koshō tapped her earbug, cycling channel. Immediately, she heard: *All Imperial evac capsules, converge on this signal. . . .*

"An Imperial broadcast! Someone's alive? How could . . ."

We have captured a Khaid vessel and come to take you home. Converge upon this signal with all haste. The familiar voice spoke quickly, concisely. It hummed with adrenaline; its familiar tone was inextricably connected in her mind, in her body, to imminent violence and battle. Susan's gaze tracked back to the threatwell—but there was nothing to be seen. The gravity-plot around the Pinhole remained quiescent.

"Mitsuharu?" she said aloud, without meaning to. Oc Chac—who had switched his own earbug to listen in—caught her eye, his head canted in a questioning pose.

Koshō replied to the unspoken question. "The Khaiden are not alone outside the Pinhole. That is the voice of a Fleet officer well known to me—it seems he is gathering up the fallen. But . . ." She paused, rewinding the message. "He can only have one ship under his command, and one taken from the enemy at that." Despite herself, she started to grin in delight.

Oc Chac shook his head in astonishment. "A tremendous feat, if true. But, *Chu-sa*, this could easily be a trick—a stratagem of the Khaid to lure us into a trap!"

"It could." Koshō straightened her shoulders, trying to quell a fierce and unexpected joy blooming in her heart. "But *this* officer was recently forced to the beach and the Fates would truly be against us if the Khaid intelligence services were so far-thinking as to capture *his* voice patterns for use against *me*. No, fantastic as it sounds I believe that *Chu-sa* Mitsuharu Hadeishi is—somehow!—beyond the Barrier, that he has captured a Khaid ship, and is using that same vessel to recover our lost evac capsules."

The Mayan's expression became dour. "Sounds brave as the deeds of Hunahpu and Xbalanque in the heroic stories of my people, but doomed, surely. There is a full Khaid *fleet* at the other end of the Pinhole, *Kyo*. And against them, one ship will not last long at all. . . ."

Susan laughed out loud. "Your twin heroes were fashioned from mortals who excelled at contests to the death, *Sho-sa*. In this living world, there is no ship commander more likely to achieve the impossible than the man whose voice we've just heard."

Then her expression darkened, lips drawing tight. "But more likely, the Khaid fleet is no longer waiting outside the Barrier. No—they have likely found a way through as well, and will soon be upon us. Then *we* will be the lone lion amongst the wolf pack."

Koshō turned to the pilot. "*Sho-i* Holloway, bring us about and prep the coil to punch gradient. We need room to maneuver. Weapons, prep your launchers!"

ON THE *MOULINS*

DOCKED WITHIN THE *CHIMALACATL*

A groan escaped Hummingbird's lips as consciousness returned in fits and starts. He opened his eyes, finding nothing but darkness. He tested the movement of his arms and legs, and found they were tightly bound. Shifting his head from side to side, the old Náhuatl determined that something—a rubbery plastic—had been stretched over his eyes. He was not gagged, which indicated to the *nauallis* that there was no one within shouting distance. In any case, he did not like to make noise when he could not see who might be listening.

On my own, am I? Hummingbird shifted his shoulders, feeling walls on either side. *A closet perhaps? But they were in a hurry—I am still wearing my skinsuit.*

The old Náhuatl twisted his head from side to side, testing the limits of his ability to move. Discovering that both knees could reach his chin, he managed to roll forward gently and get both feet beneath him. Then, Hummingbird stood up slowly and found the roof of the confined space less than a meter above his resting position. *A bit cramped, but then I am not the largest of men.*

He twisted one shoulder around to bring the sealing

strip of the skinsuit within range of his lips and then spent a good fifteen minutes trying to catch the recessed plastic tab in his teeth. Finally, after relaxing all of the muscles in his neck, back, and arms individually, he was able to do so. When the tab popped free, the skinsuit puddled to the ground in a pool of gelatinlike oil, leaving only the neckring. With a two-millimeter clearance between his bonds and skin, the *nauallis* was able to shimmy free in another twenty minutes of hot, sweaty work in the closet.

As he worked, he felt a slow, steady sense of outrage building in his mind. *A pity they couldn't accept me as a fellow brother of the Order! Srá Osá will be most displeased by their shortsightedness. Protecting humanity from itself requires broader thinking.*

Pulling the skinsuit back on was also a bit of work, but now he was fully awake and feeling quite limber. The compartment door was locked, but liquefying the suit had also deposited a number of tools from the gel matrix on the floor. He found them by feel, sorted them with deft fingers and then cut open the locking mechanism with a tiny plasma torch no longer than his little finger. Then he duck-walked out into one of the crew cabins and—thankfully—stood up.

As Hummingbird did so, the dissonance of his thought patterns concerning the crew of the *Moulins* finally caught his attention. An initial sensation of puzzlement was swiftly replaced by shock. *I've been "pushed,"* he realized. *That "Old One" is stronger than I suspected.* Disgusted, he spat on the floor of the empty room. *I've made a deadly mistake in helping an Order ship come here. They are after the same prize as the Prince. Christ the Guardian curse them down through all nine hells!*

Fifteen minutes later having recovered his clothing and z-suit, he padded onto the mess area and found the marines had been taken away. Worried, the old *nauallis* moved carefully through the rest of the little ship. Finally, he found the Imperials laid out on the floor of a cargo area above Engineering, trapped in their dead armor. Hummingbird squatted next to the squad leader with a pleasant smile. *Something to salvage. We are all "friends" here ... the Order hasn't broken fully with the Empire yet.* The marine glared back at him, sullen-eyed and gagged.

"*Go-cho* Pequah," the old Crow greeted him amiably, running practiced fingers down the desealer strip at the marine's shoulder. The wrecked armor sighed; tension released from the gelcore, and it fell away in a limp pool of black oil and plexisteel laminate. The Iroquois flexed his fingers, toes, and then rolled up—clad only in his service skinsuit, his body stiff as lightning with restrained fury. The other four marines made angry, muttering sounds behind their gags.

"We've all been played dirty," Hummingbird commented, peeling a flattened sleepytime capsule from Pequah's neck. "And I appreciate your natural desire to eviscerate someone, but your first concern must be the Prince's safety."

Released, all five marines nodded slowly, grudgingly, as they flexed oxygen-deprived limbs. For a long moment the *nauallis* met their eyes in turn, then nodded, satisfied. "Leave the Europeans to me. The Prince has a tracker in his suit. Follow the repeaters until you find him and make sure he gets back here in one piece."

Leaving the marines to scavenge for weapons and tools, Hummingbird slipped out into the dim, chaotic vastness of the landing bay. Packing foam lay scattered at the base of the landing cradle. He grimaced, seeing that the Order crewmen had brought, and assembled, a grav sled. *Prepared, were they?*

He ducked back inside the ship and returned moments later with a single-rider grav-ski. The device unfolded in swift, programmed motions. A bit of a smile shone in the old man's face, remembering long summers wasted skidding around the alleys and avenues of Coyoacán with his classmates, a tight noisy pack of boys. Then the sense of fleeting time gripped him. He hopped on and grasped the controls.

"Go now." He sped away with the wide flare of the running lights searching the enormous corridor ahead.

THE KADER

In the Pinhole

Hadeishi frowned, his jaw clenched tight as Cajeme's voice burred in his earbug. *Capsule lock is completely jammed—we're having trouble cutting through without frying the nitto-hei inside—and there are four more capsules outside we can't bring onboard until we've got these men out.*

The Nisei officer's eyes darted to the nav plot, which still showed the *Tlemitl* between them and the Khaid fleet—or what of the enemy they could see with their sensors greatly obscured by the Barrier, the radiation clouds from discharged weapons, and the sensor shadow of the broken dreadnaught. From his vantage, several Khaid destroyers were hanging off at a distance, but the rest of the enemy had disappeared.

"*Thai-i*, do we have a remote we can run out to the edge of the wreck?"

Tocoztic shook his head in disgust. The Arawak's beard was starting to grow in, which made him look particularly disreputable. "Nothing, *kyo*. We've got nothing *useful* aboard. I'd use an evac pod, but their maneuvering jets are exhausted once we get them into cargo one . . ." He gestured angrily at the plot. "Something is going on out there—I can pick up gravity-wave changes and some partial drive emission signatures—but we can't see anything directly."

Mitsuharu's expression darkened further, considering the movements of the enemy. *Out of sight is not out of my mind . . . that battle-cruiser's drive emissions could easily be visible to these new-model battleships of theirs. This* Spear *does not carry the most advanced electronics quills can buy. Not like the . . . wait a moment.*

"What about the *Tlemitl*? Are there any sensor booms or subsystems we can connect to and use?"

"The—" Tocoztic stopped himself, initial disbelief replaced by curiosity. "I don't know, *Chu-sa*, but she hasn't lost *all* power to systems—just her mains. One moment . . ."

Hadeishi swiveled his shockchair, feeling the carapace creak under him. All of the Command stations were now filled with crewmen from the pods they'd recovered initially. Cajeme and his engineers downdeck were busily shuffling off the newly recovered ratings and officers, which looked to swell the *Kader*'s complement by another eighty or ninety bodies. Most of those recovered, however, had been injured to greater or lesser degree.

Now for the second act, he thought, gaze settling on *Sho-i* Lovelace at the Comm's station, despite being—perhaps—the junior-most tech aboard. The ensign had tucked two spare console styli into her hair, which was bound up in a blond bun behind her head. The young woman's expression was distant, all attention focused on sorting out the confusion of signals picked up by their sensor booms.

Hadeishi caught her eye. "*Sho-i*? Are we still synched with the Khaid battlecast?"

"No, *kyo*. I'm getting intermittent bursts of traffic,

but we're out of the loop now." She offered a crooked smile. "I'm sure they've figured out we're no longer running with the *surtu*."

"Very well. Route what you have to my earbug on sixty-three and—"

Lovelace started to nod in acknowledgment, then became quite still. "Wait one. Wait one."

She stared at her console, gently adjusting the signal filtering, before scowling. "We're picking up a rebroadcast, *kyo*. It's the Khaid 'cast channel, but not from our immediate area. Routing to sixty-three."

A babble of excited Khadesh flooded Mitsuharu's hearing. The translator kicked in, but the hunt-lords were yowling so quickly, and overlapping one another, that the software produced only a garbled mess on the secondary channel.

"Fix a vector, *Sho-i*!" he ordered, barely able to hear himself think. "Are they behind, or ahead?"

I want that ship! popped out of the howling. *She escaped once, not again!*

Hadeishi twisted the earbug around, frustrated. *That sounds like the one named Sylahdeposu—he's quick off the mark, but who does he have in his sights? Has another Imperial combatant dropped into the area, or . . .*

"*Chu-sa* Hadeishi!" Inudo had turned in his seat. The pilot had a finger to his earbug, his voice loud over the chatter on the *Kader*'s crowded bridge. "I think he means the *Naniwa*. Comp says she is the one that survived the ambush and ducked into the Pinhole—a squadron of the Khaid must have slipped past us, following their drive track."

Mitsuharu blinked and everything seemed to slow. *The* Naniwa? *The missing battle-cruiser is—*

"How did they get through?" Tocoztic demanded of Inudo. "How can they track her—*we* can barely see her signature in this mess!"

"Do we have comm to the *Naniwa*?" Hadeishi's expression made Lovelace stiffen in her seat.

"No, *Chu-sa*! We're just picking up fragments of battlecast from a relay the Khaid dropped behind them. I'm getting five or six different emitter tags—one per ship probably." The *Sho-i* swallowed nervously. "She won't last long if she's alone."

"The *Naniwa* will fight to the last missile, the last gun . . ." Mitsuharu viciously suppressed an urge to order Inudo to take them to maximum acceleration and to the Eight Hot Narakas with the rest of the evacuation capsules. Despite this, his voice was a harsh growl which made every man and woman in Command straighten up in alarm. "*Chu-i*, I want to see a ticker on the plot telling me how long the engineers have to get those capsules inboard. Tocoztic-*tzin*, get your crews to their guns, get me status on anything we have left to throw. Pilot—lock down that drive plume signature and stand by for battle acceleration."

The howling and yammering of the *surtu* pounded in his ear, though Hadeishi felt their bloodlust only as a ticking sense of time falling away into darkness. He eyed the plot—still no sign of the enemy moving against them—but now he was certain at least one of the *surtu* was loitering in the *Tlemitl*'s sensor shadow, waiting for them to break cover.

"Comms. Broadcast on the last frequency we had for the *Wilful*. Say only, "We are visiting Osaka." Do not repeat the message."

Lovelace stared back at him, pale brow furrowed as she resolved the reference, her stylus poised over the v-pane. "Do you think Captain De Molay will hear?"

"Perhaps."

"A little boat like hers—what could she—?"

"Much depends upon the purity of one's intent, *Sho-i*. Send the message."

AMONG THE FALLEN

THREE LIGHT-YEARS FROM THE PINHOLE

In quick succession, a handful of widely spaced icons popped up enemy-red in the *Naniwa*'s threatwell. The gravity spike of the Khaid ships dropping from transluminal reached the Imperial ship only instants after they emerged into realspace. Koshō was watching, elbow on the armrest of her shockchair, eyes hooded. Command was fully staffed, everyone having gotten at least a round of the showers and an hour off duty.

"Confirming five transits," Konev announced, the icons beginning to annotate with glyphs indicating expected speed, throw-weight, and countermeasures. "All cruisers or smaller—*Mishrak* and *Aslan*-class—acceleration and emissions are within expected ranges."

"Undamaged." Oc Chac grimaced, tapping through a series of v-panes showing the wreckage being cleared from the battle-cruiser's downship compartments. "Are they fresh, *Chu-sa*?"

"Doubtful, *Sho-sa*. Their captains are pushing hard—the Khaid have little need of patience. They will be wounded, like us, but keen to bring us to ground. Time to cover?"

Holloway eyed the plot. Fully half of the threatwell was a blizzard of icons representing the dead fleet. "Fifteen minutes to the nearest wrecks, *Chu-sa*. About twelve minutes until we're inside the Khaid launch envelope."

"Deflector status, *Chac-tzin*?" Susan looked back to the Mayan. "Are we still running hot?"

Oc Chac shook his head. "No, *kyo*. We can pull another three, four gravities."

"Give us a boost, Holloway-*tzin*. But don't open the

throttle wide—we need to be able to turn once we're in the debris field."

The console under Susan's fingers began to thrum with the vibration of the antimatter reactors chewing mass. "Nav—what are our options?"

Thai-i Olin looked up from his console, shaking his head. "Active scan is showing a lot of small fragments between the hulks—no good avenues for us to maneuver down—no holes yet, to hide in."

"Find us something, *Thai-i*. Quickly now." Koshō's voice was pointed. "We have two minutes . . ."

"Launch signatures!" Konev's voice was relaxed, almost a drawl, but the tenseness in his arms was as clear to Susan as an ash-cloud over Mount Talol. "Sixty missile tracks are on the board."

"Initiating countermeasures." Pucatli—at Comms—dumped the first of her spoofer pods.

"Counter-fire, *kyo*?" Konev looked to Koshō with a fierce gleam shining in his eyes. "If we concentrate, we might knock one or two out before they close to gun range."

"Save your launchers, *Thai-i*. We need to conserve every shipkiller we have left." Susan had already considered the fire rate from the on-rushing destroyers and their range of engagement. "Engage the missile cloud with kinetics and ECM starting at six minutes."

"Isn't this a brawl, *Chu-sa*?" Oc Chac looked at her questioningly, his face pale with fatigue. "Even one or two of the enemy down at this range will even the odds appreciably."

Koshō lifted her chin, indicating the 'well. "Not yet, *Sho-sa*. This is 3-v *Ullamaliztli* with only one player left on our side. You played at Academy, I'm sure—"

A warning Klaxon honked, cutting her off. A fresh icon popped into view on the 'well.

"A *Hayalet*-class battleship, *kyo*." Konev's voice was

tight as he reeled off the specifications of the new indicator. "Punched straight through from the Pinhole, right on our track."

Susan swiveled, lifting an eyebrow at Olin and Holloway. "Time to enter the maze?"

"Five minutes, *Chu-sa*." The pilot's eyes were wide with fear. "I've picked up some options but—"

"They'll have to do. Pilot, take us in."

On the plot, the destroyers continued to close, their launchers cycling a new spread of missiles every one hundred and twenty seconds. The first wave was still three minutes out, but the *Naniwa*'s point-defense was already hammering away at the incoming targets. Pucatli's spoofer pod was squealing, flooding the spectrum with distorting noise and false signals. Khaid penetrators began to flare, and then wink off of the plot.

Behind them, the *Hayalet* held course at an angle away from the *Naniwa* and her running firefight. Susan watched the vector firm up, heading in-system at a good clip.

How could they fail to notice the singularity? The sensor suite on one of those battlewagons must be the equal of ours—some daring hunt-lord sees the realization of an entire race's dreams of empire riding on that thread.

This reminded her of Prince Xochitl and the missing Hummingbird, and her heart lifted at the thought of the Khaid howling in behind those two "gentlemen," well stoked with blood lust.

They're all suited to one another, she thought bitterly. Then Susan felt a pang of conscience, just for an instant. *An Imperial officer should be mindful of her duty.*

A proximity alarm sounded—the battle-cruiser sped past an outlier of the vast shoal of wreckage—even as the first wave of Khaid shipkillers began to flare around her. The *Naniwa* groaned, shipskin hammered by the stabbing flare of fusion detonations. Now the plot was filled with the tracery of outgoing kinetics, the flash of bomb-pods erupting and Command was loud with the swift, urgent voices of her crew reacting. Konev's counter-missile wave banged away, shaking the secondary hull with the violence of launch rails cycling.

Adrenaline flushed her limbs with a quivering, bright energy. The only thing missing was Hadeishi's voice in her earbug, calm and controlled, his presence radiating a contained focus as he put the ship through her paces. *I am alone.* Susan felt a tight, stabbing pain in her diaphragm. On the plot, the density of the wrecks was soaring, and Holloway's brow was dappled with sweat as he maneuvered. *Here we go.*

Koshō detached a series of v-panes showing the movement of the Khaid battleship towards the Sunflower to her Executive console.

A good six hours for them to reach the artifact, she saw. *Long time to stay in this dance.*

A shipkiller blew only three compartments away, shredding the *Naniwa's* shipskin and venting a huge gout of atmosphere and flotsam. In Command, the overheads flickered, half the consoles cut out and someone cursed violently as their v-display shorted, spilling smoke globules and hot sparks into the air.

Oc Chac was at the man's side in an instant, a portable extinguisher spitting foam into the splintered console. "Damage control, this is Main Command, we've lost a 'net node and five consoles."

Susan saw the wreckage occlude the pursuing destroyers as Holloway put them into a jinking curve, fleeing past another of the dead behemoths. "Weapons, tight pattern—rear launchers only—delayed fuse while we're in scan-shadow."

"*Hai, kyo!*" Konev cycled his launchers, stylus darting across his console. Preconfigured munitions packages punched outbound, venting from the eight rearward rails at nearly a hundred g's.

At the same moment, Olin's voice cut across the Russian's. "New contact! New contact! *Aslan*-class cruiser to ventral—range sixty thousand kilometers—enemy is launching now, thirty missile tracks incoming! Impact in eighty seconds!"

"Now, *Sho-sa*," Susan said, her voice preternaturally calm. "Now we're in the brawl."

THE *KADER*

Command was awash in confused voices as the last of the evacuation pods was winched into the cargo hold. Hadeishi tapped his med-band, injecting another dose of anti-inflammatory to suppress a spiraling migraine. Five or six conflicting channels of information were vying for his attention, and the low-level confusion amongst his scratch crew kept jarring his attention away from the Khaid battlecast. The enemy had started to frequency-hop, but Lovelace was keeping up, though the translator always seemed to be five or six words behind what he could make out himself.

One of the new officers—his name had escaped Mitsuharu in the latest round of introductions—signaled cargo one was sealed, and the armored partitions were rotating closed over the bay doors. The *Chu-sa* switched to Cajeme's team, catching the exhausted-looking Yaqui as they were hauling two corpses from the pod, along with one midshipman who looked like she might live.

"*Nitto-hei*—how many pods do we have aboard?"

Cajeme stared back blankly for a moment, then shook himself, saying: "Eleven, *kyo*, we have eleven."

"Get them prepped to eject," Hadeishi said sharply, a hard edge in his voice. "A Weapons team is on their way to you now—there were fifteen thermonukes in munitions storage—I want those pods refitted as fast as you can."

"*Hai*"—Cajeme wheezed, his face black with carbon from the backwash of the cutter he'd been slinging for the past eighteen hours—"*kyo*."

Mitsuharu turned his attention back to Command, feeling his shoulder blades itching in anticipation. *They're coming . . . more than one of them.* "*Thai-i* Tocoztic—any progress on connecting to the *Tlemitl*'s sensor array?"

The Islander shook his head, expression mournful. "Nothing, *kyo*. We're locked out hard—the *Sho-i* tried breaking in, but found not a single loose beam."

Lovelace nodded, looking equally grim. "We found some survivors, *kyo*. One of the compartments is still intact and—"

"Do they have shipnet access?" Hadeishi cut her off coldly, his mind rotating the problem through every angle he could conceive. "Do they have power? Sensors? Anything?"

The young woman's face went blank, stung by his tone. "*Chu-sa*, they're on emergency power, but yes—they have 'net access and access to the node in their fragment. . . ."

"Put me through." Hadeishi turned to the plot, lips a tight, compressed line. "Pilot, are we ready to maneuver?"

Inudo nodded, his face wan with exhaustion. "Drives are hot, *Chu-sa*, standing by."

"Survivors on channel sixty-three, *kyo*," Lovelace said, her voice far more formal than she'd offered before. Hadeishi wasn't even aware of the change, his whole attention focused on the wavering, jittery v-pane which popped up on his display. Two z-suited figures were framed in the pickup, a room filled with floating debris behind them.

"This is Mitsuharu Hadeishi, *Chu-sa* of the *Kader*. I am your new commanding officer. I need you to open a 'cast feed to my Comms officer—*Shoi-i* Lovelace—and do *everything* you can to allow her to relay through your subsystems. Do you understand?"

The sharp, harsh edge to his voice galvanized both men, though he knew they must be running low on air, were probably out of water, and had little chance of surviving even to see another watch pass. A ragged "*Hai, kyo!*" echoed back to him across the circuit. The Nisei officer nodded sharply to his Comms officer. "Get me a sensor feed from the far side of the hulk—there's another Khaid out there, we need to find it immediately."

Then he paused, considering the plot for a long, endless three seconds and then—resolving an internal struggle—his stylus sketched out a new maneuvering vector on the plot. "Pilot, get us underway. I want maximum acceleration while holding to this path. Weapons, stand by to engage the enemy. Expect a missile exchange at a blade's distance."

Inudo stared at the new vector, then nodded jerkily to himself. "Plotting course, *Chu-sa*."

Frowning thunderously, Lovelace stared over at the pilot, whose expression had gelled into a stoic mask. "*Chu-sa* . . ." The Mirror officer caught Hadeishi's eye, her face filled with raw appeal. "The drive trail from the battle-cruiser is fragmentary now—and the Barrier *moves*! We couldn't possibly—"

"We don't need the *Naniwa*'s trace, *Sho-i*." Mitsuharu nodded to the plot as the console under his fingertips began to shiver with the engines igniting. "The Khaid fleet has already blazed the trail for us—their emissions will be impossible to miss."

"Underway, *kyo*." Inudo's report was mechanical.

"Building v—we'll be out of the shadow of the *Tlemitl* in five—four—three—two—"

"Contact, *kyo*! We have contact!" Tocoztic's blurt of alarm overrode the Pilot. "Bearing eleven high, she's massing like a battleship! Cast analysis says she's the *Kukumav*!"

The noise level in Command jolted upward, but now Hadeishi felt everything extraneous—even the joyful howl from the Khaid channel—drop away. "Weapons—launch everything you have, dead on. Pilot—get us out of here!"

The cruiser's hull shuddered, groaning as the drives kicked up to all nodes combusting full-bore and the launch rails and hardpoints belched a cloud of shipkillers and a hammering stream of kinetic warheads. Tocoztic's countermeasures display was already alight with the incoming Khaid missile storm, which outmassed theirs by five or six to one.

"Cast relay active, *Chu-sa*!" Lovelace's fingers were flying across her panel, the *tik-tik-tik* of her styli a seamless stream, like the clicking of spinning gears. "We're synching to the *Tlemitl*—wait one, wait one—she needs authorization!"

A fresh v-pane popped up on Hadeishi's console, showing the Fleet authentication interface. Cursing to himself—there was no chance the *Tlemitl* would have the authorization glyph cluster for a cashiered reserve officer—Mitsuharu framed his face in the pickup window, got a green rectangle and then keyed his sequence. The v-pane flickered, showing an IDENTITY REJECTED message for a fraction of a second, and then suddenly blanked. In its place, an oblong glyph of intertwining roses appeared, holding a black-on-white flame. Hadeishi felt a shock of recognition, though he'd only seen the icon once before, while another was manipulating a ring-zero system.

Hello, old friend. The voice on the comm channel was so unexpected, yet so familiar, that Mitsuharu could not place it for a seeming eternity. *I knew you would come, if anyone could win through, and you would need every tool at your command.* The sigil vanished, Hummingbird's voice faded, and Lovelace drew back at her station in alarm, watching as the *Tlemitl's* fragmentary shipnet unfolded before her on the Comms console.

"We're in," Hadeishi barked, watching the intercept solution for the Khaid missile storm wind down towards their destruction. "Lovelace—shift control to Tocoztic— Weapons, you have full control over anything still working in the hulk of the *Firearrow*—dump it all! Everything! Now!"

The *Kader's* hull shuddered again as the point-defense guns lit up, filling the rapidly shrinking interval between the Khaid shipkillers and the fleeing cruiser with a wall of hyper-accelerated depleted uranium pellets. Bomb-pods began to stutter in sun-bright flares, stabbing at the shipskin with invisible beams of high-energy X-rays. The first wave of shipkillers rode in hot behind the suppressive fire, tearing through the *Kader's* counter-measure.

Hadeishi felt the cruiser heave, hull hammered by a dozen impacts. His status displays flashed wildly, shading red. Dozens of compartment alerts howled as pressure vented from the secondary hull. The primary hull shredded, gouged open by massive explosions.

Tocoztic, his face bone white, stabbed a command glyph on the v-display relayed from the ruin of the *Tlemitl*. "Dumping ordnance, now!"

All along the flank of the *Tlemitl's* carcass, hard-points woke up, draining local emergency power, and went into remote mode. The launch rails and missile racks surviving the dreadnaught's dissection cycled open. They could not hurl their weapon loads into battle at high v, but approximately eighty shipkillers separated from the hull and immediately locked onto the *Kukumav*, which was building velocity past them at a relatively low speed. At the same time, the kinetic weapons began firing, spitting a cloud of ballistic munitions towards the Khaid ship.

For her part, the *Kader* punched deeper into the Pinhole at maximum burn on her engines, her flight punctuated by the flare of shipkillers and penetrators detonating across her hull. The *Kukumav*'s gunners cycled their launch rails, subcommanders howling new targeting orders. A cloud of debris, atmosphere, and chaff spewed out behind the damaged cruiser.

Hadeishi watched the streaking missile tracks on the plot with cold eyes. Inudo was pushing the maneuver drives for all they were worth—and making gradient inside the Barrier itself was obviously impossible. The transit metrics were off the scale.

"Forty seconds to the second wave," Tocoztic announced, sweat gleaming on the sides of his face. "Point-defense is down to thirty percent, shipkillers are exhausted. One salvo of penetrators and two spoofer pods left—"

"Weapons, drop pods," Mitsuharu snapped, switching his attention to the navigation plot. The track of the Khaid fleet was marvelously clear—their battleship drives coughed high-order radiation with reckless abandon—and he was praying the Barrier had not already shifted enough to swing a lattice of knives into their path. The two spoofer pods spun out from their launchers and Lovelace was waiting to key them up as duplicates of the *Kader* as soon as they had separated from her signature. "Pilot, cut drives and rotate fresh armor!"

Another ship icon popped up on the plot—a hundred thousand k behind the *Kukumav*—pulling high g acceleration. For an instant, Hadeishi thought it might be the *Moulins*, but then shipnet crunched the emissions signature and a whirl of hostile glyphs surrounded the contact.

"*Mishrak*-class destroyer *Han'zhr* on the board," Tocoztic barked.

"Rotating aspect," Inudo followed as the main drives cut out.

Mitsuharu snarled, lips drawing back. The *Kukumav*'s second missile volley slammed into the *Kader* at a bad angle. Perhaps a quarter of the shipkillers had swerved away, following the two spoofer pods, but the remainder rained in on her aft-ventral quarter. Inudo had swung them round hard, bringing an undamaged section of shipskin into line with the attack, but the guttering flare of penetrators and bomb-pods ripped aside their point-defense and tore at the primary hull in a wave of explosions.

Command lost power entirely for a microsecond, and Hadeishi felt the carapace lining the shockchair splinter as the g-decking failed. He slammed hard into the frame, and then bounced back. Secondary mains cut in, and their consoles flickered back to life in time for him to see the *Kukumav*'s icon flicker. The weapons cloud from the *Tlemitl* had hammered her, shredding armor and turning hard-points into plasma-consumed hells. The battleship swerved away, rotating to bring fresh guns to bear on the remaining missiles boosting towards her.

"Pilot," Mitsuharu croaked, seeing that Inudo was still alive and clinging to his console. "Hold course and get us out of here!"

THE ALTAR OF THE UNDYING FLAME

BURNING AT THE SUNFLOWER'S HEART

Prince Xochitl reached the top step of a pyramidlike stair ascending from the enormous floor. He glanced down at the others still toiling upward on the wide, gleaming steps, and then strode onto a platform marking the summit of the pylon. By the pale light of the distant accretion jet, he began to comprehend the scope of the massive chamber. *Scaled for giants! Or the gods themselves!* The floor stretched away for kilometers in both directions. *In a place like this, clouds will form. Rain will fall. Lightning might strike. Surely a First Sun artifact!* He turned slowly, taking everything in. He became aware of a strange, singing hum permeating his suit and vibrating through every surface on his body.

Piercing the center of the pylon was a six-meter-wide shaft, a nine-pointed star in cross-section which plunged down into darkness. Poised directly above this unfathomable hole was a second pyramidal shape, apex pointing down from the unseen ceiling. At the junction between these mirror-like pyramids, the platform measured at least thirty meters on each side. The surface was composed of a metallic alloy bearing the endlessly repeating design of two nested, equilateral triangles, while each side was circumscribed by three raised, angular consoles. Their upper surfaces were glassy-smooth, though Xochitl's exo was beginning to annotate the featureless expanse with faint glyphs indicating minute imperfections of the surface.

At much the same time, his z-suit environmental sensors began to register that the tremendously cold air in the chamber had warmed a degree, and the atmospheric mixture, which had been almost entirely nitrogen was now beginning to percolate with oxygen.

Perhaps there . . . The Prince's thought broke off as the others clambered up to the last of the steps and stopped to goggle in wonderment as he had done.

Gretchen hardly noticed the Prince. Her consciousness was suffused with data pouring into her perception from all sides. Here, everything was thick with meaning. Even node $3^3$3 seemed barely able to keep up with the flood of information. Something in the flow—so many glyphs and icons and ghost-images were popping up around her she could barely process the visual stimuli—caught at her. *This isn't right—there's something broken somewhere—no, not broken, a translation matrix is throwing errors.*

"How . . . how does this all work?" Xochitl's voice came as if from a great distance.

Gretchen struggled to focus on the man standing in front of her. When she could separate out the visual channel, the Prince was sweating behind his faceplate. Gretchen knew beyond doubt that his "mask" was gabbling unknown languages into his mind and troubling his vision with intermittent flashes of undecipherable symbols. She felt pummeled by the same forces. Xochitl reached out, seized Gretchen's suit-collar, and dragged her close. "Where is . . . where is the command interface?"

Anderssen felt immortal, weightless, and unassailable. Xochitl's problems did not concern her—or were so remote to her experience he was negligible in any calculation involving her attention. "Didn't they tell you what it looked like?" Part of her regarded him coolly. "When they sent you out here? No diagrams, no pictures of your goal?"

"No! Yes—a theory—just to find a control interface." Xochitl blinked, looking away. He batted jerkily at the air between them. "Is this hot light in my mind—or is it—"

"It is she," Sahâne accused in a wheezy growl as he finally reached the top of the long stair. The marines, growing more and more nervous for the Prince's safety, twitched toward the Hjogadim. The alien looked worse, as the inside of his helmet was smeared with bruised-plum-colored vomit. "It's been this female all along. She and the queer old ape with the bright eyes. They are the ones that brought us to this terrible place."

Gretchen nodded calmly. She hoped no one would see her hands clench into claws. The golden overlay was seeping so quickly through her synapses that the ability to command her body was running thousands of cycles behind her consciousness. *These biological interfaces are so slow!* "This is so."

"I think," Sahâne said, making a sign of command at the Prince. "That you should kill it right now."

Xochitl jerked around with a gasp, combat automatic flying out of his holster, and there was a sharp *snap-snap!* A cloud of flechettes slammed into Anderssen's chest, knocking her across the platform to crash into a console near the outer edge of the pylon. She gasped, spat blood from a split lip, and clawed weakly at the smoking wound.

Seeing that the Prince had taken action, the marines lunged forward to throw themselves between Xochitl and Sahâne. The Hjo coughed out a bitter laugh. "Tell your servants to step away, *toy*. Tell them to—"

"No," Xochitl grated out, crashing his exo again. With relief he found his vision abruptly clear of the strange artifacts. The muttering drone in his mind fell quiet. "Those patolli beans only get one throw, and you've used up all your luck, you worthless coward."

Sahâne blinked in surprise and hastily made another sign of command. The Prince shoved past the marines. "No Hjo-designed exo," Xochitl said tightly, his automatic sighted on the creature's faceplate. "No *magical* control of me. No more wastrel Sahâne, he was lost in some *accident* in the back of beyond." The México lord essayed a grim smile. "No one will ever miss you, assistant-under-attaché to the ambassador. Let's see how long your bio-armor lasts against this—"

The whine of a grav-sled echoing on his comm brought the Prince up short.

Out of sight and out of mind, Gretchen crawled away, leaking atmosphere in a deadly hiss from her punctured suit, nerveless fingers scrabbling into the ruin of her field jacket to drag out the corroded bronze tablet. The device was now pierced with dozens of pinpoint, smoking holes. The golden glare in her mind had dissolved into confusion with hundreds of voices chattering away. Random images flared across her retinas. Then the memory of a raspy, irritating old voice speaking impeccable Náhuatl forced its way through into her stunned, shocky consciousness: *The second enemy of perception is seeing too much. You must learn true focus for the first time in your life.*

Then, those were not *my thoughts! All the events I could see! Everything was so clear in the golden light—* Anderssen's hand twitched in horror and the bronze block skittered away across the floor of the platform. Sliding on the smooth metal, the tablet encountered little or no resistance.

Meters away, the others jerked around as the tablet sailed across the shaft opening and was sliced cleanly in half by an invisible thread running vertically through the open space. Both halves vanished into the depths without a sound.

"The singularity is down there," Gretchen gasped out. She rolled over and punched her med-band override. She felt a sharp pinching in her chest and the cool flood of meds rushing into her bloodstream as the little device reacted in confusion, thinking the collapse of the neural overlay represented her own imminent demise. A raging headache from fighting the gold-tinged invader in her consciousness faded with the onslaught of pain-killers. "Down at the root of all this . . . a string tied to a stone cast into a deep dark pool . . . *aaaaah!*"

Anderssen felt her own native sight awaking, pricked by the stabbing pain in her chest. *Focus*, she commanded and went limp on the platform. Her sightless eyes stared up into the darkness. *Focus*, she commanded, and her mind fell quiet.

Distantly she heard one of the marines say, "Someone's coming up the steps."

Another—this one very close by—said, "Her band has redlined."

AT THE PINHOLE EXIT

The *Kader* limped out of the Barrier passage, coughing clouds of debris and leaking radiation. In Command, Hadeishi watched the plot stonily as the Khaid destroyer *Han'zhr* nimbly avoided the last of their makeshift mines and closed to gun-range with a flare of her engines.

Tocoztic coughed hoarsely, his z-suit patched up with

quickseal, and stabbed a series of glyphs on his console. "Another contact emerging from the Barrier, *Chu-sa*." He squinted at the v-display, which was fluctuating as shipnet nodes crashed and rebooted themselves in quick succession. "Looks like another *Mishrak*. No ident confirm . . . I don't think the 'net is going to hold up through another hit."

Mitsuharu nodded, jaw clenched, and surveyed the wrecked bridge. A penetrator had chewed through part of the Command compartment, killing more than half of the men standing watch. Lovelace had been carried away by the corpsmen, but Inudo and the weapons officer were left. "Pilot, can we still maneuver?"

"Barely anything left, *kyo*. Adjustment thrusters are wrecked, we only have one drive nacelle in operation and there's nowhere to go." The Nisei pilot indicated the navigational scanners with a shaky hand. "The nearest object here is about three light-years away and our hypercoil is shot to hell."

The race is over, Mitsuharu thought bleakly. *The* Naniwa *is nowhere to be found and our sensor suite is reduced to almost nothing . . . two destroyers are more than a match for this cripple, and there's nothing stopping that* Hayalet *from coming through the Barrier after us.*

"Pilot, cut thrust to zero."

Then he switched his comm to ship-wide channel, hoping the crews of men struggling to keep them spaceworthy were all within range of a repeater or a shipnet node in operating condition. "All hands, this is *Chu-sa* Hadeishi. We can see Fuji-san, but there is still one last kilometer to travel. All hands to arms, all hands to battle stations. Form up on your section leaders, check your sidearm loads, and regroup to the Command deck."

Mitsuharu paused, checking the v-panes arrayed on his console. Some of the ship's automatic systems were still in operation. He'd lost touch with Cajeme and the engineering crew on comm, but the 'net v-eyes in cargo one and two showed ranks of evacuation pods lined up and ready. Mentally saluting the little Yaqui, the Nisei officer punched in a launch code, then watched with half-lidded eyes as both cargo bays vented to space. The pods scattered, some of them retaining enough maneuvering fuel to kick off preprogrammed escape vectors.

Dandelion seeds on the last breeze of autumn.

Tocoztic had been watching, his display updating with scattered icons. "Capsules away, *kyo*. They'll be on the Khaid sensor plot already."

I don't think they're going to take the bait, Hadeishi thought, feeling his stomach clench. A horrible pain was starting to pierce his heart, stealing the strength from his limbs. *Another ship lost . . . another crew killed.*

On passive sensors, the two Khaid destroyers were unmistakably clear as they closed in on the coasting-cruiser, each properly spaced to overlap point-defense while retaining a clear field of fire for their missile racks and hardpoints. Mitsuharu hoisted the *Yilan* shipgun from the scabbard at the side of his shockchair and checked the magazine charge. *Six hundred rounds, armor-piercing.*

Then he thumbed an override glyph on the console, sending the main reactor into shutdown and cutting all internal power. The dimmed lights flickered and went out. In the sudden darkness, Mitsuharu toggled his suit-comm alive and said: "Stand by to repel boarders."

Musashi crouched beneath the battlement of Shimabara Castle, his armor in tatters. A huge ringing sound filled his head, as though an enormous gong had been cloven by a giant. Blood was everywhere, streaking the rough-hewn stones. At the edge of his stunned vision, a gaping section of the wall had been torn away by the impact of a Mongol bombard stone. All of the samurai

*on the parapet had been cast to the ground as jack-
straws. He groped fruitlessly for his bokutō, but the
weapon was nowhere to be found. Despite the stunned
weakness of his limbs, Musashi rose up, finding a katana still scabbarded in the belt of a dead man. By the
time he'd reached the steps leading down into the courtyard below, the first of the Mongol spearmen were
swarming over the lower curtain wall. The sight of them
sent a shock of vigor through his limbs. Here was an
enemy within the length of his blade!*

IN THE DEAD FLEET

ABOARD THE *NANIWA*

Oc Chac, Helsdon, and Konev cursed in unison, lever-
ing at the hatchway into Main Command with a magnetic ram. The compartment frame had warped in the
last exchange of shipkillers, though their continued survival spoke volumes to the resistance afforded by the
hexacomb armor between the primary and secondary
hulls. Koshō hung back, one arm tucked around a stanchion, paying only partial attention to the efforts of the
bridge crew to force an exit from the ruined compartment. Her earbug was still live, and she could monitor
the chatter from Secondary Command, which was in
operation. She could have used one of the escape hatches
that led to an evac pod, but there was still work to be
done, and her ship to fight.

Chu-i Pucatli was nearly helmet-to-helmet with her, a
field comp tucked into his elbow while the Comms officer tried to keep track of everything happening else-
where on the ship.

We've broken contact, Chu-sa, reported the second watch pilot from Secondary. *That last exchange blinded the destroyer and we've gone to ground between two of the leviathans.*

"How much clearance do we have?" Susan did not like the thought of getting too close to something that might wake up at any time, though she admitted to herself that *beggars cannot be choosers.*

Enough, kyo. But once they start hunting, we'll have to run for it and drives are at sixty percent.

Koshō shook her head in displeasure, eyeing Pucatli. "Are you picking up anything from their 'cast traffic?"

The Comms officer's lips twisted into a puzzled grimace. "Fragments, *kyo*—I think something's happened in-system from us." The younger officer clipped his z-suit to the stanchion and crossed his legs, pinning the field comp in place as he floated. "Most of our sensors are blocked by the wrecks, but—"

"What about the remote we dropped at the Pinhole?" Susan folded her arms, glaring at Oc Chac and Helsdon working on the door. Being denied the threatwell or any kind of proper information feed was making her almost violently nervous. The *Sho-sa* was now cutting into the doorframe with a plasma torch, which was generating a huge cloud of sparks and smoke droplets. "Do we still have a t-relay connection?"

"*Hai, kyo.*" Pucatli was working the comp as fast as he could, but no good answers were coming back. "But it's six light-years from the *Chimalacatl*—so we've nothing on sensor or visual. Gravity plot now . . . here we go."

The *Chu-i* turned the comp, showing Susan a navigational plot. Multiple tracks arrowed inbound from the Pinhole, showing a line-pattern indicating they'd gone superluminal to leap across the six light-year interval to the immediate region of the Sunflower. One of the traces ended abruptly—and the timestamp on the vector indicated they'd ceased to exist less than fifteen minutes ago.

"See that, *Chu-sa*?" Pucatli could not help but grin, teeth white behind his grimy faceplate.

"That last *Hayalet* stepped too close to the sun," Susan stated flatly.

"Boom-boom, *kyo*," the Comms officer observed, rubbing fine particles of ash from his screen.

Now we know what happened to this fleet, Koshō thought, feeling the weight of the dead pressing against the hull of her ship. *Did they try and attack the artifact? No—they weren't warships. Whoever—whatever—controlled the weapon system turned upon them.*

She turned up the filters on her z-suit against the electrical smoke now obscuring their vision. *Anderssen and Hummingbird must have had some way to slip us past before, when we were so close to the artifact. Damn the old man . . . somehow he knows how to control the weapon.*

Thirty minutes later, in Secondary Command, Susan stretched gingerly and sucked down some water. She'd taken a bad crack on the shoulder while the command team had scrambled downdeck. Most of her ship was seriously damaged, though they'd been lucky enough not to lose the shipcore entirely.

"The main squadron will be coming back this way, Fujiwara," she said to the Home Islander sitting at the Pilot's station. "We need to move closer to the *Chimala-catl* at every opportunity. The Khaid will fear it now, and we'll take every advantage the Goddess sends us."

Oc Chac looked up from the other end of Secondary. "*Chu-sa*, won't we fall prey to the same fate, if we move too close to the device?" His gloved fingers tapped restlessly on the back of his helmet. "That Khaid ship was destroyed well out from the artifact—when we dropped off that freighter we were much closer—" The *Sho-sa* suddenly stopped, having reached an unpalatable conclusion. "How will we tell what our safe distance is *now*?"

Susan looked pointedly at Helsdon. The engineer grimaced, wishing he could clear the taste of ashes from his throat, and immediately fell to work at one of the consoles. "For now," the *Chu-sa* said, "we will assume it's safer near the Sunflower than in the crosshairs of a Khaid missile battery."

Oc Chac nodded in agreement, and then pointed wordlessly at the compartment status v-panes showing a wild mixture of red, orange, and yellow on his display. Koshō leaned in, feeling a slow trickle of despair at the state of her fine new ship.

"Release emergency air to decks thirteen and fifteen. Close down atmosphere to the rest of the compromised compartments."

Turning back to the threatwell—what a relief to have some view of the battle, even if the display had substantial arcs of darkness where there was simply no data to be had—Susan tilted her head, puzzled for a moment by the latest positions of the enemy.

"*Chu-sa*, they're regrouping—the destroyers hunting us are shifting vector out of the shoal." Pucatli sounded wary, and Koshō shared his concern.

"Assume they *are* taking stock of the situation, *Chu-i*. They will need to set some priorities—so keep a close eye on any movements in our direction. See if that remote at the Pinhole can pick up their 'cast traffic."

Then she sat, at last, and drank some more water and managed to force down a threesquare. Everyone else remained furiously busy with damage control and trying to get updated inventory and arranging for the wounded and the dead. Susan sat quietly in the commander's shockchair, watching the 'well update.

"Can you project their rendezvous point?" Susan asked Fujiwara as the minutes crawled by.

The pilot shrugged. "No guarantees, *kyo*. Comp has tagged this one"—he highlighted one of the icons—"as the *Kartal*—an *Aslan*-class heavy cruiser—and presumably the Flag for the remains of their squadron. She's building vector away from the *Chimalacatl* and away from us. The others might be converging on her, but there's no guarantee yet."

Koshō nodded, considering the dimensional model herself. After a minute, she said: "They may have found the chase too hot to follow—or they may be resolving internal differences of *surtu* hierarchy. Set course for the Sunflower—but keep us well back from the destruction point of those two Khaid ships."

Then she smiled tightly at Helsdon, who had looked up from his console for a moment.

Blanching, he set himself to work again.

"*Kyo?*" Pucatli looked up from the Comms console, where he was sharing space with the duty officer. "We've synched a channel to the remote at the Pinhole. You should see this . . ."

Susan tapped up the feed on her own console and pursed her lips, whistling in surprise. The relay telemetry showed three ships erupting from the aperture, engaged in a long-distance missile duel. All three of them popped up on the display with the familiar collection of Khaid glyphs. The pursued—a light cruiser tagged "*Kader*" by shipnet from the 'cast traffic they'd captured during the initial fighting—was taking a beating, shedding a coiling cloud of debris and weaving drunkenly. In comparison, the two pursuers seemed sleek and fast, shrugging aside any counter-fire with contemptuous ease.

"A clan dispute, *kyo*? Did one of the ship commanders try a coup?" Oc Chac peered at her display.

"No." Susan's hand clenched on the armrest beside the shockchair. *He tried to reach me.*

"No," she continued. "This must be the Khaid ship captured by *Chu-sa* Hadeishi. He found himself in the same predicament as we did—and passed through the Pinhole as well."

"To no avail, *Chu-sa*." The Mayan shook his head sadly. "See, they've lost that last drive—they're ballistic now. If they don't lose containment, the Khaid will finish them off with a single shipkiller."

Koshō nodded, feeling sick. The *Kader*'s maneuvering drives had sputtered out, leaving the cruiser a hulk coasting into the void. A cloud of tiny pinpoints popped, spilling away from the dying ship.

He's ejected pods, she thought, feeling an enormous distance open in her heart. *Reactors are off-line. She's just scrap metal now, falling into infinity. Not even worth—*

The two Khaid destroyers cut their drives as well, and on the plot, the paths of the three vessels began to converge.

"Why are—" Pucatli fell silent, seeing that Oc Chac was nodding to himself.

The Mayan scratched at a tiny fringe of beard he'd started to accumulate. "The coil on that ship might still be intact, *Thai-i*, and her reactors are still working—even if they've had to shut them down. Some quick work by the engineers on those two *Mishrak*-class boats might salvage the whole ship. No reason to waste a shipkiller *and* a working starship."

Oc Chac looked to Koshō, a speculative expression on his face. "And the captains of those two destroyers haven't read *Chu-sa* Hadeishi's service jacket, have they?"

"No." Susan sat up, feeling an enormous, crushing

weight begin to dissipate. "They have no idea the evacuation pods are empty. No idea at all."

Then she scowled forbiddingly at the *Sho-sa* and the rest of the crew. "Back to work! We need our drives back on line, missile racks refreshed, guns working!" She clapped her hands sharply, making a fierce explosive sound that made everyone in Secondary jump in alarm. "*Banzai!*"

THE PYLON OF THOUGHT

Burning shapes impressed themselves upon Gretchen's perception, even with her eyes squeezed tightly closed, even without the power of the bronzed tablet flowing through her nervous system. A shining rainbow streak coiled around the Thread tethered at the center of the shaft. The low consoles and the floor itself were filled with quiescent corkscrewlike patterns of brass and silver. Far above, the roof of the enormous room was flowing with filmy curlicues drawn in white, rose, and violet. Dimly, she felt these were the sleeping patterns of control systems, comp nodes, and other undecipherable systems.

In her ghost-sight, the phantasmal bodies of uniformed Hjogadim congealed from the air, busy at the control consoles on either side of the platform. There were other beings with them—slighter of form, indigo-blue-pelted, with thin, ancient-seeming faces and depthless eyes. These creatures stood apart from the Hjo operators though they were intensely focused on the work underway.

Are those the Vay'en themselves? she wondered for an instant, before *something else* climbed onto the platform.

The powerfully built physicality of the Hjogadim was barely visible as a vaporous skeleton. The organic frame was obscured by the scintillating golden glare of *something* coiled at the top of the inhuman spine.

A serpent of fire, was the first image springing to mind. *Naga-kanya, the bringer of wisdom. Where are the five heads?*

The crack of assault rifles and the darting transparencies of the Prince's marines were ephemeral to her. The shapes of the ancient past were far, far clearer. She rolled to her knees, taking in the valley-sized chamber below in one sweeping glance. Hundreds of thousands of ancient ghosts thronged the rows of platforms. Countless golden-haloed Hjogadim lay within the crystalline cradles, while swarms of slightly built blue-black creatures tended to the machines. Platoons of armored Hjo— massive in powered red-and-black battle armor—stood ready at the intersections between the triangular sectors. The hiss of her suit atmosphere escaping failed to register upon Anderssen's conscious mind. Despite the cold pricking her chest as her clothing turned brittle in the near-zero atmosphere, Gretchen crawled unhindered to the edge of the shaft at the center of the pylon.

Far below, the singularity swelled in her sight: a pulsating void streaked with fire as a constant, thin stream of matter plunged down to annihilation. The Thread descended beyond the limit of her sight, a cable of nine atoms stretched enormously thin, forming an unbreakable path into the abyss. The wavering mercury-sheen of some kind of force field blocked the full glare of annihilation from blinding her. *Is this their heaven? They are below, somewhere between here and the event horizon. Millions of them, basking in the crucible of creation—are they healing? Giving birth to a whole new generation? Sleeping until it is time to wake again? Is this a natural cycle? A serpent's egg warmed by the cascade of dying mass from three carefully-balanced suns?*

The stuttering roar of an assault rifle firing wildly only meters away broke her concentration. Gretchen scrambled back into the shelter of a console, gasping as bones ground raw in her chest and side. A Fleet marine staggered across her field of view, blood hissing to vapor from rents in his armor. Across the gaping maw of the shaft, she saw Prince Xochitl and Sahâne crouched behind another console. The Prince's attention was on his attackers, his visage grim, teeth bared in a snarl of defiance. As she watched, he ejected an ammunition spool from his rifle and slammed in a fresh one. The Hjogadim, its long snout wrinkled up in fear, stared wide-eyed across at Gretchen. *Is he capable of pleading for mercy?*

A priest, she remembered. *Like those toiling on the field of abandoned husks below. But that isn't right . . . a technician. A medical technician?*

Xochitl nosed his rifle around the corner of the console and squeezed off a burst of flechettes in the direction of the stair.

But the cubbyholes in the halls were all empty, Anderssen thought, her mind drawn inexorably back to the puzzle at hand. Wheezing, she lay back and fumbled quickseal from a thigh pocket. Even in her elevated state, she could now feel bitter cold biting at her heart. *Where did all the Hjo bodies . . . oh, the garbage disposal port. Outside, then, and into the maw of the black hole. Discarded servants.*

A little black cylinder bounced up onto the platform and before anyone could react, exploded. A web of glittering silver filaments sprayed out, tangling Gretchen, Sahâne, and the Prince. Xochitl cursed in two languages as he struggled to draw a monofilament knife.

The gray-eyed navigator from the *Moulins* appeared

in Gretchen's field of view. Absurdly, she was relieved to see no trace of a golden glow emanating from his helmet. *A regular old human, thank Christ the Sacrifice!*

Piet gave her an evaluating look, swinging a short-barreled assault rifle in her direction, but when his eyes fell upon the México—still struggling to cut away the webbing—his face contorted into open hatred and the Frisian squeezed off a burst into the Prince's faceplate. At such short range Xochitl's glassite faceplate shattered as the armor-piercing rounds struck, spraying blood across Sahâne's helmet. The Prince's corpse contorted violently, but the México's last movements barely moved the tangleweb. The Hjo squealed, as though he were the one who had been murdered. Gretchen felt a paralyzing shock run through her body.

That was as cold and calculated an execution as I ever pray to see.

Two more crewmen from the *Moulins* appeared. They quartered the platform, checking the bodies of the fallen marines in a businesslike way. Their battle-armor was scarred and pitted, but seemed to have held up far better than that of the dead Imperials. Their insignia—a red cross formed of three smaller crosses surmounting a descending spike—gleamed hot in the pale light of the accretion jet. Now, seeing them in motion with arms, armor, and heraldry revealed, Anderssen grasped who they were: *Knights of the Order of the Temple of Jerusalem—the Templars of New Malta! But—they're allies of the Empire, servants of the Emperor—aren't they?*

Though her abdomen was beginning to warm, her z-suit working overtime to replace the heat lost through the punctured chestplate, she felt a chill memory surface. *The Jehanan warred upon one another, each clan seeking to seize the false secrets of the* Kalpataru *for themselves, and so their unity was destroyed and—in time—their civilization fell into ruin, burned away by thermonuclear fire.*

"Which one do we need?" Piet inquired of his companions. His rifle muzzle indicated Gretchen and Sahâne in turn. "Her . . . or him?"

"I suggest you keep both of them alive," the voice of Green Hummingbird urged over the comm. The old Náhuatl stepped up onto the platform, tattered brown cloak drifting behind him. "Particularly now that the Prince is dead. You will need this Hjogadim to explain why Xochitl had to be killed. The Grand Master will want to know the *Tlatocapilli* was sent to seize this place for the Empire in defiance of the Pact."

Three black-snouted rifles swung 'round, fixing on the old man. The *nauallis* nodded genially to the Templars. "Though my lord Sahâne is entirely competent for the task at hand, Miss Anderssen has your master's tablet in her safekeeping. Help her to a console, if you will."

That's Mrs. Anderssen to you, Crow, Gretchen thought blackly, refusing to budge from the nice comfortable floor even when the tangleweb strands were cut away. Hummingbird and the wavering ghost-image of the serpent-headed Hjogadim Lord interpenetrated in her Sight. At that moment she perceived they were cut much of the same cloth, though they stood millennia apart. *Equally calculating and barren of compassion, using entire civilizations as their . . . what did Sahâne call us? As their toys?*

Piet reached down and dragged her up, grimacing at the ruin of her chestplate, now bubbled shut with quickseal foam. "She's been shot," he said in an annoyed snarl.

Hummingbird was at Gretchen's side in an instant. He gently prodded at her z-suit, checking the med readout. She met his gaze with a cold, angry stare. He drew back minutely. She felt his thumb, hidden under her arm, adjusting the channel on her suit comm.

"I'm sorry, Anderssen," he said, face turned away

from the three Europeans. "But these men have not the least respect for my authority."

"I'll bet," Gretchen growled, feeling faint. The ghostly Hjogadim lord was stalking amongst his servants, and the entire great chamber was lit from below by a wavering bronze-colored fire. Even without looking over the edge, she knew every Hjo body in every cradle was yielding up its guest, a serpentine ribbon of living flame, all of them flowing into the thread leading down into the singularity. "That was a dirty trick with the tablet. . . ."

"I warned you the first time we met," Hummingbird said, voice tinged with melancholy. "There are many things best left undisturbed."

"Will she live?" Piet broke in, leaning over the old man's shoulder.

"She will," Hummingbird said. Gretchen realized he had switched the comm channel back. "But she is badly wounded. . . ."

"Give me the Old One's tablet, then," the pilot said eagerly. "I can serve as his messenger, if she cannot."

Gretchen managed a sickly grin, and on the other side of the shaft, Sahâne made a barking sound like a dog choking on a too-large bone. *Was that laughter?*

"Tablet?" she said innocently. "I don't have any tablet."

Piet went quite still. Hummingbird's eyes did not leave her face, but they grew large with surprise.

"*Kyo?*"

Susan opened her eyes, alarmed that she'd fallen asleep in her shockchair. Oc Chac and Pucatli were at the Comms console, and the *Sho-sa* seemed quite agitated.

"What has happened?" Koshō sat up, feeling every bone and sinew complain.

"Our remote at the Pinhole is gone." Pucatli shook his head in disgust. "We've some telemetry from the aperture right before we lost contact, but it makes no sense."

"Show me." Susan rolled her neck and flexed her fingers, trying to force some warmth back into them. Secondary Command seemed to have lost pressure and temperature control while she'd been sleeping. Oc Chac rotated a large v-pane towards her, and then tapped up a series of glyphs to replay the feed.

"We'd picked up what seems to be a Khaid light cruiser about sixty minutes ago." The Mayan's stylus indicated a faint outline against the riot of color glowing from the Barrier clouds. "Lying dark, under full emissions control. Watching the back trail of the main squadron, of course. Doing a good job, too—the *Thai-i* only caught him out by replaying the gravity plot from our passage through the region."

Oc Chac patted Pucatli on the shoulder. "Then we get a gravity-spike from the Pinhole—see, here? Massing like a dreadnaught, *kyo*. As though the *Tlemitl* picked herself up and came after us. But then—wait, I'll rewind again." Susan had started, watching the emissions signature on the plot suddenly break apart.

"Not one ship, but hundreds of smaller ones." The *Sho-sa* shook his head in puzzlement. "Look at all the drive flares! Like they came in packed together, then deployed in a cloudburst. We're still crunching the signatures in comp, trying to match a known profile but—"

Susan's eyes narrowed in speculation, a fingertip drifting across a line of metrics displayed on the console. "I've seen that kind of signature once before, *Shosa*, but not in such numbers. This is something like a Maltese assault carrier launching its complement. But I've never heard the Knights had something which could simultaneously deploy over three hundred fighters!"

"Don't know, *kyo*." Pucatli grimaced, indicating the flood of contacts now racing across the plot. "But they're at high-v and rolling right down the drive plume laid by the Khaid battlegroup!"

"Huh!" Koshō's attention switched to the Khaid light cruiser, which had suddenly exposed a pinpoint hotspot on its shipskin. "We're in line with a comm laser?"

Oc Chac nodded, keying up a directional indicator. "Snap transmit to the main fleet, *Chu-sa*, but see—it's already too late."

A brace of drive signatures suddenly flickered into view on the telemetry; ships a fraction the size of the Khaid light cruiser racing past the long black hull, and then the stuttering flare of shipkiller detonations rippled from one end of the warship to the other. In the remote's camera view, a flurry of white-hot pinpoints appeared in the darkness and then the bright, sudden blossom of the cruiser's containment failing enveloped the ship.

The tiny ships had already vanished, just before the remote's telemetry stopped cold.

"They found our remote, too." Susan clasped her hands behind her back, teeth clicking thoughtfully. "*Shosa*, did you notice how well shielded their drives are? Like ghosts . . ."

The Mayan barked a hoarse, exhausted laugh. "Like they weren't even *there*, *Chu-sa*. Until they were on that cruiser and firing."

THE KADER

Humanoid shapes moved abruptly in the shadows, armor glinting in the intermittent strobe of emergency lights. Some sections of the old *Spear*-class cruiser had their own generators to run critical subsystems, which meant there were pockets of atmosphere and occasional overheads still working. Hadeishi was crouched down behind a shattered section of interior wall, watching the advance of the enemy through a remote v-eye tucked into a dead lighting socket. A good dozen Khaid marines were leapfrogging up the main corridor into the habitat ring, five of the aliens in powered armor in the lead. Mitsuharu guessed they were a combat team detached from the main body of the attackers, who had managed to fight their way into the shipcore.

The Nisei officer turned, signing *Stand by* to the four Imperials behind him with their motley assortment of weapons. When he checked the v-eye again, the Khaid were shifting smoothly from door to bulkhead frame to door, their heavy shipguns shining oily in the flickering light.

Now. Hadeishi flashed a quick sign, and then tripped the switch on a portable fuel-cell generator they'd lugged down from the Command ring. Electrons flooded the local circuits and every light and door activated. The room hatches being forced by the Khaid suddenly cycled open, sending at least one of the invaders sprawling into the compartment beyond. The overheads flared to life, shedding a bright warm glow over the wreckage strewn along the corridor. The Khaiden marines swiveled, guns quartering the nearest openings—and found nothing. Their advance paused for an instant as each hunter assessed every possible threat within his field of view.

Heated to flashpoint by the lights in the overheads, twenty or thirty pounds of fuse paper—all they had left from the landing site clearing supplies the Khaid had been dragging around—ignited with a rippling *bang-bang-bang* and the overhead panels popped free, swinging wildly in the oozing clouds of smoke. The Khaiden marines reacted violently, six of them ripping loose with suppressive fire to shred the ceiling tiles and shatter the remaining lights. The vanguard loped forward, looking to clear the "ambush" zone, while the rear-guard fell back to the closest intersection, ensuring their line of retreat was secured.

Hadeishi popped up as the lead Khaid sprang past a fallen beam, and the *Yilan* tucked into his shoulder stuttered, flash-suppressor spitting flame in a brief, brilliant cross. At point-blank range, the armor-piercing munitions tore up the chest, faceplate, and shoulder of the hunter's armor, knocking him back into the Khaid following behind. The other Imperials also let loose, all fire concentrated on the same lead figure. By the time the hunter had collided with his companions, the armor had been punctured twice by the hundreds of rounds and he drifted limply away.

"Go!" Mitsuharu barked, ducking back. One of his men tossed a grenade—their last—into the midst of the enemy vanguard and then kicked off, sailing down their escape route. The other Imperials were already gone as the grenade cooked off in a sharp, hot blast. The Khaid hunters were thrown back by the pressure wave, but it was an even chance any of them suffered any lasting damage. Their armor was too tough for the lightweight weapons Hadeishi's crew had managed to scavenge. The blast did collapse the roof, however, which had already been weakened by an engineering crew.

The spitting howl of a squad support weapon replied— Mitsuharu didn't remember the code-name assigned by

Fleet intelligence—but the flechettes tore a horizontal gap across the fallen debris and hot sparks chased him down the hallway.

Twenty minutes later, the *Chu-sa* ducked under a haphazardly strung line of glowbeans and went to one knee, his face seamed with worry. The main medbay had been abandoned an hour ago, when the Khaid attack into the shipcore had focused on the secondary command ring, which also held the medical section. The surviving Imperials needing a corpsman—and there were many now—had been hauled out by grav-sled or z-line to the armored compartment managing the boat and cargo bays in the primary hull, which had escaped the initial assault. On a properly equipped Fleet ship, Hadeishi might have had one or two spare shuttles tucked away in the boat-bays. But the *Kader* had nothing spare, so they'd cut power to the bays and vented as much debris and garbage as could be found through the doors to discourage the Khaid from trying to land in them.

Lovelace was tacked to the floor, her body wrapped in a survival blanket, leaving only the status readouts of her z-suit visible. Her rounded face was pale behind the faceplate, eyes closed. On her wrist, the med-band was a softly glowing bracelet of amber and green.

"Not dead yet," Mitsuharu said softly, squinting at the tiny readout. "But you're not going to last without proper facilities."

"Sorry, *kyo*." The Mirror Comms officer's voice was a broken rasp. "They sealed the hull splinter in with me, but I can feel the knife twisting when I breathe."

"Don't talk then." Hadeishi sat, his back against the wall, her wrist held lightly between thumb and forefinger. "We've all run out of time in any case. And the Khaid are sadly lacking in regen pods. They don't eat their own dead, but do employ a species of shipbug blessed by their priests for the very purpose."

"I taste terrible," the girl said; her voice very, very faint.

Mitsuharu nodded, watching her respiration flutter. The pale blue light of the glowbeans painted her cheekbones a deathly hue. "I'm sure you do, *Sho-i*. It was an honor to serve with you. I am sorry I did not listen—you tried to keep me from this fool's errand."

"We—" A bubbling wheeze stopped her for a moment, but then she managed to say: "We were dead if we tried to run out past those two destroyers. You bought us another sixteen hours, at least."

I did that, he thought. *To no good end, save to bring down a few more Khaid before the black sea takes us all.*

One of the lights on her med-band began to pulse red. Feeling a terrible sense of *déjà vu*, he gently dialed the band to send the Comms officer unconscious. *Plum petals are falling, sickle moon sharp as—*

The poem faltered in his memory, the pace and tenor of the chatter and background noise on his comm suddenly changing. Hadeishi looked away from Lovelace, eyes closed, letting the voices of his men, his subcommanders, the sound and feel of the ship penetrating his back, his hands, the soles of his feet wash over him. On one of the channels, Tocoztic's familiar voice—his breathing labored—said: "Is this getting easier, or is it my imagination?"

Mitsuharu stiffened, rising from the floor. "All units report. Are you currently in contact with the enemy?"

"No, *Chu-sa*," worried voices replied. "It's been quiet on either side of us for maybe five minutes."

Just as Hadeishi thumbed the all-channel push control on his z-suit comm, the partially open bay doors flared into a white-hot bar. The debris cloud outside was ionizing as a particle beam ripped across the surface of the *Kader*. The impact reverberated through the frame of the ship seconds later, transmitting itself to Mitsuharu as a keening shriek rising from his boot-soles. Screams on the comm channels were snuffed out abruptly as the beam punched through the central ring of the cruiser.

The boat-bay doors crumpled as the primary hull twisted, suddenly torqued by a series of explosive blasts. Hadeishi dropped to the floor, crouching over Lovelace's body, and felt the walls and floor ripple. Glassite shattered as the boat-bay windows tore from their frames. A second colossal impact followed as a shipkiller rammed into the gap torn by the particle beam. The missile vented plasma into the shipcore, immolating the dozens of Imperials still trapped within the secondary hull.

The concussive wave transmitted to the primary hull as well, tearing the bay doors away entirely. The old cruiser split open, though Mitsuharu knew only that he and Lovelace were thrown against the far wall of the compartment along with everyone else in the makeshift medbay. Cries of agony filled his ears, but the *Chu-sa*'s attention was fixed on the violently glowing dust-clouds now visible through the gaping hole where the boat-bay had been. What tiny bit of atmosphere had remained in the management compartment now vented out into hard vacuum, crystallizing as frost on their suits.

Hadeishi's suit visor flickered, trying to focus on the abyss outside, then suddenly picked out—and enhanced—the outline of a Khaid destroyer sliding past at ten thousand kilometers, a long black shape with a blue-white flare where the drive nacelles were burning at one-quarter power. The first thing springing to mind was the image of a missile hatch cycling open as he watched . . .

"We've got to get out"—he forced himself away from the wall, one arm snaking behind Lovelace's shoulders to pull her with him—"of here."

Before he could drag her away a stabbing white glare

flooded the compartment, momentarily polarizing Hadeishi's visor to black.

"What is—" someone shouted on the channel, before being drowned out by a tidal wave of static.

Hadeishi felt his skin burning painfully from residual heat the z-suit could not disperse and gasped, blinded by even the microsecond of exposure to the antimatter reactor annihilating itself. When his vision cleared, the compartment was filled with drifting corpses, the walls discolored by the blast of radiation.

"Report," he croaked, "any survivors, report!"

For a minute, or more, there was silence—stunned, wordless silence—but he could hear someone breathing harshly. Then a handful of voices babbled back, reporting status of their teams and their compartments.

"*Chu-sa*, what happened?" Cajeme's voice was suddenly clear and sharp; and the thought of the little Yaqui's survival released a tiny fraction of the bone-crushing despair Mitsuharu had been struggling to wade through.

"A *Neshter*-class destroyer," Hadeishi managed to croak out, "blew to atoms within visual of us. I do not know why, or how, but nothing else has hit us in the last sixty seconds, so I claim victory."

THE PYLON

Gretchen flinched away from a sudden, titanic plasma blast. The air erupted with blinding flame and a whirlwind of shrapnel. She lost her balance, teetering at the edge of the platform. Both Piet and Hummingbird lunged forward, gloved hands seizing her arms. Only then did she realize the burning cloud was passing through the two of them without harm. Eons in the past, the technicians at the consoles were strewn about like matchsticks. The mighty Hjogadim Lord burned like a torch while the golden serpent suddenly, violently, escaped from its physicality. The great hall, to its farthest corners, boiled with unforeseen catastrophe.

Anderssen blinked tears from her eyes, trying to focus on the present. Meanwhile, Piet had torn away her utility rig and was digging through the pockets.

"I saw her stash it . . . back in the ship," his voice rasped over the comm. "It must be here somewhere!"

"It is gone," Sahâne barked in amusement. The Hjogadim gestured towards the shaft. "Cast into the abyss."

Piet glared at the alien. "Then you will serve in her place."

Sahâne nodded and rose to his feet, helped by one of the other Templars. To Gretchen it was plain that something in the Hjo had found surety at last, banishing his chronic fear. "What will you have me say?"

Confused, Gretchen eyed the Europeans, Hummingbird, and the alien. *A message? To the dead? No . . . to those sleeping below? But they cannot hear us—not without a Voice—uh oh . . .*

Piet paused, squaring his shoulders, and then recited: "That we await their coming and are prepared to aid, as did their servants of old. That we pledge true service, where so many failed them before. That we have need, for a great peril will soon return."

Sahâne's snout twitched in amusement, but he nodded.

Out of the corner of her eye, Gretchen caught a glimpse of a thin blue-black furred shape shrouding the pilot like a ghostly cloak. *How could anything have survived that plasma blast?* She turned in amazement to get a better look. But the apparition was already gone. The ghost-world was fading now, consumed by the chaos of ancient battle. Too many fleeting events to leave a lasting mark on the substance of the consoles or the time-worn floor. Only one last glimpse of the Lord Serpent wicking through the air as a burning ribbon. Then it plunged into the cowering body of a still-living blue-black technician.

In a last burst of memory, the slim, now-radiant alien escaped over the edge of the pylon.

A vampire, Gretchen realized, falling back into the waking world, her limbs clammy with shock. *A parasite of some kind, that . . . something like that was in the tablet! It was controlling me, guiding my mind! Xochitl was right—and there are hundreds of thousands more of them, down there, in the abyss . . . the deities of the Hjogadim.*

"I will say these words, to the Gods," Sahâne announced, breaking her train of thought. The priest made an elegant, human-style bow. "If you give me leave to do so."

The three Templars shared a glance and nodded, almost as one. Piet gestured with his assault rifle, pointing Sahâne towards the nearest console. "Waste no time, then."

Gretchen watched curiously as the Hjo paced deliberately to the largest, most centrally located console and then pressed fingertips to forebrain, a swift, mumbled litany on his lips. *What is he? . . .* Anderssen felt suddenly the fool. Her ghost-sight quickened, and she saw the air around Sahâne come alive with flickering glyphs and signs. *His masks are on overdrive and—spouting nonsense? They must be trying to decipher the control systems . . . but are too new to understand these older mechanisms.*

Despite the confusion of symbols, the subaudible hum in the floor changed pitch. At once the consoles flickered awake, glowing with dappled green and gold. The air in the enormous chamber stirred. Long lines of lamps began to shine among the abandoned cradles. Anderssen crawled to the nearest panel and felt it becoming aware under her hands, waiting for guidance. She realized that despite the echoes of destruction reverberating in the ghost-world, the gargantuan machine around her was intact and functioning.

Automated maintenance, she guessed. *Little bots or nanites always working to clean and fix and repair . . . gathering up the bodies of the dead, taking them away to be properly disposed of . . .* A frown creased her forehead. *But not by the great doors? Wouldn't they . . . ah, but everything there is in a great untidy pile. Collected by the automated janitors, for something else, something larger to take away. But it couldn't? Because the doors were locked tight, sealed. . . .* She suppressed an automatic reaction to look around the platform for the corpse of the last technician, the one that had sealed the doors, trapping himself inside, and then expired in due time. *Not here, not here . . . some chamber where he'd cached a bit of food and water, until he knew the tomb was forgotten and no one would return.*

So, treachery. *Battle and slaughter in the midst of the great undertaking. Millions of stasis racks, all empty. Storage for the bodies drained of guiding flame. Waiting for their masters—their operators?—to return. . . .*

Gretchen's tongue awoke. "I don't think you want him to do *anything* with that console, Löjtnant Piet."

The pilot turned, politely curious.

"His race views ours as *slaves* and *toys*. I do not think the honorable Lord Sahâne will treat us kindly once he's figured out how to work the controls of this fortress." She forced a grin. "I think war-machines will come and we will all die. And then *he* will be in control of this place, and all that it contains."

Piet stared first at her, then at Hummingbird, and finally at Sahâne. Gretchen was woefully aware of his sudden confusion, and fear, and the absolute depth of his ignorance. *If a penny will not do, then a pound must suffice.* She coughed wetly. "We don't have much time, but I think I can deliver your message to his Gods—to the Vay'en who are sleeping far below us, in the singularity." Another cough, this one unforced. "Even without the bronze tablet."

Sahâne's eyes were black as ink, his long face unreadable.

Piet blinked at Gretchen, and then eyed Sahâne suspiciously. Nodding, he raised his weapon. "Away from the console, creature."

The Hjogadim moved back, slender hands raised.

"And him, too, get *him* away from *everything*," Gretchen said, feeling her weakness returning, indicating Hummingbird with a tilt of her helmet. "You mustn't trust him *at all*."

The Templars were quick to action. They forced the *nauallis* away, to the top of the steps. Hummingbird went without complaint, though his eyes were fixed on Anderssen, his entire body tensed.

No, old Crow, I won't tell you what I'm going to do. Not now, not ever again.

She suppressed a start of alarm when the still-open secondary comm channel squeaked in her ear. *Oh oh, not much time left!* Rubbing her gloves together, Anderssen placed her hands on the console.

The control surfaces gleamed like water under her touch. The glyphs swam to and fro in her unsteady vision. She closed both eyes, letting her mind grow quiet, feeling the pattern of the ancient machinery radiating against her outstretched hands. *Somewhere here . . .*

"This is truly a construct of the Vay'en?" Hummingbird's voice was reasonable, quiet, and far distant from her hurrying, busy thoughts. "A curious turn, to find the Hjogadim here in such numbers. . . ."

"I do not know of these *Vahyyyen*," Sahâne replied testily. "My people built this fastness long ago, for our signs and symbols are everywhere. Even the passage-signs are in archaic Hjogadim, just as you might read in the Perfect Path. You trespass! This female of yours cannot have the first conception of how to—"

Gretchen moved along the control surface, following fragmentary memories, until a collection of glyphs under her hands suddenly felt *incorrect.*

A constellation of meanings, she perceived, *where specific arrangements of the glyphs equal actions. Not verbs and nouns, but hieroglyphs. Like in the transit core outside.* She adjusted two of the outermost symbols, letting them flow under her fingertips into their long-accustomed, proper orientation.

A rippling groan permeated the air, rising up from the floor below the pylon. Everyone tensed, but nothing happened immediately. Anderssen craned her neck over the edge to see that the endless rows of cradles had tilted upright. Their restraining wings were unfolding. *Ready for the next fifty thousand passengers!*

"I did that," she said idly to the onlookers. Then she returned to letting her awareness expand and hoped against hope to grasp the meaning of these . . . *That is odd.* Two whole sequences of the controls were suddenly and clearly out of joint. *These feel . . . stuck.* She tried to move them back into what was so-obviously their proper configuration. Intermittent thought-images from her gold-tinged dreams surfaced, colliding with the glyphs on the control surface, but yielding faint guidance to her. *Yes, this first is a control constellation which means death. Transfiguration. Yielding to chaos.* But still, neither set of control symbols would move. *The controls are jammed,* she realized with a sinking feeling. Her focus turned to the second set.

This is birth; borrowed memory told her, *rejuvenation.*

Images of a blossoming flower invaded her vision—
opening, wilting, dying, budding, opening, wilting—*no,
not just any bloom, but a perennial. But why*—

Gretchen grasped the totality of the puzzle in one
shining instant. Many details were lacking, but the shattered pot suddenly fell together in her hands. *What cold
calculating horror.* She knew what must be done. *Hummingbird is going to be displeased with me.*

Anderssen laughed aloud, drawing a strained look
from everyone arrayed around her.

NEAR THE SUNFLOWER

"Time to safety limit?" Koshō felt a great lightness steal
over her as the *Naniwa* slipped past the last of the gargantuan wrecks. They were once more in open space,
with nothing between her battle-cruiser and the distant
speck of the artifact but vacuum. Somewhere ahead the
ionized clouds of two *Hayalet*-class battleships marked
the edge of the thread-weapon guarding the Sunflower.
She hoped they would be able to use that—somehow—
to their advantage in dealing with the rest of the Khaid.
Her attention snapped to Helsdon, who was still crouched
over his consoles, stylus tapping intermittently as he
tried to tune the sensor array to detect the quantum distortions caused by the alien weapon.

Her other earbug was filled with bursts of chatter
from out-system, where Pucatli's sensor booms were trying to capture and decipher the enemy battlecast.

"The Khaid have counterattacked," Oc Chac reported. He, too, was watching the sensor plot closely.

Thai-i Olin laughed nastily. "If what I've heard is

true, these Maltese would match Xipe himself in flaying them to the bone."

"The Khaid assault anyone who assaults them," Susan replied softly, her mind filled with disquiet. "They are ambitious. Destroying even one Order ship would win the survivors enough respect among the *Kovan* planets and stations." *Those men on the little ship,* she suddenly realized, *were Order Knights. The* Moulins . . . *Hummingbird arranged all this!*

An instant of pure fury was ruthlessly suppressed. Susan breathed in sharply, steadying herself. *Hummingbird arranged everything. Even the Khaid. Everything. The deaths of all those Mirror scientists and their support ships. He used me. He even used Sayu! Gods of mountain and stream, his ambition is without limit! He's traded an entire Fleet battle-group—all of my dead crew—a superdreadnaught fresh from the yards for that thing.*

In the threatwell, the *Chimalacatl* loomed, growing steadily larger with every passing second.

"Up speed a quarter-point," she spoke sharply at Olin, startling the México officer. "*Sho-sa*, prepare a combat team—if any of our marines are left alive—for a boarding action."

No one is going to miss a spare Judge amid all this slaughter. No one.

THE THREAD

Gretchen turned to Sahâne, her hands light on the console, fingertips floating a millimeter over the softly glowing hieroglyphs. "Holy One, it is blasphemy for me to complete this task. This is the abode of your Gods and you are their priest. Stand by me, give me your blessing, and I will rouse them from the long sleep. Let them guide your people again, if they wish."

The Hjo goggled at her; suspicion, fear, and slowly growing wonder lighted his eyes. "You lie, toy. You will . . . you will . . . what *will* you do?"

"Look around, Holy one. You saw the bodies of the fallen at the last door. The Guard Imperial fell here—to the last man—defending this place. The enemies of your people could not pass that portal, not against their sacrifice. The traitors fled, unable to reach this"—once more she spread her arms, taking in the entire panorama of the accretion disk, the pylon, and the endless rows of cradles—"sanctuary." She leaned towards him, voice fading to barely a whisper.

Almost against his will, Sahâne stepped within an arm's reach. Gretchen continued. "But your Gods *did not die*. They are sleeping far below. Those Hjo who remained faithful to the end did that much. They sent the Wise One to safety."

Sahâne's fur rippled erect. His voice was hushed, barely audible even over the comm. "He . . . he is here?"

Anderssen met his eyes and nodded assent. "Why else should the Banner Crimson and Black fly *here*, save he was present?" *And perhaps he was,* she thought, remembering the Lord Serpent. *Perhaps he was.* "Will you help me lift him up, into the land of the living?" She tilted her head towards Löjtnant Piet. "Their message is for *him*, you know. They seek *his* help, to be guided, as The People are guided."

Sahâne looked at Piet in puzzlement, and then he nodded as understanding slowly took hold. "I . . . I see. I did not know—that you believed as we believe."

"All," Hummingbird interjected very smoothly, before Piet could answer, "seek Guidance."

"Then what can I do?" Sahâne's nervousness was palpable.

Anderssen took his hand, feeling a cool shock as her fingers passed through the aura of glyphs surrounding the young alien. "We will move these constellations like . . . so . . ."

Codes unlocked at the priest's touch and the great machine trembled awake. The Thread emitted an audible wail. Enormous energies, long held in abeyance, were released. Mechanisms spun to life, twisting the pattern of space, dragging at infinity like Herakles against the Promethean chain.

Gretchen heard someone's swift, measured breathing rasp on her suit comm and the soft clink of metal on metal.

We're out of time.

Far far below, at the mouth of the abyss, two structures moved—one up, one down. The consoles flared alight with warnings, flashing glyphs and symbols of all kinds. Sahâne goggled at the displays, dark eyes filled with the hot glow of the lights. Simultaneously, his exo bleated a warning just as Anderssen's fingertips—no more than a millimeter from his body—*adjusted* the drifting pattern of glyphs which controlled the alien's body armor. The z-suit helmet suddenly detached with a *thonk!* as the retaining ring popped loose. The Hjo screamed, clawing at his neckring—atmosphere warmer than the sub-freezing atmosphere in the chamber rushed out, frosting the inside of his helmet solid white.

Her blood surging with adrenaline, Anderssen took the first chance for protection and heaved herself over the console just as Löjtnant Piet, shouting in alarm, lunged forward to catch Sahâne. The other two Templars turned hastily towards the near stairway, their guns coming up. Hummingbird hurled himself to one side, but too late as they both squeezed off a burst. Flechettes pocked the *nauallis'* chest and shoulder, punching him back. His footing lost, Hummingbird toppled down the steps, directly past the Jaguar Knight crouching at the edge of the platform.

Koris sidestepped the Judge nimbly. One powerful arm pitched a bundle of short-fuse grenades onto the platform. Löjtnant Piet turned awkwardly, Sahâne's armored body clutched to his chest. The Hjo's z-suit was rippling into spiked bio-armor while his clawlike hands struggled to replace the helmet. The grenade-bundle exploded less than a meter from Piet and Sahâne in a stunning blast of flame and armor-piercing shrapnel.

The Hjo bio-armor crumpled. Sahâne's helmet flew backward and the plasma-flare boiled the priest's flesh from his skull. The blast flung Piet and the corpse into the Thread. Like the bronze tablet, both Templar and Hjo were diced neatly in half before disappearing from sight.

The blast also slapped aside the other armored Templars. One hurled forward down the steps to crash into the Jaguar Knight in a tangle of arms and legs. The other slammed against the edge of a console, but bounced back, shaken but unharmed. The Templar vaulted the nearest control panel and skidded down the side of the pylon, showing fabulous dexterity in remaining upright. Two more marines opened fire on the Order Knight as he alighted, but neither was clad in battle armor.

Gretchen looked away as she heard the two Imperials die over the open circuit on her suit-comm. She clung by her fingernails to the base of the console, her feet dangling over a hundred-foot drop. Anderssen could see that the fight on the stairs was over, the remaining Templar having shattered Koris' faceplate and flung him aside. Anderssen pulled back from the edge of the platform, wheezing, her damaged z-suit once more hissing air. Lacking the time to fumble out another cylinder of quickseal, Gretchen dragged herself up to the viewing screen. The surface was undamaged, and a quick glance showed pulsating warning symbols surrounding a new control constellation. *An override,* she guessed, her hand poised over the half-understood symbology.

Is it right for me to make this choice, Gretchen's conscience ventured. *For an entire race? One I've observed only in fragmentary dreams and through teaching-illusions? Guided by an untested hypothesis which could be so, so wrong? . . .*

Lord Serpent stared back at her out of memory. A brilliant, golden glare of unfettered, unparalleled power. Brighter even than the plasma-blast incinerating its host. *Eat then, of the fruit of knowledge, and you shall know the truth.*

Anderssen's fingers moved on the console and the override blinked out.

The entire great machine groaned once more as the Thread whined to life. Far below, one structure rose, the other fell. Out of the corner of her eye, almost obscured by the helmet, she caught a glimpse of the last Templar turning towards her, assault rifle swinging up. It was Captain Locke. Gretchen swallowed against a dry, dry throat; a prayer to the Virgin of the Roses on her lips.

"Traitor—" Locke jerked as a very small hole appeared in his faceplate. Water vapor, blood, and atmosphere jetted out, condensing into dirty-red frost. The Templar pitched to one side, quite dead. Gretchen saw Hummingbird, one arm shattered, crouched at the edge of the platform, a tiny black gun in his hand.

"You do carry a pistol," Anderssen said, crawling towards him. She was feeling so very, very cold. Her medband shone solid red. "I always knew you did."

"Not mine," Hummingbird wheezed, his pupils huge

from the meds coursing through his system. Shaking, he tossed the pistol aside. The weapon clattered away, fetching up at the foot of one of the consoles. "There is a grav-sled below, Anderssen, we can—"

He stopped, suddenly apprehending the bleak expression on her face, the cold, lifeless light in her eyes as she staggered up on both feet. Her field tool was in one hand as she limped towards him, the trenching spike extended.

"You just saved my life, Crow, but we are *not even*."

Alarmed, the *nauallis* edged away from her advance, barely able to crawl.

"You drew that damned bronze block across my path as a lure, letting the teacher inside infest my mind—you brought the Prince and Sahâne here against their will, just so you could cut out their hearts on this hell-bound altar—yes, a nice symmetry, bringing three keys to the doors of the tripartite temple." Her voice rose, ringing harshly on the suit-comm. "And you've your back up—these soldier-priests with their superb armor and unflinching resolve—but—by my eyes—they are *all dead* now, Crow, and only you and I are left."

"Anderssen!" Hummingbird's voice was ragged, but he managed something of his old strength. "Stop this foolishness! You need me to get out of here; we need each other to survive the next ten hours, we—"

"There is no *we*!" Gretchen lunged, slamming the field tool down at his face with a convulsive, rage-fueled stroke. The *nauallis* rolled away with a gasp at the last second, his face blanching white, and the pick screeched on the Vay'en metal of the floor. Hummingbird scrambled up, broken arm clutched against his thin chest. For the first time, she saw a glint of real fear in his limpid green eyes. The scarred, impassive face was suddenly showing signs of humanity. He scuttled back, finding him-

LAND OF THE DEAD 445

self caught in the wedge-shaped corner of two of the consoles.

"Doctor Anderssen, you know the kinds of things I must do. You know my purpose. I have never misled you about my aims. This place—"

"Is exactly the kind of trap you've always gone on about!" Gretchen snarled, circling to put herself between him and the stairs. "A fortune no one can spend, a tool no one dare wield. Do you grasp the enormity of what lies below us, incubating in the forge of creation? Do you know how long you would last under their influence?"

Hummingbird—sidling along the console—stopped, a questioning expression stealing over his scarred old features. "Do *you* know? Have you seen them, comprehended them?"

What? Oh Lady of the Seven Stars, he has no idea what is going on here! Anderssen hefted the field tool, finding a surety of purpose in the heavy, oiled metal. "Goddamned Crow, you didn't even know what you might unlock when you set the Prince against this place? What were you hoping to gain? The weapons technology behind the barrier of knives? Some fragments of the wisdom of the Vay'en themselves?"

"At the most," he said, voice settling into something like its old calm, "the annihilation of the Prince, the Khaid, even the poor Ambassador and my own life in the bargain. A clean set of books—nothing falling into the Emperor's hands to upset the balance at home—and *time*. Time we desperately need."

"Against what black day?" Gretchen eased closer, the tool raised, her eyes fixed on his midsection. "Opening this tomb door would vomit up the annihilation of our entire species—isn't that your eternal fear?—well, here you were right!"

She lunged again, snapping the tool around in a fast, sharp arc. Hummingbird bolted, twisting his shattered arm into the path of the spike. The point gouged into his z-suit, bouncing from a metal plate and snagging in the gel at the elbow. Gretchen wretched the tool away, but the *nauallis* slammed his working forearm into her faceplate, cracking a metal wristband against the glassite with a ringing blow. Stunned, Anderssen skipped back, desperate to retain her weapon.

"I never meant to wake the powers sleeping here!" Hummingbird gasped. "I was used in turn, Doctor, by a *Senescalcus* of Templars. He—it—is stronger than I understood. It *pushed* my mind, sent me down this course— sent them along, the Knights, to ensure the message we heard from Piet's lips was delivered!"

Gretchen froze, a flash of memory resurfacing. *One survived. One still survives.*

Then she moved again, vastly relieved. The last shred of conscience which had lain upon her, holding back her fury, evaporated. Something in her expression must have transformed as well, for Hummingbird hissed in anger and darted away from her, trying to cut across the gap between the consoles and the pit. Anderssen leapt after him, feeling a joyful strength filling her body. She caught him two paces from the edge of the shaft, dodged past his outflung arm, and smashed the tool across his faceplate and shoulder. Sparks leapt back, the old man crashed to the floor, and atmosphere hissed, obscuring his faceplate.

"Ahhh!" His cry of pain echoed on her comm. Anderssen pounced, pinning him to the floor with one knee. The point of the tool ground against his armpit, tearing at the gel.

"Anderssen, please! Remember your family, remember they need you to come home—to provide for them! Isabelle, Tristan—they can still benefit—the *calmecac* schools *can* be moved to accept them. Ahhh!"

The spike punched through into his side, blood boiling away into vapor as it welled around the metal.

"There's nothing you can offer me, Crow, which will buy your life." Gretchen's voice was cold, her heart filling with a tremendous pressure as his face contorted behind the faceplate. "You can promise only ash and broken shells. Your gifts are only death and suffering—"

"Duncan," he gasped, trying to catch her eyes, his old face tight with terrible pain. "There are universities on Anáhuac who will still take him; he can be all you desired, you can—"

"My son is dead," she said, wrenching the field tool free and standing up. "My son *is dead*."

Atmosphere hissed from the gaping wound. Hummingbird's faceplate frosted over and she could hear a tight, harsh gasp of pain over her comm. The *nauallis'* body jerked spasmodically, limbs stiffening. He tried to roll over, to get his feet beneath him. Gretchen took a step back, and then jammed her boot into the old man's side, sending him sliding across the mirror-bright floor. His good hand scrabbled wildly on the surface— then he tipped over the edge, just like Sahâne and the pilot.

The comm circuit cut off, leaving only Anderssen's harsh, bellowslike rasp echoing in her ears.

It's done. It's all done.

OUTSIDE

The shuttle's cargo door swung up with a whine and spacers in white-and-brown z-suits helped Hadeishi and the remains of his crew out into a huge, brightly lit boat-bay. Mitsuharu looked over the faces of his men with a measuring eye. They were all bloody, bruised, and pale with exhaustion. *Some of these men have crewed three ships in this one venture.* In spite of the heavy losses, he felt great relief and pride at the spirit of his surviving crew. Not one of them seemed impressed by the shining new ship surrounding them, or the ranks of armored men arrayed across the floor of the bay. Enormous banners hung from the walls, showing a crimson cross on a white field. *And now another ship, another berth. Lost travelers on the road to the holy city, redeemed from bandits and rogues by the cross-men.* Then he caught sight of a familiar face and smiled broadly through the grease and carbon he knew crusted his face and helmet. "*Konnichi-wa, Sencho-sana.*"

Captain De Molay was waiting impatiently, arms crossed, one foot tapping on the deck. She was kitted out in the same white-and-brown space-armor as the ship's crew. Her rank insignia was quite polished; a squared crimson cross flamed on her breast. She saluted stiffly. *Wounds from the Khaiden ambush not yet mended.*

"*Chu-sa* Hadeishi, welcome aboard the *Pilgrim.*"

Mitsuharu nodded, and then returned the salute with a hand trembling with fatigue. "Our fortune improves. And my men?"

"We've taken almost sixty aboard already, and there are more on shuttles inbound." The elderly woman offered him a sombre expression. "*Our* medical facilities are first-rate."

"*Infirmus fui et visitastis me,*" Mitsuharu returned soberly.

De Molay stared at him in surprise, the corner of her mouth quirking into a smile. "'I was sick and you visited me.' That is—"

"The twentieth rule," he said, nodding to the cross on her breastplate. "This is a strike-carrier of the Order of the Temple; I would say a refitted Norsktek *Galahad*-class hull with—by what I saw from the shuttle view-port—an entirely upgraded drive array. Out of the yards on New Malta?"

"It is indeed," De Molay said, pleased. "And it is ap-propriate that you have attended to all her details."

Mitsuharu's thin black eyebrows lifted in query.

"In good time, *Chu-sa*," De Molay said with no emo-tion whatever. "If you will step over here, please." She guided him away from the others. Templar medical staff were everywhere in the bay, triaging the rescued Imperi-als. A line of grav-sleds was waiting to take the survi-vors away. "Come with me, there is someone who has waited a long time to see you again."

In the tube-car, Mitsuharu closed his eyes—for just a moment—and fell sound asleep against the upholstered chair.

Tap-tap-tap went the blind man's bamboo cane on the side of the road, ticking against the mossy rocks laid at the border. Musashi was dozing, nearly asleep in the shel-ter of the little shrine. Rain was drumming on the slanted, tiled roof, but his head was dry on a bundle of cloth hold-ing the rice-paper book he'd been so laboriously writing in. He opened one eye halfway as the shuffling mendicant ducked under the eaves. "Ah, pardon," wheezed a tired voice. "Just getting out of the rain."

"Welcome, brother," Musashi replied, moving his legs out of the way. Both shins were bound in bandages. "I'd offer you tea—if I had any—or a rice ball—if I had one. But I've neither, so you're welcome to the dry roof at least."

The blind man laughed, his stout face creasing into a merry smile. "The tamghachi *have left this whole province hungry—or so they tell me in the inns, when there is nothing to eat."* He settled down on a little bench, head bowed over his cane.

Outside, the drumming sound of the rain was supplemented—then replaced—by the rattle of hooves on the metaled road. At first one horse, then a dozen. "Hm." The blind man dug vigorously at one ear with a blunt finger. *"Someone is coming in a great hurry. I wonder—could it be the militia? I've heard there is a murderer loose—he slew a tax collector some days ago."*

"Interesting." Musashi yawned, hands behind his head. *"But the militia does not ride war horses."*

Hadeishi awoke to find a sandy-haired man with knight-commander's tabs standing beside his gurney. The familiar sounds and smells of medbay surrounded them, and De Molay was loitering behind the Templar. Her gray eyes wrinkled up in amusement at the look on Hadeishi's face when he recognized Ketcham.

"You were in a bad way the last time I saw you, *Chusa* Hadeishi," the European observed.

Mitsuharu smiled wryly. "Aside from far too much radiation exposure, I believe my wounds are only of the heart, Præceptor Ketcham. You found another ship, I see, and one better suited to you than wildcatting with an illegal ore refinery."

"I did." Ketcham scratched the back of his head, failing to suppress a huge grin. "You seem to have gotten back into the hot-chair, too, by hook and by crook."

"By stealing my ship," De Molay grumbled. Her good humor made the elderly woman seem a dozen years younger. "Twice!"

"I returned it," Hadeishi said quietly. He looked around the room, hoping for a comm panel.

"Much the worse for wear!" De Molay objected, jutting out her chin pugnaciously.

"He has that way." Ketcham laughed. "You will want to know, *Chu-sa*, that Commander Koshō is well, though busy aboard her ship, which is somewhat . . . battered. We intend to ship your men across to the *Naniwa* as soon as she has atmosphere restored on all decks, and proper facilities prepared."

Mitsuharu felt his heart ease at the news of the battle-cruiser's survival and lay easier on the gurney. "Then I can sleep at last."

He closed his eyes, feeling the tug of tremendous weariness, and wondered idly if it were possible for him to sleep for a full week. Then he sat up again, frowning at the two Templars. They had not moved, and were waiting for him expectantly.

"My men, you say, to the *Naniwa*. Where am I bound, if not with them?"

De Molay produced a data crystal, bound with gold and white bands. "If you recall, *Chu-sa* Hadeishi, you signed aboard the merchanter *Wilful* as an engineer's mate. After *Wilful*'s unhappy experience with marauding Khaid, you assumed emergency captaincy until such time as you engineered the capture of the Khaiden light cruiser *Kader*. You served as *de facto* captain aboard her until the vessel was evacuated. From our point of view, you are still captain of the *Kader*, but her fate is yet to be decided. And you are still our employee, bound by contract. One possibility is to scuttle the cruiser and add her remains to the debris along the Barrier. Another is to affect sufficient repairs to allow transit to the nearest Temple shipyard where she may either be reborn, or recycled. In any case, she is your charge. These orders—" She tapped a fingernail against the crystal. "Affirm your employment and responsibilities."

De Molay reached for his hand and closed his thin, newly scrubbed fingers over the crystal. It seemed tremendously heavy, possessing a weight in his mind far in excess of the tiny dimensions.

Hadeishi's glance shifted to Ketcham. "What time is it and when does the next watch begin?"

De Molay turned a snort of laughter into a sneeze.

Ketcham shook his head, putting on a forbidding expression. "You, *Chu-sa*, are on medbay time. Down here, I'm XO of the *Pilgrim* in name only. When the Infirmarian lets you go, you can take your duty station. Until then—well, you'll have time to sleep at last."

ABOARD THE *NANIWA*

IN COMPANY OF THE *PILGRIM* AND
HER SUPPORT FLOTILLA

Chu-sa Koshō nodded in greeting to the two Imperial marines standing watch outside medbay pod twenty-seven, and then stepped inside without a pause, followed by *Kikan-shi* Helsdon. The pressurized door whispered shut behind them and Susan paused a moment, letting the portal seal, before turning around, hands clasped behind her back. The *Naniwa*'s commander looked civilized again—she'd had a shower, been out of her z-armor for nearly a day, and gotten a few hours of sleep. Helsdon, now sitting nervously in a corner chair, looked little different than usual. The engineering teams had been working around the clock to repair secondary hull damage and return normal living conditions to the hab rings and command compartments.

"Anderssen-*tzin*, good afternoon."

Gretchen looked up from her field comp, face mottled with bruises, her tangled blond hair tied back in a ponytail. Her bare arms and neck were shining with quickheal, and her ruined civilian z-armor had been replaced by a matte black Fleet skinsuit while she remained in medbay. She was sitting on a bed of crates, spare insulation, and blankets—the regular pod bed had been moved somewhere else. A portable lamp hung from the ceiling, shedding a bluish-white glow. On her field comp's screen, a relayed feed from the main navigational array was unspooling, showing the singularity and its attendant stars. The icon of the Sunflower was nowhere to be seen.

"It's gone." The Swedish woman set the comp down, shoulders slumping in weariness. "Dragged down by irresistible gravity. The last sanctuary of the Vay'en is no more."

Koshō glanced to Helsdon, who shook his head in ignorance. The Nisei woman pursed her lips, frowned once, and then tilted her head questioningly at the xenoarchaeologist.

"I do not know who these *Vahyyyen* might be, but I am very interested in determining what happened to Prince Xochitl and Ambassador Sahâne. Can you tell me?"

"Oh," Anderssen blinked, and then rubbed her face, trying to remember. "I had forgotten all about the two boys . . . they are dead, Captain. One of the Templars shot Xochitl in the face with an assault rifle, and Sahâne— well, he was burned alive by a plasma burst and then cut in half. Old Crow, he—" She nodded to herself, feeling light-headed. "He was shot, then stabbed, and then fell down a very, very deep pit. But—but I could not say for certain he perished, not being able to see the bottom of that pit. It was quite deep."

Susan's expression congealed into a cold, immobile mask. "My marines found you drifting on a jury-rigged grav-sled outside the artifact, Doctor Anderssen, in the company of a half-dead, blinded Jaguar Knight who had been *Cuauhhuehueh* of the Prince's guard detachment. The ship Xochitl commandeered—the *Moulins*—has disappeared. Do you know what happened to the freighter?"

Gretchen shrugged. "One of the Templars survived the melee with the Prince and his men. He must have taken it out of the landing cradle—she was gone when Koris and I reached the garbage disposal port."

"I see." Koshō's jaw tightened in frustration. "Do you know how the freighter avoided our notice—assuming the ship left the vicinity of the *Chimalacatl* and boosted outbound, to join the rest of the Templar battle-group? Helsdon here and my techs have gone over the sensor logs at least three times—finding nothing."

"It was a military ship," Anderssen offered. "Disguised as a freighter. But the crewmen were all Order Knights and they were using—at the end—powered armor and modern weapons. Better than the Prince's men had, from what I saw."

Susan looked to Helsdon, clicking her teeth. "Then the *Moulins* could have been equipped with the same stealthing technology the *Pilgrim*'s fighters were showing off against the Khaid."

"No reason," the engineer coughed, covering his mouth, "to believe otherwise, *kyo*."

"Why are you asking me, Captain?" Anderssen was watching them both with an odd, distant expression. "I'm just an archaeologist caught up in something far, far bigger than she expected."

"I need any information you can give me, Doctor, because I'm beginning to wonder if *we* will be allowed to leave this place." The Nisei officer indicated the ship, the rosette, the universe with an encompassing wave of her hand. "I know these things: that my ship is alone, wounded and in desperate need of resupply. A presumably friendly fleet—including a strike carrier easily the size of the *Tlemitl*—has come to our aid, is providing medical assistance, and has sent across dozens of wounded rescued from other Fleet ships lost in the recent series of battles. But at the same time, you tell me that Knights of the Temple have murdered an *Imperial Prince*, the ambassador of a friendly realm, and also an Imperial Judge, and . . . I wonder if we are next, if the Knights decide to clean up this little mess before they go on their way."

"Oh." Gretchen leaned her head on one hand, eyes half closed. "That is a problem, I guess."

"It could be . . . serious." Koshō stood beside the bed, her attention fully upon the Swedish woman. "You came here with Hummingbird. I *know* he was at the center of all this. I have a horrible suspicion that he *arranged* all of this. But I do not know why—and I hope that you will tell me, for the sake of my crew, if not out of courtesy to me."

Anderssen regarded Susan sidelong, her expression still and distant for nearly a minute. Then she lifted her head, attention returning to the present, and she looked at Koshō with great curiosity. "Captain, do you remember that this is the third time our paths have crossed? Each time, great events have been in play—at Ephesus III, on Jagan, and now here. . . . I wonder, is *Chu-sa* Hadeishi here as well? I know you've your own ship now, but—"

"He is." Koshō's stoic expression was suddenly and subtly transformed, cycling from glad relief to concern to suspicion and then grim certainty. "He *is* here. Hummingbird brought him here. Hummingbird brought *me* here, and the Prince, and—what in the Nine Hells was he doing? What were *you* doing with him?"

"Do you really want to know?" Gretchen spread her hands. "You will find no ease to your worries!"

"Tell me." Susan's voice sounded stretched and brittle.

"The Crow found me on New Aberdeen," Anderssen

said, "and he needed help with something beyond his 'capacity to evaluate.' *I* thought he needed my technical skills as a xenoarchaeologist—but that was a gravely incorrect assumption. *He* never said—he never does, you know?—what he expected me to do."

"And you just came when he beckoned?" Koshō sounded disgusted.

Gretchen shook her head, all expression draining from her tired face. "No. I had been waiting for him, or someone like him, to come nosing around. After everything that happened on Jagan, when I came home empty-handed, without a bonus check from the Company, I found that my boy Duncan had been killed while working on a trawler in the Northern Cape Sea. That—"

She stopped, her attention suddenly far away from the medbay and the two officers. Susan waited, watching the subtle play of emotions on the blond woman's face, until Helsdon stirred, looking at his commander beseechingly.

"Anderssen-*tzin*, we don't have much time. Please tell us what the Hummingbird was doing here."

"Oh." Gretchen shook herself, grinding the heel of one palm into her left eye. "I have a recording, I think. My suit comm was on when he told me. You can hear it from his own lips."

She tapped up a sequence on her field comp, and then slid the volume to three-quarters. The sound of static and harsh breathing filled the little room, and then the old Náhuatl was saying: *. . . the annihilation of the Prince, the Khaid, even the poor Ambassador and my own life in the bargain. A clean set of books—nothing falling into the Emperor's hands to upset the balance at home—and time. Time we desperately need.*

The recording stopped and Anderssen made a face. "We came here in little tramp freighters and mail-boats before the *Moulins*, which seemed like more of the same. Hummingbird didn't have anything on his side but some fancy comps in a case, me—for whatever I was worth—and his own invincible self assurance. Do you hear him? He was hurt when he said that, and afraid— not of dying, no, but of failing at the task he'd taken upon himself."

She stopped, running her finger across the navigational display. The *Chimalacatl* was already gone, torn to shreds as it fell. Comp projections showed the delicate balance holding all three of the brown dwarves was beginning to fail. In a hundred years, or a thousand, the entire rosette would succumb to the black hole and obliterate all traces of the Vay'en and their works.

"I thought," Gretchen continued, "when I sent them down into oblivion, that I defeated him. But listening to his voice now, I think I did exactly what he wanted . . . even better than he could have managed himself."

Susan made a soft, strangled sound. "He wanted the Sunflower destroyed?"

"More than that," Gretchen replied. "He needed—or the Judges needed—to ensure that not only was the artifact obliterated—but everyone who had come seeking its power was slain, denied, or convinced it did not exist. The Prince is dead, the Khaid massacred, the Order Knights left with empty hands . . . we are witnesses to the immolation of the evidence. The nav plot shows that the entire Barrier will be swallowed up in time, pulled into the black sack and made to vanish."

She laughed nervously. "Only three people remain who saw the heart of the structure, who know what happened there—me and an Order Knight who escaped, the one who departed in the *Moulins*. He will certainly carry the news to his masters—and I wonder how they will react?"

"They came well equipped," Koshō admitted grudgingly. "The *Pilgrim* is the core of a full-scale squadron and seems more than capable of mopping up the leftovers of our ill-fated expedition. If we're on the books to be marked off—we won't last long."

"If you give me to them, they will let you go." Gretchen's statement carried an odd weight of certainty. "I think they are very keen to know the fate of the Vay'en, and the *Chimalacatl*, and what transpired within."

"That seems, to me, Doctor Anderssen, an excellent reason *not* to put you into their hands." Susan offered a tight, bitter smile. "I am still an officer of the Fleet and the Emperor's servant. If we escape, then duty requires that I report what transpired in this benighted place. It seems unwise to leave *all* of the witnesses in the hands of the Temple. But what becomes of you after we return—I cannot say."

"It does not matter." Gretchen's expression was bleak. "I've done all I can. Like Hummingbird, my death or disappearance evens the books, leaving almost no trace of our passing."

"Untrue." Koshō lifted her chin, indicating the icons of the Templar ships on the plot. "They are still here—they have possession—but what do they gain from all this, Doctor? Are they now an enemy of the Empire?"

"No." Anderssen scratched the back of her head, where a sore had developed from wearing her helmet so long. "They came seeking to ally themselves with something—with someone—they thought remained in this funereal place. Hummingbird alluded to needing *time*. He believed—and the Templars believe—some enormous calamity is fast approaching. One which we—humanity—cannot withstand without the assistance of the kind of powers which once dwelt here."

Helsdon stiffened in his chair, fear stark in his features. "My God, woman, this place was built by a race with the power of the Gods! We won't have this level of technology for thousands of years!"

Susan nodded in agreement, her complexion growing waxy. "Do you know what they fear? Do the Templars?"

"They believe they know." Gretchen smiled sadly. "I do not. But I can tell you the Order Knights are being used, as you and I were used by Hummingbird, by *another* agent—another puppet master hiding in the wings, out of our sight. This seems to me a skirmish—an opening move—where greater powers than the Empire are jockeying for position on the field of combat."

"These Vay'en," Koshō said, after considering the Swedish woman's words. "The Templars believed they were still alive, after millions of years? That they could be woken, or summoned? And bargained with?"

Anderssen nodded. "Yes. It is even possible they were right—but none of the Vay'en remained, only their machines and devices. Of course, given the disparity of power between us, I don't think *bargained with* would be the appropriate term. Subjecting humanity to slavery and servitude—yes, that would have been the likely outcome."

Helsdon glanced at Susan, who nodded, wondering what the engineer intended.

"Doctor Anderssen—what happened to disrupt the equilibrium of the system? Did—did *you* do something?"

Gretchen looked at him, seemingly puzzled, before saying, "Ambassador Sahâne attempted to harness the machine. But his exocortex was insufficient to the task. There was an interruption during the process—and what he intended did not come to pass."

Susan's forehead creased sharply. "Why was the ambassador here? Did he know something about the artifact? Did his race—these Hjo—know something?"

"*He* knew nothing." Anderssen sighed. "But his race—yes, they had once served the Vay'en—long ago, they were servants, soldiers, bureaucrats . . . the linchpin of the Vay'en demesne. Like the Prince, like me, his presence had been *arranged* by those who set all this in motion. Three of us were needed to unlock the mechanism, so three were delivered by Hummingbird."

Helsdon cursed under his breath, rubbing his palms on his thighs. "The Barrier. The *Naniwa* and the *Moulins* could reach the Sunflower because all three of you were aboard!" He laughed, a little hysterically. "All my work to identify the Barrier threads—for nothing! Good thing we didn't get too close while the security system was still operational!"

"Wait—" Koshō's eyes narrowed in suspicion. "The builders of this place were obviously fond of threes and multiples of three. I can understand the ambassador, if his people had once been the servants of the Vay'en. But how did *you* and *Sayu* qualify as keys to the structure? You're not Hjo!"

"I was." Anderssen knuckled her brow-line with one fist, feeling an enormous migraine coming on. "Hummingbird had exposed me to that corroded-looking bronze tablet—let me use it as a comp—and the Vay'en 'instructor' within began to rewrite my neurology. The tablet led us through the Barrier—you saw the effects as it revised the ship's interfaces and systems—the same was happening to me, though I didn't realize it until too late. While I was under its influence, the *Chimalacatl* treated me as a Hjo as well."

"And the Prince?"

Gretchen pursed her lips, examining Susan's face with great care. "Did you care for him?"

"Me? For Sayu?" Koshō looked horrified. "He pursued me, momentarily, at Chapultepec when we were in the lower form. But I was not what he expected, so— nothing came to pass. After that, there was open rivalry between us, and—I must confess—he often came up short." She paused, remembering. "Later he did better—

after third year he seemed to collect himself. Then he was the popular one, the pretty one. Captain of the *Ullamaliztli* team—everything expected of a scion of the Imperial house."

Anderssen nodded to herself. "Like me, he had an overlay which allowed him entrance, made him seem enough of a Hjogadim to qualify for the machine. I don't think he realized, even at the end, why he was here. Whoever sent him must have known what would happen . . . but you know, Hummingbird was surprised to encounter Xochitl out here. Surprised when the big battleship arrived." She ran her fingertips along the outside of her field comp. "You said the Crow *arranged all of this*—but I don't agree. I think he was trying to manage a situation that kept escalating out of his control. Some of it—yes, he brought me here, he had something to do with the Templars being here—the rest? It seems doubtful."

"He arranged—he arranged the Khaid." Helsdon looked more uncomfortable than ever. "We've found traces in the comm system of t-relay activity between the *Naniwa* and the Khaid fleet during the fighting outside the Pinhole."

"Ah." Gretchen nodded, remembering. "I helped him assemble a t-relay when we first came aboard."

"And he arranged for *Chu-sa* Hadeishi to be here." Susan's expression was positively glacial. "Both to further his own ends—and as leverage with me, if needed."

"Yes." Anderssen was watching the Nisei officer again and smiling faintly. "I didn't like the Crow—hate might be too weak a word—but he had something in mind for you, Captain Koshō, and for me as well. You'd served with Hadeishi for a long time, hadn't you?"

"Five years," Koshō said grudgingly, regarding the archaeologist with suspicion. "What do you mean—*in mind*?"

"So you'd seen Hummingbird come and go over those five years, always dropping in unexpectedly, getting your ship and your captain into some kind of dodgy situation? Always on off-the-books business for the *Tlamantinime*?" Gretchen didn't wait for a response from Susan. "He had the same pattern in mind for you, and for me. Once you had your own ship—this ship!—you'd be put on frontier duty, patrolling alone at the edge of cultivation—one step out into the darkness—with no support, no backup, and no oversight."

She paused, running one hand through her tangled, greasy hair. Koshō looked like she'd swallowed a sour pickle. "Where is your political officer, Captain? Where are the Mice? I haven't seen any—isn't that *very strange*?"

"We—" Susan halted, considering. "I had assumed Oc Chac, my new *Sho-sa*, was the Mirror representative aboard—but you're right, there should be a whole complement on a ship this size." She glanced at Helsdon, who had retreated again and was swallowing nervously. "All of the other ships in the squadron were drawn from units tasked to support the Mirror science teams. They would have been crawling with political officers. But not us?"

"You see? The *Tlemitl* was free of them as well. Hummingbird mentioned at one point—I don't think he realized I was listening—that the Prince's ship had entirely new security systems—none like those used by the Judges, or the Mirror. I doubt that would have been allowed if there were proper political officers aboard!

"And after all of this business was done—if you survived—then you'd be sent off on patrol, and then *I* would be the one dropping in unexpectedly when *I* needed a ship for some dirty work."

Koshō grimaced. "You're one of the *Tlamantinime* now, are you? I thought there were no female Judges."

"There aren't." Anderssen bit at the edge of her thumb. "But once I heard the Crow and two others talking—a female counterpart to the *nauallis* exists—and they were pressing to take on a similar role along the frontier. I think that now—driven by fear—the old strictures are breaking down. I think Hummingbird hoped I would become his apprentice—take on his responsibilities—and the two of us would replace him and Hadeishi, if they died or grew too old to act."

"How interesting." Susan's displeasure radiated from her as a sharp, prickly heat. "I have no appetite for his schemes—and now that he's dead, then all of this can die with him."

"Can it? If he spoke truly—if the Templars were correct in their belief—then *someone* must walk the fences, watch in the shadows, do all the things Hummingbird and his brother Judges have been doing."

Koshō shook her head. "He arranged the deaths of thousands of Fleet crewmen. He, and whoever decided to poke this nest of ants with a stick, and whoever dispatched Sayu to his death. Do you want that kind of hideous *karma* upon *your* soul?"

"No." Gretchen's voice faltered. "It's already cost me my boy. A wise woman once said—almost immediately after meeting the Crow—that he stank of 'broken shells and ash.' She was right—he would not hesitate to sacrifice a fleet, a planet, even a whole species to achieve the ends he thought necessary. But I begin to perceive there are other players in the game, perhaps those on the very summit of the Heavenly Mountain, who will sacrifice even more to *win*, or just survive."

She tapped the navigational plot. "Alliance with the Vay'en would have cost us our humanity. Even if our bodies endured—they would have been no more than husks filled with a living flame—and every human being

alive would have been their slave. Yet someone, somewhere, believes it was absolutely necessary to do so."

"This implies the annihilation of our species at the
hands of this unknown threat is the alternative." Susan
flexed her hands angrily. "One of the first lectures
Chapultepec beats into the heads of the lower form is
that the realm of the México, for all its power, pomp, and
majesty, is a tiny principality in a galaxy filled with mam-
moth empires. It is easy to forget that we are weak and
ill-regarded." She laughed bitterly. "They do not tell you,
however, anything about these great powers . . . that is
ring-zero information. Only the Emperors will know
how low on the mountain we truly are."

"Hummingbird implied the same to me, when first
we met." Anderssen closed her field comp. "When you
work for the Honorable Company, it's very clear your
purpose is to poke and pry and dig in the dead cities and
ruined worlds, not for scientific benefit, but for tools—
weapons—knowledge from the ancients that will benefit the Empire. Make it stronger, make it more powerful.
Climb another step on that mountain. . . ." She sighed,
shaking her head. "The Mirror was trying the same thing
here. They found *something* and wondered if it could
make them great—but they were only a cat's paw. The
Templars came prepared. Hummingbird came prepared.
Even Xochitl was sent by someone who *knew what was
here already*."

"What about the Khaid?" Helsdon ventured. "Why
bring them into the equation?"

"The Judges—or Hummingbird—must have decided
that the Mirror fleet had to be destroyed. And *they*
didn't know the Order was also in play with a powerful
fleet." Gretchen smiled ruefully at Koshō. "He had great
faith in you, Captain, expecting you and your ship to
survive when everyone else was slated to die. The arrival

LAND OF THE DEAD   465

of the *Tlemitl* threw all of those plans into question—he was almost frantic when the Prince arrived."

"And the Knights of the Temple," Susan said, her lip curling in distaste, "stood by waiting to clean up the survivors—on either side!—and take the prize."

"And now they have it." Helsdon's pale face was drawn with worry. "*Chu-sa*, we're not ready to fight or even run. Perhaps—perhaps we should give her over, if that will obtain our safe passage?"

Gretchen nodded in agreement, but Koshō's expression turned obstinate. "She's all we have for a bargaining chip—I'm not going to *offer* her to anyone." She raised a slim hand to forestall Anderssen's rejoinder. "Consider this as well—at least three *Imperial* factions were involved here—the Mirror, the Judges, and presumably the Emperor himself—who else could have dispatched Sayu with a newly minted super-dreadnaught? It is very likely the Knights are *also* divided amongst themselves—if not, why send some of their agents in secret, and others arrive with such overwhelming force as to seize the prize openly? Also weigh that they have *not* attacked us, though at least a day has passed since the missing Templar from the Sunflower should have reached the *Pilgrim*."

This gave Gretchen pause, and she settled back, searching her memories. "That is . . . possible. Hummingbird had not intended to reach this place aboard the *Moulins*—we were supposed to meet another ship— one carrying an ally, he said—but the Khaid had intercepted them. I think—I got the impression we were going to meet Captain Hadeishi on that other ship. And he's here, now, right?"

"Yes." Susan nodded, her eyes dark. "I've been told he is aboard the *Pilgrim*. They took him aboard, along with many survivors from the Imperial ships destroyed outside the Pinhole. I've spoken with one of his officers—a Mirror technician, actually—who was brought over from their medbay. He was on a ship called the *Wilful*, commanded by a woman *Sencho* named De Molay."

"Really? How curious . . ." Anderssen opened her field comp again. "Yes—I thought that sounded familiar. A famous Templar surname, actually. So two Templar spy-ships—and a fleet to back them up—but maybe only *one* of the freighters was intended to be here. The other—the crewmen on the *Wilful*—they had an insignia, a tattoo actually, of a—ah, here it is: the *Croix re-croisetée au pied fiché*, in crimson on a white field."

She turned the comp so Koshō and Helsdon could see a cross composed of three smaller squared crosses—for the crossbar and crown—then the long end of the cross was more like a spike, or spear, pointing downward.

"Striking," Susan commented, "but not the insignia of the Knights of the Order. They bear a cross with equal arms and rounded ends, fit to a circle, not a rectangle."

"This one," Gretchen said, tapping up a second image, which matched the Nisei officer's description.

"So there are your two factions, *Chu-sa*." Anderssen shrugged again. "Probably representing a political split within the Temple hierarchy; each espousing the same goals, I'm sure, but embracing markedly different means to reach the end." She tapped the *croix fiché*. "Three crosses, each composed of three arms, surmounting a spear. I—I saw something like that when I was aboard the *Moulins*. The sense of it was a warrior brotherhood, standing watch on the edge of infinity, much like the Judges. . . ."

"Three of three?" Helsdon blinked. "Like the patterns on the surface of the *Chimalacatl*?"

"Aping the Vay'en and their symbology." Gretchen scowled. "The Hjogadim were the same way, thinking the oversize robes and scepter of their overlords would grant them the power of Lord Serpent! Fools. The strength of the Vay'en was—is—beyond our ability to grasp." She laughed harshly, thinking of the hundreds of thousands of Hjo corpses desiccating in the garbage disposal chutes throughout the massive artifact. "The same fate awaits us—our puny little principality—if the great houses, the Emperor and the Order all fall out amongst one another over the prize. It is better the Sunflower is gone—safer by far for everyone. Much better."

Hearing a change in the Swedish woman's voice, Ko-shō's jaw tightened and she glanced sideways at Hels-don. The engineer was watching Gretchen as well, and the same dawning suspicion was showing in his face. "You destroyed the artifact, Doctor? You—what *did* you do?"

"And why? Just to protect humanity from some hypothetical civil war?" Susan seemed genuinely curious. "Are you certain such a fate would befall us?"

"Look around you, Captain!" Gretchen rang her knuckles on the damaged wall beside her. "An Imperial Judge betrayed the Prince's expedition to the barbarians! Just to keep the Emperor's hand from the hilt of this infernal blade! The unity of the Temple is already divided, one faction intriguing against the other—and it will not end here, no—it will not end until Anáhuac is a burning ruin and all our colonies and settlements are laid waste." Her voice had gained a harsh, hectoring edge. "Because even should we seize this power for ourselves and learn its use—*others* will come which we cannot withstand, even with this weapon! Remember the lesson from the Hill of Grasshoppers!"

The Swedish woman winced, feeling her bruised torso twinge. Angrily, she stabbed at the field comp with her stylus, invoking a projected image of the rosette—the three brown dwarves, the distant demarcation of the

Barrier, the singularity—then she cupped the holo in her hands. "The Vay'en *assembled this*. They dragged these suns into position, spun up a black hole of their own, wrapped in the wall of knives—everything within ten light-years is here by the will of Lord Serpent, who perished nearly a million years ago!" She caught Koshō's eye with a piercing, exasperated glare—then jabbed a finger at Helsdon. "We can barely perceive their works with our instrumentality—and you expect the Mirror, or the Fleet, to grasp their technology?"

"In time." Susan lifted her hands, conceding the point. "But what else can we do? Even if we are beneath the notice of these great powers, that must surely change. When that black day comes, we'd be remiss in all duty if we had not prepared as best we could. Even to the point of waking—as you say—a power like the Vay'en and seeking their alliance."

"Foolish. Very foolish." Gretchen buried her head in both hands. "At least this temptation is banished— none of the sleepers will return from the pit." She made a casting-away motion. "The balance in the system has been destroyed. Structures you cannot perceive have descended deep into slow-time, quite close to the event horizon of the singularity. The tidal stress on the Thread broke apart the *Chimalacatl*—the Pylon, the great chrysalis chambers, the warehouses for the hosts—all gone."

"We saw." Helsdon sounded sick, but his face was alight with interest for the first time. "How—how did they do it? Hold something in balance deep in the gravity well? A platform—for the Vay'en themselves?"

"There were two lattices," Anderssen replied, growing weary. What little strength had returned to her while recuperating in medbay was beginning to flag. "One fell while the other raised—not much, in the scale of their works, but enough. Enough for them to feel time quicken again."

"Who?" Helsdon frowned, glancing to Koshō for support. "You said the Vay'en fell to oblivion—but something else rose up out of slow-time? What else was dwelling in this place? Something that will issue forth, as these Vay'en would have done?"

"Not yet, maybe never." Gretchen made a vague motion towards the floor. "Eventually they might escape the gravity well, as their ancestors did. Or not. They have"—a small, fierce smile flitted across her face—"free will at least. They'll have to choose, just like the rest of us."

"Who? If the Vay'en perished in the singularity, what was on the *other structure*?"

"Their children."

Helsdon and Susan stared at her, uncomprehending.

"That clever little bronze tablet Hummingbird gave me? He must have thought it a personal comp, or a ship-comm of some kind. But it was a teaching device for immature Vay'en. It tried to reprogram *my* mind and failed because my poor old ape brain just wasn't capable of following the lessons. But it was a piece of the puzzle—and a twisty, nasty one at that. You see, the tablet was very old, even to the Vay'en. It was something they'd put aside—a failed, melancholy experiment—in favor of another, more promising way to cheat death."

Koshō said nothing, hands clenched tightly behind her back. The Swedish woman's voice had a queer, atonal quality and her face seemed marked by some last remnant of a hot golden glow. Helsdon drew back, shaking hand reaching for his sidearm.

"The Vay'en were—are—energy creatures," Gretchen continued. "We would consider them sentient wave structures. And I would guess they could manipulate electromagnetic fields in close proximity to themselves with great dexterity. But in turn, their *own* physicality could be manipulated by quantum resonance. With the tablet, they were trying to bring their offspring 'up to speed' by exposing them to the already established mentation pattern of an accomplished elder. The mind in the tablet had been a poet, I think. Some kind of great artist. They wanted to keep his essence alive, even when chaos claimed him at last.

"In the beginning, the Vay'en evolved in the interface around a black hole. They could live far beyond its confines, but from all we saw, it seems they returned there to breed." Gretchen halted, watching her two companions digest what she'd said.

Susan spoke first, musingly. "It was a nursery."

Anderssen nodded, digging around for a threesquare in her blankets.

"They were betrayed, then," the Nisei officer continued. "Their most loyal servants turned upon them at a most crucial juncture—their great fleet shattered by their own weapons. The Vay'en had to descend into the singularity to birth a new generation? But the Hjogadim trapped them too close to the event horizon, in slow-time. Then the treacherous Hjo abandoned the artifact and fled—to assume custody of the Vay'en dominions—to become Gods themselves."

"Plagiarists," Anderssen mumbled around the chewy bar. "Doesn't sound like the traitors told anyone, though. A 'Guide of Thought' still rules the Hjo, from what I gather. But the Guide is not a Vay'en anymore, just some old fart of a Hjogadim pissing around a palace. So do the great powers pass!"

During this Helsdon had said nothing, but now the engineer stirred, moistening his lips before venturing: "You are saying the elder Vay'en had discovered how to live forever by impressing their memories and personality patterns upon the newborns of their *own kind* as they emerged from the birth-caul. They murdered their own children, so they might live on themselves?"

"Not just kin-murderers, either. They had no care for others of any race." Gretchen's voice was flat with anger. "You saw how Sahâne viewed *us*. A pale echo of the attitude of his Gods. I think when the Vay'en departed their puppets en masse and descended to renew themselves, the Hjo rose up, seizing their *one* moment to escape. We have stumbled across the traces of a successful slave revolt."

"But they didn't all rebel, did they?" Koshō lifted her chin at the nav plot, where the vast shoals of broken leviathans still drifted in the abyss. "Even within the shield-reed, there must have been those who remained true to their masters."

"Yes, many remained loyal. Quite a vicious little struggle they had. It was brother against brother . . . so much for the legacy of the glorious Vay'en. A squalid play of infanticide, kin war, and murder played out on a galactic scale, just to forestall death *one more day*."

"And now? What will happen to the children you've released from slow-time?"

Anderssen shrugged, managing the faintest smile. "I don't know. It's not much of a gifting day present, but they are freed from a cruel past." *And free of Lord Serpent, I hope.* A nagging feeling of unease began to steal over her. *Did that one escape the rebellion? How would you kill something like that? How long do they live?*

"Was that what Hummingbird wanted?" Susan's old anger began to return, thinking of the old Náhuatl. "Was that the choice of a *nauallis*? You said the end result was much as he desired—"

"His desire?" Gretchen snorted incredulously. "No, this was a tired mother's choice, one who has seen both happy children and sad in full measure. No child was ever so blessed as to grow without the hand of expectation on her neck! Those which are let be, flourish, while those who are pressed hard wither. The Crow had no comprehension of what I felt, holding any of my babies in my arms. This was his great failing, I think, having no children of his own."

With this, Anderssen finally lay back on the bed, her eyes turned to the ceiling and some distant vision. Koshō watched her for a minute, and then for five. But the Swedish woman said nothing more. At last, the *Chu-sa* turned away, motioning for Helsdon to follow.

When the door had cycled shut, Susan tapped open a comm channel to Oc Chac, who was acting duty officer on the bridge. "*Sho-sa*, can you connect me to Captain De Charney aboard the *Pilgrim*? Extend my regards and let him know we're ready for the rest of the wounded to come aboard."

Then she turned to the engineer, who was waiting silently, head slightly bowed as he tried to digest all they had heard in the medbay. "*Kikan-shi*, find Hennig and let him know we'll be underway and out of this cursed place as fast as his crews can get the hypercoil in operation."

Koshō's face was calm and composed but her eyes were dark with troubled thoughts as Helsdon departed in haste. She could think of only one thing to do, given the intricacy of the situation. *It's at least seven days to get in range of one of the big t-repeaters on the Rim. If we push it, six. If I can manage a secure channel to Oba-san Suchiru, then perhaps an accommodation can be made between the Mountains. Emperor Ahuizotl cannot be pleased to learn I've lost his son—not even an honorable corpse to bring home—as well as any possible prize from this tar-pit.*

The thought of facing her grandmother with a disaster of this scale made Susan's stomach clench, but despite this she walked steadily to the nearest lift, nodding to the doctors and corpsmen hurrying here and there in the medbay. When the doors cycled closed, she was perfectly composed, her white uniform shining in the gleam of the overheads.

"Main Command," she requested.

Hadeishi pressed two fingers against a battle-steel door and heard, muted and distant through the metal, a chiming sound. A moment passed as he stood at ease, hands clasped behind his back, and then the door receded into the bulkhead with a soft *hsst!* Within, kneeling behind a low desk of teak and rosewood, her fine-boned face pale in the light of a single task-light, Susan Koshō was considering an array of v-displays, all filled with reports, forms, and colorful graphs displaying the state of her ship.

"Yes?" she said, not bothering to look up.

"Somehow," he said, amused, "you've brought your office through in fine shape, *Sho-sa*. Mine always seemed to take the worst of it, riding such a rough passage. Everything would always be ruined. . . ."

Koshō's head lifted, eyes widening at the sight of the thin, weary-looking Nisei officer. She stood, tucking a stylus into the twisted bun of hair behind her head, and stepped around the end of the desk.

"You're here?" She paused a polite distance away, the carefully impassive mask of her face subtly transforming. Without meaning to, Susan began to smile. "You were very foolish to come through the Pinhole after us—there was no safety to be found in our company."

"So we discovered!" Mitsuharu bowed, dark eyes

twinkling. "But things would have been worse if we ran the other way. . . . I had no choice, really, knowing you were here."

She nodded, looking him up and down. Then she shook her head, seeing quickheal gel shining on his neck, his wrists. The trim brown and white uniform seemed to fit him well enough, though it was strange to see him out of Fleet colors. "You've been in the infirmary again, *Chu-sa*. And I've seen your poor ship—kindling and splinters are all that remains."

"Yes," he said ruefully, shrugging thin shoulders. "She had a brave heart, though, even to the end."

"Your crew is aboard," Koshō offered, "under the best care we can provide." She stepped closer, pursing her lips disapprovingly, and took the hem of his jacket sleeve between thumb and forefinger. "Lost all your clothes, I see. Is this a loaner?"

Hadeishi shook his head, straightening the half-jacket. "I've a new commission, *Sho-sa*. Brevet-captain of the *Kader*—that same poor wreck lying in tow off the *Pilgrim*—mine now that I'd found her, brought her to worse state than when she fell into my hands. But—"

"A ship, still. A starship." Koshō stepped back, her expression turning wan and drained. "I can offer you nothing better, *Chu-sa*. Not even as an unfounded promise."

"I know." Hadeishi smoothed back his hair from forehead to nape in a terribly familiar gesture. "It is strange—not to be in dress whites, not to hear the piping when coming aboard." He looked around her cabin, at first sad, but then whistling softly in appreciation. In comparison to his old quarters on the *Cornuelle*, the *Naniwa*'s accommodations were refined, even luxurious. "This suits you, *Sho-sa*."

Koshō looked around at the gleaming wood-paneled walls—the tatami-patterned g-decking—and laughed softly. "Pretty—but all this doesn't give me another meter of armor, another sixteen hard-points. . . ."

"Don't think it useless!" Mitsuharu admonished. "You must find rest *somewhere* or your alertness will be dulled."

"How does it compare to a Templar ship?" Susan slid a panel aside on one of the walls, revealing a compartment holding a black iron kettle and a rack of cups. "Tea?"

"*Dōmo, Sho-sa.*" He knelt gingerly on a nearby mat, settling with a hiss of pain. Koshō began measuring *matcha* into the cups. "What I have seen of the *Pilgrim* matches the best the Fleet has put underway. Their captains—well, I've experience with two—are able."

"Hm." Susan whisked steaming hot water into the green powder. "Are you oath sworn now, to the Temple?"

"No." Hadeishi tilted his head inquisitively. He could see Koshō's attention was fixed on the molten jade swirling in the two cups, but something in her voice sharpened his interest. "I've command of the *Kader* under the terms of a commercial contract as a serving crewman on a Temple-owned ship—as salvage officer. But I am not yet a Knight of the Temple, or even a poor brother. . . ."

She turned, holding a small enameled tray in her hands, and knelt as well, pale blue cups and rice cakes between them. "You wish to be?"

"They have use of my poor talents, it seems. As a salvage driver, if nothing else." He shrugged, and then lifted his cup. "*Dōmo arigatō, Sho-sa.* It is good to sit with you again, even in such a strange place, so far from home."

She inclined her head. "You're welcome, *Chu-sa.* Magister De Charney would be a fool to refuse your talents. Not as a tug captain, either! I've recently reviewed all of the Mirror briefs on the *Fratres Milites Templi*—and while they have an excellent reputation in counterpiracy activities, and even in some border skirmishes—there is *no* evidence they have put main line-of-battle vessels like the *Pilgrim* into service before. Nor deployed ships displaying a countermeasures system which can handily defeat our sensors!"

With this, she paused, watching him carefully. For the first time in their long association, Mitsuharu suddenly felt a distance between them. *She's suspicious? Of me? Hadeishi set down his cup. And why not? I've arrived in the colors of a foreign power.* Having been aboard the strike carrier for only a day, the Nisei officer had already grasped the leap in power and confidence of the Knights. Seeing the ship's crew at work in the command spaces, in the medbay, even in the shuttle which had brought him over to the *Naniwa*, an old, old story from the naval history of old Earth had come to mind. A Danish admiral had once said, when judging his people's many enemies: "Nothing shows the temper and ability of a nation more clearly and concisely than the crew of a ship of war—be it an aircraft carrier or an attack submarine—everything else can be disguised, hidden, faked ... but not the natural camaraderie and interplay of an experienced crew."

"Susan, I am still an Imperial officer. My name remains on the List, my commission stands. I can tell you this much of the Knights: the *Pilgrim* is a match in gunnery, speed, crew, and systems for any carrier in the Fleet. Her crew is dedicated, resourceful, and enthusiastic. And yes, I have seen with my own eyes—I have in fact *used* to excellent effect—an emissions dampening system which rendered a Temple-owned freighter *invisible* to Khaid sensors at point-blank range."

Koshō did not answer immediately, setting down her own cup and adjusting the tray carefully. When she did look up, Hadeishi felt a tiny cold shock. Her expression was pinched and wan. "Do you think—" She paused, reordering her thoughts. "Has the Order decided to break with the Empire? Is the *Pilgrim* on a combat footing?"

"Combat?" Mitsuharu shook his head. "No, they've stood down. There are fighter wings on patrol . . . but I've seen *nothing* which indicates they are hostile to us."

Then she did seem to relax, a brittle tension flowing away from her, and she raised the cup again. "Greetings, *Chu-sa*. I did not think I'd see you again, when we parted at Toroson."

"I either!" Hadeishi laughed softly, feeling his heart lighten. "Who could have guessed we'd come together again in such a remote fastness, or by such a circuitous path?"

"Who indeed?" Koshō offered a faint smile, though her eyes were shadowed again. "It must have been fate."

The temple bells were ringing the length and breadth of Kyoto, filling the warm night air with a glad clamoring sound. Uncounted voices were raised, singing a song of welcome and unbridled joy. Musashi nodded to himself, scratching at his stubbled, gray beard, and turned away from the huge mass of people thronging the courtyard. He passed under an orange tree whose branches were filled with chattering, laughing children—all peering wide-eyed at the steps leading up into the hall of Shishinden, hoping for a glimpse of the new Emperor—and then forced his way against the press of citizens flowing into the royal complex from the streets. Once beyond the Imperial precincts, the traffic eased and he sighed with relief. He shrugged his shoulders, loosening his muscles, tucked both arms inside his kimono, and found his feet on the great Nara road, heading west. The night sky was clear, showing the moon in quarter-crescent, and the stars were twinkling like jewels strewn on black velvet.

Breathing deeply, feeling free for the first time in a decade, the old man started home.